SON OF HYDRA

A NOVEL

SHELLEY DARK

Copyright

Also by Shelley Dark

Hydra in Winter: An Island Escape in Search of a Greek Pirate (2024)

Cover design by Rony Dhar 2025

Contents

I dedicate this novel to my husband John—
thank you for knowing
when to read,
when not to read,
when to argue,
when to listen,
and when to pour the wine.
This novel might have my name on it.
But *Son of Hydra* is yours.

And in memory of Dimitris Mavrideros—genealogist and
gentleman, whose generous spirit and insight into Ghikas' likely
origins helped bring this story to life.

A Reflection

Heraklis Kalogerakis–Vice Admiral
Hellenic Navy (retd)

This is a book that, once you start reading, you cannot put down. A 'historical novel' that recounts significant events of another era—events that cannot be judged by modern social standards.

Poverty, hunger, social inequality and the spirit of freedom, can drive people into unexpected situations. To answer the questions that arise in your mind while reading, one must mentally travel to that region of the Eastern Mediterranean, during the time when piracy flourished, and understand the political and military ambitions of the great powers.

Although in Greece the privateers (corsairs) contributed to the success of the Revolution, piracy in the Aegean and Eastern Mediterranean was strongly suppressed by the official government and completely eradicated in 1831 by Ioannis Kapodistrias, the first governor of the new Greek state.

As for the 'migrants,' it becomes clear that anyone can take root and thrive wherever they go—provided they find work, love, and understanding. These were precisely the elements that the exiled Hydriot seamen found in Australia.

Happy reading.

Greek Names and Spelling

In Greek, names change their endings when you're speaking to someone—a small shift of intimacy. Ghikas becomes Ghika, Nikos (an abbreviation of Nikolaos) becomes Niko.

In *Son of Hydra*, all Greek words and names appear in English letters rather than the Greek alphabet. Their spellings are chosen for readability—and to keep the cadence of the Greek language alive on the page.

A short glossary at the back of the book explains the Greek words and phrases in the story.

Historical Note

Hydra (Ύδρα) is a small Greek island east of the Peloponnese and south of the Argolic Peninsula, about an hour and a quarter by hydrofoil from Athens. Rocky, rugged and mountainous, with a population of about 2,000, it has little arable land and no natural water. To the casual visitor, it's an idyllic summer haven for the fashionable set and an enclave for artists and writers, yet for all its twenty-first-century glamour, the island remains fiercely proud of its history.

Albanian refugees fleeing religious persecution first settled Hydra in the fifteenth and sixteenth centuries, as Venetian control of the area ended and Ottoman rule began. With limited resources, its inhabitants turned to the sea: they fished, carried goods, and became recognised merchant traders and shipbuilders.

A turning point came in 1774, when the Treaty of Küçük Kaynarca between the Ottoman and Russian empires allowed Hydra's ships to sail under the Russian flag and access the Black Sea grain markets. Hydra flourished, and its crews—already famous for their seamanship—ran the English blockade of European ports. They risked seizure, imprisonment, or the destruction of their ships to supply Napoleon, who is said to have given, as a reward, the silver candelabra in the Hydra cathedral. Fortunes soared, the island grew wealthy, respected, and influential, and the population swelled to 20,000—earning Hydra the nickname "Little England"—at a time when England epitomised empire and naval dominance. Hydra had become a formidable maritime power.

Contemporary visitors admired the Hydriots as industrious, proud, athletic, well-dressed, and defiantly independent, known not only for their skilled seamanship and uncompromising spirit but also for their taciturn nature, hard partying, and habit of firing guns in the street. Meanwhile, the women of wealthier families lived secluded lives within mansions behind high courtyard walls, yet were remembered for their grace and poise when they welcomed guests.

The war to win Greek independence from the Ottoman Turks began in 1821, when that empire spanned half the Mediterranean world and its Muslim rulers governed the Christian regions of Greece. Hydra—together with the islands of Spetses and Psara—armed its merchant fleet for battle, and ordinary sailors became freedom fighters. Hydra, with the largest fleet, led the squadrons that turned the tide against the Sultan's navy. Only later did Britain, France, and Russia join the cause; in those first critical years, the three islands faced the combined might of the Ottomans and their Egyptian allies alone.

But by 1829, before Greece had won its independence, seven of Hydra's sons were convicts in New South Wales.

This is the fictionalised story of one of them.

It is not through wealth, nor through status,

but through deeds, that a man is known.

—Sophocles, *Antigone*, c. 441 BC

———————————————————

1

SYDNEY

The End of the Earth

———————————————————

SYDNEY COVE, New South Wales
    September 1829

'You will be a nobody. A nothing.'

A curse more than a warning.

I would lie awake night after night, swearing my father would choke on those words. I'd fight beside my brothers at sea, marry well, own more ships than he ever dreamed of, and fill my warehouses from Hydra to Smyrna.

He'd be the one forgotten—not me.

But the war is almost at an end, Greece free at last.

And me? Convict 197, on the other side of the world, ankles scarred, sweat stinging my back, a British ensign flying above my head.

His curse fulfilled.

I tighten my grip on the rail.

In two days, some shore-bound clerk will decide where we go—with no thought for our skills, our friendship, or the storms we've survived together. They can't even pronounce our names. We're just numbers, assigned and forgotten.

Once, I was the one giving orders—and in this world, a man's worth lies in what he commands. The rest is ballast.

The *Norfolk* groans on her anchor, turning broadside to the shore. So this is Sydney. This is what the British Empire scraped from the bottom of her boot. Shacks and scrub and a handful of buildings pretending to be grand, hovels scattered like driftwood. Rutted tracks crawl up the hills to escape the town. And there. Columns. Greek columns. Here, of all places.

They said Sydney was the end of the earth. It even smells like it.

There are five of us, and I dread the moment they separate us. Andonis —the fever still in him, ribs like twigs—can't take another beating, and Damos never knows when to keep his mouth shut. Kostas will hold his tongue even if it kills him. And Nikos—God help him—will think it's his fault.

On Avlaki's cliffs, I dared them to jump. Five boys. Hands locked. We leapt together.

I swore I'd never leave one behind. I still swear it.

My stomach churns. I do the thinking for all of us. Without me, they're dead men walking.

'The arse of the world,' mutters an Irishman along the rail.

The boys laugh—they've picked up English from guards and convicts. Father made me learn it properly, to read his letters, impress the English captains who came to dine.

It's served me better behind bars than it ever did at his table.

Andonis props himself against the rail, skin the colour of tallow, eyes half-shut against the glare.

'You're staring again,' he murmurs in Greek, his voice a rasp, one eyelid drooping.

'Making sure you're still breathing,' I say.

A faint smile answers me. His good eye widens—the other pupil stays a pinprick, wrecked in that fall from the mast when we were boys. The smallest of us, and the toughest. But since the beating in Portsmouth, and the catarrh that sent him to the surgeon late in the voyage, he moves slowly, his breath short. The salt beef has blistered his lips, hollowed his cheeks.

Ninety-three days from Portsmouth—a record, according to the captain —and all of us still upright. Two crew lost, accidents both.

'Three dry docks, look, Ghika,' he says.

'Yes, carved from the bedrock,' I say, crossing my arms. 'And only one in use. Plainly short of skilled hands. Captain Greig will speak for us.'

No one asked us to help when a crewman flailed in the rigging off Portsmouth, but Kostas was up the shrouds before the man finished cursing —and the rest of us after him. They let us work on deck after that day, carry out repairs. We earned that.

'They need shipbuilders,' I say. 'And they might know the name Voulgaris.'

He shakes his head. 'Means nothing here, Ghika.'

I scan the dockyard—sails flap like laundry, lines tangled, men everywhere. A yard should hum. This place bleeds incompetence.

Kostas scowls, eyes bulging like a monk seal. 'Don't get us flogged, Ghika.'

I rub my thumb across the calluses on my palm, pressing until each finger curls. An old habit.

'If I didn't look after you, you'd be rowing in circles.' I say it lightly but they know it's true. 'I'll keep us together.'

Damos watches me, reading my thoughts as he always does. His gold earrings flash in the sun—he's as good-looking as Kostas is not. 'You think they'll send us all to the dockyard?' he says.

He hooks his thumbs into the rope at his waist.

Andonis murmurs, 'Don't raise our hopes, Ghika.'

Damos jerks his chin toward the guards. 'You speak their tongue. We don't. What happens when they split us? When they flog Andonis senseless, chain Nikos to a post?'

Nikos' eyes snap open; I steady him with a hand on his arm.

'No one is wearing irons,' I say, more certain than I feel.

'If Ghikas hadn't been with us, Damo,' Andonis says, 'we'd never have made it this far.'

'We wouldn't be here at all,' Damos shoots back. He blames me for everything—the life sentences he and Andonis face, the arrogance he thinks damned us all.

But when the wind turns foul, he might curse me to hell, but he'll stand beside me.

'Enough,' says Andonis.

I meet Damos' gaze, my head throbbing. 'I'll fix it.' My thumb twitches towards the calluses.

'Stop that,' my father used to say. 'You make a fool of yourself.'

His measure of a man—wealth, obedience, honour.

I failed on all three.

—

We're permitted to stay on deck—a mercy, given the stench below.

I sit cross-legged near the rail, thumbing through a tattered copy of *The Sydney Gazette* the captain has allowed to be passed around. From the date, I realise I turned twenty-two three days ago. No one remembered. Not even me.

Andonis drops beside me, raises one knee, pulling threads from the hem of his trousers. Nikos flicks splinters into the sea, absorbed in the small satisfaction of watching them float.

'What does it say?' Nikos leans close.

Even the headings sound like warnings.

'A man cutting grass in front of Government House gets ten days in gaol.'

'For cutting grass?' Nikos gasps. 'What kind of grass?'

'They call it *lawn*. And convicts who run to the bush and rob others are called bushrangers—six hanged a servant and then shot him dead.'

Damos pulls a face. 'Fools. Should have run him through with a yataghan.'

Kostas spits over the side. Shadows stretch across the deck; the heat's gone. I flick further down the page, searching for something amusing to lift our mood.

I keep reading aloud, the others half-listening. Then laughter carries across the water—women's voices, bright and sharp. We all turn toward it. White dresses flash.

Damos grins. 'The Irish girls,' he says.

I glance back at the paper. 'Here,' I read. 'The *Red Rover*. Two hundred Irish girls aboard—free and virtuous, it says.'

Damos laughs. 'Not for long.'

Every man aboard has watched her these past two days, since she dropped anchor near us. I've thought about women these past two years. Of course I have. Not usually in daylight. But these girls are servant girls at best. Thieves or prostitutes at worst.

Andonis leans forward, arms on his knees. He has spoken little today, the heat wearing on him. Now, though, he lifts his head. 'Poor waifs,' he murmurs. 'Should have stayed in Ireland.'

Kostas folds his thick arms, eyes on the shore. 'Not for the likes of us. Best remember that.'

Damos hooks his thumbs into his belt and grins. 'Why not? Fine gentlemen, every one of us. Ladies of Sydney, form a queue.'

We drift to the rail, drawn by laughter and light voices calling across the water. A sound I've almost forgotten.

'Oi, love! I'd marry you in a heartbeat!' one of our convicts calls.

'You can't afford me, sir!'

More laughter ripples between the ships. Bright as birdsong. Even I smile.

As the laughter fades, my gaze lands on one girl, smaller than the rest, chin high, back straight. Not calling out like the others. Different. Her silhouette, touched by the sun, stands apart. Proud. Defiant.

The sun catches her hair.

For a moment, I can't smell the harbour or hear the men.

For a moment, I'm at home. On Hydra again.

My sister Katerina could silence a room with one look. This girl has the same steel in her.

And God help me, she's looking straight at me.

'Ah,' Damos drawls. 'Ghikas' head's turned.'

'I'm only admiring her rigging,' I say.

'She'd cut your throat,' he laughs.

'A Voulgaris doesn't choose his wife from a cargo manifest,' I say.

She doesn't look away. Chin high. Still. Unmoved. Something twists in my gut. Not hunger, not fear. Worse. Wanting.

No. I'm spoken for. When my sentence is done, I'll return to Hydra, reclaim my name, restore my family. I'll marry well—as I was meant to. Strength marries strength. Bloodlines, gold, alliance.

She's still there.

Still watching.

Something in me unclenches. For a second, I'm not proving anything to the men beside me—just feeling the quiet, like when Yiayia hummed at her mending, with no need to speak.

And for the first time in months, I feel something beyond survival.

I feel alive.

—

The bay lies quiet now. Both ships still. The girls too—faces lifted upward to the sky. Moonlight streaks across the water, painting the rigging silver.

Above us, an indigo sky is sprinkled with stars—no Cassiopeia, no Bear, no Little Dipper—all gone with the northern world. But the Milky Way is here—Hera's milk spilled across the heavens when she tore the infant Herakles from her breast—brighter here than anywhere. When Andonis and I were ship's boys on my father's vessels, we vowed one day to sail straight across it.

Low on the horizon gleams a constellation new to us: the mast-shaped Southern Cross—its long arm always pointing south.

The girl on the *Red Rover* watches the same stars. I know it.

The thought calms me.

A shout cuts across the water. The white dresses vanish below, quick as fish diving to the dark.

She's gone.

A footstep behind me.

'Get below!'

I'm still looking for her when the hatch slams shut above us.

—

Boots thud overhead. The wooden bar lifts with a heavy clunk, the hatch swings wide, sunlight floods the hold.

'On deck! Move!'

From across the way, Damos' voice cuts through the waking. 'What have you set down for us today, Ghika? A public flogging?'

I can't help laughing. 'Only for you, Damo.'

Men reach for their boots, leather white with salt, soles rotted by months at sea. I don't bother. Bare feet grip better.

We climb topside. Sunlight bounces off water and the ship lists gently at anchor, creaking with the tide. Men clutch tin cups of weak, tepid tea. The guards toss us chunks of stale bread, hurled from the sack like fish guts thrown overboard.

Nikos turns his over in his hand, frowning. 'Is this bread or ballast?'

Damos gnaws at his. 'You choose, Niko. Breakfast or a bludgeon.'

Kostas squints into the glare, eyes red and watering. Damos has been fighting his stomach for a week—and losing. Nikos is scratching. We all are.

'Look at us,' I say. 'Greek gods.'

They blink.

My shirt's in tatters, trousers held up by rope, a rash up both arms, chilblains bleeding. Cheeks peeling, beard knotted, and I smell like something that died in a barrel.

Silence.

Then Damos snorts. And chokes.

Andonis tries to laugh but ends up coughing.

Nikos grins. Kostas lets out a grunt—then another—and then a roar.

Laughter breaks over us like a squall—wheezing, helpless, uncontrollable. For a heartbeat we're not convicts or cargo. Just men.

We're boys again, laughing at the gods. Daring them to do their worst.

Even the guards grin.

'Line up!' The command cracks across the deck like a whip.

Laughter dies mid-breath. The guards shove us forward.

A folding oak desk has been set up by the mainmast. Neat brass hinges. A clerk sits behind it, scratching names into a ledger with looping strokes. Next to the book—a second sheet, not part of the register.

That's Hely's list. The Superintendent of Convicts.

And there he stands, red-faced, bored.

The Irish brothers are first.

'John, to Bathurst. Thomas—the Lumberyard.'

'No!' Thomas cries. 'We're brothers!'

The guards seize him. He fights and his brother joins in. The response is immediate and vicious.

'Take them below. Twenty lashes apiece when they're ashore.'

Andonis grips my arm. 'Steady. Don't be a fool.'

The sun climbs higher. The deck groans in the heat. Minutes drag like hours.

Nikos starts to scramble up the ratlines—a skill we perfected as boys—legs swinging out with each grab. 'É, Ghika! Look—that looks like one of your family's *archontiká*!'

He is pointing at a grand, two-storey house on the rise.

I'm below him in an instant. 'Niko—down. Now.'

He grins. The guard turns.

'Now,' I hiss.

He lands beside me and claps my back hard enough to send me overboard. I catch the rail.

'Smell that?' he says. 'Like figs in the sun.' His eyes shine as he lifts his face to the breeze. The white horizontal scar on his forehead—from a swinging boom—catches the light.

A passing sailor laughs. Everyone likes Nikos.

Kostas exhales through his nose, rare irritation surfacing. 'Figs?' His voice is low but edged with anxiety. 'We're lining up like animals ready for slaughter, Niko, and you're thinking about fruit?' He flexes his hands.

We'll be next.

'I wonder if your *yiayia* is baking today, Ghika,' Nikos says, half to himself. 'She always gave me *amygdalota*.'

He remembers the sweetness. I remember the table, Yiayia brushing crumbs from my sleeve, my mother's laugh, orange blossom on the breeze.

Names are called—age, crime, and trade; each man's destination decided in a single breath. The clerk's stained fingers dip the quill in the ink, scratches in each column, moves on. Another fate sealed.

Our turn.

My tongue sticks to my teeth. Every word is rehearsed. I'll convince him.

Hely doesn't bother to look up. 'Ah, the famous Greek pirates.' As if it's a disease.

Pirates. I look around, half-expecting someone else. That's what the English call men who fight without their permission.

He raises his eyes slowly, from our feet to our faces.

I step forward. Calm. Clear. Practised.

'Sir. Ghikas Voulgaris. From the island of Hydra. These men are my crew. Sailors. Shipbuilders from boyhood. Keep us together in the dock-yard, and we can—'

Hely flicks his wrist. As if swatting a fly.

I am about to list our skills. Tell him that our island is the centre of the Greek fleet, remind him that England and Greece are allies, remind him of Navarino. But the words die.

My throat closes. A drop of sweat slides down my spine.

A redcoat says too loudly, 'His family owns half the Mediterranean.'

Nikos nods, eager, loyal—he's told anyone who'll listen, thinking it will help. It's had the opposite effect.

I quiet him with a hand on his arm.

Hely tilts his head. 'Is that so?' Not derision. Boredom.

'Fourteen years, this one,' the clerk says.

I push on. 'Sir, Captain Greig will vouch for our work—rigging, hull repairs, mast fittings—'

He raises one tobacco-stained finger. Slow. Final.

I should play the grateful convict and fall silent. But I can't help myself. '—canvas, caulking, splicing—'

He taps his fist on the wood. Once. Twice.

I imagine ramming a quill through his hand. Or snapping his fingers backwards one by one.

He writes on his own sheet. Not the ledger. Not the register.

He leans back. 'Our task is complete.'

No reason. Just dismissal. A wave of the hand. As if we're already dead.

I don't move.

He thinks it's over. I nod once, as if we've reached an agreement.

Then I turn.

The guards shove us aside.

Behind me, Damos mutters, 'He didn't fancy your name much, Ghika.'
Nikos grips my arm. 'We go to the same place, yes?'
A breeze stirs the sweat on my back. The *Norfolk* creaks.
I search the deck of the *Red Rover*.
A guard shouts. We move.
I look back once more.
She's not there.

2

HYDRA

Son of Nikolaos

HYDRA

July 1822, *seven years earlier*

The smell of *stiphado* invaded my senses before my eyes opened—sizzling rabbit, cinnamon, cloves, and onion drifting up the stairwell. When Mamá cooked *stiphado*, it meant the fleet was back. My stomach growled.

Downstairs, the breakfast table would be set with olives, cheese, and warm bread. My little brother Makris would be first there, a harbour chart open beside his plate. At six, he knew the port depths from Poros to Piraeus —as our father demanded. As was expected of a Voulgaris. Seamanship was our language. Father said it was Hydra's greatest defence —more reliable than any gun.

On the steps outside the window, a mule-driver shouted, and the swish of Despina's broom was sweeping the courtyard clean, killing anything that moved — spiders, beetles, ants. I hated that. Two thousand dead men I could stomach, but not that small crunch underfoot. But she'd leave the early figs on the windowsill for Makris.

I rolled off the bedding and crossed to the basin. Despina had laid my clothes on the marble slab, as always. I ran my fingers over the cool stone, tracing the veins. I hauled on my *vraka* and fixed it with my red *zonári*. The white shirt went over my head, then the *geléki* vest—thread catching the light like fire on water. Clothes of a shipowner's son—the son of Nikolaos.

Hydra had been at war for fifteen months.

When the revolution began, we had no warships. Not one.

The shipowners—ours, Spetses, Psara—tore the bellies out of their own merchant brigs and bolted cannon to the decks. They paid for crews, powder, and provided the hulls for fireships. That passed as the Greek navy. And they sent their sons to fight.

Father said that was patriotism. He said it was why men like him should lead Greece. Men who risked their fortunes had earned the right to steer the future.

The English meanwhile patrolled our waters. Not prepared to help, yet calling us pirates when we attacked enemy ships.

I could barely hear the mule driver down the hill now.

Three months ago—in April—the Ottomans crushed the uprising on Chios. Burned the villages, hanged the priests, and chained the women and children for the slave markets in Smyrna and Constantinople. Forty thousand dead. Maybe more.

Yesterday the fleet had come home with the news that Psara's youngest captain, Kanaris, had sailed a fireship straight into the Turkish fleet at anchor and lit up their flagship like a pyre. The head of their navy, the Kapudan Pasha, went down with it, and two thousand men.

We'd wanted revenge since April. Now we had it.

Every cannon on Hydra had fired. The square was crowded—flags, speeches, salutes. My brothers were already on shoulders by the time I arrived. Father stood with the other councillors cheering Admiral Miaoulis.

A shipowner's son is meant to be at Mandraki when the fleet comes in. I understood why. The men on those ships were heroes. They deserved to see us waiting for them.

And I was late.

And even as I shouted myself hoarse, I knew Chios still lay in ruins. The Turks still held it. Those who'd survived the massacre were facing typhus, dysentery, smallpox, starvation. And when our ships returned soon to blockade the island—as they must—it would be the innocent who suffered first.

But Hydra was celebrating. And I was fifteen. Trained. Restless. Nailed to the dockyard by a father who thought that time alone would make me a man.

I wanted to fight. I wanted Greece whole again.

I stepped into the coolness of the dining room, shutters half-closed against the morning sun, the thick stone walls and high ceilings holding back the heat outside. The long table was set. Bread waited under cloth. Figs shone on a clay dish.

Makris had beaten me there. He'd smuggled a short length of rope to the table again, and he slid it toward me.

'Reef knot,' he said.

I tied it without looking. 'Bowline?'

He grinned. I flicked it neatly.

'Enough,' Mamá said, setting down the olives. 'Eat while it's warm— and take that chart off the table. That's why your father pays masters at the academy.'

'It's not just navigation, Mamá,' Makris said. 'Gunnery angles. Mathematics. Marine law. Even surgery.'

'Don't let them practise their surgery on you, little brother,' I said.

Mamá added a plate of white cheese and nodded for us to begin. She and Yiayia would eat later, as always. This was the men's meal.

'They say the wind carried the smoke and ash from the Turkish flagship and blew it all over our fleet,' she said.

My elder sister Katerina bounced into the room and kissed my cheek. My older brothers had homes of their own now, close by. They'd married, started families. I saw them often, but not usually at breakfast. Mamá would send Despina with dishes for their wives.

'No daughter-in-law should cook when her husband comes home,' she said.

Yiayia entered last, holding the pan, oil still spitting. I reached for a crispy fish tail.

She slapped my hand. 'You'll burn yourself! Fifteen years old and still a silly boy, Ghika.'

I winced and clutched my wrist. 'Yiayia, you've crippled me. How will I command a ship now?'

'Command?' she snorted. 'We'll tie you to the mast ourselves as a warning to the Turks.'

'You think it's over?' Mamá asked quietly, setting down a clay dish. 'Nikolaos says the Turks are trapped by our blockade, but so are the remaining Chiotes. And disease doesn't choose sides.'

Yiayia clicked her tongue. 'War is war. And the Sultan is bleeding.' She looked at the table with satisfaction. 'Please begin.'

Giorgios said, through a mouthful of fig, 'You're in trouble, Ghika.'

I tousled his hair and tossed an olive into my mouth. 'When am I not?'

Katerina laughed. She'd been radiating joy for weeks, ever since Father arranged her betrothal to a shipowner from Spetses. The war had slowed everything, but the match was made. Even in revolution, alliances were brokered.

'Will you play *tavli* with me tonight?' she asked.

'If you don't cheat.'

'That's called strategy.'

Makris was out of his chair and pulled at my vraka. 'Can I play too?'

I lifted him into the air and spun him around. 'Only if you promise not to win.'

Despina moved behind me with the bread.

'Always stirring the pot, Ghika,' she said.

'You'd be bored if I didn't, Despina.'

'*Kyra* Despina,' Mamá said gently. 'Have respect.' But she patted my shoulder as she said it.

'I belong on a warship, Mamá, not shifting timber. Not crewing supply ships. I could out-sail my brothers when I was twelve.'

'You're too reckless, too brave.'

I made the sign to ward off the evil eye. Praise like that can attract misfortune.

Anyway, my father wouldn't let me near a warship—he said I was too unpredictable. Volatile. They weren't just ships, he said; they were family assets.

Now they carried cannon, ran supplies, blockaded Ottoman ports. Trade was gone, and fortunes were dwindling.

Although it might take more than a war to eat up my father's fortune.

—

Footsteps sounded on the stone stairs. The room fell silent. Even Yiayia stopped what she was doing. Mamá adjusted a dish that didn't need adjusting.

He entered without a word, his eyes sweeping the table. They stopped on me. 'Where were you? You missed your brothers' return.'

'I saw the first brig and ran up the mountain to see if the other ships were coming. I took water to Yiannis on the way.'

It was true. Yiannis kept his sheep high in the hills. I'd stopped to fill his barrel, like I always did. But I'd also ducked into the old hut. The one we used as a fortress when we were boys. My friends were living there now—to ease the burden on their families. We were meant to be installing a cracked lintel. A builder had offered it free.

'We have sentries for that. Was your mission of mercy also to see your friends?'

I said nothing.

'A son who watches from a hill is not ready to command.'

I felt that in my chest.

His gaze didn't leave mine. 'My reception room. Now.'

Sweat trickled down my forehead as we climbed the stairs. His silences unnerved me more than his fury, and I didn't know which awaited me this time.

He stopped under Grandfather's portrait—dark curls, white teeth, brown skin, the fine straight nose the three of us shared. Mamá called it noble.

I touched my vraka with one hand. The other found the silver amulet at my chest—Saint George, the patron saint of Greece, seated on his horse, lance poised to strike the dragon. It had been my grandfather's, passed down through my mother, who swore it kept him safe at sea. She said it would protect me too.

I opened my mouth to explain, but he spoke before me.

'The *Icarus* came under fire. She needs repair before returning to Chios. She's at Palamidas. Ask your uncle which cousins he can spare. Go now. Sleep at the summer house. Do not return until the work is done.'

He tethered me to repairs—far from the open sea and battle.

Palamidas was a secondary shipyard. My prosperous cousins didn't need work, but my friends' survival depended on it.

'Forget your useless friends. Their fathers are bilge water.' He waved me out. Dismissed like a deckhand.

A surge of defiance anchored me in place. I was no child to be ordered about. I would hire my friends instead—it was the right thing to do.

'Their fathers have fought bravely for Greece.'

My father frowned, his grip tightening on the armrest of his chair.

'You forget yourself,' he said. 'They fight for coin.' He folded his arms. 'We sacrifice ships. While they squabble over wages, we fund the provisional government. Unity makes a nation, Ghika. Not mutiny. And we need unity, with English ships staring into our harbour.'

I clenched my fists until the nails bit into my palms. 'The men are not mutinous. They're hungry.'

His face flushed, a vein pulsing at his temple.

'They risk their lives,' I said. 'Is it wrong to ask for pay? What happens to their families if they don't come back? What happens to their wives? Their children?'

'The same as happens to us. You speak of fairness, Ghika, yet you disregard the perilous position we're in. Your reckless antics with those boys only fuel their insubordination.'

I wouldn't be silenced.

'Patéra, when a sailor dies, his wife inherits his debts. And his sons inherit hunger. When a shipowner dies—'

'His sons inherit command.' His voice cracked like a whip. 'You think your friends are loyal. They're loyal to themselves. To their bellies. Not to Greece. And certainly not to you.'

'They're like brothers to me. I won't turn my back on them.'

He stared at me. And then, slowly, the fight left his body. 'You leave me no choice, Ghika. Until you learn where your true loyalties lie, you are confined to the house and the shipyard. No more running to the hills. Men face responsibility.'

The weight of it hit me.

He thought responsibility meant obedience. I thought it meant looking after the men who sailed our ships, and being heard when I said so.

He would listen to me—if not here at home, then I'd show him on the quay, in the yard, anywhere that men worked for us.

—

As I descended the stairs, Giorgios was coming up. Taking my hand, he whispered, 'Is Father punishing you?'

I drew my finger across my throat and his eyes widened with horror. I cuffed him lightly and laughed.

Downstairs, the dining room had returned to chatter. As if my future hadn't just been rerouted to Palamidas.

I forced a grin. 'Well, I'm relegated to cleaning ships' heads at Palamidas.'

Giorgios made a retching expression.

'Who will help me write a letter of resignation?'

Mamá came to me and placed a reassuring hand on my arm. She spoke softly. 'Your father only wants you to understand the responsibilities that come with your name.'

I sighed, nodding. 'I know, Mamá. If only he could see things from another viewpoint.'

'Your father was once very much like you, Ghika. And he never forgave himself for what it cost him. He's only trying to help you.'

Makris looked up from his book, a grin on his ink-smudged face. 'Maybe now you'll have more time to fish with me.'

I snatched a handful of olives from Mamá's bowl and kissed her cheek.

Yiayia crossed herself. 'I'll burn a candle for you. Stay safe.'

'I'll bring back fish from Palamidas,' I promised.

As I bounded down the steps to the quay, two at a time, I imagined my fleet after the war—sleek black hulls with white stripes lined up in the harbour. Maria's smile at sunrise. Sons at our feet.

My cousin Dimitris' voice sliced through my daydream. 'Ghika! Splendid victory at Chios, was it not?'

Dimitris, with his overly ambitious moustache, was older than me by two years, and was everything Father wished me to be—a walking measure of my shortcomings. When his father, my uncle and the island's governor, died when Dimitris was only ten, he turned tragedy into opportunity. At sixteen, he'd assumed control of his father's fleet; now, he not only commanded his own ship but also sat on Hydra's governing council. At this rate, he'd rule Greece.

'On your way to the quay?' he asked, voice as polished as his future.

I forced a smile. 'Patéra wants me to oversee repairs to the *Icarus*.' I felt myself blush at the lie. I'd follow orders, not give them.

'Responsibility suits you. I hope you live up to it.' He stroked his moustache as if it held the answer to every question.

So sure of himself.

'I will hire my friends,' I said. It came out before I could stop it.

His look told me he was taking me seriously. Good. Let him see I had a mind of my own. Just because they had the wrong names didn't mean they were worthless.

He ran his thumb and forefinger along the edge of his moustache, considering. Then he said, 'The *Icarus* would be better served by our cousins. Do you wish to prove your friends' loyalty—or yours?'

I frowned.

He leaned in and dropped his voice. 'A man who fights for Greece does not count his wages before the war is won. Ghika, be cautious. Their fathers do not share our allegiance.'

I was not a spineless sea slug. 'I'm not employing their fathers,' I snapped.

He said nothing.

I knew what happened to men who spoke out of turn. One of the island's heroes, Antonios Oikonomou, had expelled the governor and stood on the quay the year before, declaring that Greece was at war. The elders hadn't approved—too afraid of losing their Ottoman privileges and trade. The crowd cheered. The council didn't.

They had him arrested. He escaped. Made it as far as Argos. That's where they found him. That's where he died.

By then, the shipowners had declared war themselves.

That was how Hydra handled defiance. But I was a Voulgaris. I could bend the rules.

Heat came off the cobblestones as I hurried toward the harbour, and off the square, whitewashed houses stacked like spectators on the amphitheatre of hills around the port. Gulls swooped in graceful circles over the forest of masts: *caïques*, *hydraiki*, schooners, brigs. Our mighty three-masted polaccas were a mile along the coast at Mandraki Bay with the rest of the fleet.

On the quay, my best friend Andonis was lifting an empty water barrel onto his shoulder, the others trailing behind for more. I lifted one and swung it aboard before anyone could ask. My father said I'd be ready for a warship when I could see what needed doing, judge what mattered most, and do it. Not for praise but for honour—*philotimo*.

So for now, I shifted barrels, patched splintered hulls, ferried supplies. Work. But not war.

My friends weren't idlers either. Before the war, their fathers had worked for mine, and they'd been sailors ever since they could walk— quick, capable, and trusted.

Every man chased a place on a warship. Few were chosen. I hadn't earned mine yet. Or perhaps my mother was influencing my father to keep me out of danger.

'*Kaliméra*, Ghika.' Andonis—a qualified purser and the same age as me—grabbed me in a hug. 'Why did our ancestors settle on an island with no water? And what kept you?' he added, grinning.

'Father kept me,' I said. 'We had a 'talk'. I'm banished to Palamidas.'

He stopped smiling. 'What about the lintel?'

'That plan's been scuttled.' I made a face.

He squinted with his odd eye. 'Why?'

I shaded mine from the glare bouncing off the water. 'I'm to help patch the *Icarus*. And stay there until it's done.'

Damos cut in, unable to help himself. He always had something to prove. 'I saw her being towed yesterday. They're letting you near her?'

I didn't give him the satisfaction of seeing me flinch. 'Damo, if you worked as much as you talked, you'd be running Palamidas, not hammering nails.'

The words sounded hotter than I meant, but I didn't look away.

His father sailed for Marseilles when he was six and didn't come back. He'd carried a man's load ever since. He was a qualified ships' carpenter and knew ships better than I did—maybe better than anyone our age—but he was the wrong class, and the wrong temperament. Too impertinent with authority, too quick to take offence, too ready to speak

his mind. He resented that doors opened for me that stayed closed
to him.

'You want us to help.' Andonis wasn't asking.

If the yard needed hands, standing by my friends—and proving myself
to them—was worth the risk. And if Father called that mutiny, he could
come say so to my face at Palamidas.

'Yes. Let's go.'

'Right,' said Andonis. 'We'll collect our pay and our bags.'

Kostas crossed his arms. 'I want to make music, not sawdust.'

I rolled my eyes. Kostas hated mess—sixteen years old, the same as
Damos—and the *bouzouki* was already his life. When his fingers touched
the strings, no one spoke. But you couldn't support a family that way. I
kept telling him.

'I'm in low spirits, Ghika,' said giant Nikos, kneeling on a seashell on
the flagstones. 'I've lost a shell.' He looked up and broke into a warm
smile. 'I've missed you. I'm thirsty.'

'I've missed you too, Niko,' I said, and I meant it. Nikos needed
someone to tell him where to put his feet. He couldn't be more different
from my father, whose Christian name he shared.

As I filled his cup at the rain barrel, the sizzle of *souvlaki* from a
nearby stall made my mouth water. My father had recently lectured me
about my 'generous' spending habits. But my friends couldn't work with
empty stomachs.

That was something Yiannis understood. He caught us stealing grapes
from his vines when we were six. He didn't shout or raise a hand. He only
laughed. After that, we brought him treats from Yiayia, helped with his
sheep and goats, and watched him cook *tiganites* on the hot stones. His
view of the world clashed with my father's—and, sometimes, with mine.

He had no ship, no fortune—but his common sense and wisdom spoke
straight to me. I never forgot his words, delivered over a honeyed hotcake
with walnuts from his tree. 'Do you know how I judge a man, lads? By
whether he shares his bread.'

That was a rule I could follow.

Even now we were close to manhood, we still visited him.

But now, bellies full, we tramped along the coastal cliffs under the blis-
tering sun, past the battlements where a hundred cannon pointed seaward,

sweat running down our faces and soaking our shirts. I lobbed olives for them to catch in their mouths, laughter shaking my sense that I was doing something I shouldn't.

I launched a playful assault on Andonis with a wild yell. '*Eleftheria i thanatos*!' Give us freedom or give us death. The battle cry.

Andonis frowned. 'And if you die, Ghika? Maria Kountouriotis will marry someone else.'

'I've heard she will marry your cousin Dimitris,' said Damos. 'He's richer than you will ever be.'

'He is a *koufiokéfalos*,' I said. An empty head. Although I was calculating—the Voulgaris fleet, even split among more brothers, could stand its ground against the Kountouriotis'. Our house on Kiafa Hill had been built by the same Genoese craftsmen; the courtyard bloomed with colourful exotics planted in soil shipped from the mainland. Inside, the same marble floor tiles ran black and white like a chessboard—Makris and I used to race down the hall and skid in our stockings. The reception room had a marble fountain—a trickle, but enough to cool the air. The cedar ceiling curved like the hull of a ship turned upside down, and when we had company, the servants lit rose oil in the copper lamps.

Mamá used to say even the cat walked with pride in our house.

But yes, it was bold to wish for Maria's hand. But as Yiayia always said, *to thrasos einai i misi andriosýni*—audacity is half of a man's bravery.

The steep Avlaki cliff beside us dropped straight to the rock ledge on the small bay, a perfect diving platform. We spent summers there as children, sun-browned and sleek as dolphins.

'Come, we'll jump from the rocks!' I said.

Andonis shook his head.

'You were limping for a week last time,' Damos said, laughing.

In the distance, the island of Dokos rose like a whale from the sea, stretching away to the powdered blue hills of the mainland and Ermione, where my family's farming land supplied food for the Voulgaris houses. Our island was rocky and steep, with little arable soil.

From when I was young, Father had sent me to the farms in different periods of the year—to learn how to run them. I hated every minute. I trimmed vines wrongly, fed the donkeys too much, dropped olives into the wrong basket. But I never forgot how the foreman checked a tree—how he ran his fingers under the leaves to test for rust.

Kostas said, 'What about Maria's father's own wedding? When a bravo stabbed her grandfather with a *bichaq*? And killed him outright.'

I flicked my hand in dismissal—that was over the Russian alliance. A very sad event, but nothing to do with my marriage.

'Maria's family doesn't lose sleep over a trifle like bloodshed,' I said. But my stomach churned. It made my father angry, this aversion of mine—only women fainted at the sight of blood.

Andonis said, 'Marriage isn't just a business proposition.'

'Love is for fools, Andoni,' I teased him. I danced along the path, fingers clicking in rhythm. Island marriages were arranged, and ours would join two of the richest families—a strategy like a well-planned sea battle. I'd seen Maria a few months ago when I delivered a message to her father. As she descended the stairs, our shoulders brushed, her scent hitting me like a fresh sea breeze blowing across lavender.

'*Kaliméra*, Ghika,' she said. Two words, and the step under my foot vanished. I was nine again, kneeling in the lemon grove behind the Kountouriotis house. She'd laughed; told me I'd have to earn her.

I promised I would. From that day on, whenever I scaled a mast, it was her face I saw when I reached the top. Maria wouldn't only be my betrothed—she was the measure of my future.

But the memory of her was gone, leaving me filled with longing. Andonis spoke again. 'Have you spoken to her?'

He knew that was impossible. Women like Maria left their fathers' houses only on special occasions, and only with chaperones. 'You know I haven't. Have you spoken to Anastasia?'

I was teasing, too. Andonis' shyness concealed his deep affection for Anastasia, the daughter of a servant in the house of a ship's captain. He had loved her since we were small boys, and I wished for his happiness. But she didn't seem to have the same affection for him—her eyes were always moving, always on the lookout for a better prospect. There were nicer girls than Anastasia.

—

We descended the slope to the moorings at Kamini, lured by the sparkling blue water. Fishermen and their wives mended nets on the rocks, arms glistening in the scorching heat. Andonis' family *caïque*, the *Niki*, sat among others, half out of the water. A trusty old vessel—no warships here.

'Race you in!' I shouted, throwing down my bag and sprinting across the hot stones. My friends were behind as I ran into the water, dragging my legs through the shallows until I tumbled forward. As I hit the water, the icy shock stole my breath, but laughter bubbled up in its place. We stood there, hands scooping up liquid diamonds, launching them in sparkling arcs through the shimmering air. The fresh wind in my face, against my wet shirt, stirred a thrill of excitement.

'É, Andoni,' I called, shaking the water from my hair. 'How about a quick sail in your father's old tub?'

He furrowed his brow as he looked at the low roll of cloud on the horizon, lightning flashing inside it.

'What about Palamidas?' he said.

I shrugged. 'The *Icarus* can wait an hour.'

'The wind's picking up,' said Kostas, flat and certain.

'Your cousin Dimitris told my uncle you weren't fit for command,' said Damos. 'Are you trying to prove him right?'

I flung a stone into the sea, heat rising in my neck. 'Did he, now?'

'And that's not a wind. That's a *bouríni*,' said Damos. A rare summer storm. A *bouríni* spelled danger.

The air smelled of rain on dirt. Intoxicating. The sky had that sharp, polished look it gets before a storm, as if the gods had taken a whetstone to it.

Nikos hurled another arc of water at me. I dodged, laughing, and slapped Andonis on the shoulder.

Kostas shook his head. 'I'm not going.'

Andonis would follow me.

'Come on, Andoni,' I said. 'Do you think Admiral Miaoulis waits for permission?' His jaw tightened.

I reached for my amulet and grinned. If they wouldn't listen on land, I'd make them listen at sea.

The waves were turning the sea to froth. The wind was rising.

3

Prisoners' Barracks

SYDNEY, New South Wales
   September 1829

The first launch has already pulled away from the *Norfolk*, riding low with convicts. Two others bob alongside ready to load.

'I'm ready,' says Nikos, shifting his grip. 'Shall we go?'

On deck, redcoats stand watch, muskets slung, eyes on us as we descend the rope ladder one by one—each man carrying his life in a bundle.

The boat noses up to a narrow wharf extending way out beyond the reeds below the Governor's residence.

Over on George Street, the bustling main street of the town, the King's Wharf beats like a pulse, convicts and redcoats shouting, barrels clanging, crates thudding, the scrape of goods being unloaded from ox-drawn drays. Goods flow on and off ships in a constant rhythm of labour and trade.

We line up at the end of our jetty, met by men with authority who jot down notes, assessing our worth. A gentleman steps forward, a chain glinting at his waistcoat as he writes in a notebook. His gaze moves across us, appraising.

It stops on me.

'One of the Greeks, eh?'

'Yes, sir. Five. From Hydra.'

'Hydra.' He nods slowly, thoughtful. 'You're a braw boy. You grow vines for wine there? Sheep, citrus?'

I straighten, surprised. 'Exactly, sir. Sheep on the hills, vineyards and orchards along the valleys.' A lie. Hydra has barely a donkey track between it and God.

He gives a faint smile. '*Seep*?'

I flush. There is no 'sh' sound in Greek, and I cannot master it.

'Don't worry, lad, it's not how you pronounce the word. It's how you look after them that counts.'

'We are sailors, sir, skilled at building ships—' I stumble on 'ships'. 'Put us in the dockyard and we'll earn our keep.'

He nods again, lips pursed, clearly satisfied. 'Good. That's good. Your name?'

'Ghikas Voulgaris.'

He writes it down. No more questions. Just a flick of his watch chain as he moves along.

Andonis leans close. 'Who was that? He didn't speak to anyone else.'

'I don't know,' I say, still watching him go. 'But he carries himself as if he owns half of Sydney.'

A redcoat waves us forward with a flick of his musket, as if swatting flies. We march—not through the town, but around it, to the east of the Governor's mansion. Dust as thick as flour catches in our throats. Sweat trickles down my arm, past the manacle scar on my wrist. The smell of roasting meat drifts on the breeze and my stomach knots.

Someone's eating well. It won't be us.

In the distance, a vendor cries, 'Fine sand mullet! Snappers, all alive! Kingfish, whiting, oysters ho!' The voice rises and falls in nasal tones I've learned to recognise on the *Norfolk*—a Londoner.

To the right is a muddy watercourse choked with weeds and refuse; on this side, a lumber yard faces the main street—stacks of timber, sawdust swept into heaps. The Sydney Gazette back on the *Norfolk* said they've cleared the rooms to lodge the *Red Rover* girls. Until they find work. Or husbands.

The Governor's domain lies up the hill. We march past his mansion—

modest enough—and neatly fenced vegetable gardens. Stables with polished brass. Cabbage rows so neat they must have been measured with a yardstick. We slow without meaning to. Andonis squints at the patch. Damos mutters something low under his breath.

A guard marching beside us barks, 'Eyes front! His Excellency counts every cabbage in that patch himself.'

Another grumbles, 'And he'd put a toll on the privy if he could.'

'Ask that poor bastard Sudds what happens if you step out of line.'

A snort from behind. 'You can't. He's dead.'

'Darling hates the Irish,' the first one says, lowering his voice. 'Hates bushrangers. Flogs a man for coughing.'

'Or for thinking about it,' the second mutters.

Dry grass crunches underfoot and sweat sticks the shirt to my back. Beside me, Andonis drags his feet, breathing shallow—ever since the flogging, he tires quickly, but he will never admit to pain—so I stay close, ready to press a hand against his back when he falters.

When we reach the barracks, I spot a familiar figure—Mister Hallan from the *Norfolk*—a government architect lodged in a passenger cabin. The kind of man who toasts Greek liberty, but would spill none of his own blood for it. Fresh coat, gleaming boots. A servant holds his luggage. Now he stands outside the Colonial Architect's office, shaking hands, wearing the kind of clothes I once had tailored in Nafplio—with a shoemaker who knew my name.

Hallan steps inside without glancing at us. Days ago, we ate the same wormy biscuit. Now he is served—and I carry. I was raised to command ships, not take orders like a deckhand.

I'd better become accustomed to it.

The handsome red-brick barracks looms on our right—encircled by walls, domed sandstone guard towers on each corner. Redcoats stand near the entrance, muskets slung across their backs, eyes tracking us as we approach. A military band in grey uniform plays faintly in the distance, the tune swallowed in the dust of the large open area.

'Greenway designed this,' a guard says. 'A convict. How's that for justice?'

A convict? A man like us designing buildings? What else might a convict become here? Maybe class lines in the colony aren't as uncrossable as they look.

The gates swing open and we file in. A stench rises from a wastewater ditch running through the grounds.

Superintendent Hely waits in the courtyard. On one side, a giant of a man, the handle of a coiled whip resting against his leg, face heavy and watchful. On his other side, an almost pretty, elderly gentleman, grey curls brushed forward, skin the colour and texture of bread dough, a froth of cream silk at his throat.

Hely's voice rings out across the gravel. 'Welcome to the Prisoners' Barracks.' As if we're cattle ready for slaughter. 'We've already met,' he says. 'All paperwork comes through me. Convictions. Sentences. Assignments. Applications to marry. Tickets of Leave.'

He says that last like it's a prize.

A pause. 'Deaths.' Another pause. 'You will not be shackled unless you reoffend. Those who do will work on a road gang or the treadmill. In irons. Run, and you will be caught and hanged. Or sent to Norfolk Island. Or killed by the blacks. Or starve.'

The treadmill? I turned the word over. A mill?

'Your day is run by the bell. Rise on the dawn bell. Sleep at the night bell. Work in between.'

He turns to the older man.

'And now a word from Mister Alexander Macleay, Secretary to the Governor.'

'Gentlemen,' Macleay begins. 'This colony is built on order, industry, and reform. Those not yet assigned will receive their orders on Friday.'

He scans the lineup—curious, not cruel.

'Follow the rules. Work well. Conduct yourselves with honour. There are opportunities here—for those who understand their place.'

I hear the words. I don't believe them.

I take a chance. 'Sir.'

Macleay blinks.

'We are five men, sir. From Hydra.' I nod towards my friends. 'We request assignment to the same employer.'

Anything, as long as they don't separate us.

A flicker of recognition. 'Ah, yes. The Greeks.' He looks at Hely. 'The dockyard needs men.'

Hely's face stays blank. But relief floods through me.

They leave, and the giant with the whip follows.

Convicts loiter nearby, watching us like men checking a hull for dry rot. We don't fit in. Skin too dark. Tongue too foreign. Greeks. Pirates, not thieves.

But we have the strength of numbers. They keep their distance.

We're issued slops—canvas trousers and a coarse shirt, PB stencilled large for Prisoners' Barracks, and a brown arrow on the chest. Yellow-grey waistcoat. The shoes are crude, the leather stiff, unyielding—a far cry from the soft kid leather at home. I look down at my own—what's left of them. Soles coming apart, but the leather has moulded to my feet. They won't last much longer.

I pull on the new pair. I'll have blisters by nightfall.

Nikos holds his up, beaming. 'We have gifts, Ghika!'

I haul on the trousers. 'A fine fit. If I were a barrel.'

We don't have long to enjoy them.

A door bangs open. Boots on stone. The giant steps in and waits for silence.

'Deputy Superintendent Lane. Mister Lane to you.' Voice clipped, eyes hard. 'You Greeks don't want splitting? Easily fixed. I'll chain you together.'

He laughs. No one joins in.

He uncoils the cat-o'-nine-tails and lets the blood-stiffened cords dangle. 'Three punishments if you break the rules. Solitary. The treadmill. Or this.' He lifts the whip. 'Most lads prefer my friend. Painful but quick. Merry entertainment.'

Upstairs, hammocks hang in long narrow rows in dormitories—if one man moves, the whole line sways. Some hammocks have shirts or blankets bound tightly with rope and tied on.

Kostas studies the room. 'Keep your belongings close. Or you won't see them again.'

We are handed chunks of soap that stink of tallow and lye. A joke, considering that when we find the wash area—a shallow basin set along the back wall of the courtyard—it's fed by a trickle of murky water. The stench of the privies clings to the air, ripe in the heat.

A man grins at us from the corner of the yard, chewing on a scrap of bread. My skin crawls.

A bell rings for the midday meal. Hundreds of convicts trudge back from work, wiping sweat from their faces. We follow them into one of two mess rooms on the southern wall, the kitchen in between. Six hundred men, two sittings.

A rough-looking convict ladles sludge onto our tin plates, the spoon clanking against the pot.

Mamá's pot was blackened outside, but silver within—filled with fluffy pilaf, scented with cinnamon and cloves. I close my eyes. For a moment, I smell home: fish grilling over coals, warm bread torn by hand, my mother pressing a piece into mine. Then it's gone.

Nikos eyes his bowl, then mine. 'If they have fish, Ghika, will you buy me some?'

I laugh. 'With what, Niko? My good looks?'

On my plate is a lump of salted beef, barely softened by boiling, in a watery gruel thick with sediment. The chalky grit crunches between my teeth.

We sit on a crowded bench. No one speaks.

At the next table, spoons scrape against tin plates. I catch the words, '*Red Rover*, that's what I heard'.

'Lucky bastards in the town,' one says. 'Two hundred of them, and we're stuck in here.'

'Won't be long before they're married off,' another says, shoving a lump of meat into his mouth. 'Not that I'd take one. Harlots, most of them.'

He elbows his mate. 'You'd take one without teeth.'

I think of the girl and hope she finds a kind employer. Strange that I recall her. Stranger still that I care.

Something brushes my coat. I catch a wrist—thin, quick, already pulling back with my handkerchief in his fist. Attached to the head is a tangle of filthy blond hair.

'Searchin' you for weapons is all. Meant no harm.' The man grins.

Before I can speak, he's gone—vanished like a crab on wet sand.

At the evening bell, we return to the dormitory. The room stinks worse —bodies, breath, wet cloth.

A man with a ginger beard cleans his teeth with a piece of straw. 'Plenty more where they came from,' he says, nodding at a rat. 'Kill a hundred, a hundred more take their place.'

I rub my arms, an itch starting under my skin.

'Who was Sudds?' I ask.

'A British soldier. Stole a bolt of cloth because he heard convict life out here was better. Governor put him in twenty-two pound irons to prove a point. Marched him too long in the sun and left him in the stockade; the heat did the rest.'

A pause.

'That was three years ago. But no one's forgotten that's what Darling's like.'

The dormitory captain paces between the rows, eyes on us in the darkness. He and his mates own the hammocks nearest the door—where it's cooler, with easier access. Our hammocks are in the farthest corner, against the wall. The air is staler here; the heat trapped.

A convict jerks his head toward the door. 'Use the bog before lights out. Rise after that and you'll be flogged.'

I help Andonis into his canvas. Then Nikos. Then myself. The row swings. Curses fly. A knee hits my ribs. A heel clips my back. Lice and fleas live in the seams.

At last I'm in.

Kostas hums a tune and slaps time on his stomach.

'Stow it,' someone mutters from the dark.

'Let him be,' says another voice. 'Better that than the chains in me head.'

Kostas hums louder. Plucks at the air like it's a bouzouki.

He finishes the tune and the dormitory falls quiet, the silence broken only by the sound of scratching and snoring. I lie there, thinking.

Then I hear a whisper. Nikos.

He's giving away his blanket. I grab it back and wedge it under his arm. The man grins in the dark. He'll be back.

'Not everyone is your yiayia, Niko,' I whisper.

'He only wanted my blanket, Ghika.'

'And what next?' I nudge his shoulder. 'Your boots? Your food? Your shirt?'

'He must be cold,' he says. Warm. Kind.

I press my hand to my face. 'Next time, tell him no. It's yours.'

'Why?'

Because I may not be there to hold them off forever.

Back on Hydra, I left him once. We ran from a gang of older boys. I thought he was behind me. He wasn't. I found him with blood on his knees, sobbing. I never made that mistake again.

Tomorrow, I'll teach him.

—

Breakfast is 'hominy'—a porridge made from Indian corn, yellow and bitter—and a small portion of salted beef. The bread is coarse, sour, rock-hard, and crawling with weevils. I chew and force myself to swallow. Hunger will be worse.

After breakfast, in the yard, three men close in on Nikos. They circle like dogs scenting blood. One shoves his shoulder. Nikos—the loveable idiot—smiles.

'Where'd you find those shoes?' one asks in a lazy drawl.

Another chuckles. 'Think you could give me a pair, boy? And your shirt? Look at mine.'

Nikos spreads his arms to show off. 'These are new ones!'

He thinks they're admiring him.

The big one strokes his chest.

I'm already moving.

But then something flickers in Nikos' eyes. He looks down at the hand. Then up.

He remembers. Maybe the blanket.

'No,' he says. Still gentle. Still Nikos. 'You should not treat people so.'

'Should I not?' says the biggest.

'No. You're unkind.'

I push forward, planting myself between them. 'Leave him be.'

The big one reaches past me and grabs Nikos by the wrist.

A fist jabs my ribs. Testing me.

Nikos steps toward me and his head jerks sideways—blood smeared along his lip. He blinks, startled. He doesn't even know who hit him.

If I protect him every time, he'll never learn. But if I don't—

They move.

One hooks an arm around Nikos' throat. Another drives a fist into his stomach. He doubles over with a grunt. Someone else grabs his arm, twisting, forcing him down.

I throw myself forward, wrenching one of them off, but another grabs my shirt, dragging me back. A fist crashes into my jaw. My head jerks sideways—pain bursts white behind my eye.

Nikos is gasping now. He shoves the man away and swings wild and wide, like a boy with a scythe. He swings again, sending two reeling.

They step back.

I drive my elbow into my man's gut, shove him back and stagger free.

It's done. One wipes his mouth, curses, walks off. Nikos hunches over, panting. His hand bleeds.

'Ghika, I didn't like that,' he says.

Neither did I.

'I didn't like it,' he says again, and walks away.

His back is straight. But I know he's shaken.

So am I.

I don't feel proud. I feel sick.

Maybe I've made him a target.

—

I ask what the treadmill is. It's an English invention of torture—of course. A great wooden wheel like a paddlewheel. Men grip a rail and climb its steps for six hours—driving a mill to grind wheat into flour.

That afternoon, we're back in time to see men returning from the carters' barracks where they keep it. Their legs buckle, feet struggle to find steady ground. Sweat streaks their slops, dust cakes their skin. Their palms are raw and peeling from clutching the crossbar. Some cradle their fingers like broken birds.

Damos says, 'By God, you'll never see me in that company. Let some other poor bastard grind the King's grain.'

Night falls, and a voice at the dormitory door murmurs my name in the darkness.

I freeze. One of the men from this morning? I tense to rise.

But Nikos' voice cuts through the darkness. Loud. Calm. Certain. 'No, you will not. Not tonight.'

Silence. Footsteps, fading.

I let out a breath.

I wait for Nikos to make a joke. He doesn't. After a while he speaks— quietly, as if reminding himself. 'If they send me somewhere different from you, Ghika—I know what to do.'

I stare at the dark ceiling.

He's learning.

God help him. He's learning.

—

The next morning, the muster bell sends us to roll call, where Lane barks out the work details. The guards pull the shackled men into groups— they're under heavy guard, bound for road gangs, farms and quarries beyond the town.

A voice calls for the dockyard men. We step forward and the work bell sends us down George Street toward the harbour. Redcoats pace beside us, easy. There's nowhere to run.

On our left, a row of shops lines the street—tailors, bakers, ware- houses. A fishmonger guts a catch on a wooden block, tossing scraps to a dog at his feet. Ahead, carts and drays lurch over ruts, barrels rattling as drivers curse. A woman in a bonnet sweeps her front doorway, casting a wary glance our way as we pass. A man rides past on horseback, urging his horse through pedestrians.

Sydney is no Hydra. The English built this town for function, not beauty. The sea breeze at home carries the smell of fresh fish and citrus, lime-wash and wild herbs drying in the sun.

A woman in a torn bonnet lifts her head as we pass. For a heartbeat, I think it is she, the girl from the Red Rover. Same chin, similar way of standing like she owns the ground. Then she turns, and it's not her. The Red Rover girls haven't disembarked yet. Or perhaps they have.

We halt at the gates.

'Concentrate on the work, Ghika. Leave the running of the dockyard to them,' says Andonis.

At first, we perform brute labour—hauling rope, shifting cargo, carrying steaming buckets of pitch, backs bent under heavy loads. Nothing I haven't done a thousand times before—only I'm used to giving orders. We work without stopping, sweat soaking our shirts, arms burning with the effort. I cover for Andonis when his energy flags so the overseers don't notice.

At close of work, the guard says we're at liberty—we must be back at the barracks by the bell.

We pool our coins and find a barber shop near the wharf. The sharp scent of lather, the sting of razor against my jaw—each stroke scraping months of grime from my face—feels like shedding the past.

I watch the dark brown curls drop to the floor. 'What do you do with the hair?' I ask.

'Burn it,' says the barber. 'What else?'

I nod. Satisfactory. Everyone knows that a man with a piece of your hair has part of your soul.

He sweeps the clippings into the brazier. Nothing escapes.

When he sets me upright, I run a hand over my cheeks—rasped raw—and brush my fingers along the tight braid at the back of my neck. Cool air touches skin I haven't felt in months. I could almost pass for respectable.

We head back to the barracks with blistered hands and cleaner faces.

Two mornings later, the shipwright leads us to the joinery shed. He barely glances at us as he jerks a thumb toward a cracked beam—not bad enough to warrant replacing. We are to reinforce it—chisel, fit braces, fix with treenails.

Damos runs a hand along the split, testing the depth with practiced fingers. The overseer watches, arms folded, as if debating. He indicates the tools and walks away. Two redcoats remain nearby.

We set to. Damos measures and marks the braces, then swears softly when the beam is out of true. He recalculates, adjusting the cut. Andonis steadies the plank while he saws. Kostas and I chisel and file to refine the fit, shaving the edges until the braces seat cleanly. Nikos prepares the treenails—hardwood dowels that swell tight when driven in. He rough shapes them first, the grain coarse and uncooperative. On the second go, he shifts his angle, letting the blade follow the grain. Cleaner taper. Tighter seat. By the third, he's fast. Efficient. Not pretty—but solid. They'll hold.

The overseer returns partway through, says nothing, leans on a post and watches. Every move feels scrutinised. The hammering starts slowly—align, test, align—then quickens to a steady rhythm as the treenails are driven in, locking the braces against the split.

When it's done, the shipwright gives one nod. 'There are more,' he says, pointing to a heap.

It lands like a stamp of approval.

Damos wipes his forehead with his sleeve, satisfied. 'That's high praise. Will someone please fetch my wages? You'll need a handcart.'

We laugh, but it lingers. There's talk that skilled convicts are allowed to take private work. Maybe even earn wages.

The guards talk as they watch us sweat.

'Wentworth's at it again,' says one, shifting his musket. 'Now he reckons convicts should be allowed to buy land. Sit on juries. Next thing, they'll want a seat in government.' He's sneering.

His mate shrugs. 'Maybe they should. Some of 'em are smarter than the blue bloods running the place.'

'Wentworth should stick to lawyering,' the first one says.

Wentworth, I gather, is some sort of barrister with a newspaper called *The Australian*—and he doesn't support the current governor. *The Sydney Gazette* does—their own civil war, on paper. Apparently Wentworth's father was an explorer. Found a way through the mountains to the west. The son is carving his own path.

A third guard spits. 'Macquarie let men rise by skill. Darling says that's dangerous. Wants to keep the classes in their place.'

I can hear my father now, agreeing with Darling—not because criminals might earn respect, but because rank is slipping. Labourers giving orders. Tradesmen commanding ships.

But I've seen skill. You don't need a name to have good sense. You don't need a title to do a fine job. If this colony won't use men like that, it's the colony that suffers.

And it's not just men. At breakfast, someone said a convict woman—a

Mary Reibey—owns half the wharves. I've seen her name on a ship, a warehouse. They say she started a bank.

If this place can raise her, maybe there's hope.

Unless, of course, you're Greek.

Damos says he heard that the Red Rover girls are due to disembark this week. I pretend not to listen. But every time I see the harbour, I make sure she's still at anchor.

If I see the girl again, I'll know her.

I feel a sting on the back of my neck. Slap it. Blood. I gag, as I always do. Nikos laughs as if it's the funniest thing he's ever seen.

'A gadfly, Ghika,' he chortles. 'The flies favour your blood still.'

Andonis leans against a piling, breath shallow.

'Ease up, Andoni,' I mutter.

He shakes his head. 'I must keep up. It's the only way.'

I don't argue.

When I glance up, I catch the shipwright speaking in a low voice with an overseer, eyes flicking our way.

A man at the far end of the shed works alone, back straight, movements clean. No one is watching him, and still he works as if the world depends on it.

We too are proving our worth. We move like men who've done this before. And we don't wait for orders.

If we keep this up, they won't send us anywhere else. We're gaining status.

This is working. My plan is holding.

4

A Rising Wind

HYDRA

July 1822

Together, we heaved the Manolis caïque—the *Niki*—into deeper water. I grabbed the gunwale, oiled wood slick beneath my palms.

'Don't worry, Andoni,' I said. 'We'll be back before the storm breaks.'

We leapt aboard—young, fearless, certain—with Andonis at the tiller, hands as steady as his gaze. The lateen caught clean and tight, and we surged away from Kamini, steering straight into the teeth of the storm. The hull sliced through the chop as I hauled the sheet, palms burning even as spray cooled my face.

Andonis could have tacked wide. But we didn't sail that way—we were Hydriots—sons of men who ran wheat past the British and sailed our ships so close to the wind that one wrong move meant death. Our sailors were famous for it.

The British thought they ruled the seas; we sailed circles around them.

One day soon, I'd captain my own ship. For my family. For Greece. For freedom.

I licked the salt from my lips as white-toothed smiles lit our brown faces. We whooped into the wind. It ripped our shouts away and I felt like a god. On the choppier water of the channel, we picked up speed. My chest lifted with the sail—my friends, my island, our life.

The light changed. Curtains of rain swept across the rising white caps. Damos flinched at a clap of thunder. Nikos laughed again and hunched his wide shoulders, face tipped back to catch the first drops in his mouth. The wind roared. Every gust hit harder. The sail strained. The mainland was obscured in blackness.

'Time to turn for home!' Andonis shouted.

'Not yet,' I shouted back. 'Wait.'

He glanced at me—for a second—but held the course.

Then a gust hit. Harder than before. The *Niki* lurched. A wave reared up ahead. We weren't racing the storm any longer—we were within it.

'Now!' I shouted, seizing the tiller.

Andonis scrambled away, face wet with spray. I turned her back toward the island. Faster and faster, we crash-skimmed across the deepening waves, leaving sense in our wake.

Rain crossed in driving sheets.

A ripping sound. The sail flapped like a wounded bird, twisting, useless. We lost steerage; the *caïque* turned side-on to the swell. Before I could turn the rudder, a wall of water slammed into our port side, tipping the hull vertical. I clung on as the wave drove the *caïque* broadside before it; the mast speared into the sea and snapped—one brutal crack—sheets and canvas trailing.

Andonis yelled, 'Ghika!'

He dropped into the churning sea. My best friend in the world. Salt water shot up my nose, tumbled me until I didn't know which way was up.

When I surfaced outside the inverted hull, my shirt ballooned, my vraka dragged like lead.

I counted heads.

Nikos. Damos.

'Andoni!' I howled at the wind, searching.

He must be underneath.

I gasped and dived, slid under the gunwale, and kicked upwards until I broke into an enclosed space—a capsule of quiet beneath the hull. I sucked in a breath—bubbles, then a head, bursting up beside me.

Blood streamed from Andonis' eyebrow, streaking the half-grown fuzz he called a moustache. He opened and closed his mouth, gulping water tinged with red.

I gagged, as always, at the sight of blood. Not now. We had to get out. 'We must dive!'

He was slow to respond.

I yelled again. 'Take a breath!'

I dragged him below, kicking sideways, pulling him until we resurfaced in the foaming water outside the *Niki*, both coughing and gasping.

A wave crashed over us. Andonis reached one arm around my neck, pulling me close, climbing on top of me, pushing me under. The chain around my neck tightened as he grabbed and pulled. I twisted and broke free, coughed and choked, desperate to breathe. Silver links flashed—my amulet.

It sank out of sight.

He was panicking, pushing me under again, thrashing, desperate. We could both drown. I broke free, pulled my fist back, and cracked it against his skull. He went limp, face down in the water, curls a black halo. He wasn't unconscious but he no longer fought me. I dragged him through wave after wave. Now and then, on a swell, I'd glimpse another head bobbing in the chop. My arms were cramping. I couldn't keep going much longer. At last, I could see the shore. I kept swimming—then my feet touched rock.

The other boys waded in and helped me haul him from the pummelling waves and we fell on the shore at Kamini, near his father's house. I lay gasping for breath, the warmth of solid rock beneath my back, occasional drops from a sun shower on my face. Andonis, chest heaving.

Kostas. Damos. Nikos. Me. Five. I made the sign of the cross.

We'd made it. That was all that mattered.

—

Andonis coughed and heaved out a stream of water. And then he said, 'Ghika—what have you done?'

What had *I* done?

We'd seen worse weather than that. He could have stayed on shore. But he allowed himself to be pulled in—and now he blamed me? I wanted to hit him, shake him.

'We'll fix this,' I blurted. 'I'll fix it. It's only a boat.'

Then I saw his face. Stricken.

'You shouldn't have done it,' said Kostas.

'We need to fix your cut, Andoni.' Nikos' face was white.

Andonis nodded, then shook his head, eyes closed.

'You swim worse than you sail,' I said.

He opened them again. 'I swim better than you rescue.' He winced as he touched the side of his head with the tips of his fingers.

Then he reached out to touch my hand. I grasped it. We sat, elbows on knees.

This wasn't supposed to happen.

—

Their small family home was only a few minutes' walk away. Steam rose off the path, fallen limbs and leaves washed into lines by the deluge. Water ran in the gutters.

Andonis' little sister was playing outside their house, and she ran to hug me around the waist. 'Ghikaki, will you play knucklebones with me?'

I ruffled her hair.

His mother, God help her. Seeing Andonis walk through the door, she cried out as if wounded, crossed herself, and held up two fingers to ward off the evil eye. Arms wide, she said over and over, '*Moro mou.*' My baby.

'You dare to return without the *Niki*?' We turned—*Kyrios* Manolis.

His voice was ragged with fury and loss. He looked at me. Not Andonis.

'You are fifteen years old. Old enough to understand we are at war—every *caïque* is a lifeline. That wasn't only a fishing boat—it ferries wheat to be ground into flour to make the bread for your breakfast. I carry water supplies from the mainland.'

As if I'd known the storm would capsize us. I bit my tongue.

We left Andonis there and went to the taverna. What else could we do?

Kostas blinked several times as if collecting his thoughts, then spoke with his usual measured gravity. 'Ghika,' he said, 'It was wrong to challenge Andonis. We were supposed to be repairing that warship.'

'Condemn me if you will, Kostandi,' I snapped. 'Did I tie him to the mast? Did I drag him aboard? He knew the risk. He made his own choice. And unlike some, he doesn't whine when things go south. Perhaps that's a lesson for you.'

'Easy for you to say,' Kostas said. 'You never learn, Ghika. Your father fixes everything.'

Nikos placed a hand on Kostas' arm, soothing the storm. 'Kostandi, please don't blame Ghikas. We were only having fun. Please, no fight.' He shivered, his massive frame suddenly vulnerable. 'I'm catching a chill.'

My stomach was churning at the thought of telling my father. I needed to cool off. Clear my head. This would all blow over.

I paid for their drinks and took my leave. But instead of sprinting straight home, I slipped into our tiny church to light a candle for Andonis' family.

My father would sort out the money. The Manolis family would recover. So would Andonis.

But there were no boats to be bought. That was the real problem.

When I finally shouldered open the heavy gate into our courtyard, lamplight spilled across the marble doorstep, lighting fallen olives on the flagstones, casualties of the *bouríni*. As I locked it from the inside, our cat brushed against my leg. Lifting her, I whispered, '*Ómorfo korítsi.*' Pretty girl.

The amulet. My mother would be inconsolable.

I shoved the door open so hard that it hit the internal wall like a gunshot.

Yiayia was in the kitchen, alone, the fire low. I told her what had happened.

'Your father will fix it,' she said, not looking up.

My stomach dropped. 'Fix what, Yiayia?'

She placed a bowl of olives on the table with slow precision. 'He will pay *Kyrios* Manolis for his *caïque.*'

Relief surged through me. And dread behind it. Like iron in my gut.

'Ghikaki,' Yiayia said, abrupt. 'You must stop being so reckless.'

'I know,' I said.

Later, when he had heard the news, Father's voice was quiet in the reception room.

'You were not at the shipyard. You were not with your cousins.'

He set down the broadsheet—he was proud of Hydra's *Voice of the Law*—printed on the island.

'Instead, you went sailing, and now an entire family cannot eat. And the *Icarus* is supposed to sail for Chios. You might as well surrender our fleet to the Turks.'

My jaw clenched. He kept speaking as if I were a child.

'I'll work,' I said. 'I'll pay them back.'

'With what?' His voice was bitter. 'A boy's wages? Your grandfather built our name with his own hands. And you gamble it for a thrill?'

Of course he'd mention my grandfather. He still hadn't spoken to his sister since she challenged his inheritance.

'Patéra, we can still get the *Icarus* to Chios on time.'

The silence dragged.

At last he said, 'Do not presume to raise the subject of your betrothal again. Maria's father requires a husband who thinks beyond pranks. Someone who understands responsibility—like a man.'

This landed like a blow. Maria. My future wife. Gone. Just like that. The sound in the room thickened—the scrape of his chair, the rasp of his breath—but everything inside me was noise.

I forced myself to meet his eyes.

'You may no longer see your friends. Your focus will be the shipyard. Your duties. And you will learn what it is to carry the name Voulgaris.'

I curled my fists. This was banishment. A father's duty was to correct, to guide. But he was casting me adrift.

I returned to the kitchen, still thinking about Andonis. He could have stayed on the shore if he didn't like it.

'Father said I can't see my friends. And he's halting negotiations for my betrothal. Maria will marry someone else. My life is over.'

'Ghika, your destiny may not lie with Maria Kountouriotis,' said Yiayia.

'But you married the love of your life, Yiayia.'

She was silent for a moment. 'My father chose your *papou*.'

I pressed her. 'Did you love another, Yiayia?'

She ignored that. 'I learned to love your grandfather. The plague took the best.'

That had been in 1792. The old people of Hydra still spoke of it.

She rose, signalling the end of our conversation.

My father left nothing to chance—not business, not family, not even love. After losing his first wife in childbirth, he found himself with three sons and a newborn daughter—my elder brothers and my sister Katerina. He told us he arranged his second marriage himself, choosing Mamá for her excellent qualities. He had known her since she was a child, well acquainted with her noble family and their estate near the Thermisi salt lakes on the mainland. He didn't marry her for the size of her dowry, though it was handsome. He chose her—and loved her absolutely.

Every time he entered a room, Mamá was there, slapping fluff off his jacket, straightening his cuffs, pulling at embroidery threads that weren't there. He'd puff up and stretch his neck like a kid goat. I wished they would reserve such displays for their private moments—especially considering the difference in their ages—but I had to acknowledge the love between them.

Jokingly, she'd tease my father, 'You aren't Greek, Niko. Your family's only been here for a couple of centuries.' She spoke of her noble Frankish ancestors, with a story of a long-ago grandmother who leaped to her death from a castle parapet to avoid violation by a Turkish officer.

'Greece should be grateful for the steel of our Albanian warrior blood,' he'd reply with a smile.

He had taken charge of his fate.

So would I.

Dear Maria,

It is my fervent wish to formalise our childhood promise. I humbly pray you will persuade your father to recommence negotiations for our betrothal.

Yours in hope,
Ghikas

· · ·

I entrusted it to our servant Lambros to deliver. Then I slipped out again, shoulders hunched against the cold.

Yiannis, the old shepherd, was settled beside his fire, the flock penned beneath the olive trees.

'Well, Herakles?' he said, without turning. 'How deep is the pit you have dug this time?'

I can't recall who initially dubbed me 'Herakles'. One stormy afternoon, a barrel and a coil of rope went overboard. I'd heaved in the rope, then dived in to rescue the barrel.

'Opa, Herakles!' someone had shouted.

Herakles. Son of Zeus. The strongest man alive. It stuck. Not only for strength. For making things happen. For leading. Herakles always led the charge, always came back bloodied but victorious. That's who I was.

I told Yiannis everything.

He listened, silent, as the fire crackled. When I finished, he folded his hands and said, 'You were foolish, Ghika, but then you were brave. But courage without care is like a knife without a sheath—it cuts those you love as well as your enemies.'

I shook my head. 'My father will never let me near a warship now.'

He looked at me now, calm. 'You have only yourself to blame. You must learn something better than seamanship.'

I stared into the fire. 'They looked for the hull, searched the shore for wreckage. The sea took everything. And Maria will marry someone else,' I muttered.

'Maybe. Or maybe she's waiting for the man she trusts you'll become.'

He stood, gripped my shoulder, solid as stone.

'Be better, Ghika. But not because someone tells you to be. Not for her. Not for your father. For yourself.'

I didn't need another lecture.

As I turned to go, he added, more quietly, 'Your father may have paid for the boat. But money may not heal the rift between you and Andonis.'

I nodded stiffly and stepped out into the dark, knowing that the next dawn would find me at the shipyard mast, hammer in hand.

I waited with impatience for Maria's reply. It arrived two days later.

· · ·

Dear Ghika,

My father desires my future husband to be a man of excellent character and substantial means.

I cherish our childhood friendship.

His obedient daughter,

Maria

She remembered. She hadn't forgotten. That meant something. Maybe I just needed someone to believe I could be better than I was. I'd give her father no reason to refuse me.

When I next saw Andonis, I opened my mouth to apologise, to explain, to make it right between us—but his gaze stopped me cold. He stared at me for a long moment. Then, without a word, he walked away. Not a backward glance.

As if I'd never been his brother at all.

Say something, I wanted to shout. *Our friendship is worth more than a boat.*

He'd always answered before.

Always.

This time, he didn't.

Fine, he was angry. So was I. If he wanted to blame me, let him. I'd outwork them all.

I laughed it off in daylight. But by night, as I lay awake, hot and restless, the waves rose again and again in my head.

5

Quartered

SYDNEY, New South Wales
September 1829

Andonis turns towards me, the old warmth in his eyes. We're walking back up George Street from the dockyard, shirts stiff with sweat and covered in sawdust, Sydney's afternoon light making slanted shadows on the road.

'Congratulations, Ghika. Your plan is working.'

The certainty in his voice settles something deep in my chest.

'Yes,' says Kostas, nodding his head.

We pass the blacksmith's forge, door propped open, heat pouring out. Nikos slows to watch a man shoeing a restless grey horse—flanks flecked with sweat, one hoof held high.

The overseers value us. We work well together. If we continue like this, and take on private work in our spare hours, we can rent a room in town— free of the filth, free of the men who would bully Nikos. Most assigned men live with their employers—but I'm sure the authorities will allow it if we prove ourselves reliable.

I've persuaded men with more power than these before.

I feel it—the rare, solid weight of something settled. For the first time since we arrived, the future looks solid.

The sound of footsteps behind us.

'A plan, is it?' The voice is light with curiosity.

We turn to see a man in a dark coat, collar white against his sun-browned neck. He holds a brown felt hat with both hands.

Father Therry.

He has been visiting the barracks each day since we arrived, moving through the yard, speaking with the convicts—Catholic or not. I have seen him at the wash trough, at roll call, even sitting on the barracks steps with a man who had received news from England of his wife's death. Even the hardest men stop to talk to him.

I have spoken to him myself, but only by way of introduction. I don't need a priest. I pray morning and night, but privately.

And yet, here he is, falling in beside us, fixing me with a steady, interested gaze.

'I see you each day,' he says, nodding. 'Five men, always together. You must have endured much.' He has a warm, friendly smile.

'Brothers in everything but blood, Reverend Sir,' I say.

The priest smiles. 'Ah. Then you are fortunate men. A bond like that is rare.'

'We've been through enough together,' I say. 'Since childhood. We sailed together. Fought together. Ate from the same pot.'

Damos says, 'Bled together, too. Not that Ghikas ever looks, for he cannot stand the sight of blood.'

Andonis smiles and adds, quietly but firm, 'Ghikas is our spokesman.'

Father Therry nods, thoughtful.

'And so you have a plan?'

'We do,' I say. 'Everything is lined and caulked.'

It's an exaggeration, but it won't be for long.

Father Therry is still smiling, but there's something else now. A hesitation. He studies me for a long moment, as if weighing something.

'I trust you won't find today difficult,' he says.

Andonis frowns. 'Why?'

The priest's voice is gentle. 'Do you know your assignments are being allocated today?'

The moment jolts me. I stop short. Yes, I know it's Friday.

Damos stiffens. 'What about them?'

'In my experience, it's rare for the authorities to allow a group of men to remain together. There's always the fear of insurrection.'

Father Therry studies me.

For a moment I say nothing. Then, 'That will not apply to us, Father. The authorities know we are harmless.'

He nods. 'I trust your plan holds, Ghika.' As he turns to leave, he places a hand briefly on my shoulder. 'You have the look of men who do not ask for help. If ever you need a quiet place—or someone to talk to—you'll find me at Saint Mary's. No obligation, of course. But the door is open.'

I nod. 'Thank you, Father.'

He walks on towards Saint Mary's.

—

Mister Hely will confirm our assignments—place a rubber stamp on what is already settled. We have proven ourselves.

And yet, as we wait in his office, I remain close to Andonis, as if physical proximity will anchor us together.

Hely barely glances up from his paperwork. 'Damianos Ninis—you remain at the dockyard, and remain lodged at the barracks. But you will learn to obey orders.'

The breath leaves my chest. Damos doesn't always follow the shipwright's instructions. But that's one at least. He claps me on the back. Four remain.

I knew it would happen according to plan.

Damos opens his mouth, but Hely lifts a hand in warning.

He looks up, around, at each one of us.

'There's been a great deal of competition for your allocations,' he says. 'Kostas—your industry has impressed. Your strength and determination have not gone unnoticed. And your integrity.' He pauses. 'I have land north of Sydney with an orange orchard. The region is accessible only by ship. You leave tomorrow.'

The words land like a volley of cannon fire. Mister Hely is taking Kostas away, for himself. Himself. Kostas wouldn't recognise an orange branch if it whipped him. Normally, his face is unreadable, but his eyes flick to me, betraying a need he cannot voice. His jaw tightens.

I must stop this. I step forward. 'But sir—'

'Silence.' Hely's voice is clipped.

My solid, quiet friend. To be sent away to a position he'll hate. He trusted me.

Hely continues. 'Andonis Manolis. Nikolaos Papandreou.'

My pulse jumps. Together? Andonis and Nikos? The knot in my chest pulls tighter. They both need me. I need them. Kostas is gone. Now these two?

'Mister John Macarthur is a member of our Legislative Council,' Hely says, as if we have not already heard of the man. 'And a breeder of fine sheep. He and his sons grow vines at Parramatta and Camden Park, in a fertile river valley called the Cow Pastures. You both go there.'

Andonis' eyes meet mine. I clench my jaw so tightly I taste blood. Nikos looks the same—he doesn't understand.

This is the end of us.

'Ghikas.'

I snap my attention back. 'Yes, sir. Assign me with them. I'm skilled with vines—'

'The Colonial Secretary assigned you to himself.'

Macleay.

Hely doesn't look up. 'But that has changed.'

No one else is going to Macleay. I've spoken to a convict who works for Macleay—he's creating a garden on fifty-four acres east of the town. But he holds grazing land too.

The floor shifts. What did he say? Changed?

I blink. 'Sir, with respect—'

'No.' He raises a hand without looking at me.

Heat rises in my face. At home, a man shows his palm only to a mule, a child, a servant—never to a man worthy of respect.

'You met the Deputy Assistant Commissary on the wharf when you disembarked.'

The man with the watch.

'Stewart Ryrie. He and his sons are developing land at Arnprior, on the

Shoalhaven River. He has requested Mister Macleay reassign you to him. Mister Macleay has agreed. You will work as a shepherd.'

For a moment, the world narrows to this room, to the parchment in Hely's hand.

We are to be separated.

I look at Andonis. He attempts a reassuring smile. It starts, falters, and dies.

A shepherd.

I force myself to swallow. I have been many things—a son, a sailor, a pirate. But never something so small.

I was born to command men.

Now I will herd sheep.

'How far from Sydney, sir?' My voice scrapes dry against my throat. How far do you send a man to silence him?

'Two hundred miles south, I believe. At the farthest edge of what Governor Darling rules to be Authorised Settlement.'

I can't breathe. Two hundred miles. They might as well kill me.

Hely is already flipping paper, moving on to the next life to be sorted like a piece on a game board. Then he looks up again.

'It's possible to earn a Ticket of Leave,' Hely says, 'granted for good conduct. If you work well and obediently. And if you have a master willing to recommend you. For a fourteen-year sentence, you may apply after six years. For lifers,'—here he looks at Andonis and Damos—'eight years.'

He places his hand flat on the desk.

'A Ticket of Leave allows you to leave your assigned service. Find your own work. Earn your own living. But only in your assigned district. Report to the magistrate every three months. Fail to obey the conditions, and it will be revoked.'

I don't care about tickets. I am being removed from my friends.

Two hundred miles removed.

I should have seen it coming.

We made ourselves useful. Reliable. Respectable.

Of course men like Hely and Macarthur would carve us up like spoils.

I heard a convict spit the word yesterday—*the Exclusives*—as if it tasted foul. He meant the old army officers and civil servants who treat the colony like a private estate. As if they're entitled to all the land, and men to work it. They call the freed convicts *Emancipists*.

They're ranged up against each other. As if one were born clean and the other can never wash the stain off.

We're below both.

Andonis' eyes meet mine—a silent conversation in a single look. And for the first time since we were exiled to this far-flung colony, I understand the depth of our isolation.

Here, we are not just prisoners of the system.

We are lost to each other.

—

We wait in the quadrangle. Heat radiates from the gravel and the brick walls. My shirt clings to my skin.

Kostas left yesterday. His parting words, 'Ghika, it matters not where they send us. They cannot break our bonds.'

Damos is next. Knowing his headstrong nature, I worry.

'Go safely, Damo,' I say. 'Keep your mouth shut and your back straight.'

He flashes a grin and pulls at the belt around his waist. 'I won't be rotting here, Ghika. You only have fourteen years. Andonis and I are here for life. The first chance I have, I'm jumping a ship out of this place.'

'Damo. It's futile. You'll be caught and punished. You must obey orders.'

He grins, grimly. 'I don't obey yours.'

We both laugh.

Andonis and Nikos will travel together to Elizabeth Farm at Parramatta, on a dray sent by Mister Macarthur.

I keep my composure, giving instructions: work diligently, stay out of trouble, write letters.

But Nikos is already crumbling. His mouth moves, but no sound comes out.

Then he suddenly lunges at me and holds me in a vice-like grip. 'Ghika, you won't forget me, will you?'

His fingers dig into my back. I hold him hard to stop his shaking. I wish I could take his terror from him, and hold it within me.

When I pull away, I punch my heart. 'You are printed in here, Niko. Nothing can rub you out.'

His lip wobbles. 'Who will read to me?'

Pain sears through my chest.

I close my eyes and swallow. I shake his shoulders. 'You'll be fine, Niko. Stand behind Andonis.'

'But he doesn't do the voices,' Nikos whispers. 'And he misses bits.'

He is trying not to cry, and failing. My own throat is raw.

'You'll be fine, Niko,' I say, trying to make it sound true.

He nods, miserably. Then he lets go. But his hand trails down my arm as he steps away, and that last touch undoes me.

Only then does Andonis step forward.

Andonis pulls me into a tight embrace.

'*File mou, sto kaló,*' I whisper in his ear. My friend, go to a good place. 'And don't look back.'

His fingers dig into my shoulder.

He pulls back to look at me, voice hoarse. '*Siderenios.*' Be as strong as iron.

When he presses even harder, I welcome the stab of pain to mask the one tearing me apart.

'Look after Nikos,' I say. 'If he gives away his blanket, tie it to him.'

He nods, unable to speak.

As the gates close, I etch their images into my memory. I may never see them again. They are taking my purpose, my direction.

For the first time in my life, I'm utterly alone.

—

Near the sentry box, two convicts with canvas bags slung over their shoulders watch me. Are these men also assigned to the Ryrie boys at Arnprior? I extend my hand to a pale, pasty fellow with unruly blond hair and red-rimmed eyes. A white froth of saliva bubbles at the ends of his broken-toothed smile.

'Joseph Little.' He doesn't pronounce the t's, and his voice has a nervous pitch. He continually looks over his shoulder as if someone is chasing him. 'You c'n call me Joe. Will you work for the Ryries?'

'Ghikas Voulgaris, yes,' I say.

Still, after two years, I wait for a flicker of respect at my name. None comes.

His handshake is limp, hand grimy. 'You're one of them Greeks,' he says as if talking about rats in the privy. Then he clamps his mouth shut as if he's used up his words for the week.

He scratches his neck, glances around, then digs into his shirt and pulls something out.

'This might be yours.'

It's my handkerchief.

'Smells Greek.' He grins like we've been friends for years.

He hands it over, damp and creased. I consider telling him to wash it first. Then I take it—on the grounds that I may not see it again.

I draw myself to my full height. 'You have a trade?'

He stares, blank.

'Anything to earn your bread.'

His shoulders relax. 'Oh. Pickpocket.'

I laugh. I asked for that.

The other steps forward. 'And I be Martin Armstrong.' His voice booms—loud, exuberant, impossible to ignore. Wild eyes, a cloud of chestnut hair, crooked teeth, and a handshake that could crush bone. He laughs, full-throated and unrestrained, then claps Joe on the back. 'Hands like iron, me. I can do a bit of everything—none of it legal.'

I nod. 'Good. Walk ahead of me. If we look like a rabble, we'll be treated as one.'

He stares. 'What? In a line?'

Joseph sidles up. His smell alone is a crime. 'Are you in charge, then?'

I fold my arms. 'Someone needs to be. Today, it's me.'

Armstrong nudges him. 'Oi, you letting this Greek tell you what to do?'

Joe grins. 'Might do.'

This is who I'm shackled to now. I've lost my brothers—and they've given me this. A braggart. A halfwit. Londoners. Criminals. No name, no blood. Worthless scum—the kind of men you wouldn't trust to clean the head.

My brothers chose to follow me. I'll have to drag these.

If they have a use, I'll find it.

I look past them, toward the sentry box, where Mister Hely is striding toward us, gravel crunching under his polished boots.

'Mister Hely, sir,' I call out, stepping forward. 'Do we have an escort?' If I'm with hardened criminals, there'll be one.

He barely slows his stride, handing me a piece of paper with an address. 'You don't need one. There's nowhere to run. The Ryrie residence is down near the wharf facing George Street. Enter the yard from the lane.'

I glance at Joe and Armstrong. Joe is picking at his nose. Armstrong has his finger in his ear.

These aren't my men, and I am not their captain.

'Leave now,' Hely says.

I follow them, jaw clenched.

They show no respect. I'll have to teach them.

—

The gates of the prisoners' barracks close behind us, and we are swept into a human current of convicts, gentlemen, and guardsmen heading down George Street towards the wharf.

As we descend, a column of women parades into view, shepherded by a puffed-up official and a peacock of a police officer, chest ablaze with medals. A contingent of constables forms a protective guard.

These are the Irish girls arriving. I crane my neck to see them. They walk two by two like lambs to market, hems dragging through the dust.

Our companions jostle forward in a stampede. The unruly crowd of ruffians hinders the girls' movement, shouting obscenities. The waifs maintain an air of respectability, even primness, wearing bonnets and gloves, cloaks drawn tight despite the heat.

A flock of gulls, with no chance of flight.

One girl stumbles.

My heart clenches. It's her. The same girl I saw on the ship—small, serious, bone-white with fright.

The sole of her shoe has detached from the upper and it flaps like a gawping fish as she steps forward. With one hand, she clenches her bundle tightly against her stomach, elbow close to her sides. With her other, she steadies the girl beside her, though it is she who needs steadying.

Frightened, she looks up, her mouth set in a fiercely determined line. She stands upright, even when the crowd jostles her—as if she refuses to be intimidated.

God help me, she is the most beautiful thing I've seen in two years. In my life.

I forget the smells. I forget the noise.

She trips again and a man laughs. 'That one'll be easy!'

She jerks backward, as if slapped.

I don't think. I move. 'Joe, wait here. I'll be back soon.'

'We don't have time for a bit o' muslin. What about Mister Ryrie?'

He's right. I should walk away. I've lost too much because of reckless choices. But I stride towards the women—they're almost at the lumber yard.

'I won't be long. If I am, follow the shouting.'

As I reach her, a hand touches her shoulder, and the leering man beside her rumbles, 'I be visiting your bed tonight with a gift for you, my pretty one!'

She recoils. The girl beside her is crying.

But then he touches her, and my hand moves before my mind does.

I grab the blackguard by his collar and drag him close. Broken veins sprawl across his cheeks, a mottled map of his inebriation. He gasps a strangled wheeze.

The girl's eyes widen in fear—not of him, but of me.

As I cast the lout aside, the others move on, and as she turns to catch up, she stumbles again.

I run ahead of her.

She stares as if I am a monster, clutching the girl beside her.

She has the most remarkable green eyes I have ever seen. It's as if I have dived into the sea at Avlaki. I reel at the shock of cold water.

For two years, I have seen nothing but filth, loss, violence. I have forced myself not to feel.

The girl reminds me, suddenly, of everything I have lost.

I feel the edge of panic. I must stay with her. I must.

I walk backwards to shield her, arms outstretched. My heart is hammering.

Her blush catches me off guard.

I grin.

A flicker of a smile. A single dimple. Then it's gone.

In the warmth of that second, I bump against someone, and stagger.

She bites her lip, dimples appearing as she holds her chattels tight against her stomach. A rogue curl, light brown, has escaped her bonnet.

A constable's musket pushes me aside. I allow it.

She is being swept along with the rest of the women, across the stone bridge spanning the boggy stream, and into the lumber yard.

I'm losing sight of her.

The onlookers fall back at the gate, a spent wave.

I should be thinking about Arnprior. About sheep, the scrub they speak of, and what I'm facing.

But I yell instead. 'I'll fix that shoe! What's your name?'

Over the crowd, I hear her. 'Mary.'

I watch until they are out of view.

My chest feels tight. I'm hot.

That girl isn't looking to be rescued. But something in me insists I must.

Then I remember. By this afternoon, I will already be halfway to God knows where.

And Mary doesn't even know my name.

6

A Question Of Loyalty

HYDRA

Summer 1824

I helped carry the injured from the *Makedonia*—lanterns bobbing across the dark water as the skiffs came in. She'd limped into Mandraki Bay during the night, decks splintered by Turkish grapeshot.

My arms ached. My eyes stung. As we heaved a stretcher along the boggy foreshore, someone called for lint.

Three weeks before the Turks attacked Psara, Kasos had begged for help. We'd had twelve brigs ready to sail—and the government in Nafplio delayed the gunpowder.

I shifted my grip on the handles, arms straight, palms burning, jaw set.

By the time our ships reached Kasos, it was too late—two thousand dead, as many taken in chains. Some were ransomed; most were sold in Egypt or Crete. The island was ash.

Then Psara fell to the Ottoman fleet. From the start of the war, our navy had been Hydra, Spetses, Psara. Psara held out until the last man and their harbour ran red. The last defenders lit the powder stores and blew themselves apart—wives and children with them.

Those who'd escaped earlier were still arriving on the islands—Syros,

Spetses, anywhere that would take them. Few came to Hydra; we already had twenty thousand people, no water, and barely enough houses for our own.

A girl was crying in a nearby skiff. We lowered the stretcher at the medical tent, then I hauled her over the gunwale. Someone pushed a water-skin into my hand; her cracked lips found it and she drank.

Admiral Kanaris had taken what was left of his island's fleet to Aegina —and that became their new anchorage overnight.

Now the Egyptian fleet was gathering off Crete. Samos was next— everyone was saying so—then us.

A man shouldered through the crowd, shouting a name; the girl's head snapped up and she flung herself at him. He wrapped her in his coat, nodding thanks over her head as I turned back to the skiff.

Admiral Miaoulis of Hydra was our hero. And our deadliest weapon was the fireship: we painted old hulls with pitch and packed them with brushwood and gunpowder. On moonless nights, iron-nerved crews would sail in silence toward enemy ships, light the fuses at the last moment, and leap clear—sending them crashing amidships in a blazing inferno. Burning timber rained from the sky after the blast, the enemy ship razed to the waterline with no survivors. Kanaris was the master.

The men who lit the fuses never slept easily again. And still they volunteered.

'Pitch, Ghika!'

I walked towards the slipway. The *Argos* lay tilted on her side, timber props jammed under her belly. Caulkers worked on the seams from staging planks.

I waved and ducked into the warehouse. Only a few casks left. The war had drained us of supplies—food, timber, pitch.

I rolled a full one towards the doorway and paused, scanning Mandraki. Dawn's pale light outlined two canvas tents thrown up on the beach in front of the old berth house where we stored our ships' bedding, sheets and rigging.

Five men lay on stretchers beside it. A surgeon knelt beside a fire, and as I watched he dipped a strip of linen into a pot of boiling water, then lifted it out, steam rising as he draped it over a rack to cool. He tested it on his wrist, then pressed it to a man's thigh. A moan followed—of agony or relief, I wasn't sure.

My father said my work in the shipyard brought me honour. A seventeen-year-old boy with calloused hands and a hammer. These men had put their lives on the line for Greece. They were the heroes. And I was carting barrels.

Beyond them, a corvette bobbed at anchor, seams blackened and oozing tar where it had come too close to one of our fireships. A splintered mast drifted in the bay. Donkeys hauled broken spars along the shore.

Before the war, you could barely see water for all the bright-hulled merchantmen side by side, with shipwrights carving keels in the sun next to stacks of timber and pitch.

I nudged the barrel into daylight with my foot.

From next door, in a low, whitewashed warehouse between me and the yard, I heard the murmur of conversation.

'We've bankrolled this war from the start—and now the mainlanders presume they give orders? And then squabble over who pays the bill?'

'Kolokotronis thinks he's directing the entire campaign.'

'Well, he is, on the mainland at least.'

'He demands we defend the Peloponnese—while we're bleeding to hold Chios.'

'Let him defend the mainland without us, then.'

'And let the Turks retake Tripolitsa? You'd let the mainland fall? We'd be next.'

'Well, if we pull back from Chios, the war in the east is lost.'

They'd been fighting like children over sweets for two years—the mainland regions and the islands. How to fight the war. How to fund it. We'd borrowed a fabulous sum from the English—£800,000 on paper, yet after fees we saw scarcely £470,000—and still we quarrelled over powder and pay.

Even now, Maria's uncle Giorgios and General Kolokotronis—the Lion—were at each other's throats. There was even talk of locking him up.

I no longer knew which war would finish us first.

With trade strangled and the island hungry, some of our captains were already slipping out under borrowed flags, disappearing into the night and returning with English loot. We called it *koursema*—sanctioned prize-taking—born of necessity; the English and French called it piracy.

They knew it was our only means of survival—yet they had the arrogance to accuse. The year before, Captain Hamilton had swept into our harbour hunting a stolen ship. He asked no permission—turned his glass on our fleet, found nothing, and left. As if his 'neutrality' gave him a key to our front door.

A shout carried across the bay as another skiff approached. As it beached, a young man staggered out, bandages crimson with fresh blood; two women supported an elderly man bowed by the weight of a swaddled child. They passed without a word—faces grey, hollow-eyed. And our temporary accommodation was teeming with typhus.

I caught movement out of the corner of my eye: Andonis was standing two ships over, arms crossed, watching me. Since we'd lost the *Niki*, we had spoken only fleetingly. Now, seeing me here, he simply tilted his head. No wave. No smile.

I pretended not to see him.

I kept rolling the cask and left it beside the *Argos'* hull, then climbed the rope ladder.

As I stepped onto the rail, something shifted. A groan of timber. A jolt.

I looked up. The cracked boom was tipping, its weight taking the rig with it.

If it fell, it could hit the caulkers below.

I lunged—no thought, just reach—to catch it, but no man stops a falling boom. It was as good as gone.

I went over with it.

I struck the edge of the staging. Pain seared through my ribs. Then I hit the ground.

I lay there, winded, staring up into a whirl of faces—until Andonis came into focus, his eyes wide with alarm.

I bared my teeth at him.

'Still being a hero, Ghika?' he said, breath rasping. But his voice held relief.

'And you're not?' I gave a grunt as he hauled me up. I spat. 'Did it hit anyone?'

His jaw softened, and for a moment his anger melted. 'It missed them,' he said. 'Lucky you fell in the oakum.'

'You call this lucky?' I pointed at the smashed boom.

He slipped his arm under my armpit to hold me up, but I shook him off.

The yardmaster appeared, beard flecked with sawdust. 'Voulgaris—you're all fire, no sense.' He stepped closer and studied me, eyes narrowing. 'Next time, think before you act. I can't patch a man who's full of holes.'

He was right—I needed caulking.

He put his hand on my shoulder.

'You've not been to bed, boy. Go now. I'll tell your father you're working well. Now,' he said as he walked away, 'let's see the damage.'

—

Hydra, Autumn 1825

My ribs healed, but the gulf between Andonis and me did not. When I saw him down at the port or at Mandraki, he barely greeted me. Nikos still threw his arms around me and never asked why Andonis did not.

So when my father gave permission for me to attend Phineas' wedding —our servant Lambros' son was marrying Kostas' sister—I took it as a sign. An opportunity to call a truce. A thread back to my old life. Maybe things would shift. Maybe not. I just wanted one afternoon with them.

My father had said nothing of my betrothal to Maria. Not a word.

And now finally the day of the wedding had come.

Celebrations like this had been severely curtailed by war, but births hadn't stopped, nor deaths. Typhus came. Dysentery followed. Then smallpox swept the island and stayed—it left pits on our arms, our cheeks. Nikos bore the worst of it. But we lived.

Andonis, I heard, still pined for Anastasia, and she would be at the marriage celebration. People said she was stringing him along. Maybe they were right. Or maybe she liked the attention.

I'd keep an eye on her. He could act tough, but Andonis was easily wounded.

The afternoon was bright and blue as I joined Lambros' family on the meadow path to Vlychos. In our patched finery, we laughed, picked wildflowers, pretended, for one afternoon only, that war and sickness had gone. Phineas carried a bouquet for his bride. The children ran ahead, Makris hauling me up the arch of the new stone bridge the French engineer had built at Vlychos.

While we waited for the bride's party at the church, I nodded toward the sea and said to Phineas, 'If the admirals had found a favourable wind to strike Alexandria last month, the war might already be over.'

If they had, everything would have been different.

Phineas shrugged. 'Maybe. Still, slipping into Ibrahim Pasha's own port was no mean feat.'

'What's happening between Anastasia and Andonis?' I asked him.

He gave me a sideways look. 'Nothing much. She has her eye on her employer's son. Or even you, so they say,' he added with a sly grin.

I laughed. Typical gossip. Anastasia flirted—it meant nothing. She barely looked at me.

After the wedding in the tiny church overlooking the sea, as dusk painted the sky a soft shell pink, we walked along the coast to the taverna. Despite the shortages, Kostas' parents—likely helped by my father—had outdone themselves. Candles flickered on tables scattered with wildflowers, platters of roasted goat, fish, pilaf, warm bread.

Anastasia was standing with her parents as Andonis approached. He greeted her father, then her mother, and then he leaned toward her, looking at her with that quiet intensity he reserved for what—or who—mattered most to him.

She laughed at something he said as her eyes searched the room, but then she saw me, and her smile changed.

'Ghika,' she called.

I nodded coolly, 'Anastasia.'

I turned back to Andonis. 'What did you think of those five hundred Greeks holding off five thousand Egyptians at Nafplio?'

Anastasia turned on her heel and went to speak to the bride.

Andonis watched her go, hurt in his eyes.

Behind us, Damos gave a low snort. 'Anastasia is playing you like a flute, Andoni. Keeping you close to prove she can.'

I wanted to punch something. 'She wouldn't keep seeking Andonis out, Damo, if she weren't interested.'

Another nod. Andonis' eyes stayed fixed on her.

Outside, the night was cooling. But inside, the heat was rising. Sweat prickled my neck. I wiped my brow.

We joined the line of dancers curving around the taverna's perimeter—men and women linked lightly by fingertips, or for modesty, with a *mantíli* —kerchief—held between them. The steps were simple, in time with the rhythm of the *syrtos*—forwards, backwards, lift, slide, tap.

Anastasia danced between her parents at the far end—light on her feet, smiling.

As the music ended and the dancers broke apart, she leaned in to whisper something to her father. When the line re-formed, she didn't return to his side, but several places down with some of her friends. And closer to Andonis.

Maybe she'd stop playing around and hold out her *mantíli* to him.

But as Kostas and his brothers struck up the music for the next round, she stepped forward and turned to hold out the *mantíli*—to me.

Heat rushed up my neck. She'd chosen me—in front of everyone. I hesitated. And then I took the other end. Her hand brushed mine through the fabric—light, deliberate. The scent of her hair reached me, cloves and something sweeter. I kept my eyes forward, but I felt her pulse through the cloth, the heat of her skin.

The dance began. We moved with the line—slow steps, wrists raised, the cloth stretched between us.

I turned my head to her. 'Do you mean to wound Andonis?' I said just above a whisper.

'I need to speak with you.'

I kept my eyes ahead. 'I have nothing to say to you.'

When the music ended, I dropped the *mantíli* without waiting for the last beat. A clean release. A refusal.

We all clapped.

I bowed to the group, not to her, and walked outside to the courtyard fountain. The cooler night air wrapped around me. I bent to the basin, closed my eyes, and splashed water over my face.

When I opened them—she was standing there. Alone. Offering her cloth to wipe my face. She had followed me. On purpose.

No respectable girl would put herself in this position—alone with a man.

I straightened and took out my own kerchief, drying my face without looking at her. But she didn't leave. She came closer.

'You danced well,' she said. Her voice was low. Soft. Practised. She touched my arm. 'I've seen the way you look at me.'

I said nothing. But her nearness made me light-headed. For a heartbeat, I thought of kissing her—and the thought dishonoured me. I pulled away.

'You're not like the others,' she said. 'You could have your choice. I would be—a good wife to you.'

I turned to face her. 'You shame your family,' I said. 'And Andonis.'

She flinched. Then she raised her chin. 'My family lives on lentils and bread,' she said. 'My father hasn't worked since the fever. I have two younger brothers. If I don't bring home a dowry, none of us eat.'

I didn't answer. Her voice wasn't angry—just tired. The softness was gone.

'Andonis is nothing to me. You've been watching me all night. Don't say you haven't.'

I opened my mouth to rebuke her again.

'You think I want this?' she said. 'You think I enjoy flaunting myself at men who were born with—everything?'

Her voice cracked. 'I love a poor man. But I can't marry him—I need to marry well to support my family.'

She made of noise of disgust. 'But what do you know of matters like these? You in your fine house?'

She laughed, sharp and bitter.

I felt a flash of pity. Then something else—reluctant respect. She was doing what needed to be done. I couldn't fault that. Not really.

But she had no thought for others caught up in her scheming.

'Go now,' I said, 'before you embarrass yourself further.'

Her eyes flared—for a second. Fury, sharp and clean. Then she turned and walked back inside.

By the time I followed, women had formed a tight circle around her. She was crying—or seemed to be. Andonis was staring.

She was going to make me pay.

Disgust twisted my gut. I'd done nothing. She was the one chasing. Now she was acting as if I'd done something wrong?

I waited for Andonis to scoff. Roll his eyes. Dismiss her.

He looked at me. I waited.

'You take everything,' he said. He looked at me as if I'd planned it.

My mouth dropped open.

Me?

He brushed past me, shoulder grazing mine, and walked straight to the food table. Kostas and Damos followed. A wall of silence followed them.

We were brothers.

Nikos' voice cut through it. 'Why is Anastasia crying?'

He looked at Andonis and the others. Then at me.

His forehead creased, uncertain—then he turned and followed them.

Even Nikos.

Let them think what they wanted. I would not grovel. They hadn't even asked what had happened.

I didn't care what she'd said or whether she was able to cry on cue.

Something in me had changed since that night. The thought of her—the warmth of her breath, the touch of her fingers—made my stomach twist. Desire and disgust tangled until I couldn't tell them apart. Even now, if voices drop when I enter a room—the shame, the sense of being shut out as a dishonourable man, the knowledge I'd been a fool.

So that was the way Andonis and I remained—both adrift, each nursing the wound.

But mine festered. That night taught me that honour could be stripped away in an instant—even when you've done nothing wrong.

—

Hydra, December 1826

I followed my father's orders month after month. Andonis and I spoke only briefly—a few strained words when our paths crossed.

Fine. They'd made their choice. So had I. If he wanted to sulk forever, let him. I wasn't about to approach him either—not until he apologised.

I had more important things to do.

Father said the Englishman, Cochrane—the man Napoleon called 'Sea

Wolf'—would be commander-in-chief of the Greek fleet next year, in a bid to unify our fragmented naval command and the rebellious sailors. Miaoulis would step aside. I cheered Cochrane's daring but spat at his flag.

Missolonghi had fallen. Ibrahim held the Peloponnesus. Athens was under siege. The islands would be next.

We'd been saying that for four years. I was tired of waiting. Everyone was.

The white walls reflected the afternoon light, but Hydra felt cornered. Starving. Angry. The island boiled with unrest. Sailors marched for back pay. Pirate ships were slipping out under moonlight, holds empty, guns at the ready. The tavernas were full of rumours, not music. Greek pirates had killed the entire crew of a Sardinian ship, except for one sailor who survived by hiding in a barrel.

I checked the moorings. Only a couple of dozen ships left in the harbour. A few corvettes, one or two brigs. Men who were once crew now scavenged the quay for bread crusts.

When I left the quay, the fishmonger—a curiosity to me as a child, with his drooping lower eyelids revealing a glistening redness—was sweeping in front of his stall. He leaned in, lowering his voice. 'Stay off the streets tonight, *kyrie*. The sailors plan to storm the primates' hall.'

My hand moved instinctively to my *xiphos*. '*Efcharistó, kyrie.*'

My gaze swept over the quay—empty crates, idle men. Not like the old days.

Jobs were plentiful then, and pockets full. Shops had ringed the harbour, selling goods from Europe, Africa, the Americas, India—even China. Fish flapped beside mainland vegetables. There was Greek and Spanish olive oil, Madeira wine, American tobacco, sponges, oriental silks, beeswax, Mauritian sugar, African birds. Donkeys stood outside the tavernas and coffee houses, the air thick with coffee and tobacco, exotic spices, fish frying, meat roasting over braziers. The sound of music as traders and buyers shouted, haggled and laughed.

In those days, our traders had navigated the Hellespont freely to carry Russian wheat to Europe. I thought it would always be like that. But now, the Turkish fleet barred the way. Beggars sat idle on the stones.

Even the comparative luxury of the wedding last year was a lifetime ago.

'A coin, *kyrie*?'

I dropped money into outstretched hands. Men huddled outside boarded-up shops; tavernas and coffee houses stood quiet. Merchants still trading locked their doors against marauders, pistols ready, open only to those with cash. I had heard that Andonis and the boys were enduring hardship too.

I came home to find Mamá in the kitchen, the scent of *buhur suyu* on the air—the perfume of my childhood. Before the war, my father always had it sent from Constantinople for her: oil of flowers, sandalwood, cedar, frankincense, and oud. He said she should throw it out—there was no place for Turkish perfume in a patriot's house. She said he could throw himself out first. She used it sparingly these days, for there would be no more.

The scent ought to have calmed me, but it reminded me instead how fragile the old life had become.

'Hello, Ghikaki,' she said, cradling my new baby brother in one arm and setting down a plate of goat's cheese with the other. I'd heard it said that Mamá was too old to have children, so I'd been worried about her health until he arrived safely. Her eyes lingered on me, reading my face as she handed me a piece of bread and a thick slice of cheese. 'You're out early and back late, Ghika. Your father comments on it, you know.'

'He grumbles more than he comments,' I said, kissing her cheek.

She sighed. 'Why do you constantly disagree with him?'

'Because he is usually wrong.'

She shook her head. 'Then don't make him right.' She added, 'A widow asked after you today. Her little boy loves the boat you carved.'

I kept chewing.

Her smile deepened. 'You turned a piece of leftover wood into a child's joy. You have a knack with children.'

'Hire me as a nurse,' I said, still chewing, and she smacked my wrist.

Makris ran into the kitchen. 'You're my prisoner, Ghika! I'm the captain of a pirate ship!' He tapped my back with his wooden spoon 'yataghan', eyes gleaming.

'Which ship did you rob, Makri?' I said.

'The English. With a cargo of sugarplums!'

I shook my head. 'We can't rob friends.'

Although with friends like the English, we didn't need enemies.

He thought for a moment. 'I'll capture a Turk and take their *lokum*!'

I leaned in close. 'A cunning plan, *aderfáki*. You have the mind of a captain. I'd sail with you.'

My father and elder brothers were at a meeting to discuss the sailors' demands for back pay and their proposal to use the island's ships for privateering, while I did domestic duty. I took Mamá, my two younger brothers, and the baby to church, leaving Yiayia snug at home. I tucked the infant inside my coat and hunched my shoulders into the cutting wind, shielding Mamá and my brothers trailing behind.

In the tiny chapel's close quarters, Father Christos swung the silver censer, his low chant mesmerising as the fragrant smoke curled upward. Until a familiar voice beside me broke the hush.

'It's Damos. He's in trouble!'

My heart thumped in my throat—in the flickering gloom, Andonis' scarred face seemed leaner, sterner. The voice I hadn't heard for months.

He swallowed.

They had cast me out. And yet he stood here, asking for help.

I could refuse. Let them fix their own mess.

'They caught him stealing food from one of the Ionian prizes they've brought in. They'll hang him. They will listen to you,' he said.

That was all. No apology. No please.

Mamá's gloved hand tightened on my arm. 'No, Ghikaki,' she mouthed.

Why help him? Why care? But even as I thought it, I knew the answer.

I was nineteen years old. These were my men. Damos was my responsibility.

'I'll come. But after this, Andoni, you and I need to talk.'

I handed the baby back to Mamá, kissed my fingers, and touched them to her cheek. 'Mamá, I must go,' I said firmly, gently freeing myself from her grasp.

To Giorgios, I said, 'If I'm delayed, take Mitéra and the baby home. Can you do that?'

He was fourteen now, and our little church was far from the troubles at the port.

'Let me! You said I'm a captain!' said Makris.

I smiled.

Giorgios nodded, wide-eyed, eyes darting to the door. I crossed myself. Please, dear God, forgive me for disobeying my father.

—

At the harbour, the air was acrid with smoke—from bonfires, burning oil and rope, and the fumes of burning timber made me choke. In the haze, a thousand sailors had gathered for a share of the spoils, bent on civil unrest, shouting, pushing, shoving. The noise was deafening.

Gunshots cracked through the night and the sound of breaking glass amplified my dread as I searched for Damos in the chaos, eyes streaming and heart pounding.

If Father found me here, I'd be dead.

Then, suddenly—there he was. Damos. Alive, soaked and shivering, shoulders hunched, lips tinged blue. Nikos, gripping his arm, eyes wide with fright.

I rushed to him, yanking off my fur-lined coat and throwing it around his shoulders, rubbing his arms briskly to bring the blood back.

'What in God's name were you doing here during a riot? I've told you —stay away from trouble, you idiot,' I muttered. 'You nearly got yourself killed.'

Damos snorted, cocky, even with his teeth chattering. 'Why did you come? I didn't need your help.'

Nikos rolled his eyes. 'You nearly drowned, Damo.'

Damos shot him a glare, but clutched the coat tighter.

A shadow shifted beside me. Andonis stepped into the light.

I turned to face him.

His jaw worked as if he wanted to speak, but no words came. Pride and fury flickered behind his eyes.

He had come to me for help. But there'd been no need—and now they were both in my debt, and I'd done nothing.

I stared at him. 'So that's it?'

He let out a breath, short and bitter. 'If something had happened to Damos—'

He looked away.

Still no apology. Still nothing.

I thought I saw him soften. A flicker. Then it was gone.

Suddenly, Kostas was there, tone urgent. 'The mob has stormed the primates' hall. They're smashing the shops and stealing everything inside. They demand a hundred *piastres* each—or they'll take it in blood. Ghika, your family's in danger.'

My pulse pounded. My mother. My little brothers. In the church while the mob roared for blood. And Yiayia was at home, oblivious to the threat.

A roar rose from the crowd. 'Burn the admirals' houses!'

'Hang the shipowners!'

Another voice yelled, '*The Talbot* is standing off Kamini!' An English ship.

'Captain Spencer is taking the shipowners off the island. Stop them!'

Of course he was—English rescue for the men they needed. English law for everyone else.

The mob surged past like a torrent, faces grotesque in the flickering torchlight.

If they reached Kiafa before me, Mamá would face them with two boys and a baby. Over my dead body.

I darted through the frenzied crowd and leapt the stairs to the church— only to find the pews empty, the priest extinguishing the candles.

'Your family has fled to your uncle's house. They were fetching your yiayia first,' he said.

My stomach dropped. Mamá would be terrified alone in the dark streets. And my brothers.

Please, dear God. Don't let the mob reach them before I do.

I sprinted along rough paths, through dark alleys, up steep stairs. At my uncle's house, I banged on the door, ribs throbbing, fighting for breath.

Gunshots echoed from the harbour, then distant shouting.

I pounded again, harder.

'Open up!' I slammed my fist against the wood.

Please. Let them be here.

7

Prasinomata – Green Eyes

SYDNEY, New South Wales
  September 1829

I leave the girl at the lumberyard knowing full well I've disobeyed orders —and knowing I might be about to pay for it. I head for the rear of the Ryrie residence, where several oxen stand by a loaded dray. A bearded man with a pipe in his mouth, clothes a patchwork of grease and grime, is adjusting the ropes. Two horses are tethered to a hitching rail.

I arrive out of breath. Joseph spots me and grins. 'You're in trouble. We thought you legged it.'

The man at the oxen turns and bares his yellow teeth, worn down by the unlit pipe. Mister Ryrie emerges from the back door of the house with a ginger-haired young man, a small dog at their heels. He releases plumes of pipe smoke from the sides of his mouth.

'Gerkas? You were ordered to report here immediately,' he says without raising his voice. 'You did not.'

'Ghikas, sir. I was helping a young lady, sir,' I say.

'Commendable, I'm sure. But under the law,' he says calmly, 'absconding is an offence. Before a bench it will earn you a flogging—or chains and a road gang. Next time you will seek permission. Do you understand?'

'Yes, sir.'

He studies me, then nods. 'Very well. See it is not repeated.'

'Yes, sir.'

'Tomorrow, you leave for Arnprior. William, my eldest, is master there. This is James,' he nods.

James wheezes into his handkerchief. It seems a concave chest and ailing lungs have already shaped his life.

'Donald and wee Stewart you'll meet in due course. Obey them all. Is that clear?'

Mister Ryrie nods at the man with the oxen. 'And this is Ned. A free man, fine bullocky, fellow Scot.'

Then he points proudly at the dray. 'Guard that diligently. It's a pianoforte, all the way from Scotland, and Mrs Ryrie's most cherished possession. You won't see us at Arnprior until next year, gentlemen. That is all. Ned will direct your tasks for the rest of the afternoon.'

'I'm done, sir. Ready to depart at dawn,' Ned says.

Mister Ryrie casts a final look over the yard. 'Gentlemen, you are at liberty until five o'clock—no taverns mind—be back at this yard by the five o'clock bell. Miss it, and I'll not speak for you.'

Martin suggests a walk to Millers Point, past the dockyard where natives are often seen spear fishing.

I decline his offer. I intend to escort a young lady to a cobbler.

—

At the Lumber Yard, the woman at the gate snaps out a question in a voice as starched as her bonnet. 'To whom do you wish to speak?'

'Her name is Mary.'

She rolls her eyes back. 'Of the two hundred girls on the Red Rover, fifty-six were christened Mary. If I find this young lady, what is your message?'

'I promised I'd have her shoe mended.'

She lifts one eyebrow and wrinkles her nose at my clothes. 'How imaginative.' Her hand waves in dismissal. 'Wait on the other side of the road.'

I spend twenty minutes listening to vulgar discussions of the 'Red Rovers' and the intentions of the crowd of men waiting. Some will propose marriage.

Almost ready to give up, I spot her leaving the building. I reach the gate before she does, nearly wrenching it off its hinges.

She meets my gaze with those striking eyes. On Hydra we have a word for her: *prasinomáta*—green-eyes.

Something shifts under my skin, slow and tidal. It moves into my stomach.

'Ah, here you are,' I hear myself saying, mind strangely blank.

'Yes, here I be,' she says, as calm as sunrise, as if I hadn't pushed my way through a mob to burst out, red-faced and gasping, in front of her.

I blurt, 'That shoe needs a cobbler. I'll take it.'

She crosses her arms. 'Not without me, you won't. They're the only ones I have to my name.'

The lilt of her Irish accent sucks the breath from my chest. Her face shines with an inner glow and the whites of her eyes are so bright they're startling.

I put my hands together as if I am a priest. 'It is important to maintain shoes. If they deteriorate too far, they go beyond repair. I am told that shoes made in the colony last but a couple of months. It would be unfortunate if you had to go barefoot.'

I think of her bare feet.

'What's that tongue you're speaking?'

A flush of heat colours my cheeks as I realise I've lapsed into Greek. I abandon the speech and smile. My tongue is too big.

'May I take you to the cobbler?'

She narrows her eyes. 'You put the fear in me.'

I look like a ragamuffin: trousers bearing the arrows of a convict, shirt soaked with perspiration. I clutch the fabric at the neck of my shirt to hide my chest hair—the top button has fallen off. But at least my face is shaven and moustache trimmed.

A constable on guard is taking a lively interest. 'The cobbler's shop is down the hill, miss.'

I smile at him. Long moments pass while the girl studies me.

I can't tell if she's weighing my offer or watching me squirm. I bristle.

'I regret having taken up your time. Good day,' I say.

'Hold on, sir,' says the constable. 'She is thinking about it, are you not, miss? Don't abandon her yet, sir.'

I turn back.

She's still hesitating. 'I'm after coming,' she says, 'but only on account of my shoe. Don't you be trying anything or I'll scream.'

I raise my eyebrows. The constable breaks into a grin.

'I don't doubt it,' I say.

'I reckon you'll be safe with this gentleman,' says the constable. 'The Ladies' Committee will watch you Red Rover girls like hawks. Besides, he looks harmless.'

The girl remains undecided.

I wipe my hands on my trousers and gently take her hand to place on my arm. Her skin makes mine look like tanned leather.

She jerks back—unused, perhaps, to such courtesies. Or maybe she simply doesn't trust me.

She crosses her arms. I hold up my hands in surrender—no more attempts at gallantry. She lacks the refinement of our women at home, but there's something refreshing in her rough edges, her defiance.

We fall into step, heading down the hill together, her limp shoe slap-slapping with each stride. Sydney Cove spreads out below us in a gleam of water and masts, the Red Rover at anchor once more. Smoke drifts silver from the chimneys, softening the town beneath it.

'My name is Ghikas. I am Greek. From the island of Hydra.'

'Speak slowly.'

'Are you giving me orders?'

But I repeat my name. 'Ghee–kah–ss. But in Greek, when you address someone, you leave off the 's'. So, you may call me Ghika.'

She brings her eyebrows together, her gaze fixed on my mouth. Her lips, small and perfect, mimic mine. And those eyes—that unbelievable shade of green. She repeats my name without fault. I cannot help smiling. She smiles back, revealing a slight gap between her front teeth. The earth beneath me has given way, and I am suspended in the air beside her.

I inhale deeply to regain my composure.

When she stumbles again, I reach out to steady her, feel a jolt when our skins touch. A team of oxen overtakes us, on the point of breaking into a downhill trot, when the bullocky calls out, 'Whoa.' I move to shield her, but she jumps the wrong way. The dray skids to a halt, splattering muck over her skirt.

She doesn't seem to mind.

A fish vendor pulling a cart yells, 'Fish ho!'

'Do you have a surname, Mary?'

'It be Lyons.' She steps over a pile of horse droppings; a cloud of flies rises in a wave and settles again.

'And where are you from?'

'County Cork. Éire.' She adds, 'That's Ireland to you.'

'Oy-er-land, eh?' I laugh, for the joy of it.

'Is it impolite you're being?' she asks, serious, looking at the arrow on my trousers. 'And are you a convict?'

'Yes. Transported for piracy.'

Her eyes widen. 'A Greek pirate! I read about them in the Cork newspaper. And weren't they calling you an evil name? Was it smell-fungus? Wasn't I reading that in a pamphlet somewhere?'

She says it with such delight that I can't help laughing, though I've no idea what it means. Her laughter follows mine—light, effervescent, contagious.

Then I surprise myself by confiding something even more intimate. 'I lost my grandfather's amulet seven years ago. I've had bad luck since.'

'That will be your problem, to be sure. What is your work? Apart from piracy?' Her dimples appear.

'I am a sailor, but they mean me to work as a shepherd. We leave at dawn for a place called Arnprior, two hundred miles south. For fourteen years.'

'A long time.'

'Yes, but it's not forever. My old life is waiting for me at home. I need to see this through.'

'Two hundred miles? Sure, and if you went that far in Ireland, you'd fall off the edge. And what if you change your mind in fourteen years and decide to stay?'

'Out of the question. And you Mary? What was your crime?'

Her eyes flash. 'I am a free settler. Not a common criminal.'

'Like me?'

An impish look. 'No. You're uncommon.'

I throw my head back and laugh. She's like a sudden wind raising the hairs on your arms on a hot day.

The cobbler shop is near the market at the bottom of the hill, in a quaint stone building with a wooden bench out front. Mary's gaze follows a gentlewoman with a child, manoeuvring through the crowd, holding a dainty parasol.

She watches them disappear into a haberdashery. She sits then bends to remove the half-ankle boot made of a forest green canvas. Their mildewed state makes the side laces stubborn, so she sheds her gloves. The skin of her fingers is peeling.

'Ouch!' She sucks her index finger.

A parrot in a cage near the door squawks and she glances up. Her jawline takes me back to a painting at home, Amphitrite, goddess of the sea.

I kneel. 'May I?'

She pulls her feet away, tucks them under the bench.

'I have a sister,' I say.

She extends them. 'You're lucky. I wish I did.'

I ease the tight laces on the flapping shoe, but I pull too hard on the heel. The boot flies off, and her head hits the wall, and my hand lands squarely on her knee. For a heartbeat, no words, just a meeting of eyes. I have the most extraordinary floating sensation.

'Ouch again!' She rubs the back of her head, laughter bubbling up. In fact, we're both laughing.

She has folded a portion of her oversized stocking underneath her toe. No wonder the sole came loose.

'Watch what you are doing.' A stern voice.

I glance around.

'Show the young lady respect.'

A man in a cutaway coat stands on the doorstep of the shop.

Mary speaks before me. 'Please do not concern yourself, sir. This kind gentleman is assisting me.'

I stand and look him squarely in the eye. 'The young lady has nothing to fear from me, sir.'

He holds my gaze, unflinching. 'Townsend. Richard Townsend.' He speaks over my shoulder. 'At your service, miss.' He clicks his polished heels.

Mary has her shoe in her hands.

'I'll take that,' he says, with an air of self-importance. He snatches it and enters the shop.

I mutter. 'Who made him the keeper of boots?'

She wriggles away along the bench for me to sit beside her. She lacks the acquired graces, yet possesses a natural charm.

'Don't worry Captain Bluebeard. It gives us time to talk.'

'I think you mean Blackbeard. Bluebeard murdered his wives.'

She laughs. 'Yes, yes. The pirate.'

'Where in Ireland did you live Mary?'

'Most girls on the Red Rover are coming from the Cork Foundling Hospital. Or the workhouse.'

'Foundling Hospital?'

'It's a home for orphans. Or those abandoned at birth. Like me. Left in a box at the gate. I don't care, anyway. I can look after myself.'

Her resilience astounds me. On Hydra, we cherish every child. Orphan or not.

'I am sorry about your welcome this morning. Or lack of it.'

'Ghikas?' She dismisses that with a wave of her hand. 'Ghika? We don't really call pirates smell-fungus. I like the sound of it.'

Her smile lights the day.

Two men across the way struggle with a crate, tilting it dangerously. My jaw tightens. I swallow the urge to bark orders.

She ought to be back in Ireland with parents to love her.

I am drawn to her. Curious, since she is nothing like the obedient girls on Hydra.

'Have you secured a position yet, Mary?'

'I will work as a maid for a Mrs Bloodsworth, eight pounds a year.' She says it proudly.

Part of me wants to shield her. 'You'll be alone in this Sydney house. Does that not worry you?'

'I can fend for myself.'

There's a scuffle outside the public house across the way and two men roll in the dirt. We watch as two others pry them apart. One clutches his head and stumbles into the alley beside us. A tattered woman hawking second-hand garments from a barrow yells, 'Silk stockings for sale! Fine chemises!'

'This place breaks its fast on girls like you,' I say. 'Would you consider a position at Arnprior if I could arrange it?'

'Way out there? Never.' She shivers. 'I'd never live in the wilderness. I'm staying in Sydney. Don't you like the city?'

'No. Hydra is the only place I want to be.'

'And what if it's not the place you remember? Fourteen years is a fierce long time. People change on you. They do.'

'Hydra will never change. Anyway, I will go home to marry a good Greek girl.'

'Better than a bad one, I suppose. Me, I'm a misogamist.'

I sputter and laugh. 'What does that mean?'

'I will never marry. Men find a way to put a pall on every day.'

We are speaking of other things when the gentleman returns. 'Your shoe,' he says.

'To be sure, that must be new, sir!' she says.

He beams. 'The cobbler said it wasn't worth repairing. But I told him to do it anyway.'

'And what is my debt?' she asks.

'Please. That is my gift.'

'No, sir. I will pay.' She presses a coin into his hand. 'I will not be in anyone's debt.'

I had intended to settle the account—yet I'm glad she declines his offer. She will not be owned. And I do not know what to do with that.

'Back to the lumberyard for me,' she says. And to the gentleman, 'Thank you again, sir.'

'I've an appointment at the Bank of New South Wales, or I'd escort you, miss,' he says.

No doubt he'll be counting his money.

'I will accompany Miss Lyons,' I say.

I curse myself—now he knows her name.

As she and I retrace our steps, the strains of the regimental military band drift from the barracks. We leave the cobblestones of the harbour-side and start up the hill. She hums a tune, and I smile at the sweetness of her voice, a smile she catches.

'It's called *The Last Rose of Summer*. My friend Lizbet would sing it to me at home.'

I will leave Sydney tomorrow and I may never see her again.

'Do you have a religion, Mary?'

'Reared Protestant in the Foundling Hospital right enough, but born Catholic, so I was. A mongrel, I suppose you'd say. And you?'

'We are of the Greek faith, but there is no church for us here. But a Roman Catholic priest has shown us kindness since we arrived. Father Therry—he's Irish, like you. He could give you guidance—'

'On what? My lack of virtue?' She laughs. 'Hah. So you're a Catholic, now? You'll be going to hell sure as sin, Ghika.' She laughs.

'Don't joke, Mary. It's a serious matter.'

'I'm not joking—the matron always said I was wicked.'

She's so honest. Without guile. But she speaks with the determination of a man. If she were one, I would admire this quality. But she isn't. I worry for her.

She's quiet for a while, then says, 'Tell me about where you lived.'

I glance at her.

'On your island.'

I hesitate. 'Stone walls. A courtyard with olive trees. My mother kept lemon trees in pots. There was an orchard, and we could see the harbour.'

Her eyes stay on the road ahead. 'Your parents worked for a fine gentleman by the sound of it.'

I say nothing.

'Must have been nice.'

'Mary, are you sure you will not come to Arnprior? For your safety?'

'Safety? Me? I've done fine so far.'

She has survived. It's not the same as being safe.

'It's dangerous for a woman here,' I say. 'Especially one alone.'

'Sure I'm not afraid. I'd rather my freedom than your safety, so I would.'

Is she trying to be objectionable? Or does she mean this?

'You won't feel that way when it's dark, and you're alone, and someone is following you.'

She shrugs. 'Then I'll deal with it.'

So foolish. She says it as if danger were a game. But there's a flash, for a second, of something raw. Alone.

I say, 'Are you trained to fight? To box?'

'Of course I am not. But I can run. Anyway, that's life. You were brave facing that lout for me. But I don't need saving.'

'Mary, you've done well, considering your own background. But you would do better to curb your rebellious nature. You need protection.'

She stiffens. I can see I've upset her. But she is quick to take offence when I only mean to help.

'Is that so? Well, I've managed quite well since I was left in that crate. You don't need to be telling me what's wrong with my background. Or my nature.'

'It befits a woman to take correction. How else will she improve?'

Her voice rises. 'Improve? You mean to fix me, like my shoe? I'm not yours to repair. You speak as if you're a gentleman, but here, you're no better than the rest of us. Perhaps worse, for thinking you are.'

A fist to the chest. That same hollow, burning shame. Feeling worthless. As if I were sixteen again, standing before my father, trying and failing to explain.

I will not take this from a girl. I keep my voice even. 'You are being unreasonable. A woman needs guidance and protection.'

Her face turns a burning pink. 'Then let me be perfectly reasonable, Mister Greek Pirate. Even if no other man walked the earth, I would not seek your guidance—nor your protection.' She crosses her arms.

'Is that really how you feel?'

She nods—defiant, stubborn.

'Then we are fortunate. For even if you were the last woman, I would offer neither.'

The words are sharper than I intended. She doesn't flinch, but her chin lifts as she wheels away.

I'm glad to be rid of her, yet something in me wants to call her back. I don't know if I want to argue or apologise.

She is halfway to the building when she stops, turns on her heel, and comes back at me.

I brace.

She marches right up. 'Listen,' she says. 'I didn't mean it about the last man on earth.'

My mouth opens.

Then she grins. 'But you're still a smell-fungus!'

She whirls, and she's gone.

Even our Greek war hasn't prepared me for her.

8

A High Stakes Game

HYDRA

December 1826

The gunfire on the Hydra quay grew closer now, louder. I pounded on my uncle's gate again. A servant appeared on the terrace, then vanished, surely to unlock it.

Please, *Panagia mou*, let Mitéra and my brothers be here.

Another face appeared—my father's. Thank God he was safe.

'Patéra! Where are Mitéra and the baby? My brothers?'

His words exploded white in the frosty air. 'Where were you when they needed you? Fraternising with ruffians?'

'*Babá*, please. I was helping a friend.' I kicked myself for using the word 'daddy'. 'The mob is out of control,' I said. 'We must go to Kamini. The English will take us off the island.'

His lips were blue with cold and fury. 'A friend who takes precedence over your family? You left your mother and brothers in the church. Did you not see where your duty lay, as a son, as a brother?'

I clenched my jaw. 'Patéra, they were not in danger. I had to help him.'

'Your duty was to your family.'

I shot back, 'And what about your duty? To your men? There's a reason the sailors are rioting.'

Disbelief swept across his face. He barked, 'You are a disgrace. Find Despina and Lambros. Bring them here.'

Mitéra emerged, the baby in her arms, a single tear betraying her. That undid me. I had never seen her cry. I wanted to be her pride—and after all her training, a man she admired. My father's iron grip guided her away.

He always found a reason to shut me out. I hadn't done anything wrong.

I returned to my father's house and found Lambros and Despina safe.

At daybreak, Lambros and I descended to the harbour. The quay was a scene of overturned stalls and smouldering fires.

The old fishwife, ever ready with news, was waiting. 'Your family is unharmed. They stayed at the Kountouriotis mansion last night.' She added, 'The shipowners have agreed to pay one million *piastres* in back pay—but the English insist their ships and goods be returned, and Zacca be given up to them. Four English ships, the *Glasgow*, *Cambrian*, *Brisk* and *Talbot* are all standing off the island, and are threatening to fire on the town. This trouble isn't over.'

Armed with her brightest-eyed fish and a crusty loaf, we arrived home as my family returned. My little brothers burst into the kitchen.

'Ghikaki, the sailors rioted!' Makris was puffing.

'They lit fires and shot muskets!' Giorgios held up his arms to mimic shooting.

Mitéra's hand touched mine—gentle, relieved, sad.

Outside, I heard my father's voice. 'Lambros, summon Ghikas.'

My guts twisted.

In the reception room, my father looked at me, not with anger, but disgust.

'Ghika, you carry the family name,' he began, his voice steady. 'You are an heir of your grandfather Dimas Voulgaris. That means something. You chose to stand with strangers last night, instead of your mother and brothers. You were not the son I raised. Tonight, we celebrate your brother's promotion to captain. You may attend. Or not.' He lifted the broadsheet as if to read.

The rustle of the paper sent a pulse of rage through me. He sought my obedience—that was all he cared about.

His own brothers had left him behind years ago. Uncle Giorgios had been governor of Hydra. Uncle Frangiskos' house was right on the harbour. His was up at Kiafa.

I was nineteen years old—it was time I stopped bending to my father's will. I clenched my fists at my sides and walked out.

As evening settled in, I found my elder brother—to offer him my sincere congratulations and tell him of my decision.

'Ghika, your relationship with Patéra is fraught, I know,' he said, placing a comforting hand on my shoulder. 'There will be other dinners.'

I embraced him and headed to the port.

—

My friends sat around a brazier outside the coffeehouse, smoke curling upwards in the freezing air. The quay had been swept clean, debris removed, but not from the hearts of the shopkeepers. They were bitter. The English had given Hydra two days—either Zacca returned the Ionian prizes and their cargo, or they'd reduce the town to rubble.

A truce, they called it. A pistol held to the temple.

When Andonis saw me, he sprang to his feet with a hoot of happiness, a smile splitting his face. 'Well, look who's lighting up the night sky! It's Ghikas!'

I grinned back.

Damos danced his way across to me, slipping my coat from his shoulders as he came. 'É! The Phoenix rises! Thank you for this, Ghika. It's good to have rich friends.'

'I live to serve, Damo,' I said drily.

Kostas laughed.

Nikos, eyes wide with excitement, threw his arm around me, 'Ghika, I found a whole bag of raisins! And now you're back! It's like the old days.'

He offered me a sweaty handful.

I took one. 'Thank you, Niko. I'm better off here than suffering another lecture from my father. Let's go to the taverna.'

I glanced up towards my family home, where laughter and celebration continued without me.

I slapped the table. 'É! Three *rakis* each! Make a line on the table!'

We drank to each other, to Damos' escape, to Hydra, to winning the war, to being heroes.

Andonis raised his cup. 'Or as Yiannis would say, to being compassionate men.'

Compassion. Easy to toast. Harder to live.

Nikos' cheeks were flushed. 'We're together again! Let's drink to that!'

'Ghika?' Andonis said. 'Remember how Yiannis used to flick his *komboloi,* and ask what we'd be when we grew up?'

Yianni used to flip the loop of his komboloi beads, slapping them backwards and forwards, making circles in the air, his fingers a blur. Swing, stop, sort. Swing, stop, sort.

I grinned. 'You said you'd captain your own brig.'

'I still will.' He really looked at me then. 'You said you'd marry Maria. Build a fleet bigger than your father's. Die a hero.'

'Almost there,' I said. They laughed.

I didn't want to help anyone any longer. I wanted power. Respect was the size of your fleet. And glory only mattered if someone was watching.

Even now, I was still trapped. My father's shadow on one side. My friends' expectations on the other.

The *raki* dulled the sting, not the truth.

I wanted to be free of him—yet still make him proud.

I wanted to stand on my own—and still have my friends lean on me.

Pitiful.

But they needed me.

'Tonight we make fun.' Andonis scraped the tobacco dregs from his pipe and threw them onto the coals of the brazier, where they exploded in tiny bursts of flame and disappeared with a 'pffft'—like my dreams.

As the night wore on, Andonis breathed raki fumes in my face as spirits spilled from his cup. 'We have missed you, Ghikaki.'

Kostas played the bouzouki. I made my way to the centre of the taverna, arms wide, swaying to the beat of the music. As a slow clapping began, I bent to sweep my arm across the floor, each movement leading into the next—forward step, back glide, side slide, knee bend. One by one, others joined, forming a chain of arms over shoulders. On and on, as we found a rhythm, the music faster and faster, moving together as if we were one, building to the last almighty crescendo, when Kostas struck the strings with a bang. He flung both arms up, bouzouki held high, and we fell to the floor, laughing.

I wanted to place this memory in a bottle and seal it with wax.

I could keep us strong, keep us together.

Near midnight, Andonis clapped a hand on my shoulder. 'Come with us, Ghikaki. Come live with us!'

I hesitated.

'Not tonight. I'll visit you tomorrow.'

Damos swayed and grinned. 'Damn your treacherous eyes, Ghika.' He hugged me.

We walked a little. Said our goodbyes. They continued on.

I wandered back to the taverna. The coals were black, the patrons gone. Alone on the quay, I slumped into a chair. A drifting mist softened the moon, but its light still stretched across the harbour, a rippling path on the water. My head, heavy as a cannonball, rolled forward. When I awoke that same rippling line of moonlight reached toward me like an accusation.

A burst of laughter came from the taverna's back room—a forbidden area where I had never been—the exclusive domain of cut-throats who played the *blaktzakis* card game for money.

But these men cared nothing for their fathers, or sins like gambling, or the Ottoman law that banned it. Or for the philosopher Aristotle who said it was akin to thievery.

Didn't the greatest victories come from the greatest risk?

I fumbled in my vraka. We had played this game as children, wagering with pebbles scavenged on the beach. I had consistently ended the game with a pile.

'They'll see,' I mumbled. 'Tomorrow I'll walk into the hut with enough for all of them. Enough to feed their families. They'll call me Herakles again. Like they used to.'

The moon vanished behind a cloud, and the breeze, drunk with power, rattled the taverna's shutters.

I lurched toward the back room and fell against the door. Inside, a smoky haze hung in the air. A circle of men lounged on floor cushions, smoking the *nargile* pipe, eyes on the floor strewn with cards.

They paused only briefly to glance my way. A dark-skinned man with rings on every finger and a forest of chest hair sprouting from his open shirt grunted as he threw his cards. He shoved a heap of coins at his rival. Laughter rippled as they clinked *raki* cups.

My eyes fixed on the staggering piles of gold coins scattered in front of each player.

A player raised his eyes to mine. 'Do you lack the courage to play, *kyrie*?'

Kyrie. That's what I deserved. Respect. They didn't look down on me. They didn't tell me I was a disappointment.

My heart pounded. Sweat beaded at my temple as I stepped closer.

Another man leaned forward. 'Or do you lack the funds?'

My voice quivered. 'Funds? I have both.' My fingers trembled.

'Well, then,' the first player said. 'Let's see you stake the Voulgaris fortune.'

Two men moved sideways, creating a narrow space. Another pushed a cushion into it.

The room closed in. The cards flew. Hand after hand, my hope dwindled as money changed hands. Each defeat tightened a knot in my gut. I doubled my wager, desperate to claw back losses, only to see them match my every move.

I froze, palms slick. My hands, steady at sea, shook with the cards.

I had one good hand—just enough to keep me playing. Just enough to make me think the tide had turned.

I was in debt for more than I could afford.

But maybe the next round would change everything. One coin, one deal. That was all I needed.

My pulse pounded in my ears.

I wasn't quitting. Not when they were watching. Not when I could win.

A ripple of laughter rolled through the room. A single coin spun across the wood before joining the gleaming heap. The dark-skinned man's rings caught the lamplight as he shuffled the cards.

'What's the matter, Voulgaris? Afraid?' His voice was velvet smooth.

'No coin left? Sail with us, son of Nikolaos. Turn pirate, and your debt disappears.'

A hush fell over the table.

'Double, or I am quit,' I said, voice tight.

A low murmur spread. The smaller player's eyes gleamed.

'Now that is courage,' he whispered.

He dealt the cards.

By the time pale light filtered through the narrow window, my original stake had vanished. I had borrowed more money than I could repay, enough to feed my friends' families for a year.

I rose, legs heavy as anchors.

The small man's chillingly polite tone sent shivers down my spine. 'We shall speak of your debt. Another day. Take this coin for good luck.'

—

Later, I woke to Giorgios shaking me.

'Ghikaki, will you help me mend my boat?'

My head pounded, my mouth was parched; my skin was clammy with sweat. I struggled to swallow. I glanced down at my dishevelled clothes from the night before, and a wave of nausea surged through me.

My voice emerged as a croak. 'Not now, Giorgi. Later.'

I pulled my pillow over my head.

I had no idea how I'd pay it back. None.

But I couldn't tell my father. He'd never forgive me—and he'd never let me forget it.

I stumbled to the window, barely reaching it before I retched violently, heaving long after my stomach had emptied itself.

Weak and ill, I flopped back on the bedding. The coin lay there, mocking me.

I was roused by the soft, persistent sound of scraping and tapping in the garden below. When I rose to look for the source, Giorgios was sitting under an orange tree, engrossed in mending his toy boat, concentration evident in the wrinkles on his brow. His fingers worked meticulously.

I watched him from the window, shame burning behind my eyes at his dedication to repairing his toy, something so small yet significant to him. I didn't deserve him.

Part of me wanted to crawl back under the covers. He looked up and waved, then continued.

I descended to join him, splashed my face at the stone basin near the back door, and knelt at his side.

'Let me help,' I said.

He looked up and smiled.

We worked together—his hands sure, mine shaking.

My father had always found a reason to shut me out.

This time I had done it to myself.

9

Learning The Land

SYDNEY TO ARNPRIOR, New South Wales
October 1829

We begin our journey from Sydney to Arnprior on the Parramatta Road, where we encounter carriages, carts, men on horseback and pedestrians, from soldiers to beggars. The Parramatta coach rattles past several times, then we pass it again as it stops for passengers or goods.

James says, 'If you wish to escape, go ahead. But if you do, William will deal with you.' His eyes show a hint of amusement. 'Trust me, you'd rather any fate than William.'

He slumps in the saddle, exhausted from his speech, and wipes his mouth.

'Do you reckon he means it? Let's escape!' whispers Joe, fingers fluttering like a sparrow.

'I suggest we do not.'

In Sydney yesterday, Mister Ryrie and James carried themselves with the easy confidence of men used to respect. Gentlemen. William, surely, will be the same. Not like Ned, who barks orders like a tavern-keeper turning out drunkards.

Arnprior. I imagine a fine house with columns of wood or stone, with outbuildings and sheds and enclosures for the sheep. This William will come down the grand steps, look us over. A man of breeding will surely recognise another. He'll shake my hand and assign me suitable tasks.

Given my background, we might even be friends. If a man knows quality, he knows it when he sees it. I mean to be seen.

The sun is oppressive; the road is dusty, and the incessant buzz of insects almost overrides the jingle of harness. Trees giving off a menthol and camphorous tang purge themselves by shedding long slivers of bark from silver satin trunks.

Ned's voice is full of frustration and clear resentment towards us as convicts. His oaths are our constant companion. I am told to walk the off side of the team while Ned keeps to the near—the equivalent of starboard and port. I am called the offsider.

'By Saint Andrew's cross, I'll make you regret your dawdling, you filthy scoundrels!'

'There is no shade in this infernal hell,' Joe says.

We occasionally meet other travellers—men on horseback, carts, and buggies. Children stare listlessly from the backs of the drays, bare legs dangling. The women, few in number, are a sad sight, bonnets limp in the heat, trailing alongside their men, or bouncing on unforgiving planks under the glaring sun. They clutch the sides with both hands, knuckles white, heads bowed, eyes hollow.

I am reminded of the Irish girl, Mary. Were these women once as spirited? Is this what the colony has done to them? Will she have it beaten out of her too? I hope not.

I was too blunt that day. She was rude, yes—but I let her provoke me. I should have answered with dignity.

I owe her an apology. Not that she'd want it. That jaw of hers—she could bite through iron.

If ever I see her, I'll give an apology anyway.

As the days pass, the road narrows until it's barely wide enough for our passage, choked with ruts, washaways, fallen branches, and loose stones. We meet a team of surveyors who tell Ned that one day this will be a fine road. Ned grunts and says, 'When? In a hundred years?'

The oxen are harnessed by day, hobbled by night, and Ned controls them with his whip. They remind me of Kostas—slow and obstinate, but brave, steady, loyal.

'For the love of Jesus Christ, canna you see that branch, you blethering idiots?' Ned shouts at us. 'Do you want it to put the bullock's eye out, you muttonhead? We're mired again, you lazy sods! Why do they send me fools and simpletons?'

During one of our rest breaks, Martin murmurs, 'William Ryrie sounds like a demon. Ned says he doesn't use the lash himself—but he has the overseer, Bartholomew, do his work for him.'

'No gentleman whips another,' I say.

Martin laughs. 'Unless your pockets are filled with banknotes, Ghika, I doubt they'll class you as one.'

I almost say something, but he'd never understand.

Once, I almost called him Damos. And twice, I've called Ned Andonis.

Saying their names won't make them appear.

Black dirt lines Joe's fingernails, and he constantly scratches himself or probes his ear. One evening, when it's his turn to cook, the others eat their food like hungry wolves, shovelling in great mouthfuls without hesitation. I manage to eat it, but later I double over and retch in the dust.

'Bit weak in the belly, Ghika?' Joe's face crinkles into lines as he wheezes with laughter.

And like that, my moral superiority vanishes—undone by a bowl of stew.

After several weeks, James, with a glint in his eye, points ahead, down a rise. 'That's Arnprior. And there's the Shoalhaven—the best river in New South Wales. We're home.' He gallops ahead.

Ned lowers his voice. 'He calls it home. Ryrie took this land off some poor bastard named Davis,' he mutters, glancing sideways. Then louder, for anyone listening, 'Fine place, though.'

Through the gum trees, on the river flat below us, the breeze ripples the blue-green waves of a wheat crop. I already know Indian corn is a darker, fresher green.

There are no rivers at home. No crops. There are no grand buildings here. This place is nothing like home.

The oxen need no urging.

Away to the left, a simple homestead squats on a flat rise above the stream. Only as we draw nearer do I spot James' mare hitched to a rail behind it, one hind leg cocked in rest, her weight on the other. A grey stands beside her, switching at flies with his tail.

Ned points at a confusion of huts further up the slope. The bowl of his pipe jerks up and down as he speaks. 'Them huts are for you lags.'

We unharness the oxen and let them go in a paddock enclosed by a post and rail fence. With our bags over our shoulders, we trail behind Ned up the hill. Sapling poles hold together the bark slabs of the huts. Some have rough stone chimneys; some have fireplaces outside. Open doors reveal dirt floors.

Ned leads us to an abandoned ruin. Roof collapsed, walls buckling. 'Build your own or fix this. Your choice.'

The hefty wooden jamb has collapsed on one side, blocking the door-way. Martin tosses it aside.

I turn to Ned. 'If they expect diligent labour from their convicts, they ought to provide more suitable lodgings. A man works better with adequate rest.'

At home, they might have listened. But Ned guffaws.

Here, I am simply another convict. I am trying to help—but maybe it seems to others I'm trying to prove something.

When I enter the hut, I jump backwards. An ugly monster of a lizard stares at me with unblinking eyes, tongue flicking in and out.

'Only a goanna. Don't hurt 'im, he won't hurt you. Some lags feed 'em. Stupid gits. They bite.'

The animal's wrinkled grey body raises itself on clawed feet. A collar of loose skin sags at its neck; double bands of black ring its belly. After a ponderous turn, it wanders out through a hole in the wall, lifting each thick leg as if over an invisible obstruction.

'I will take this hut,' I say firmly, taking charge. 'Who will share? Anyone with carpentry skills?'

I look around fiercely enough, daring anyone to laugh at my pronunciation of 'share'.

'Who said you choose first?' says Ned.

'I did,' I say.

'I will share with Ghika,' says Joseph.

'We'll have it fixed in no time,' says Martin, slapping his hands together.

I duck to avoid a fallen beam and knock my head on another. Too low. Too tight. They laugh. I step outside to breathe.

They have followed me. 'Any chance of some female company around here?' says Martin.

I imagine the Irish girl's reaction to that language. That look that could shame a general.

Ned laughs. 'A cook? A chambermaid too?' He relents. 'There's a female on Durran Durra—the wife of a convict. You'll not be seeing her. When Mrs Ryrie and young Jane arrive, they will breathe a woman's touch intae the place. But they'll not be cooking for the likes of you scabs. No more will I.'

He talks tougher than he acts, inviting us into his hut where he tosses hunks of rank green pork and turnips into a pot, boils them until barely cooked, then dumps the steaming mess onto battered plates.

'Dig in. That's the last meal you'll be having from me. After this, you're on your own.'

He leans back against the wall, pipe in hand, as we begin to eat. Only then do I notice—he has nothing for himself.

A hollow opens in my chest. I'm banished, stripped of everything I care about, and now my friends are gone too. Yet here, in a shack of rough boards and bark, with a foul-smelling pot and a snarling bullocky, I find the same *filoxenia*—love for the stranger—I was raised to honour. At home, it's a rule. We offer our best to a stranger first.

And this rough-swearing man has given me his last share.

I scrape half my plate onto an empty one on the table and indicate it's for him. He grunts, picks it up and eats. I brace myself for the rancid pork and turnips.

'Tell me about this man Davis,' I say. 'The one whose land Ryrie took.'

'Davis had a land grant from an earlier governor, but William and James had newer ones. William won in court. He tore Davis' stockyards down, let his cows go, ripped the roof of his house clean off.'

'Surely that's against the law.'

'Yes, he had to pay Davis one hundred pounds for using force. But it's ended up Ryrie's land. That's how it works here.'

We spread our blankets on the ground outside his hut and I'm asleep instantly.

Hours later, I lie awake staring up at the stars.

I asked her if she'd come to the country—to protect her morals, I said.

I imagine her in a white apron, embroidery in her lap, sitting in a rocking chair.

I've seen the homestead now. There are no armchairs here. Just dirt, flies, and men who boil green pork and swear at oxen. No protection. No sanctuary.

It's fortunate she said no.

I shut her from my mind. I won't see her again.

The next morning, as we follow Ned to the storehouse, I catch my first glimpse of William. He resembles a lean English racing hound, with the same copper hair as James.

He moves like a man who is used to giving orders and having them obeyed. He isn't big, but the riding crop slaps once against his tall leather boot—a casual motion. He pulls his waistcoat down over the waist of his white duck trousers, gaze flicking over us like a butcher inspecting livestock.

Behind him, James begins to speak—but William lifts a hand, stopping him.

He turns to Ned.

Ned doesn't rush. He knocks his hat back to scratch his head, eyes us with practiced disinterest, then nods toward Martin. 'That one—strong back, no trouble. The Greek, he'll talk back, but he works. The thief's skittish, but he's quick.'

William gives a single nod, accepting the assessment without question.

Ned has no land, no title—just calloused hands and a foul mouth. Yet James listens when he speaks. And now William does too.

We line up.

'Right James,' says William. 'Introduce me.'

James flicks his handkerchief into his pocket and points at Joseph. 'That's Joseph. I've heard he'd steal his own shoes.'

Joseph's face drains of colour. William stares at him until he shifts his feet.

'And this is Martin Armstrong,' James continues.

William, eyeing Martin's build, steps forward and grabs his arm, sizing him up. 'Let's see if you live up to your name.' He's lucky Martin is so affable.

'And this is Ghikas. Ghika. I told you. Father had him reassigned from Macleay. He—'

'Why? What is useful about him? Apart from his size?'

James shrugs. 'He's Greek. He knows vines.'

I step forward with my hand outstretched.

William ignores it. 'Greek, eh? What was your crime, Hercules?'

He means Herakles. I expect it to be said with respect, but here it's a joke.

'Piracy, sir.'

He explodes into scornful laughter. 'Good God, James. Father expects us to turn this into a sheep run. What does he expect us to do with a pirate?' And to me, 'Will you build us a ship to sail the Shoalhaven?'

I keep still. My jaw tightens. I've dined with lords. This man wouldn't step over the threshold of my father's house.

Martin suppresses a laugh. I do not add I am a *palikari*. It means nothing here. The only freedom fighters they know are Irish—political prisoners. And they're considered troublemakers.

James answers for me. 'He's the strongest of them,' he says. 'He knows sheep and growing vegetables. And he says he can ride.'

I didn't say we rode donkeys.

William gives me a long disdainful look, runs his gaze up and down my body. Crawls over my skin.

'Then perhaps he understands pruning and winemaking. Not all Greeks are barbarians.'

I've taken worse than this man can dish out. But heat rises in my face.

I speak clearly, choosing my words. 'Greeks were drinking wine while the Scots were learning the wheel, sir.'

A breath of silence. No one moves.

He raises the riding crop.

Stinging pain slashes across my cheek.

Not a duel. Not a fair fight. One man with a whip striking another who can't strike back.

I tuck my thumbs into my palms to keep from retaliating.

He stands there, breath heaving. For a moment he looks as if he regrets having done it. James looks away.

He knows I could have stopped him. Broken his puny arm. That enrages him.

'You lump of Greek shit.' He takes a deep breath and looks around. His eyes lock back onto mine. 'You think I sweat blood in this godforsaken hole to have a convict speak to me like that? You are lower than a worm in the dirt. Speak out of turn again, and I'll show you what respect means.'

One final glare, and then he walks off. James follows.

My cheek throbs.

William has two and a half thousand acres. Enough to make him a gentleman here. His brother the same. But the house is rough-built, the land—apart from the river flat—thin and stony. Open forest barely cleared. I've seen poorer land, but not much. Only Hydra is worse.

Ryrie carries himself like a gentleman, but there's no fortune behind it. This is the man who strikes me.

If you push back, you earn the whip or the crop.

At the Sydney dockyard, we worked hard and earned respect. That's why I ended up here—usefulness. But I've learned not to trust people. Not when it matters.

So I'll do it again—learn the land, run their sheep, keep my head down. Be useful. Needed.

If I'm to be a shepherd, I'll be the best bloody shepherd Arnprior has seen.

10

The Ultimatum

HYDRA

Summer 1827

My debt gnawed at my insides like woodworm in a ship's hull.

And while I lay awake sweating over coins I didn't have, Greece was being torn apart. Not by the Turks—but by division within. Greeks against Greeks. The councils bickered, the politicians lined their pockets, and the committees sent orders that contradicted one another before the ink was dry. Gunpowder sat locked away while ships begged for it. We quarrelled. The enemy advanced.

Even old Kolokotronis—the Lion of the Morea—had to swallow his pride and nod while the foreigners took charge. It made my blood boil. Foreigners giving orders to men who'd been at sea since boyhood— Englishmen who thought courage could be measured in discipline and rank.

General Church for the army, Lord Cochrane for the fleet. An Englishman and a Scot to save Greece. It looked fine on paper—the Great Powers applauded—but no captain from Hydra ever took orders from a man who couldn't reef a sail. Athens fell last year, and the Acropolis above it surrendered last month under Church's command.

The National Assembly at Troezen had chosen a governor—
Kapodistrias. A Greek from Corfu, but his years in the service of the Tsar
had made him, to us, more Russian than Hellene.

Precise, frugal, incorruptible—he prized order above daring. Rigid as
iron, mistrusting every motive but his own. He had no love for Hydra and
the feeling was mutual.

Still—someone had to stop the bleeding. Someone had to unify the
fighting forces and keep the regions from warring with each other. But we
knew his kind. He'd build a new Greek state—and make Hydra bow to it.

And here I was, hiding from card-players with long knives.

I stood on our terrace, watching the sun set over the masts, gilding the
rooftops. Hydra's houses glowed like honey, each window a lantern against
the escarpment. I would be called in to eat soon. I had to decide.

I could tell my father. He might pay, if only to protect his name. But
mine would be ruined—branded a nothing and a nobody forever. And he
and the other shipowners were too busy smoking the *nargile* pipe with
Cochrane—waiting for his broken-down steamship—to worry about me.
My father called it diplomacy. I called it grovelling.

There was gold in the cellar. Every shipowner stored coin in their water
tanks. I knew where it was. But I wasn't a thief. And I wasn't a beggar
either.

My uncles? They'd tell him before I'd finished speaking the sentence.

I had no ship to sell. No goods to trade. And no time left.

No way out.

Tell Dimitris? My clever cousin? I'd rather fall on my *yataghan*.

My father dragged Dimitris across every conversation like a rusty
anchor. 'Look at Dimitris,' he'd say.

I wanted to shout, '*I would, if he'd stop blocking the light!*'

I brushed the dust from my vraka and went in to supper, half-resolved
to confess, when father said it again. 'Why can't you be more like
Dimitris? Now there's a man of worth. A born leader.'

'I'm not Dimitris, Patéra,' I said, teeth grinding.

'You never will be.'

My mother shifted uncomfortably in the chair, one hand pressed to her
lower back.

My voice rose. 'He inherited everything! On a silver platter!'

My father's face darkened with rage. 'You dare to speak back to me, boy?'

'Please, Niko, not now,' my mother pleaded, eyes full of tears. 'You and Ghikas—it's tearing us apart.'

My mother—speaking against him. I'd never seen it.

'Tell that to your son,' he bellowed, storming out.

Carrying the baby inside her shortened my mother's breath. Our arguments were hurting her.

'I'm sorry, Mamá,' I said.

She touched my cheek. 'Why can't you two be at peace?'

Later that night, I told her I was moving into the hut with my friends.

'Your place at the table will always be set, Ghikaki,' Mamá said.

'That's wonderful news, Mamá,' I said with a laugh, squeezing her hand. 'Because I'll be back tomorrow for breakfast.'

Yiayia hugged me. 'You're a good boy to consider your mother like this, Ghika. May the *Theotókos* light your way.'

I went to Katerina's room to say goodbye. She wasn't sewing for her trousseau as I thought, but sitting with her embroidery in her lap, twisting a thread around her finger, staring out the window.

'It's what I wanted, Ghika. A good match. But I don't want to leave home.' She turned, eyes wide. 'I'm frightened.'

I sat beside her. 'Remember what you used to say to me when I was afraid to go to sleep?'

She smiled faintly. 'My star shines brightest on the darkest night.'

'Exactly,' I said. 'If you ever feel alone, say the words. And I'll be there. As you were for me.'

—

Work at Mandraki was its own distraction, and I helped Giorgios patch a hole in his dinghy—fixing something small, feeling small.

We'd finished re-rigging the *Herakles*, a sleek schooner part-owned by Dimitris. I ran my hand along her rail. She gleamed in the sun, my favourite ship—re-caulked, re-rigged, two new guns polished like a promise. If life was fair, I'd be her captain. Instead, I was rolling tar and tightening pulleys, a shipwright's boy in my own yard.

I was to take her back to the port that afternoon. News had reached Hydra that the Egyptian Muhammad Ali was sailing his fleet from Alexandria—Dimitris wanted her back in the harbour.

The other workers were sitting in the shade eating olives and cold fish. One yelled, 'Ghika!'

I heard the scrape of boots on stone before I saw him.

Antonio. Hydra's most feared bravo. Striding along the shore like he owned it.

He came to a halt, rested his hand on the silver handle of his *yataghan*, black eyes locked on mine, earrings glinting like baitfish. But before he spoke, he glanced out to sea—for a second.

As if someone might be watching him. As if this wasn't about me.

Every nerve cried, run!

I didn't move.

He drew the blade and ran one finger down its edge. Slowly. I gripped the pulley block, knuckles white.

A smile widened across his face. 'You'll pay your debt by the Fast of the Dormition.'

Only weeks away. The *yataghan* gleamed—sharp as a harpoon's tip. Sweat ran off my chin.

He stepped in close. I caught the tang of cloves on his breath. This wasn't rage. This was pleasure.

'Or I'll cut off your balls. Then carve your back into a fish net.'

He leaned in further, voice low now. 'I answer to men who don't wait. They want their money. If it's not in my hand by that day—when I'm done, you'll pray to die.'

The blade pointed at my groin and flicked upwards.

His boots crunched away across the stones. The others sat watching, mouths open.

I had a date—weeks away, not months. And it had a face.

—

When I returned to the hut that starry evening, the others were on the grassy terrace, backs against the wall. Damos was holding court as usual, hands flying. Nikos and Kostas were hanging on his every word. Their laughter rang out like the old days.

My mind was still elsewhere. Still staring down the shape edge of a blade.

'I was kissing her passionately,' Damos said, 'when I heard footsteps—'

Nikos gasped. 'No! Her brothers? Were they going to cut off your—'

I stood. 'Not that story again!'

'Sorry if I bore you, Ghika,' Damos said, winking.

I didn't answer.

Andonis saw my face.

'What's happened?'

'Nothing,' I said. 'Long day.'

Inside, the air was stale with the day's heat, but at least it was quiet. Nikos followed, book in hand. He flipped to his favourite page—grotesque illustrations in a mildewed surgeon's manual. By candlelight, his finger traced the outline of a swelling in the scrotum, caused by sliding down a ship's stay rope. The treatment? A trocar. Directly into the flesh.

'Look, Ghika. They're sticking a *xiphos* into his balls!' He pointed, laughing with delight.

Laughter came easily to Nikos. I couldn't even smile.

Andonis' voice came from outside. 'Ghika. We need to talk.'

I leaned against the doorframe. Nikos stood beside me, my shadow.

'I got back from Nafplio today,' Andonis said. 'The Egyptian madman has burned everything. They wear no shoes. Bleeding feet. No bread. The children cry like animals.'

Kostas fell silent, his fingers still on the *bouzouki*—his grandfather's fine instrument, carved from Carpathian spruce. He'd played it for hours at his sister's wedding. Until Anastasia.

Another total disaster.

My life was a shipwreck.

Andonis went on. 'There's an American relief ship there. Giving out grain and medicine. But it's not enough. Our families will starve.'

I didn't reply.

'Kapsalis at Kamini is hiring out his ships for privateering. I say we lease one.'

Antonio's threat still burned in my gut. The Fast was only weeks away, and I had no plan, no coin, no help. And now Andonis—who wouldn't swat a fly, even if he'd betray a friend—was talking about piracy as if it were a grand adventure.

The last time he had the chance to stand by someone, he didn't even ask what happened. Just turned his back and walked away.

'You've got heart, Andoni, and the head for command, but it's not enough. Kapsalis will not hand you a ship without captain's papers or a letter of marque. And what happens when it's time to board the prize, supposing you find one? When you must fire the cannon, or gut a man on the deck? The last time you touched a yataghan you were showing off behind the bakery. Damos is all talk, Nikos will think it's a game, and Kostas,' I nodded at the *bouzouki*, 'he plays.'

Kostas raised an eyebrow but continued to strum. I wanted to take it back. But bitterness held my tongue.

Andonis leaned closer. 'We can do it. What else can we do, Ghika? Watch our brothers and sisters starve?'

I shrugged. 'Kapsalis won't hand over a ship to fools.'

He leaned back. 'Will you borrow one from your father? We can strike the Ottomans, Ghika. Feed our own. At least this way, we fight. Not only for bread—but for Greece.'

I didn't answer. Yes, it was my dream to fight for Greece. On a warship. That was the honourable path. The one my father would respect. But he would never give me a ship.

Kostas stopped playing. 'Tell us what to do, Ghika,' he said. 'You always have.'

'This time, I have no answer,' I said. 'I'm going to see Yiannis—on business.'

I climbed the hill, heart pounding.

I couldn't help Greece if I ended up face down on the quay in my own blood.

Let them talk of hunger and war.

I had to find a way to stay alive.

11

The Greek Dismount

ARNPRIOR, New South Wales
October 1830

The muscles in my shoulders scream with each swing of the sledgehammer. Hour after hour, day after day, the same motion. Sweat trickles down my forehead as shards of stone fly up with every blow.

'He's coming,' Martin says.

Bartholomew, usually content with drinking tea from a pannikin in the shade, now paces, whip in hand, eyes narrowed—as if he enjoys watching men flinch. He doesn't speak. He doesn't need to. The whip in his hand says enough. We're working at the base of a rock cliff on the Shoalhaven River, breaking rock for the extensions to the Arnprior homestead. Beside us, the river ripples under the midday sun.

I blink the grit away. Every swing sends pain shooting through my shoulders and down my arms. My palms are raw. Sweat stings my eyes.

Again. And again.

Bartholomew strides over to Joe, hand tightening on the whip. Joe swings wildly, nearly striking his own leg—which only invites Bartholomew's fury.

'Steady yourself, man, before you do others harm!' he shouts.

I bite down hard on my lip, feeling a small victory in restraining the anger that boils beneath the surface.

In the distance, Ned's familiar voice curses the oxen as the dray approaches. Bartholomew relaxes slightly; the tension eases—if only for a moment. I've seen that whip fall too many times on some poor devil's back.

Martin passes Joe the waterskin before he drinks himself. Waits for Joe to pass it back.

—

Tonight, inside the hut, the air is greasy with boiling brisket and over-cooked cabbage, and the oil lamp's pale glow barely reaches the corners. Joe, fixated on the meal, stops eating for long enough to entertain us with tales of his pickpocketing. We've learned to return whatever he steals from other huts.

'I need a wife,' says Martin. 'To clean up after me. Stop me from talking to myself.'

Joe, voice low and glum, says, 'I had a sweetheart once. She tossed me out like an old rag.'

Martin stops chewing. No amount of soaking ever really frees the meat from its brine, leaving our lips perpetually pinched. Fresh meat is a luxury.

'Why, Joe?'

'Because of me thieving. What about you, Ghika?' says Joe.

'Yes, your turn,' says Martin. 'Tell us about the Greek beauty waiting for you.'

I was brought up to believe that women are precious creatures, not topics for idle chatter. But tonight I indulge them.

'My father will arrange my marriage,' I say. 'That's the way we do things.'

Joe chokes on his tea. 'God's truth, Ghika?'

I feel the first prickle of irritation.

Joe leans forward, voice tinged with disbelief. 'You'd marry a stranger?'

'Her family and position—that's what matters.'

Martin asks, 'It's about money?'

'It's about family, and honour and tradition,' I say, heat rising in my face.

'But what if she's ugly or barren?'

Their disrespectful laughter fills the room. It's not worth my time to argue.

'In Greece, we say the rarest treasure hides in the plainest jar.'

Joe pulls a face.

Martin says, 'Well, what if you find the treasure here? Someone who makes you forget Greek girls? I'll wager you'd stay here then!'

I think of Mary and push the thought aside. Anyway, I'm smell-fungus. I smile.

Joe lifts the kettle. 'You'd have to be careful she didn't steal your sugar ration. My da always said watch the women—they're the light-fingered ones. But he couldn't talk. He nabbed a king's deer and they hanged him for it. Ma said it was the only thing he ever did right.'

He laughs.

Martin says, 'I have a daughter back in the old country. Her mother used to take in washing. Then I got caught stealing from the same house twice. She'd be grown by now.'

He stares into the fire.

'She's better off forgetting me.'

I stand. 'When I go, I won't be looking back either. Goodnight, gentlemen.'

I lie on my cot and face the wall.

—

William doesn't waste breath on encouragement. He sends me out for a week with each of his five shepherds—before I'm given my own. I follow behind.

They don't speak much—just enough to show me how to count the ewes out in the morning with the sun in our eyes, how to listen for a bleat that's too frequent, too faint, or changes note.

I learn to watch for flystrike, scab, footrot, lice, foot abscess, poisonous plants and boggy ground. I can tell which ewes have just lambed and learn how to search for the lambs they hide. I study tracks, learn where there's good feed, and find the safe watering points. I begin to understand how a mob behaves, and take my turn at watch when we sleep out overnight.

'There's always a leader,' says the shepherd, 'called the marker. Where she goes, they'll follow. Lose her and you'll lose the lot. A good marker sheep leads the mob out to pasture in the morning and back to the yard at dusk. I paint mine so I can see her easily, and she wears a bell.'

I learn which sheep always lag at the tail. I learn to pick up stragglers who fall behind.

I practise turning a sheep on its side, checking the fleece for maggots, pulling burrs from the breech wool around her tail.

On my first attempt, I land in the dirt with a mouthful of wool.

I keep quiet, learn how to open and shut a split timber gate, fix a broken one, mend a fence, treat flystrike. I learn to wave a staff to move the stubborn ones. It's essential we count the same number back into the yard at night as we let out in the morning. The penalty for losing a sheep can be ten lashes. No one lets me forget it.

One shepherd drinks vinegar. Another smokes a clay pipe that never leaves his mouth, even when he swears. Another's hands shake so much he can't hold a cup. I learn by watching. And by being yelled at.

—

By the time I'm sent out on my own, I'm glad to escape. But even this freedom is an illusion. I'm shackled to the Ryries and Arnprior, overseen by Bartholomew, forced to follow orders. Go here, go there, do this, do that. Mind the wild dogs. Watch the blacks.

Night plays its own symphony: the gentle clinking of a marker sheep moving—the creak of timber, the urgent chirp of a cricket. By firelight, I re-read creased letters from Andonis. The gaps speak the loudest—no mention of homesickness, loneliness, endurance, or punishment. Nothing of his health.

I pore over every word about their work and the seasons. Nikos is well. Damos has visited Camden Park—he's sick of the 'drudgery' at the dock-yard and dreams of a transfer to Camden. I can't imagine how he'll manage that—but if he did, he'd only unsettle Nikos with his teasing. Damos' letters to me are scrawled—full of jokes and probably dictated to another convict for a fee—but he's made friends. Kostas has settled in too, though he rarely sees Superintendent Hely. His letter is as spare as his speech. No mention of music.

They need me to organise them. If we were all together, I'd—

But we're not.

No. They're doing well enough without me.

I'm proud of them, but I'm also a lagging ship, watching others sail ahead.

Lately, I've taken to sketching—rough lines in charcoal on scraps of paper. A way to hold on to Hydra. The house I'll build, the ship I'll own, sheep pens for Yiannis. Each drawing charts my passage home.

The firelight blurs the lines—until a bleating cry snaps me back to the present.

The flames are low, and in the dim light the sheep are a restless sea of white, bunched at one end of the fold. As I peer through the rails, I spot the cause of the commotion: a lamb, somehow forced out, is now the focus of a circling dingo. Its lean, shadowy form is moving with a predator's patience while the lamb makes frantic attempts to reach its mother.

I grab a stick and rush at the dog. It hesitates. I shout, swing my arms. It melts into the dark—but the threat remains. Gently, I lift the lamb, its heart hammering against my palms. Once I place it back inside, the others settle, their cries falling to a low murmur.

Sleep eludes me. Bartholomew's taunt about my inexperience echoes in my mind. 'You're no shepherd.'

Yiannis once said, 'A shepherd's worth is measured by the sheep he brings home.'

I'm proving Bartholomew wrong. Yiannis would be proud.

At dawn, I sit up on my blanket, stretch, and drop a piece of rock-hard bread into my pannikin of water.

Kangaroos graze in the stillness on short grass near the creek. A thin mist lifts off the water, outlined against the twisted trunks on the far bank.

The ridge above the creek is bare, blackened from a recent burn. Among the ash, crimson blooms burn red as coals against the dull green of the bush. It seems too vivid for this place, too alive. I can't recall the name —it's a plant that flowers only after fire. I think of Mary then. I can't say why. Maybe because it's survived.

Overhead, the sky fades from confectioner's-sugar rose at the horizon to ice blue above.

I toss leaves and kindling onto the embers, coaxing the fire back to life. Eucalyptus smoke swirls around me; I cough and wave it away.

The remaining lump of bread is as hard as stone, but I force it down. My oilskin tea pouch hangs limp and empty. I shudder at the thought of the meat back at the hut—mouldy salted beef, stinking pork, rank kangaroo. If Ryrie allows it, we might be issued a couple of sheep this week. Fresh mutton.

I think of the fishing boats back at home—and of the natives who fish this river, too.

There are about thirty of them who come and go, living in a collection of bark dwellings on the riverbank, near the crossing—a place they call Kurraducbidgee. Ned says they're Walbanga, one of the Yuin tribes from the coast. I don't know how he knows—maybe they told him, or maybe he decided it. Either way, that's what he calls them. And he says *bidgee* means river flat.

They come and go as they please, and mysterious, even though they're accustomed to us whites. Some say the small Arnprior group belongs to the fierce warrior tribes from the coastal regions, not the southern ones. They understand English well enough, though they feign ignorance when it suits them.

William gives them odd jobs, mostly washing sheep. They're full of laughter, quick with jokes, but like a passing breeze, they're here one day, gone the next.

At first, their sudden appearances between the trees—standing tall on one leg, eyes dark and intense—made me uneasy. If a sheep goes missing, I'm responsible. I wave them off, shout at them, and they vanish.

But they return.

They speak to me in a strange tongue and point to my bread; I share it. In return, they offer a cooked lizard tasting of charcoal and smoke.

They don't yell at the earth; they listen to it. A far cry from the way we bend it to our will. The squatters have dispossessed them of their land, of their soul, but not their authority. It's in the way they stand, in the quiet watchfulness of their eyes. They don't raise their voices. They don't bark orders. Even now, with nothing left, they hold themselves like kings. It unsettles me. And if I'm honest, it makes me feel smaller than I like.

Mister Ryrie says we're lucky here in the St Vincent district that they only quarrel among themselves, but he keeps a gun by the bed all the same. For bushrangers, he says, not the natives.

Convicts, it seems, must fend for themselves.

By the time the sun sets on Saturday afternoon, I have brought the flock home. A few sheep still straggle on the flat below the house, while the rest trail their noses along the ground uphill, in silent communication with the earth. Mister Ryrie comes walking down the slope, hand fishing in the fob pocket of his waistcoat.

He and Mrs Ryrie arrived from Sydney in March and now live here permanently. His white collar is starched and buttoned tightly, neck wrinkled above it. He checks his watch as usual, gives a click of approval and slides it back. I wonder if time races by for an old man with a young wife.

'There's good feed where you've been, Jigger? The sheep are holding their condition.'

I've become used to his heavy accent, and this new nickname he's given me. Everyone calls me that now.

'Yes, sir, but the grass is short—the sheep like it better than when it's long, but there's less of it.'

'Looks like rain coming.'

Weather means as much to a sheep farmer as it does to a sailor.

We both study the sky.

I wave my stick at a dawdling ewe. She skips a couple of steps and drops her head again.

Mister Ryrie lifts his arm to stop another turning back. 'Mrs Ryrie says we must prepare more beds for the summer crop. She wishes your help.'

Just as my father did when his first wife passed away, after his own loss, Mister Ryrie has wed a younger woman. Mrs Ryrie is only a few years older than her husband's sons. It's said by the other convicts that he sailed from Scotland for New South Wales with his new young wife and grown-up family, only days after he married her.

'Yes, sir. Best to plant some now, and the rest once the risk of frost is over.' I understand a late cold snap last year wiped out half the seedlings. 'We must clean out the sheep yards for old manure.'

Mister Ryrie smiles. 'I'm pleased you bade us prune the grapes when you did. That warm spell in September has brought them on fast.'

William rides up, slides easily off the saddle and allows the reins to trail on the ground. He doesn't look at me. I recognise myself in his arrogance. We have seen little of him since I've been here, thankfully. He's been off exploring a way through the mountains to the coast, and droving Ryrie sheep down south, where the family has an interest in more land.

'Bartholomew must go. He flogged a man,' he says to his father.

Mister Ryrie sighs. 'And yet, Will, we're short-handed as it is. Now I've left government service it will be harder to find men—free or assigned. The convict allocations go to the governor himself and his cousins—he gave one a full gang. I've written twice for more, but unless we're building a bridge for His Excellency, we'll wait.'

And then he appears to remember what William said. 'Why did Bartholomew flog the man?'

'Insolence,' says William.

'I know he has a short temper, Will. But he's not a wicked man—he's as gentle as a lamb with his children. Have a talk to him.'

William jerks his head. 'I already have. Next time I will dismiss him.'

Mister Ryrie sighs again. 'There's talk in the *Gazette* of a convict rebellion near Bathurst. Armed men, escapees. They've hanged one already. At least Bartholomew keeps ours in order.'

William clears his throat—sharp, deliberate. It's clear he thinks his father should not speak of such things in front of me. Then, he says, pointedly, to me, 'One of your rams is sick.'

The tone is pure accusation. My hackles rise.

'I'm aware of it,' I say. 'It's a cut to his mouth. It's healing.'

William turns back to his father, as if I'm not present. 'Is he trustworthy?'

'I have earned trust, sir,' I say firmly.

William whips around, smelling a challenge. 'By doing what, exactly?'

He's full of swagger. And I'm supposed to call him 'sir'?

I weigh my next words. 'By doing my job well, and respecting my employers.' Then, 'Who are not my rulers.'

The skin of William's face turns a brick red. His eyes dart to his saddle, where the whip hangs.

Mister Ryrie cuts in. 'Enough, both of you. Jigger, take your sheep home. William, I'd like to speak with you.'

I walk away, my belly simmering like yesterday's stew. I follow the flock up the hill towards the fold, the liquid shape ebbing and flowing. A lamb is lagging, limping; I pick it up, pull out a burr, and carry it in my arms. Being a shepherd isn't so bad; it's the scrutiny that's suffocating. William must know I'm looking after his sheep well.

I miss Yiannis' advice. I wish I'd said goodbye to him before setting sail on the *Herakles*.

I lock the gate behind the sheep.

As I approach the garden, two men are laying shingles on the homestead roof. Mister Ryrie's sons built four rooms, and now, with their father in permanent residence, he is extending the house in stone, local hardwood and some cedar. It is not grand, but gracious, low to the ground with several fireplaces, fit for a family. Mister Ryrie allows me to work in the garden, and speak with Mrs Ryrie about chores to be done—a privilege no convict has been allowed, or so the other convicts claim. They're forbidden to approach her.

I consider this a silent judgment that I am more than the common rabble. Perhaps Mister Ryrie sees beneath the grime to the manners drilled into me as a child—or simply respects that I mind my tongue and carry myself with a measure of dignity. And perhaps Mrs Ryrie sees it too.

In a world where convicts are meant to be invisible, this small allowance sets me apart.

Neither Mrs Ryrie nor the children glance my way. Though close to my age, she reminds me a little of my mother—faraway blue eyes, porcelain skin, long dress flowing in the soft light of dusk. Some plants thrive on transplantation, others wither.

I enjoy the gentler pursuit of gardening, and flowers. I used to lie on the path leading up to Yianni's hut, near the pine trees, admiring the tiny fritillaries swaying in the breeze. They grew in winter, and only on Hydra —delicate bell-shaped blooms held on tiny stems, barely tighter than the low green grass, intricately patterned in purple and white, as if painted by the gods.

Mrs Ryrie speaks to young Jane. 'Do you feel the promise of spring?'

Or scorching summer.

Jane notices me. 'Ghika, will you raise the jump for my pony?'

No 'please'. If we were on Hydra, I'd give her a lesson in manners. But we're not.

'Certainly Miss Jane. Tomorrow.'

John and Alexander are running through the beds, trampling last week's seedlings. My grip tightens on the gate latch.

Mrs Ryrie glances down, frowns. 'Boys, those are summer greens. Please desist. I have bathed you.'

They keep running.

The baby, David, struggles to be put down from her hip.

Alexander grabs my leg. 'Geeks. Up, up!'

I hoist him onto my shoulders, holding his legs to secure him.

'Mind you don't linger too long outdoors, Isabella, my love.' Mister Ryrie is passing. 'The air's sharp tonight.' His look is one of gentle concern for her persistent cough.

Mrs Ryrie responds with a twirl of her hand. 'Do you think we'll find rose bushes for sale in Sydney, Stewart? I'd love to train them along the columns of our Indian verandah.' Her fingers are a vine curling around a post, and then she allows her arm to fall.

It reminds me of home—the ease between a man and his wife, the quiet affection.

I miss that.

My father used to whistle softly when my mother entered a room, lips tucked between his teeth. No one else existed. She'd pretend not to notice. Then she'd smile, slightly, as she turned away, to acknowledge his admiration. I watched them my whole life.

I miss my mother's touch. Yiayia pulling me close by the chin. A brother's arm around my shoulder.

I think of Mary. A slip of a girl I met a year ago has assumed an importance out of proportion to our meeting. I swear a single look from her could knock the air from my chest. She's probably married by now.

Mister Ryrie's words jerk me back. 'Jigger will do it.'

And just like that, I'm reminded of my place.

They speak about me, not to me.

I nod, because here, that's all that's expected.

—

Sundays are for prayer, rest, washing, and mending. We repair the huts, tend the convict garden. On Sundays, my thoughts turn homeward. I wonder if my older brothers have survived the war, if Giorgios has achieved his captaincy. Whether Makris is safe. Whether Katerina is happy on Spetses. Whether Yiannis is still alive—and if, in quiet moments, he spares a thought for me.

One Sunday, Joe bursts in, eyes wide. 'Ryrie's about to ride Diablo! They say he's tried it before. Last time he broke his arm clean through!'

I feel a surge of excitement—I don't wish the man harm, but I wouldn't mind seeing him thrown.

We drift down the hill and climb onto the rails of the circular breaking yard. Diablo is in the ring, scraping the ground and snorting, sending clods of dirt flying.

Bartholomew leans forward on the rail a little further along. 'Hey, Greek. Why don't you try?'

I don't bother answering. Fighting with a dog only makes you a dog yourself.

William throws a saddle over Diablo's back, wipes sweat from his brow as the horse prances.

'Ah, I forgot,' says Bartholomew loudly. 'Bravery's not the Greek's strong point.'

Joe, on my other side, nudges me. 'Pity it's not Bartholomew in the saddle. Will Ryrie be tossed?'

I'm about to wager a guess when William calls out, 'Hey, you!'

I look over at him.

'Yes, you. Hercules. Come down here.'

My stomach tightens.

Bartholomew again. 'He hasn't got the guts!'

He knows I've only ever ridden donkeys and Ginger, the old

Clydesdale—and it shows. Let him think I'm all talk. If I can't match them in skill, I'll do it in courage.

Alexander the Great was Greek—like me. They said no one could ride the unbreakable horse, Bucephalus—but Alexander did. Maybe I will too.

I slide off the rails and William hands me the reins. Diablo is a keg of gunpowder, muscles quivering, ears flattened. I stroke his sweat-slick neck. He jerks back, but I hang on to the reins.

Bartholomew yells, 'It's not playtime, pretty boy!'

'Aye, hop on, Hercules,' says William. 'Or are you only good at wagging your jaw?'

With the reins in my left hand, I grab a clump of his mane, bend and slide my foot into the stirrup. Diablo sidesteps, and I hop to maintain balance. I swing my leg over and settle into the saddle.

'Kick 'im in the guts!'

I tap his ribs—and I'm flying.

The ground slams into me. I rise, spit the dust from my mouth, and mount again.

Diablo bucks, bolts, twists—I am thrown. Again and again. But I climb back on. Every time.

After twenty rounds of the yard, he quiets under me—the coiled kind of quiet. I ease a hand along his sweat-slick neck. I angle him toward William as if the thing is done.

Joe throws his arm in the air. 'You did it, Jigger!'

Diablo explodes.

I see the sky. Then nothing.

—

When I regain consciousness, I'm staring up at a ring of faces.

'Haud on, Jigger,' says William. 'You took a wee knock to the head.'

It feels as though I've rammed my head into a mast. Blood runs into my mouth; the iron makes me gag. I clamp my jaw. Don't give Bartholomew the satisfaction.

Joe's face drifts into focus, face as white as the Parthenon statues.

'Jigger, I thought you was dead! You hit that post like a cannon ball. You've got a lump on your skull the size of an emu egg!'

William is grinning. 'Och, you rode him for a while, Jigger. That trick at the end, laddie—what do you call that? The Greek dismount?'

I sit up slowly. Everything hurts.

Bartholomew leans on the fence. 'So much for Greek nobility.'

'You noticed it then.' I wipe the blood from my lip and smile.

The next morning, black and blue and barely hobbling, I join Martin to grub out stumps in the new cultivation. He glances at my bruised face and grins.

'Jigger, you've tamed Diablo and Willie.'

If that was taming, God save me from breaking them.

I'm considering the absurdity when he adds, 'What about Bartholomew?'

I groan. 'One at a time, Martin.'

12

HYDRA

The Plan

HYDRA

July 1827

The moon was high, silvering the terraces as I climbed to see Yiannis, one foot in front of the other. The night stank of dust and goat shit. Below me, Hydra's white houses glowed like bones.

I couldn't gather my thoughts—Antonio kept intruding.

That damned blade. I could see his men dragging me behind a warehouse. One to bind me, one to cut. My back flayed open like a fishing net. Antonio was right—I'd beg for death. Part of me wanted to bolt. Sign on with a relief ship. Vanish on the mainland.

They found Oikonomou. And they'd find me. Their tentacles reached everywhere.

Antonio didn't only want repayment. He wanted my skin with it.

I kept climbing.

Yiannis was sitting outside his hut, a clay cup cradled in both hands. He looked up only when I stood in front of him.

'You look like you've seen a ghost, Herakles.'

I hadn't heard that name in months. Once, it had meant strength. Now, I could barely meet his eye.

'I've done something stupid.'

'Again?'

I didn't smile. His eyes narrowed.

'I owe money. I played *blaktzaki*. They sent the bravo, Antonio, to tell me I have until the Fast of the Dormition. Or—.' My voice failed me.

Yiannis sipped from his cup and set it down beside his foot. He leaned forward, elbows on his knees.

'I thought of going to the mainland. Disappearing for a while.'

'Ah.' He rubbed his palms together slowly. 'You think that's better than owning up to your mistake?'

My jaw clenched.

'Why are you here, Ghika?'

'I need your advice.'

'No. You don't.' His voice was quiet. 'You already know what you should do.'

'No I don't,' I snapped. 'You're the wise one.'

'You've known since the moment Antonio spoke. But you don't like the answer, so you came to me, hoping I'd give you another.'

I swallowed hard.

'You must go to your father. Tell him. Like a man. Like a Voulgaris.'

'He'll disown me. I'll lose everything.'

'Then don't tell him. Wait for Antonio to carve his initials into your flesh. That's the other option.'

I looked down. 'I thought you might—help.'

Yiannis let out a slow breath through his nose. 'You want help? Then listen to me, Ghika. Sometimes mistakes don't have a fix.'

My breath came faster.

'Tell your father, or dig your grave. The choice is yours.'

He stood. Picked up the cup. Walked past me to the olive tree and tipped the dregs at its base.

'Right. Time for sleep. I'll throw a mat on the floor for you. Come.'

I followed him inside, where he brought out a blanket and unrolled it on the ground.

'Sleep on it. We'll talk in the morning,' he said.

—

I didn't sleep. I lay on the cool stones, staring up at the dark rafters, listening to Yiannis snore.

If I fled to the mainland, I could grow a beard, change my name, disappear. Then I thought about starving with strangers. A living hell.

I wasn't raised to slink off like a rat.

I thought of my father's words. 'Words are whispers to the wind if not followed by actions,' he's said.

The sky was paling when I stepped outside the following morning. Yiannis was still asleep, grey head on sheepskins in the corner.

I stood there a moment, watching him breathe. Then I slipped out and started down the hill.

Hydra was silent. Even the cicadas hadn't begun.

I would tell my father. I hated the thought, but I rehearsed the words as I walked.

They cheated me. They're dangerous men. They'll come after you, too, Patéra.

Each one sounded weak. Like a boy whining to his tutor. Coward's talk.

Tell him the truth. Tell him you thought you were smarter than they were. Gambled like a fool and betrayed the family name in a single night.

The stone steps narrowed. My breath caught.

I tried again.

Patéra—

Nothing followed.

The harbour came into view, and among the other ships, there she was —the *Herakles*. Tethered, gleaming, waiting. She looked better than she had in years. I had made her that way. The sun caught her rails, her clean lines. I could almost see the dark glint of tar at the seams. Tar I'd put there.

And now Dimitris would take her. Not me. She was his again.

And then I saw it—Andonis, wanting to hire a ship. Me, laughing— saying no shipowner would ever agree. Yiannis, telling me to go to my father.

Maybe I didn't have to.

The *Herakles* was the answer to everything.

I would simply take her. My namesake.

This was a command decision—the action my father had demanded. With one blow, I'd make my family proud.

I hesitated. Was I fooling myself?

No. This wasn't like taking the Niki for a dare, or wagering money I didn't have just to prove I could win. Those were the rash mistakes of a boy.

I'd instruct Andonis to find the right men while I planned what we'd need—water, provisions, weapons, charts. I'd leave nothing to chance. I wouldn't rely on luck. I would choose my moment.

The sun was rising fast now, gilding the terraces, catching on stone and whitewash. I barely saw it. I turned back the way I'd come, my feet hitting each step with a thud.

Andonis was still lying on the terrace, one arm thrown over his face. Kostas sat hunched, fiddling with a length of line, while Nikos blinked up at me from the shadows.

'You still want a ship?' I said to Andonis' form.

He moved his arm, squinted.

'I have one,' I said.

He sat up slowly. I dropped beside him, still catching my breath. He frowned, rubbing his eyes.

'They won't lend us a ship. We take one.'

Andonis' eyes widened. 'That's theft.'

'No. It's taking a risk.'

I leaned in. 'They'll never give us a vessel. But if we take the *Herakles*, attack an enemy ship and bring back treasure—and we will— they'll pretend they backed us from the start. They'll call us war heroes.'

Damos let out a sharp laugh. 'Ghikas is right. That's exactly what they'll do.'

I could see it—the war inside Andonis. He wanted to do this the right way. But we didn't have that choice.

'Twenty-five men,' I said. 'Thirty at most. As for the proceeds: one quarter to me for procuring the ship, a quarter to Dimitris and his partner as owners, an eighth to the provisional government, and three eighths to the crew.'

Andonis looked across at the mainland, doubtless thinking about what he'd seen yesterday. Then he looked at the others, all hanging on his words. His jaw tightened. For a heartbeat, he stared into space. He took a huge breath, held it, and let it out.

His fingers curled around a tuft of grass and pulled it free.

'All right. I'll do it.' He tossed the grass aside and nodded towards the port. 'I will captain and hire the crew,' he said. 'You will be my second in command. I'll take the same share as the crew. Nothing more. We split it evenly—to feed our mothers and brothers.'

I nodded. 'Agreed. I'll provision the ship.'

Nikos was counting on his fingers, his lips moving.

'We'll be rich!' he grinned.

Andonis raked a hand through his hair. 'We have no choice. But—' He hesitated again. 'Can we trust you?'

Could I trust them? Cold anger turned my voice to steel. 'You always could.'

'Of course we can trust Ghikas,' said Nikos. 'I won't go unless he goes.'

One by one, they agreed.

Andonis looked around the circle. 'We leave on Monday, the twenty-third of July.' He touched the cross at his throat. 'May the *Theotókos* sail with us. If She does, we will be rich.'

Kostas' gaze lingered on me. 'If She does not, we will hang.'

As we sat there, watching the day begin, I felt the old twist in my gut. I had seized control.

But the stakes had climbed.

I could lose everything.

13

Timber

ARNPRIOR, New South Wales
October 1832

Early one morning, I'm digging an overgrown bed in the convict vegetable garden. What was his name, that 'gentleman' who appeared the day I took the Irish girl to the cobbler? Townsend, was it? A proper *malakas*.

I laugh out loud. That swear word hasn't passed my lips since Andonis and I were boys. Yet the image of that dandy—so charming, so polished—lingers, and I can't shake it. I drive the shovel in so hard that only the handle remains visible. I wrench it loose with a grunt.

Malakas. It suits him.

Why did he rile me so? Of course, the girl. With her shoe flapping, skirt muddy, face set like she'd bite the next man who offered help.

William Ryrie's laughter interrupts my thoughts. 'Digging your way back to Greece, Jigger?'

I look up.

'You've worked wonders on this soil, with all the manure you've carted. The vegetables are thriving, and the flowers too. And your pruning has brought more sun to the grapes. You're a true horticulturist. Thank you.'

Is that what you call someone who carts sheep shit? I make the sign to ward off the evil eye anyway.

'The earth here on the river is generous,' I say. Soft earth makes soft men.

The tomatoes are red and fat. The broad beans shoot higher than my waist. William is too busy with his ledgers or plotting his next expedition to think about where his food comes from. Imagine him on our rations: meat, corn flour, cornmeal, salt. While he takes a dram of whisky at night, we're eking out tea and sugar to make ours last a week.

But at least he pays me for extra work, and it goes straight into my pouch. The other convicts spend theirs on rum or rations.

'Found any farthings lately, Jigger?' they say.

A grape vine curls around the fence post—William has had some success at winemaking. He examines a translucent leaf, unfurling it over his finger.

'You've impressed the night watchman. He says you count sheep through a race faster and more accurately than any shepherd he's seen.' William is congenial today, but that's what he's like—a compliment followed by a kick in the guts.

I grunt. My flock is one of five on Arnprior and my lamb survival rates are the highest.

'Bartholomew wants help over at Durran Durra,' he says. 'Barking. Take Joe too. Martin will watch your sheep today.'

Martin has no instinct for shepherding. He does not see a problem until it's too late. The thought of entrusting my flock to him unsettles me, but my muscles knot worse at the thought of a day with Bartholomew.

Durran Durra belongs to James Ryrie and is the same size as Arnprior, but with no common boundary. Still, we move stock freely between the two. The muddy creek on Durran Durra is unreliable, but the run borders the Nadgigomar range, where the Aborigines strip their bark—they make two horizontal cuts, one vertical, and the sheet lifts clean. They use it for dwellings, or trade.

It is easier for us to debark a tree already felled, but only after good rain when the sap is rising, like now. Any attempt during dry weather will fail.

But working under Bartholomew's scrutiny is like dancing on the blade of a knife. They say one of the convicts once broke into his hut. Threatened his wife. Bartholomew arrived with a whip and nearly killed the man. He watches all convicts like dogs off the leash.

He has a set against me and constantly needles. If I lose my temper, I'll end up before the magistrate, and suffer the lash—or worse.

'Yes, sir,' I say, masking my concerns.

William nods. 'Off you go. Bartholomew is waiting.'

—

'I asked for skilled men,' says Bartholomew.

He's slapping his hand on the leg of his trousers with his usual impatience, sleeves rolled up to reveal arms criss-crossed by raised white scars. A memory flashes through my mind: a convict down in the dirt, Bartholomew's whip cracking. You feel it before you hear it.

'You can ride double on Ginger. And Bulgary, stay on this time, eh?'

In the horse paddock, Bartholomew catches a big grey mare called Valda. Saddling her proves a challenge: he struggles with the surcingle while the cunning mare inflates her lungs, and once he tightens it, she lets her breath out, so it loosens. His first attempt ends with the saddle slipping down her ribs. Finally, saddle secure, he tries to mount, but she swings her rump around and skitters away, leaving him hopping alongside. Meanwhile, Joseph and I, already on Ginger, watch with amusement. Bartholomew swears and lugs Valda's ear. Once he's on, she dances sideways, all the way to the river crossing at Kurraducbidgee, champing on the bit while he continues his cursing.

The Argyle Road from Sydney sweeps down the hill behind us. On the other side of the river, stretching south for miles, a large block of forty-two thousand acres of the best land belongs to the Anglican church. Here, God lives in the big houses, dines with the landowners, rides out with the governor, nods from the Anglican pulpit. Never the Roman Catholic.

As we approach, natives sit around a fire, watching us in silence. Bartholomew's face reddens with each failed attempt to urge Valda into the water. I catch a glint of white teeth among the dark faces as the natives stifle their laughter.

Behind me, Joe vibrates with it, although we both know better than to mock Bartholomew.

But the urge to show him up is strong. So I press Ginger forward and he splashes his way through.

Valda follows meekly behind.

I've guaranteed Bartholomew's foul mood for the rest of the day.

We ride a few miles up the tributary to join the Duran Durra convicts and their bullock team. Together we drive the oxen up a heavily timbered slope through the deep shade of tall trees until we break out into a patch of sunlight. Huge stringy-bark logs lie as straight as gun barrels, one on top of another in the straggly undergrowth. The air is heavy with the smell of freshly turned soil, bracken ferns lying mangled on earth, still damp from rain.

Bartholomew walks over to the pile of timber, inspecting each piece as if selecting logs were an art.

'If you're going to be any use here, pay attention, Ghikarse.' He points at one. 'Climb up and wrap a chain around it. The bullocks will pull it forward, off the one beneath.'

He turns his back, striding toward the team. So sure of himself.

I see the danger. That log's resting on the one beneath. If I climb on top and make one wrong move—the whole thing could roll, with me still on top.

Even my father, for all his demands, would never have risked a man in this way.

My gut clenches. I'm not a fool. I won't die for Bartholomew's pride. And it's not just me—I glance at Joe. My heart thumps harder.

Joe whispers, 'If we pulled it sideways—'

He's right. The only safe way is to bring a bullock further up the slope and pull it off. Without killing someone.

I won't be silent. 'Sir, it's dangerous. The log will roll.'

He is at the bullocks now, facing away from me. He stops fiddling with the harness, both palms flat on the beast's back, motionless. The screeching of black cockatoos breaks the silence. It's possible he didn't hear me.

My skin tightens.

'Mister Bartholomew?'

He pushes away from the ox, turns to me, hands on hips, panting, face red, a strange intensity in his gaze.

He grinds the words out through his teeth, 'Do it.'

So this is the price of obedience: risk your spine, or take the lash.

This pale, red-haired bastard is telling me to put myself at risk while he watches. I have a hot urge to lash out, challenge his authority, to break free from this unjust chain of command. The temptation to defy him rises in me like a wave.

But this would not be a single act of rebellion; it's my entire future. A flogging can cripple. A second offence can mean the gallows.

He tries to provoke me. I won't give him that satisfaction. With a deep breath, I swallow the storm of emotion.

Joe pulls my arm. 'C'mon Jigger.'

As he makes a bridge with his hands, he whispers, 'I thought you were going to kill him! Pity you didn't.'

I climb on top of the log, careful not to move it. Sweat trickles down my brow; my hands shake as I grip the chain. Every beat of my heart feels like thunder in my chest, drowning out the world around me. I can't let anything happen to Joe. I slip the hook into a link of the chain.

The log is rocking.

'Joe, walk away.'

I watch him go before I slide off. As I ease myself sideways, the log shifts beneath me, trembles—then gives a violent shudder and rolls. The uphill end flicks sideways as it crashes down.

I go with it.

The earth shakes.

Silence.

I'm on the ground with my shirt snagged beneath the log. Bark chafes my skin as I wiggle the fabric free. I'm winded, but not hurt. Someone is shouting. It's Joe, fists clenched, face flushed with a rage I've never seen.

'You bloody mongrel! You could've killed Jigger!'

'Good,' shouts Bartholomew. 'Now, bring that chain here. The bullocks are waiting.'

Before I rise, Joe charges, his shoulder colliding with Bartholomew's stomach. Both men go flying, tumble together in a flurry of limbs. Bartholomew scrambles, reaching for the whip he's left on a stump. Joe covers his head. The whip arcs through the air, a snake striking its prey, landing across Joe's head and shoulders, a sharp echoing crack.

I'm there before Bartholomew swings again. My grip closes around his wrist. 'That's far enough.'

'Out of my way, Greek bastard.'

He pulls away, but I grip harder. We lock eyes, and for a moment, it's us, man to man, in a silent battle of wills. His face swells with blood and he is puffing, blowing, struggling. Only when he realises he cannot break my grasp does he relax.

I release him. If this were Hydra, I'd throw him overboard.

'William Ryrie will hear about this, Bulgary,' he blusters. 'And you, Little. You will pay for this. Both of you.'

I pull Joe away, back toward the timber. He has a fresh cut under his chin from the whip and his shirt is spotted with blood. I'm always telling him to think before he acts. The look on his face tells me he's worried I'll be angry with him.

'You have the heart of a lion, Joe.'

His face lights up.

'And the brain of a pea. It's lucky your skull is thick.' I grin and cuff him lightly over the head. He puts his arm around my back.

But this isn't over. William might send us to the magistrate. And even though Governor Bourke has ruled that magistrates can't order a flogging on a whim—this could be judged cause enough. Or the magistrate could order fifty lashes.

Enough to kill some men.

I don't let myself picture the new gallows at Goulburn.

The rest of the day passes without incident, and by the time we mount up for the ride back to Arnprior, tension is sitting on us like a blanket. Bartholomew's arm sports an angry purple bruise—in the shape of my handprint. Joe is quiet, pensive.

I let Ginger plod right behind Valda, out of Bartholomew's sight.

He turns around on his horse. 'You question an order again, you Greek fornicator, and it will be you who feels the whip.'

Every part of me wants to vault from Ginger and knock him off his horse. But there are no second chances. I swallow it. And as ridiculous as it seems, I find a fleeting victory in having bested Bartholomew today, if only for a few minutes.

Joe acted out of loyalty, not sense. I wish I could shield him, but I can't. I'll explain to William. As a man of honour, he will surely understand. And at least Joe and I will face him together.

Tonight, the cut under Joe's chin is gaping. No way to bandage it. He smears it with mutton fat.

My shoulder throbs. Worse when I move.

I am reminded of Yiayia—how she'd mutter over my scrapes, press a kiss to my forehead, tie a strip of linen over a cut with fingers that smelled of thyme.

I think of the girl in Sydney. Mary Lyons. I wonder how she'd treat it. Ridiculous, really. A girl I met once. But she makes me smile when nothing else does. Maybe she's my good-luck charm. My phantom confidante. I don't care. In my mind, she's always near, arms crossed, telling me I'm a fool. And maybe I am. But it helps.

Even if you were the last man on earth.

I should have written. Sent a letter to her care of her employer, Mrs Bloodsworth. A line or two. I was rude. I'm sorry. You didn't deserve that.

Not because I care what she thinks. Because I should have behaved better.

And if William sends us to the magistrate tomorrow—

No. No point thinking that way. I close my eyes.

Her voice is still there.

I shift again. The pain flares.

She made me laugh.

I turn over. Sleep doesn't come.

I worry about tomorrow.

14

Point of No Return

HYDRA

July 1827

We'd dragged our bedding into the dust outside the hut, in heat as thick as wool. It was past midnight; even the cicadas had given up. My mouth was dry, my hands twitched. I lay still, watching the shapes of my friends rise and fall with each breath.

Up until now, none of my bold moves had ever worked.

If we attacked a prize, would we all come back?

Skin tacky with sweat. No breeze. No air. The waterskin was long empty.

If we brought back a Turkish prize, they might talk about us. Might even call us heroes.

But what if Dimitris stepped onto his terrace at dawn? Or what if we failed?

They'd call it what it was: theft.

And they'd call me what I was.

A disgrace. A fool.

A boy who cost men their lives.

To silence the panic, I ran through my preparations. I had stocked her with enough water for thirty men for fourteen days. Charts, flags, arms, ammunition, provisions: onions, figs, pickled olives, cheese. Andonis' crew would bring what their households could spare. And we'd fish.

A sliver of pale moon hung in a sky thick with stars. The Milky Way arched so brightly it felt within reach. Yiayia used to say it was the goddess Hera's milk, flung across the heavens when she tore Herakles from her breast after learning he was Zeus' bastard.

And here I was, planning to take the *Herakles*, pretending I was the legendary hero.

I wasn't the hero. I was the boy Hera flung away. Not a blessing. A rejection. I told myself I just wanted a deck under my feet and wind in the canvas.

But the worry in my gut sat like bad fish.

This morning, Katerina raised her eyebrows when I gave her a note for Maria, to be delivered after we were gone. I couldn't take her into my confidence—she'd be duty-bound to report to our father.

Dear Maria,
By the time you receive this, I will have sailed.
On our return to Hydra in ten days, I am confident your father and mine will confirm our betrothal.
Please pray for my success.
I hold your heart in mine,
Ghikas

The cicadas started up again. Without even a whisper of a breeze to cool me, at last I slept.

—

Before dawn, we gathered our possessions by candlelight and bundled them in oilcloth bags. We pushed our yataghans and pistols into the *zonária* around our waists, and stood in a circle, the five of us. Andonis raised his hand, and we touched fingers—an arch of brotherhood. Our voices echoed in the small stone hut.

'*Eleftheria i thanatos*!' Freedom or death. We were no longer boys. But still we played at being heroes.

I snuffed the candle between my fingers.

We picked our way down the steep path to the port, gravel sharp underfoot. On the ridges, the motionless sails of the windmills promised another scorching day.

'Are you sure we'll have enough men, Andoni?' I flicked the sweat off my forehead.

'What do you think I've been doing this past week? Counting seagulls?' His elbow found my ribs. 'And you? Do you have enough rowboats to take us to the *Herakles*?'

I laughed. 'No, I'll fire both pistols and shout, *swim for it!*'

He grinned and hooked his arm around my neck.

In the light of pre-dawn, she looked like any modest cargo vessel. Nothing to draw the eye. But the men who were gathering—barefoot, gaunt, clothes in tatters—looked like beggars. The baker's son among them. Was he even a sailor? My gut twisted. This was no crew. This was a rabble.

I made a sign against the evil eye.

I glanced up first to Uncle Frangiskos' terrace overlooking the harbour, then to Dimitris' a little further away, and finally higher, to the home of Maria's father Lazarus. No movement on any of them. I crossed myself and prayed the harbour would stay asleep a little longer.

A cart rattled along the quay; several fishing boats had unloaded their catch. Dawn silhouetted the eastern escarpment as old Stefanos threw buckets of sea water in front of his stall. As he took up his broom, he waved. I waved back. A quick head count. Over forty. Some were unfit to sail.

Andonis' stubborn jaw contradicted his gesture of helplessness.

'No,' I mouthed, scanning the crowd. 'Too many.'

The water would last only ten days instead of fourteen.

When I shook my head, Andonis leaned in, his voice low but insistent. 'You'd turn them away? Knowing they have nothing to eat?'

'We're not running a benevolent society,' I said. 'If we overload her, she'll wallow. We'll be a target ourselves. And look at them. Some of them are boys.'

That was the trouble with Andonis: too soft. The strong became stronger; the weak fell by the wayside.

'They're men, Ghika. They'll work.'

I looked at their faces again. Strained. Begging. 'Very well,' I said. A surrender, not an agreement.

My shirt stuck to my body as I stepped into the smaller of the two rowboats. The workers on the dock barely looked up at the murmur of our voices.

I had boarded a ship a thousand times before, but never like this. I was a *palikári* at last, striking a blow at enemy shipping.

But the moment I stepped aboard, I was also a thief. And there'd be no going back.

Dimitris' terrace was dark. For now. Empty. For now.

At last, with everyone aboard, we hauled the lines and edged her clear of the other ships with the rowboat.

'*Ou!*' The shout came from the mighty twelve-gun *Themistokles*. A Kountouriotis ship. Known to be available for privateering.

Kostas next to me groaned and dropped his head between his arms. 'I knew it.'

The crew must have slept on board. They would give chase. Dimitris would wake. The blood drained from my face. We were caught.

I cupped my hand around my mouth and yelled back. '*Ti?*' What?

'*O Theós na evlogeí to ploío sas!*'

Kostas let out an explosive whoosh of air. I waved and crossed myself. He had wished God's blessing on our ship.

I shouted back, '*Kai se esena ta idia.*' And to you, the same.

We turned seaward into the deeper channel on the eastern side of the harbour.

I breathed in salt air, metal sharp. The *Herakles* was sleek and beautiful. A fine two-masted schooner, shallow in draft, with great speed and windward ability. As we glided out past the rocks of the mole and the headland, I felt a jolt of excitement as we overtook a fishing *caïque* and sailed into the gentle chop of the open channel.

On the mole, a boy shaded his eyes and watched us go. He raised two fingers to his lips and whistled—a sound the wind carried shoreward.

Andonis kept the light north wind abeam as we sailed west towards Dokos, picking up speed. The Aegean Sea and its islands were crawling with makeshift boats—hungry men chasing smaller prizes, robbing one another for scraps. We wanted clear water, a real wind, and a real prize worth the risk.

We would sail south.

She plunged through the water; the wind whistled in the rigging, halyards thrummed, sails snapped and filled, stretching tight—and the schooner leapt forward.

After so long on land, without direction, it felt like a purpose.

My shoulders dropped. Andonis and I smiled at each other, and he put out his hand to me. We grasped wrists.

'Back where we belong,' he said.

Even in that moment of unity, a quiet dread tugged at the edges of my triumph.

'The five of us together,' I said.

I knew the *Herakles* as well as the scars on my hand. Her fore-and-aft sail configuration and square topsails required a lightness of touch. She was ideal for privateering, except for her lack of firepower. But if we were lucky, we'd fire only a couple of warning shots.

'She's a skittish one, this!' Feet astride at the helm, Andonis was grinning.

We changed course into the south on a heading for Milos, and the last ridge of Hydra disappeared.

High in the sky, a smear of mare's tails ran the wrong way, against the wind.

The crew whistled and sang in chorus and stripped off their shirts as they set to work. Torsos, pale from a lack of sun, shone like fish pulled fresh from the water. Nikos threw a bucket of seawater at me and I yelled at the shock of it. He laughed so hard he nearly dropped the bucket. I grabbed it, filled it, and threw one at him. He sidestepped, and the water hit Damos as he turned to run. Damos bellowed, snatched another bucket, and fired back. Kostas joined the fray. Within moments, the deck was a battle-field—water flying, men slipping and cursing, the slap of bare feet on wet planks. A man's foot shot out from under him and he hit the planks hard and stayed there, groaning. I barked for order.

Andonis raised his hand, water dripping off his face. 'If we're flying the Greek flag, what if an English ship asks for our papers?'

I could have bought a Letter of Marque to show we sailed with the permission of our government. I hadn't. A name scratched on a sheet in Nafplio could turn into a word whispered in Dimitris' ear before the week was out.

Let the English call it what they pleased.

Andonis held my eye for a breath too long, as if he understood I was avoiding an answer. 'This won't end with cheers on the quay, will it?'

'We'll deal with that when it happens.'

'What if we hit a *meltemi*?'

The *meltemi* was a rare summer wind that roared out of the north-west in the early afternoon, sudden and merciless. A blessing on land, a devil at sea. It built in strength as the day wore on, dropping off at night—or not. Sometimes it howled for days. Andonis and I had faced one aboard one of my father's ships. I still carried a scar on the back of my head.

I shrugged. 'It will push us south.'

He grinned at the understatement.

I made my way forward, counting heads, shaking hands, making a list. One by one, I thanked them—for their courage, their madness, or both.

Nikos shadowed me. 'Are they real pirates, Ghika?' he whispered.

I hoped they knew their way around a ship. If they didn't, we'd find out fast.

Andonis met me on the way back. 'What's the head count?'

'Forty-three,' I told him. 'Thirteen more than we agreed.'

He shrugged. We both looked at the water casks. *Ten days if no one falls sick. Eight if the wind turns against us.*

In the bright sunlight, with the white scar down his nose, the new one on his brow, Andonis looked like a real pirate. Our major worry in these waters wasn't the English or French, or even the Turks. It was other pirates. Four men were keeping watch, but we were as nervous as cats, eyes scanning the horizon.

Andonis had it planned. 'We'll intercept the shipping lanes into

Alexandria, close to the African coast. Please God we don't run into any anti-pirate patrols. The English and French are everywhere.'

I added, 'And the Americans. We'll need to steer clear of Gramcusa, too. My father says there are over a thousand pirates in the old Venetian fort. And there's nothing they'd like more than to capture the *Herakles*.'

On the open sea, sails dotted the horizon. Mid-afternoon, a big square-rigged Turk appeared, but the wind favoured us and we soon put her out of sight. More ships appeared, none close enough to be a threat.

I lowered myself over the side on a rope and painted out the *Herakles'* name.

Near the northern shore of Milos, we cast a net over the side and hauled in a thrashing mass of silver *gavros*. At anchor in a sheltered bay, the cook steamed their clean white flesh, finishing with a drizzle of precious olive oil and lemon juice—the way my mother made it.

I wondered if anyone had realised the *Herakles* was gone.

We cracked the cask of spirits and I gave each man his allotted half cup. The vapour invaded my lungs, and the first sip burned like a fire iron. My eyes watered—I doubled over, coughing.

I hadn't taken a drink since the night in the gambling den.

Damos snorted. 'Too strong for you?'

I wiped my mouth.

He leaned closer, the firelight glinting off his earrings. He touched one hoop, grinning. His father had paid a fortune for them, when he was only a boy, at the Constantinople bazaar. I'd heard the story countless times.

'See these? He used red-hot nails.'

'Here we go,' muttered Kostas.

'Straight through the lobe. No cloth, no rum, no warning—just held me down and spat on the needle. Said it kept the fever out.'

'Did it?' asked Nikos.

'Course not,' said Damos cheerfully. 'I nearly died.' He raised his cup. 'To our health!' He tipped it back in one gulp and grinned, eyes watering.

I did the same.

The night sky stretched vast and black, the new moon barely marking its place among thousands of stars. Phosphorescence flickered in our wake like embers caught in the current. My watch wasn't until four. I lowered myself into a sitting position beside a serious, pimply-faced boy who was eyeing my yataghan—a gift from my father.

The yataghan was a much-feared sword—medium-length, single-edged, adopted from the Turks. Mine was a gift from my father—a carved bone handle and a full silver bolster to guard the hand in a thrust. The blade curved forward in the Ottoman style, better for hacking than stabbing, though I'd sharpened the tip just in case. Two flared silver wings curled from the pommel—more flourish than function, but they locked the hilt tight against my palm. I honed it until no light caught on the edge, or on the false bevel near the tip.

As I ran the whetstone along my *khanjar* and then my hatchet, the boy watched, lips parted, as if absorbing a lesson.

Kostas tightened his *bouzouki* strings and strummed a few chords.

'What is your name?' I asked the boy.

Kostas stilled the strings with his palm.

The boy sighed. 'Pietros Bouff.'

Kostas resumed, playing more softly now.

'What's the problem?'

The boy hesitated, lip trembling. 'My mother is a widow. We're short of food. What will she eat while I'm gone.' His voice dropped. 'What if we're caught?'

A fair question. One I couldn't answer.

I wanted to reassure him. Tell him we'd return rich. But I didn't make promises I wasn't sure I could keep. I squeezed his shoulder instead, hoping that was enough. It wasn't.

Kostas stopped playing. 'You ought to have thought of that before you left.'

I was fetching a cup of water when a sudden raucous noise erupted amidships—doubtless the result of *raki* warming starved stomachs, and the crew were in high spirits to be at sea.

'Voulgaris!'

The speaker was an older sailor, eyes deep set and too close together, a squinting, desperate looking man, pockmarked and weather-beaten, a mop of unruly hair already streaked with grey. I'd noticed him earlier in the day, a loner, jaw muscles working, twitching.

He sat with a crowd of men now, backs to the bulwark.

'Yes?'

'They say you marry Kountouriotis' daughter.'

Cheers and whistles. I turned away.

From behind me, he shouted, 'Have you bedded her yet?'

My hand went to the empty scabbard—a naked feeling. It was back on the deck next to the boy. My face was on fire at the disrespect, the low-class coarseness. To his credit, Damos had his hand on the man's arm in warning.

I walked towards him. His jaw muscles were working, teeth bared in a filthy grin.

He stood up. The crew were enjoying this.

'Shipowners' daughters are like powder kegs. They say she takes two lovers at a time.'

I dived at the son of a whore, shoulder slamming into his ribs, ramming his head into the mast. He grunted. I dragged him up by his filthy shirt, brought my fist back—

'Enough!' A hand gripped my arm and dragged me back. I twisted, fighting to break free, to go back and finish the scum off.

I heard Andonis' voice. 'For the sake of God, Ghika. There will be no fighting on my ship. You must learn to take a bit of baiting.' Steady, measured. A captain's voice.

A few of the men were nodding. At Andonis. Not at me.

His ship? Since when?

It wasn't his words that made my blood rise—it was the shift. My best friend was speaking to me as if I were a crewman. As if he outranked me.

'Baiting?' I asked, my volume rising. 'From that squinting piece of shit?'

Andonis used his calm captain's voice. 'We are all equal on this ship. Regardless of our birth. Remember, he may save your life. Ignore his jibes.'

That stoked the flames of my fury. As if I needed a lesson in commanding a ship. From him. I shook his hand off me. 'Listen, Andoni,' I said. 'A real captain doesn't spit on the man who made him captain.'

Silence. The word 'captain' hung there, and it did not point at me.

'And a real friend wouldn't betray his mate.'

He still believed I had. I wanted to yell, '*You* betrayed *me*!'

But I didn't give him the satisfaction. I shoved my way past him to the bow and gripped the gunwale, letting the wind hit my face. Arms braced wide, I shut my eyes, willing the rage to pass.

These were Andonis' men—but did he know them? Would they obey orders? Gut us in our sleep? Bugger us? Throw us overboard?

I didn't trust them. I didn't know them. Andonis was the one giving orders now.

But if it ended in blood, the blame would be mine. I had put them on this ship. If they died, it would be by my hand.

The *Herakles* surged forward, sails snapping.

I was no longer at the helm.

The deck pitched under a swell and, for a breath, I mistook the lurch in my gut for seasickness.

It wasn't.

It was the taste of being outranked—on the ship I'd stolen.

15

In the Balance

ARNPRIOR AND CAMDEN PARK, New South Wales
1832-33

The morning following the timber incident, I'm bleary-eyed from lack of sleep. Joe is too—except he's worse—on his knees, scrabbling beneath his bunk, cramming things into his shirt. 'Where is it? Where'd I put it?' He hurls a tin cup across the hut.

Ned bursts in. 'Bartholomew's made a charge against you!'

Joe freezes, wild-eyed, face sweaty. 'It was me started it. I'm runnin' away, Jigger. I can't face hanging.'

'Don't be daft, Joe,' I say. 'Running will only make it worse.'

'I'll hide in the well!' he says. 'Or in the cart shed. No one will look in the cart shed. Will they?'

'Joe—'

He's trembling. I grab his arm.

'Listen. You didn't start it. I did. And you're not going to hang. I'll be with you. We face it together.'

He's breathing fast, panicked. He gives a nod—quick, jerky. 'No, right. Flogging, then. Or gaol. Or the treadmill. Or transportation to somewhere even worse.' He pauses. 'Is there somewhere worse?'

'Yes. Arnprior.'

His shoulders slump—but he gives a weak laugh that's more like a blubber.

I go on. 'Don't worry. I read that the crew of the ship *Isabella* mutinied this year. All of them convicted. All released with a warning and a promise of good behaviour.'

Joe's eyes widen. 'We didn't mutiny!'

'Not officially. But you called Bartholomew a mongrel, Joe.'

He brightens. 'Did you laugh?'

'I did.'

'Will you tell Ryrie that Bartholomew's lying, Jigger? You must.' He's begging.

'No, Joe. I can't do that. We must tell the truth.'

'Oh Gawdstruth,' Joe says.

'Yes,' I say. 'Exactly.'

—

As we near the storehouse, Joe whispers, 'What if I faint in front of William? Or vomit? I might vomit, Jigger.'

I keep walking. If I stop, I might vomit too.

With the weight of imprisonment hanging over us, we stand before William Ryrie in the gloomy storehouse. He's seated behind the desk, a book of figures open in front of him, quill still in his hand as if we've interrupted him.

The cut on Joe's chin hangs open.

Bartholomew stands there, arms crossed, with a smirk that makes my skin crawl.

William leans back in his chair and it creaks like a gallows.

'So, what's this with Bartholomew, Bulgary?'

He's used my last name. Not Jigger. Not lad. A bad sign.

Behind us, boots scrape on the boards. Ned's voice comes from the doorway.

'Beggin' your pardon, Mr Ryrie,' he says quietly, 'but they're decent men, both of 'em. They've not troublemakers.'

William doesn't even look up. 'This has naught to do with you, Ned. Back to your post.'

Ned hesitates, hat twisting in his hands, then nods once. 'Aye, sir.' He hesitates a breath longer than he should before stepping outside again, but the air he leaves behind feels lighter.

Joe swallows and speaks up, too loudly. 'It were me, sir. I lost my head.'

Bartholomew pounces. 'They overpowered me, sir. I feared for my life. This one,' he jabs a thumb at Joe, 'struck me. That one there threatened to kill me. I barely escaped with my life. It was a mutiny.'

Mutiny. The word hangs like a noose.

William's brow wrinkles. 'Mutiny is a serious charge.'

Bartholomew spits. 'They're dangerous convicts. I warned you before.'

A shaft of light highlights William's copper beard as he pushes back, his chair scraping the floorboards. 'Well, Bulgary?'

I choose my words carefully. 'Sir, Joseph followed Mister Bartholomew's orders. So did I.'

William speaks again, 'Did you obey his orders, Little?'

Joe's voice is small. 'Yes, sir. We done what he said. He didn't care if Jigger died.'

Bartholomew shouts, 'Will you let them talk back now? Will they decide their own punishment?'

I say, 'I restrained Mister Bartholomew from whipping Joe, sir. Nothing more.'

William raps the desk with his knuckles. 'Enough.'

He sighs and looks at the bruise on Bartholomew's arm.

'You've been warned before, Bartholomew. You use the lash too freely.'

'Because it works! You think I can run this place by coddling them?'

'Bartholomew, if I allow this, I might as well hand the whip to any man who fancies himself in charge.'

'The devil take you, Ryrie! I cannot tolerate such a situation.'

'Is that so?' says William, and I suck in my breath. He stays silent for a moment. 'If that is the way you feel, I agree. You need tolerate it no longer. You are dismissed, Mister Bartholomew. Be gone by noon. That's final.'

I exhale so deeply I feel faint.

'But sir, my wife, my children—'

'You should have thought of them sooner. Go. Pack your bags and collect what is owing before you leave.'

Bartholomew's jaw works like a hooked fish. He opens his mouth, shuts it. Opens it again. Then he snaps, 'I'd rather live with the blacks than stay here.'

His spittle hits William in the face.

William explodes. 'The blacks wouldn't have you, Bartholomew. Get out! Get out, the lot of you. I have made my decision.'

Bartholomew shoves past us with a look of pure loathing, knocking Joe off balance.

William watches him go. 'Bulgary, if I hear of one more breach—one more scrap of trouble—you'll be on the next cart to the magistrate. No talk. No second chances.'

I nod once, throat too dry to speak.

'Get out,' he growls.

Outside, I finally breathe.

I say, 'Bartholomew has children, Joe.'

Joe snorts. 'So do rats, Jigger. Doesn't mean you keep 'em in the pantry.'

I laugh. When I look up, Bartholomew is in my path. His cheeks are blotched red, veins raised.

I keep my face unreadable, but my fingers twitch. Fists or flight—both foolish.

'You'll regret this, Bulgary,' he hisses.

He leans back and spits. A glob lands on my cheek.

Then, in a lower voice, for me, he snarls, 'You think this is the end? It's not.'

Joe mutters behind me, only loud enough for me to hear, 'Spit on your own boots, you pig-faced goat.'

—

Mrs Ryrie's voice cuts across my thoughts. 'You seem worried, Ghika.'

I hesitate. 'Not at all ma'am. It's that song you were humming.'

'The Last Rose of Summer? A pretty tune.'

I should speak only of the garden. But the thought of the Irish girl alone in the city has never left me.

'I heard that you need a housemaid, ma'am. I don't know if she's available, but I met a girl who came on the Red Rover—she was in service. Honest. Capable. She might be willing, she might suit.'

Mrs Ryrie glances up from her work with the pruning shears, curious. 'The Red Rover,' she says, scooping rose hips into her apron. 'Those girls made a brave journey. And her name, Ghika?'

Martin and Joe pass, carrying wood for the well that some of the convicts are digging.

'*Kaliméra*, Jigger,' yells Joe.

I wave.

'Mary Lyons, ma'am. I barely know her. But I'd be glad to know she's safe.'

She returns to pruning. 'We'll see.'

That's what she says to her boys when she has no intention of agreeing to their demands.

As I head towards the convict huts, a trail of smoke drifts down the hill from the cooking fires. We are an odd assortment: a blacksmith, sawyers, wheelwright, ploughmen and shepherds—common labourers. A motley crew of twenty, all from the English isles, except me, the foreigner.

The mud daub on our hut is crumbling. A Sunday chore.

Inside, Joe's skinning a hunk of dark meat. I don't ask what kind.

'Have you washed that?' I ask.

'Nah. I told you, Jigger. Dirt's good for you.'

'Did you make enough for Ned?'

Ned's been ill. I've heard he had a wife once, and they say he's buried two sons.

Joe grimaces. 'Yes. I'm sick too. Me guts are rotten.'

'Some greens might help.'

'Greens are for rabbits.'

I can't help him if he won't help himself. I let go of the bottom of my shirt, and a handful of fat broad beans from the convict garden drops to the table; he adds them to the pot.

'Chimney's working better,' he notes, adding potatoes.

When I go outside to wash my hands, I see a new slab of soap. I yell, 'Joe, give this back.' I know he's grinning. I wipe my hands on my trousers.

Back at home, baths were a luxurious experience. Marble tub, fresh clothes.

Joe ladles stew into a tin bowl for Ned. I take it over to his hut. He's still pale, propped up in bed against a rolled blanket, but he sits up when he sees me.

'Is that for me, or are you taunting a dying man?'

'Depends how polite you are.'

He lifts the spoon and sniffs. 'I'll be polite.'

I leave him chewing and return to our hut. Joe serves our meal in great gouts. It's rough but good. I pick bean strings from my teeth.

—

That night, steady rain lulls me to sleep, but a loud noise jolts me awake before dawn.

'Jigger! Get up.' William Ryrie stands at the door. 'I need an arm to hold a ladder. The well is collapsing. We must reinforce it.'

'I will dress,' I say.

'I will come too,' says Joe.

'You stay here, stupid,' William snaps back.

'Joe was offering to help. *Mister* William.'

There's a pause. Have I overstepped the mark? For once, I simply don't care. Human kindness matters more than rank.

William glares at me, then grudgingly says, 'Thank you, Joe. I only need Jigger.' He turns and disappears.

Joe can't stop grinning.

'Go back to sleep, Joe.'

I arrive at the well as dawn lights the sky, to see William lower a rickety ladder into the newly dug hole, next to the pile of soil. If they strike good water, they will line the well with stone. For now, they've used timber slabs braced by pieces of sapling. However, the overnight rain has caused one slab to become dislodged. It now leans askew, resting sideways against the wall at the bottom, clearly separated from its original position.

'Hold this steady.' William, impatient, faces me from near the top of the ladder. Thunder rumbles in the distance.

'The ground's wet, sir. Shall I fetch a rope?'

If he ties it around his waist, I can pull him out if the ladder breaks, which looks likely. We ought to have brought Joe. He could have gone to fetch one.

'God's sake, man. It's not that deep. Hold it.'

William has more guts than sense. I kneel and grip the side rails and watch him descend, the ladder groaning. He reaches the bottom, and his boots sink ankle deep in mud. His back presses against a dislodged slab of timber, and a chunk of earth tumbles down.

'Sir, I—'

A cascade of dirt buries him to his knees. Another plank strikes him as he shields his head.

Silence.

My voice echoes. 'Are you hurt?'

'My shoulder. I'm stuck.'

If I go for help, it may bury him alive. Tempting.

For a split second, I don't move. Let the bastard sit in the dark, feel the weight of the earth press in like a hand over his mouth.

But his life is at stake. I curse under my breath and grip the ladder. I don't want to go down there either.

'Hold fast.' I put my foot on the top rung.

'Hurry!' He spits out dirt. 'We need to get out of here.'

A rung near the bottom snaps like kindling. My foot crashes through empty air, and hits the next.

'Be careful, you blockhead!'

A clod of earth falls from the wall. Then another. I wait. The air is foetid with the closeness of damp earth, the walls soft and fragile. I look up at the circle of sky. It suffocates me.

Our eyes meet. I see fear in his—fear I will abandon him here. Then relief, when he realises I won't.

'Wipe the blood out of my eyes,' he says.

I freeze.

'Good God, man. Have you never seen blood before?'

I've seen it. I just don't want it near me.

I squeeze my eyes shut for a heartbeat. Breathe. Take my handkerchief from my pocket.

I wipe his face. Sweat stings my eyes.

I kneel, hands clawing at the mud around his legs. My fingers find a sharp splinter of wood; it drives straight under my fingernail. I curse softly, but continue. Finally, his legs are free.

'Don't move yet.'

I still need to shift the plank. I shove it sideways. The whole wall groans. I am making it worse. The bottom sinks deeper, the top drives into his shoulder.

'Get on with it,' he grinds out, face twisted in pain.

I move the stubborn wood back and forth. At each jerk, William grunts, his face shining white-grey in the gloom. I continue until he drags himself out from behind.

'You first,' I say.

Climbing back up is an ordeal. He moves slowly, favouring his injured arm, boots slipping on the mud-slick rungs. Twice he stops, bracing himself against the wall, breath rasping.

I hold the ladder as I watch each movement. If he falls now, we could both be buried.

At last, he drags himself over the lip at the top, groaning as he hauls his body clear.

I start up. The rungs shift beneath my feet. One cracks, but holds. I climb faster. A sound comes from behind me—soft earth falling.

I freeze.

Mud shifts. Something creaks.

I can't move.

The ladder sways under me. My muscles lock. My hands clench the side rails—but I can't make my feet lift.

'Jigger!' William's voice, urgent. 'Move!'

Still I don't. I'm wedged by fear. Pinned like a beetle.

Then his hand—mud-slick, trembling—reaches down.

Grabs my forearm.

He groans as he pulls me over the edge. We roll clear as the earth gives way behind us—then the entire wall slumps inwards—wet earth sliding in a slow, unstoppable mass, dragging planks down into the void.

We stare.

The space where we stood is gone.

Efcharistó, Mother of God. Thank you.

I catch my breath, bent double.

He's coated in mud, hand gripping his injured shoulder. 'Next time, move your feet.'

'I was thinking about it, sir.'

He laughs loudly, teeth coated with saliva and dirt.

'You did well. Call me William.'

I grin.

'As it happens,' he says. 'Before long, we're bound for Sydney with a load of wool. You may accompany us as Ned's offsider.'

—

Two months later

I barely slept last night—I haven't seen Andonis and Nikos since the Prisoners' Barracks. They scattered the five of us like driftwood. I've counted every month. And now, in minutes, I'll see Andonis and Nikos again.

It's nigh on dusk as we roll to a halt, and I glance toward the Camden Park outbuildings.

Ned jerks his chin. 'Convict huts are that way, boy. Go on then. I'll unharness the oxen—you've earned it.'

Ahead, firelight flickers against trees. Will they look the same? Sound the same? Still be my brothers, my men? Or will we be strangers?

And then—I hear them. Speaking Greek.

I step forward into the glow from a campfire, my pulse hammering in my ears.

Three heads turn.

For a heartbeat, none of us move.

I have imagined this moment in a thousand ways. None were like this. None were better.

Nikos shoots to his feet, a three-legged stool toppling behind him. 'Ghika!'

He is running at me before I can brace, before I can think—arms crushing around me, lifting me clean off my feet.

I let out a breathless laugh. '*Áse me káto, vláka!*' Put me down, you great idiot.

'Not a chance!' he says, but he sets me down, grinning so wide his face might split. 'You're uglier than I remember.'

I grip his arms, shaking him. 'You're bigger than I remember.'

Andonis is already beside us. He doesn't say anything at first—grips my arm, fingers digging in. The old way.

'You're late,' he says.

Then I hear a low chuckle. Damos. Arms crossed, smiling as if I saw him yesterday.

Disbelief, shock, relief—too many things at once.

'Look at you, Voulgaris. Respectable.'

I stare. His grin hasn't changed, but his hair has thinned.

'*You're* here?'

His grin widens. 'You didn't think I'd rot at the Barracks forever, did you? They reassigned me. I work here now.'

The fire crackles, sending up slow curls of eucalyptus smoke into the night. Nikos drops onto a log, elbows on his knees, grinning as if he still can't believe I'm real. Andonis sits cross-legged on the ground, his usual quiet presence anchoring us. Damos leans back on a log, stretching his legs toward the fire as if he owns the place.

I drink them in, letting their voices, our language, their laughter, the sheer reality of them settle over me.

Someone passes me a tin mug. I take a slow sip, the warmth spreading through my chest. As we sit in the dirt, the heat of the fire on our faces, a joy surges through me.

The talk flows easily. They've trenched twenty-two new acres for vines. Hard work, but steady. No disasters. I thought they wouldn't last without me. But they've managed. Not only managed. They've done well.

But I see things. Andonis should curb Damos. Nikos needs a push towards independence.

Once I would have said something.

And once, they might have listened.

'Our circle is almost complete tonight,' I say. 'Except for Kostas.'

'You and he should work here as well,' Andonis says quietly.

The other convicts have christened him 'Ando'—and he seems to like it.

Nikos barks out a laugh, slapping his knee. 'We nearly weren't a circle, Ghika! Damos tried to escape!'

I raise my eyebrows.

Damos grins, revelling in the attention. 'Yes. I was in the *Sydney Gazette*. Care to see?' He digs into his pocket and hands me a crumpled piece of newsprint like a man offering a prize.

Andonis grins too.

I unfold the brittle paper and hold it at arm's length so the flames illuminate the words.

I clear my throat: 'One of the Greek pirates who was transported to this Colony some time back for their atrocities in the Archipelago—'

I stop reading. 'Atrocities? They make us sound like savages.'

'Don't worry about that,' says Damos. 'Keep reading.' He edges closer to me.

My eyes skim the print. 'On the brig Wellington when getting underweigh, and handed over by Mister Oliver to the constables. He is in the service of Mister McArthur—'

I stop again. 'What were you doing in Sydney?'

'Collecting provisions,' says Damos. 'Read on.'

'—said he went on board to see a friend, with whom he was taking a glass of grog and a cigar—'

We laugh.

'—the ship began to move— taking him away against his will.'

'Against his will!' Nikos falls backward and rolls about. I love that big galoot.

They lean over each other, laughing.

Andonis wipes his eyes. 'Drinking grog and smoking a cigar. Taken away against his will! What a gentleman! That's our Damos!'

Nikos, seizing the moment, says, 'Give Ghikas the other piece of paper, Damos. Go on! Don't keep him waiting!'

Damos, wearing a comically reluctant expression, finally parts with another folded sheet, which looks even worse than the last.

'This one,' he mutters, 'was published in May, right after they handed down my sentence.'

I scan the first lines, unable to resist a playful jab. 'You used to be the commander of a seventeen-gun ship, Damos? Really? That's a swift rise to fame! And your ship the *Domini Nini*? Was it named after yourself?'

Nikos bursts into laughter once more, the mirth infectious. 'Seventeen guns!'

Damos, looking somewhat sheepish, grins. The rest watch me, faces alight with amusement.

I continue reading and then look up, raising an eyebrow. 'A desperate engagement with one of His Majesty's vessels in the Straits?'

Even in the campfire's dim light, I can see Damos blushing. He clears his throat and admits, 'Well, I had to embellish. I thought they'd give me fifty lashes.'

I can't help smiling. 'Lucky they didn't hang you. What was your punishment?'

'They put me off the ship at Pinchgut. Back to the Barracks. Twenty-one days on the treadmill.'

Three weeks. That would have crushed most men.

'I made the finest flour in Sydney,' he adds. 'The town broke its fast for weeks on my labour. I added a bucket of weevils for good luck.'

Andonis turns serious. 'When he came back to Camden, he looked like he'd been through the mill himself.'

Damos grins—crookedly. 'It nearly ground me down to my earrings.' He flicks one. 'But you should see the treadmill.'

'We're glad you're back, Damo,' Nikos says.

Damos laughs. 'Ghika, do you remember the story of the day my ears were pierced?'

We all groan in unison: 'With red-hot nails!'

He's really laughing now. 'Where was I?'

We yell: 'Constantinople! In the bazaar!'

As we sit by the fire, the orange glow fades into the night. For the first time in three years, I'm surrounded by my own. My language. My people. My past.

I feel it settle over me like a well-worn coat. I've missed the weight of it more than I knew.

'How did you manage your reassignment, Damo? I thought it difficult.'

He shrugs and grins. 'I made myself unwelcome.'

Andonis rolls his eyes. 'They wanted him out of Sydney. A bad influence. You know Damos. He charmed his way out.'

Reassignment. The thought won't leave me. The very notion of being with them again, of being together.

I will ask William.

I doubt he'll grant it.

Nikos asks, 'Do you have trouble with the natives at Arnprior?' His voice drops slightly, as if the very thought unsettles him. He nudges my arm. 'Because I'm having nightmares about being speared in my sleep.'

I raise an eyebrow.

His brows knit together. 'It's serious, Ghika. And I have the summer catarrh.'

I press a hand against his forehead. No fever.

'You'll live, Niko,' I say dryly.

He exhales, satisfied. 'Good. I'd hate to die before breakfast.'

I ruffle his hair. The firelight flickers, their faces shifting in the glow.

Being together again, like the old days—it's exhilarating. Tonight has brought a warmth no fortune could buy—too much warmth, maybe. Enough to draw the gods' notice.

The gods like to strike to remind us that joy is not ours to keep.

But surely I've suffered enough misfortune to satisfy them, to keep them entertained.

I only just avoided a hearing before the magistrate at Goulburn. Tomorrow, I'll ask William for reassignment to be with my friends and no doubt he'll react with his usual warmth and generosity. Then we ride on to Sydney where I'll deliver the letter to Mary, and in all likelihood she'll refuse to see me.

Even the gods would surely call that enough.

16

The Prize

ON BOARD THE *HERAKLES,* off the coast of Tripoli, Africa
July 1827

We'd been at sea five days, eyes searching behind and ahead.

Behind us was the predator.

The British sloop-of-war first appeared south of Crete. Two masts, square sails, eighteen guns. She cut the water like a blade, fast and lean, gaining on us every time. I was sure it was the *Gannet.* I'd seen her before—her captain once dined with my father. That made slipping her all the more urgent, by trimming every inch of sail, weaving through shallows, hiding in coves.

But she wasn't the only threat. Egyptian frigates, Barbary corsairs, even Gramvousa raiders. If any of them caught us, we'd not return home.

And ahead of us, our prey.

This morning—five days out of port—we'd spotted her. A two-masted merchant brig, riding deep in the water—fat with cargo—a painted red stripe along her hull. On a heading for Alexandria to supply the Egyptian fleet. Doubtless carrying coins to buy return freight. This was a gift to us from Poseidon. We'd strike a blow against the enemy, score a victory for Hydra. A chance to prove my courage, pay my debt.

And perhaps—finally—a reason for Patéra to be proud.

I imagined his face if he could see me now. Maria's too.

Andonis had the spyglass. 'Flush deck. New timbers. Perfect.'

Excitement and dread waged war in my chest. The thought of hand to hand combat turned my guts to water.

But then I saw two ensigns snapping in the wind. English and Maltese. Malta was English territory. This ship was a friend. Her name: the *Alceste*.

My grip on my yataghan slipped. I heard Patéra's voice. 'If we want the English to help us fight the Turk, we must cease piracy against their shipping.'

Andonis' voice was steady, his shirt clinging to his skin in the heat. 'Only one gun. No one manning it.' He looked at me. 'What say you?'

I snapped, 'Are you blind, Andoni? She's flying English colours. We cannot attack. This isn't piracy—it's war. You saw what happened when Zacca towed home those English prizes.'

He held my gaze. Calm. Grim. 'Yes. They fired on the town. A woman was killed.'

Then softer, 'But Ghika—she's on a heading for Alexandria. If England is our friend, why do her ships supply the Egyptians?'

I had no answer. The English were friends when it suited them; but they'd supply the enemy for their profit.

He continued, 'We have seen no other prize. Shall we set sail for home with our hold emptier than the day we left?'

His words stung. Sweat dropped off my chin. I hated that he was right. The bravos. My father. Maria. I looked at the horizon where the square-rigger might show.

'Agreed,' I said. 'We search her. If she's bound for Alexandria, we strip her stores. But the ship itself is not a prize.'

'Prepare to board. Remain calm,' Andonis said in a loud voice. 'Man the guns.'

That was one of my mother's favourite sayings when Despina dropped a platter, or my father's guests arrived early. It made us laugh then, and I laughed now. But none of the tension left my body.

I could make out men on her deck, but still no one manned her single cannon.

My hand cramped. Every man on the *Herakles* held a weapon, a *yataghan* or a *pala*. And we all had a double- or single-edged dagger hidden in our *zonária*, and some had a hatchet as well: a *bichaq*, *khanjar*, or *qama*, for close fighting. A few had pistols.

We looked like what we were: desperate.

Nikos, especially—bare-chested, curls tied back with a black kerchief, musket in hand and his dagger gripped between his teeth. A pirate from a broadsheet.

'Have you lost your mind, Niko?' I snapped, my voice raw. 'You'll slice your tongue off.'

He rested the musket against his leg and shoved the knife back into his belt. His grin was infectious.

The *Herakles* came about, broadside on, gun trained, cannon crew ready.

Still no signal.

Andonis cupped his hands and shouted, 'Heave to! Drop your sails and prepare to be boarded!'

For a moment, nothing.

Then her mainsail caught the wind. She was gambling we wouldn't fire on an English ship flying English colours.

Andonis didn't hesitate. 'She's running.' His arm shot up and dropped as he yelled, 'Fire!'

I put my hands over my ears, saw the flash from the muzzle, a puff of smoke, felt the blast through the soles of my feet. Our cannonball shot across the stranger's bow. Men ran on her deck, shouting at each other. I counted eight on board and they carried no weapons. We were bigger, with five times the crew.

She hove to, no fight in her—a pretty little ship.

Nikos let out a whoop. 'That was easy!'

Real pirates would have swarmed over the stranger without introduction, but Andonis yelled in the *lingua franca*, the language of trade common to the Mediterranean—combining words of Italian, French, Spanish, Greek and Arabic. 'Where are you from, and where are you bound, sir?'

The captain shouted back, 'Captain Luigi Mallia of the ship *Alceste*, out of Malta, under the English flag. Bound for Alexandria.'

'Captain, bring your papers over here.' Andonis' knuckles on the gunwale were white. And to me, 'We must separate the captain from his ship before we board her.'

Nikos still danced from foot to foot, swinging his musket around. I pushed the barrel in the opposite direction.

The crew of the *Alceste* lowered a jolly boat. Their captain attempted a dignified descent, lost his footing, and landed with a thud in the bottom, arms flailing. Laughter erupted from our deck.

Kostas flung a rope ladder over our side; when the captain reached us, he hauled him aboard and dumped him unceremoniously onto our deck. Our crew, bold, yet clearly inexperienced, tried their best to look menacing. Their weapons looked like relics more than threats, but the danger was real enough. With a mix of bravado and uncertainty, they herded him toward us, prodding at his back.

The captain was a sight—his round, red face was dripping wet, double chin quivering like jelly on a plate. His papers shook in his grasp as he rubbed his other hand up and down his breeches.

Abruptly, he reached towards his pocket.

Before I could blink, Damos' *yataghan* flashed dangerously close to the captain's chest.

I gasped.

Nikos' grin slipped.

The captain, wide-eyed, raised his hand in a gesture of calm, and pointed to his pocket, then carefully pulled out a handkerchief to mop his brow.

My pulse steadied. Only a handkerchief. Lucky for him.

'You are on your way to Alexandria, so you are supplying the enemy,' said Andonis. 'Your ship is therefore a legitimate prize of war, Captain. Do as you are told and we will spare your lives.'

Another voice came from one of our crew. '*É*, Andoni, ask him if he's heard about the *Superba*!'

Andonis' head jerked around as he shouted, 'Hold your tongue!'

The captain's eyes flew open in recognition. 'I've a wife and children in Malta, sir. Please spare us!'

The worst stories always spread fastest. Three Gramvousa pirate brigs had robbed the *Superba* several weeks ago. Their crews had beaten the captain and the cook senseless, and sodomised the steward and a passenger.

Andonis growled like a villain in a terrible play, 'How much gold do you carry?'

'None,' said Mallia. 'The owners are as poor as mice.'

The man's fear was as transparent as glass. He was lying through his teeth.

'If we find any, you will walk the plank!'

I grinned at Kostas for the absurdity of Andonis' language.

'We don't have a plank,' he muttered.

Andonis shoved the bill of lading at me.

'Sumatran pepper, linen, rope, sulphur, tin plate,' I read. My mother would be thrilled with the pepper, but this was hardly the treasure we'd hoped for.

Andonis pointed an accusing finger at the captain, trying hard to look fierce. 'You're supplying the Egyptians against Greece, aren't you?'

The captain shrugged. 'I carry freight. War is none of my business.'

I rattled off the rest of the list. 'Wine, cheeses, three casks of beef, four bags of bread. Plus the provisions in their galley.'

Andonis smiled at the captain. 'Well, Captain, we will lighten your load today.'

To our crew he said, 'Boarding party—seven only. We're stripping stores, not taking a prize. Damos, Kostas, Nikos, the two Pietros, and you —' he pointed at me, 'and me. I need hands on *Herakles* in case the square-rigger appears—then we cut and run—'

We'd never take an English hull. If we meant to keep her, we'd leave the cargo where it lay and sail her home with our own crew. Zacca tried that once—and they fired on the town. The English make sure everyone pays, not just the guilty.

'We are *palikaria*,' shouted Damos. '*Eleftheria i thanatos*!'

Our crew roared.

Freedom or death.

We'd settle for cheese and tin plate.

The captain, now resigned, called to his men. 'They're boarding. Do not resist.' He slumped, burying his face in his hands.

Andonis, all business, gave his orders. 'Lookout, go aloft. Watch for the square-rigger. Sound the alarm if you see it. Those on deck, rig the yard tackle.'

The seven of us rowed over, using a hawser to join the two ships. Pietros Lalahos misjudged the gap and nearly slipped; Pietros Bouff hauled him by the belt and grinned, both of them too young for this work. Thirty-six stayed where we needed them—on the hoists, at the tiller, at the guns.

The *Alceste* crew stood motionless while the transfer of goods began. On the *Herakles*, cargo piled up and disappeared into the hold. We paused, eyeing the last items: a heap of dirty canvas dumped on ballast in the bilge water, and brimstone sulphur in bags. A necessity of war, but irritating to the skin, and flammable.

Bouff staggered under a beef cask; Lalahos coughed when dust rose from a split bag.

'Leave it,' Andonis said. 'Not worth the effort.'

We combed through every nook—the hold, quarters, galley. Sails, personal items, instruments, food, wine, charts—we took everything but the compass.

I kept glancing over the stern. Still no sign of the square-rigger. But she was out there.

'They have to be carrying some!' I said.

'Who's the ship's clerk?' Damos demanded. 'He'll know!'

From the huddle of fearful faces, a pale young sailor stepped forward, spoke in a whisper. 'I am.'

His voice wavered, eyes darting to Damos, who was seething with rage.

'Over the gun!' Damos roared.

Andonis didn't flinch. He didn't even look at the trembling clerk. Nikos was shaking.

How had we come to this?

The young sailor clung to his mate, fingers clawing for support. I could sense his terror, his dread of what outrage might come next. Damos dragged him with a force that sent him sprawling over the cannon. His voice was different. Not just hard, but eager. His hand was already at his belt, his fingers brushing the hilt of his dagger. 'Don't stand there, Kostas,' he yelled. 'Tie him down.'

My romantic notions of piracy shattered there and then. Damos was playing the part too well. The boy didn't know it was an act. His terror was real—and I was part of the crew delivering it.

He seized the boy's hair, jerking his head back. 'Where is the gold?'

The boy was white and shaking, blubbing. 'I don't know!' He shrieked in a high-pitched voice. 'Please! Don't hurt me.'

He wept.

'We won't hurt you,' I said, but the words felt empty. This was what we had become.

Nikos took a waterskin to the sobbing boy. He didn't speak. Just held the cup to the boy's lips and wiped his chin.

—

That evening, I stood at the stern, staring into the dark water that churned in our wake. The breeze that had promised adventure this morning, now bore the stench of greed and violence. I couldn't shake off what we'd done.

I heard footsteps behind me. The man from last night walked towards me, lean muscular legs propelling his easy gait, vraka torn and swinging, eyes sunken, cheeks gaunt and hollow. When he brought his hand up towards me, I flinched.

He laughed, mouth open wide. He was offering me a cup of *raki*. I hesitated. Had he already drunk from it? I could still smell the beast in him. I remembered my promise to Andonis, held his gaze, and took it. He slung an arm around my shoulder, foul breath hot in my face. Despite his closeness, I kept my guard.

'No hard feelings?' He knocked his cup against mine.

He lowered himself to the deck and placed his cup on the boards. 'Good work today.' He inspected his toothpick. 'A true Voulgaris.'

I nodded. 'Son of Nikolaos.'

'Your family stands against piracy. Or at least they pretend it. Why are you here?'

My debt was none of his business. 'I'm bored with maintaining my father's fleet. He says I think more like a sailor than a shipowner.'

He slid his fingers along the toothpick, wiped them on his vraka.

'And you?' I asked.

He rubbed his jaw. 'Raised by my aunt after my parents died at sea. I owe her everything. When the war is over, I will build a fishing boat, and I will provide for her children, repay her kindness.'

Surprising. Driven by duty, not greed. Not what I expected. He fought for those who had nothing. I fought to prove I was someone.

He already knew who he was.

'And what of marriage?' I asked.

I pictured a woman, reduced to a mere instrument for pleasure and the provision of offspring, toiling day in and day out under his oppressive rule.

'Only the rich and powerful like you can afford marriage to rich women.'

Hairs prickled on the back of my neck. He'd better be careful. But I answered. 'I have advantages that others don't.'

'I was to be married to a girl from the Mani. Our betrothal ended when she was killed in a family feud.'

He showed as much emotion as he might about a dead turtle washed up on the beach.

'I'm sorry to hear that.' I meant it. I wasn't sure why. The question slipped out. 'Did you ever meet her?'

His voice wavered, revealing layers I had not expected to find. 'Yes. Only once. It was love at first sight.'

I had seen him today as a brute. A bully. The kind of man my father warned me about. And now he was talking about love at first sight.

I didn't laugh. Not even a smile.

He tossed the dregs of his *raki* overboard, stood, and walked away. As if he hadn't shattered everything I thought I knew about men of his class.

I sat there watching the stars. Wondering what else I had wrong.

17

Mrs Macquarie's Chair

SYDNEY, New South Wales
July 1833

The next morning, as we prepare to depart for Sydney, I seize a moment to approach William Ryrie while he tightens the girth of his saddle.

'Sir,' I begin, keeping my tone even, 'would you consider my reassignment to Mister Macarthur?'

He pulls the strap up snug under the mare's belly. His tack is always well-oiled, perfect.

I continue. 'Being with my men again would mean a great deal. We work well together. And with the recent convict assignments, you have no shortage of hands on Arnprior.'

A pause—brief, but telling. I've overstepped. It's his business how many men he needs.

He secures the girth with the same methodical precision I've seen in every decision he makes. Calculating. Weighing. Like my father, measuring a transaction.

He exhales, slow and deliberate, and turns to me. 'I value your welfare, Jigger,' he says. 'But training convicts is costly. Fairness demands you remain at Arnprior. Who would achieve the same lambing rates as you do?'

I meet his gaze. 'I'd train someone else.'

'Train them to be you?' He swings into the saddle without waiting for an answer. 'Impossible.'

He touches his hat and rides off to join his father to say goodbye to the Macarthurs.

My worth is measured only in usefulness. The business of the well lies between us, but debts of blood and mud do not shift the balance of his books. I am sure he would risk life and limb to haul me from a pit, but he will not lift a pen to let me go.

Something should crack inside me. But it doesn't.

I think of Camden Park, of the ease with which Andonis and Nikos have settled down, of the way Damos sprawled by the fire as if he's always lived here. And I picture Arnprior—the slope of the hills beyond the homestead, the hut I've patched a dozen times. Joe and Martin.

I should feel rage. Or humiliation. Or loss.

Instead, I feel—untethered.

The boys have carved out a place without me. Even Nikos.

And Ryrie won't let me go. Not because he values me, but because he owns me. Because lambing rates matter more than men.

The dray jolts forward, rocking on the uneven track. Ned clicks his tongue at the oxen. 'You little beauties.'

I don't belong at Camden Park. Not really.

I picture Martin shifting in his sleep, Joe's inevitable smile as he hands me something he doesn't own, the rhythm of work I know well—something in my chest settles.

I live for the day I return to Hydra. But in the meantime, I belong on Arnprior.

William returns and rides up alongside me, allowing his horse to settle into a walk. 'My mother tells me you enquired after a housemaid who came on the Red Rover—a Mary Lyons,' he says.

My head jerks back. What did he say?

I recover. 'Only to suggest her as a maid, sir. She seemed honest and capable. And I'd be glad to know she's safe.'

He raises an eyebrow. 'I thought you were saving yourself for a Greek bride.'

I hold his gaze. 'I am.'

He adjusts his gloves. 'I asked my mother to write to Miss Bourke, the governor's daughter. She runs the Ladies Committee. Turns out your Irish girl is still in service with the Bloodsworths on O'Connell Street. She's agreed to receive you.'

The world sharpens. Every noise seems louder—the grind of the cart wheels, the clank of a chain.

I say carefully, 'That's good to hear, thank you, sir. I'll be glad to enquire about her welfare. Nothing more.'

He pulls a folded envelope from his coat. 'If she's ever out of work, or in want of country air, my mother makes an offer of a post on Arnprior. Nothing improper—only if she's considering changing her position. We don't poach servants. But my mother thought it worth giving her the option.'

He hands it to me. 'Having a young lady on Arnprior might help you to settle down.'

So that's his motive. To keep me on Arnprior.

'I'll deliver it,' I say.

He gives the faintest nod, then rides away.

He means for me to forget Hydra. To plant roots. He doesn't know me at all.

But it will be good to see Mary again. To see how she is. I hope that life in the city hasn't worn her down. Although a little less wildness wouldn't go astray.

I push the envelope deep into my pocket.

—

It's a week before I am allowed enough free time to visit Mary. I brace myself against an icy wind as I approach the grand homes of O'Connell Street.

The door opens in front of me, and there she stands.

'Ah, Mary. Ahhhh.' I am painfully aware of my newly cut hair and raw, shaved face.

She waits.

After so long, I expect the warmth of her smile, the easy pleasure of being received. Instead, her eyes flick over me as though she's deciding whether I'm a guest, a nuisance, or simply a problem to solve.

'Is it because I am so irresistible that you've come to see me? Or is it my shoes again?'

I don't know how to answer.

So I say, 'You've been on good pasture.'

She puts her hands on her hips. 'Oh, have I now? And what is that supposed to mean? I am a fat cow? Is that what you came to tell me?'

That is not what I meant—she looks healthy.

She steps backwards, impatient, gesturing me to enter.

'Come, you're letting in cold air.'

I step inside, past her into the hallway, inhaling her same smell I remember so well from our first meeting. Clean air with a whisper of flowers. The musty hallway overtakes it and I put my hand out to touch the wall in the gloom. I knock a painting sideways.

'Will you mind now, where you're putting your hands!' Mary pushes past me along the hallway. At a doorway on the left, she stops and waits. Her eyes are wilder than I remember, with a manner to match.

'Please,' she says, nodding towards the room inside.

I find myself in a parlour, the muted gleam of china contrasting with dark furniture and pink velvet that soaks up the light. I take a seat, the cushion yielding more than expected, causing me to sink considerably.

Is that the hint of a smile? She seems warm and distant all at once.

The soft light plays on her fine features.

I am reminded of the gossip Cook shared with me this morning as she wiped her hands on her apron. 'Mrs Bloodsworth? Don't be fooled by the fine manners. They say she and her husband James threw out his mother, the old widow, from her own house—poor Sarah Bellamy—left her begging the court for a lease to keep a roof over her head. Ten years past now, but folk don't forget a scandal like that.'

Mary jumps up when Mrs Bloodsworth enters, a small, dumpy woman with hair piled high on her head, pulling her mouth down so it stretches the skin between her lips and her nose. I'm still struggling out of the chair as a mark of respect when she waves me back down.

She flicks her hands under the back of her skirt and sits on the chesterfield, feet firmly planted on the floor, back ramrod straight.

Her greeting has all the warmth of the icy wind outside. 'How do you do, Mister—?'

'Voulgaris,' I say. 'Ghikas Voulgaris.'

At my name, her lips all but disappear. She nods. 'Ah, yes, the Greek pirate. How very—exotic. Allow me to be perfectly clear,' she says in a voice like a violin string, 'your conduct with Mary must be above reproach.'

Mary is beetroot red, gaze darting to the window, highlighting a bead of perspiration on her top lip.

I feel like a schoolboy caught in mischief. I clear my throat. 'I understand, ma'am. I assure you—my intentions are entirely proper and honourable. The reputation of this household, and that of Miss Lyons, is safe in my hands.'

Mary makes a choking sound.

'You will collect Mary at eleven-thirty sharp tomorrow,' says Mrs Bloodsworth, pulling a tiny notebook from her sleeve. 'Return by two-thirty, no later. No dawdling. No liberties. No loitering in doorways. Remain outdoors. No public houses. And absolutely no palm-reading.'

'Yes, ma'am,' I say. I haven't even asked. Does Mary have no choice in this? She might refuse.

Mrs Bloodsworth closes her book with a snap. 'Mary, you have work to do.'

Then, with a whirl of her skirts, she exits with all the authority of a warship changing course.

Mary walks me to the door and yanks it open.

'Please don't presume I'm at your beck and call, Ghika. I have a life outside this arranged farce.'

She remembers how to address me.

'I'm sorry, Mary. I merely wished to know how you were. Do you wish to accompany me on an outing?'

She barely pauses for breath. 'First, I am summoned because the Governor's daughter called. Then I am questioned about why such a fuss over a Greek convict. Now it's dictated when I may go out, and where.'

She looks at me now. 'Yes, I wish it. I might even go into a public house and cause a scandal.'

Now she is attempting to shock me. She has.

'I will be honoured to escort you tomorrow at eleven thirty.'

'Thank you. But please don't try to change my mind about anything.'

She gives the briefest of smiles, then shuts the door in my face.

I stand there, stunned. I should thump on that door and tell her I will *not* be returning.

But there's something compelling about that fiery spirit.

—

The following day, she appears in answer to my knock, clear of skin, face outlined by curls, a light cotton dress to her ankles—a piece of cloth around her shoulders tied at the front. Am I mistaken, or is she flushed with excitement?

'Ah, it's yourself.' As if she has forgotten I am coming.

'Were you expecting someone else?' I ask, a trace of amusement in my voice.

'The King of England himself.' She smiles and takes a white bonnet from a peg on the wall, tying it under her chin, and adds a rough brown cloak. I step forward to help, but she steps back.

'You haven't learned yet?'

I cannot help laughing, and she puts her fingers to her lips to quiet me.

'Are you wanting to take me on an outing or not?'

'I have come a long way to do it,' I answer truthfully.

We stroll along Bridge Street, and I position myself on side of the traffic as we turn onto George Street, crowded with horses and carriages.

As we set out, I say casually, 'Cook suggested we visit Mrs Macquarie's Seat.'

Mary bursts out laughing. 'You mean Mrs Macquarie's Chair?'

I blush. 'Cook said it has a splendid view of the water.' I do not add that Cook is thrilled Mary is Irish, and has packed a picnic for me and my 'sweetheart'.

'Last week, an Irishman took a *sheilagh* there, at eleven o'clock at night. It said in the newspaper. He forced himself on her and was arrested.'

'What's a sheila?'

'It's Irish for woman.'

'Ah. Well, please don't alarm yourself, sheila. It is broad daylight and I have no such intention.'

She giggles. 'If you did, I would scream murder.'

'I am sure you would.'

She smiles as I lead her away from the lively public houses.

'It's been a while since you arrived on the Red Rover,' I begin, choosing my words carefully, 'and I have thought often about your welfare, Mary. I would like us to be friends.'

She stops walking and looks at me.

'I am not looking for friendship, Ghika. Not with you. Not with any man.' She pauses. 'And if we are going to Mrs Macquarie's Chair, we're going in the wrong direction.'

Every word feels like a battle. Is she worth this relentless tug-of-war?

'We are walking to my employer's residence. To collect a sulky. For a picnic.'

'A what? A sulky? Really?' Her eyes shine with excitement. 'Ah, I do love horses! Please now, let's do that! But please, no more talk of friendship.'

We speak of her last employer in Ireland, a Mister Jenkins, a thorough-bred horse breeder who was kind to her. And she tells me about his daughter, whose loss of speech Mary helped to restore.

'Didn't you want to stay there?' I ask, curious. 'It sounds like an advantageous situation.'

'They went back to England,' she says.

'Were you sad?'

She looks down, then shrugs. 'I thought I belonged with them.'

A pause.

'But I was the help, after all. Two guineas, Mister Jenkins gave me, and they waved goodbye.'

She gives a short laugh that isn't really a laugh. 'You learn not to speak too freely to your betters. Different worlds require different tones.'

We arrive at the Ryrie's house where Fergus, a quiet old nag, is already harnessed and tied to the hitching post. True to her word, Cook has put a bag under the seat. I killed another brown snake for her yesterday—there must be a nest of them under the house.

'Jesus, Mary and Joseph, a white horse!'

I flinch at this careless blasphemy.

''Tis good luck, Ghika!'

I have heard the Irish are superstitious.

Then, to my horror, she collects the spit in her mouth and hawks it onto the ground, shattering any illusion of ladylike behaviour. Uncouth actions like this jar with everything I expect of a woman—women on Hydra *pretend* to spit to ward off the evil eye. But they don't actually do it. I'm far from Greece, and Mary is unlike any woman I have known.

She sees my shock. 'You must do that, Ghika. Or good luck will turn to bad.'

She leans in to speak to Fergus in a low voice, putting her arms around his neck, breathing into his nose.

'Mister Jenkins was a breeder of horses. I love their smell. Ghika, what if we could buy a toilet water with the odour of horse? Wouldn't that be grand?'

She makes me laugh. At the sulky, I hesitate, unsure how to assist her up without overstepping good manners. The floor of the sulky is high, with a shaft to climb over. I'd like to grab her and dump her up there like a sack of potatoes.

She looks up at me without guile. 'Will you not be helping me?'

If she isn't the most contrary girl ever born. I lift her up, gather her skirts in a bunch, and push them in after her. I don't mean to send her backwards against the seat.

She is laughing now. 'This puts me in mind of the day you took my shoe off. You knocked me senseless then too!'

She remembers. My throat closes. I drape a blanket over her legs to ward off the cold.

Fergus trots energetically as we head east, Mary marvelling at the high perspective. How beautiful the harbour. How fine the governor's mansion. How tall the ships. I am content to stay quiet, listening, looking sideways at her now and then as she swivels about, cheeks flushed. She catches me watching her, and she looks away, her expression unreadable. She is quite the loveliest thing I have seen in the colony.

We reach the Botanic Gardens at Farm Cove and Anson's Point, where I secure Fergus in the shade. We sit together on Mrs Macquarie's Chair with the panoramic view before us. Mary talks about the hangings on Pinchgut Island, shuddering as she recounts its grim history.

'Where?'

She points. 'That one with the gibbet.'

I remember skeletons on a gibbet on the cliffs at Malta, and shudder.

She spreads the blanket on the grass and lays out on a plate my favourite mutton and pickle sandwiches. Without being asked.

I lie sideways on the grass, propped on one elbow. 'Last time we met, you wanted to be an independent woman.'

'As you see, Ghika, I remain unattached. I won't be anyone's bride, no matter what society thinks.'

I laugh too quickly. 'That's good. Because if you were expecting a proposal, it's not coming.'

She blinks once, then looks at me directly. 'And if I wanted a proposal, Ghika, I'd ask for one. But I don't.'

She's careful with my name. That voice—low, breathy. It slips straight through me, leaving something hollow behind. She blushes and leans forward to take a sandwich as I reach for the cordial. Our foreheads collide, and we are thrown off balance. I catch her and her hand finds mine.

'I'm sorry,' I say.

As our eyes lock, the longing rises—sharp, uninvited. I crush it before it takes shape. To kiss her would be an irrevocable breach of trust, an affront, a betrayal of my unknown bride on Hydra. I have no right to such thoughts. It will not happen again.

'Did you know it's a beautiful voice you have, Ghika?'

She turns my hand over. I should remove it, but I don't want to upset her. I divert her instead.

'Mary, have you thought any further about taking a position in the country?'

She releases my hand as if it burns.

I pick up a sandwich and take a bite, not noticing what is on it. She sighs and brushes crumbs off her skirt. Thank goodness. I thought she would explode again.

'I will not be told what to do.'

'Mary, Sydney is a small town. A woman's reputation is everything. And marriage—well, it's the proper end, the safe path. I say that only out of concern.'

She draws in a breath. I've misjudged. I try again.

'Mrs Ryrie—the mistress of Arnprior—has sent an offer of employment.'

When we stopped to water the oxen at Parramatta, William told me the contents of the letter.

Mary is looking a little thunderous, but I plough on. 'I'm told you'd be paid ten pounds a year. You'd have a room. You'd have the company of two other elderly maids who came with the family from Scotland. The fresh air might do you good, until you settle in Sydney as a spinster.'

I wince. Too late. She spits out her cordial.

'Sorry, sorry. Not spinster. Misogamist.'

'Is it yourself who'll be telling me what's proper for me, Ghika? Are you the shepherd of lost lambs?'

'Mary, *The Monitor* printed an article in May,' I say, keeping my tone casual. 'Two girls from the Red Rover were taken in by an old rogue—he claimed they'd make the gowns he sold at market. Turned out he was running a sly house.'

She lifts her brows.

'A brothel.'

She rolls her eyes.

'And because they're free settlers, there's no recourse. There's no protection for them, no guardianship—they won't even be sent to the Female Factory. That's only for convicts. One was only seventeen.'

I pause. 'This place doesn't look after women like you, Mary. Not if something goes wrong.'

I don't know why I'm still speaking. She's already shaking her head. She says, 'So why are you and I dining alone then Ghika? Does this not risk my reputation?'

She has a point. On Hydra, this would be unthinkable. Even here, in daylight, on public land, with her employer's permission, some might think this stains her name. Not mine.

But I continue, 'Your mail coach fare would be included. Stay three months. If you wish to return to Sydney after that time, your fare will be paid.'

I hand her Mrs Ryrie's offer of employment. I take another bite. Cook knows how to make a mutton sandwich.

She places the envelope on the blanket without a glance. No thanks. Not even a nod. My jaw tightens. Does she think these favours fall from the sky?

'When were you put in charge of my employment?'

'Only God knows why anyone would help you. You are so—*eknevristikó*.'

She lifts her eyebrows.

'Annoying.'

She crosses her arms and purses her lips. 'I have given notice to Mrs Bloodsworth, and I go to Mrs Hercules Watt, not a block away from my present position. They are charming Irish folk. Mister Watt was once a convict, but he prospers in the trade of hides. He and Mary have three children.'

She blows out her breath. 'Is that satisfactory to you?'

This Watt could be a scoundrel. 'You would work for a convict, Mary? And what makes you think him so agreeable?'

'Mister Greek god, have you forgotten you are a convict? And if it is not about hard work, this trip to the country that you see in my future, what is it about? Do you see me sitting about stitching samplers?'

She regards me, solemn, thinks for several seconds, then speaks in a calm voice. 'I cannot believe the size of your head. What makes you think I need improvement?'

My heart sinks. Misinterpreted. Again.

She doesn't allow me time to speak.

'I'm not looking for a placement in the country. I want to work in a haberdashery.' She leans in, eyes twinkling with mischief. 'I know a gentleman who intends to open an emporium, and I'd work for him. The gentleman we met the day at the cobbler, remember? He recognises potential where you see only a project, Ghikas. Not everyone believes they have the divine right to 'improve' others.'

I slam my glass down so hard that the drink splashes over my hands and the blanket. I'm not sure what she says next. I knew Townsend would pursue her. God knows what schemes that scoundrel has already hatched. What lies has he spun to ensnare her? He'll provide the capital for an emporium? Hah. And she believes him.

It hits me too late. I've offered her protection. He has offered her a measure of independence.

'The man may be pompous,' I say at last, forcing calm into my voice, 'but at least he has wealth and position.'

She lifts her chin. 'I'd rather kindness.'

I take a few seconds to allow my pulse to subside before I speak calmly.

'Mary, do you have any experience of trade?'

She traces an ivy leaf with her finger on the plate.

Suddenly she swipes the bread crust off it on to the grass, as if she'd like to smash it over my head.

'I have a *galore* of experience.'

She glares at me.

'And not only in *trade*.'

Her meaning is clear.

She flings her arms wide. 'Full of it, so I am! Fit to burst!'

She crosses her arms over her chest in defiance, as if to say, *There. Now you know what I am.*

My heart sinks.

'So, what will you do with this offer?' I say.

'Consider it.'

'Mary, I only speak out of concern for you. Please do not let us part on bad terms.'

She continues to stare at me for a long time.

'Ghika, I believe you. I accept your friendship.'

I cannot resist a Parthian shot. 'I said right at the beginning that was all I offered.'

In truth, she confuses me. I care about her welfare. But deep down, do I want more than friendship? It's as well she's not coming to Arnprior.

—

I sleep at the back of the George Street house and the following morning, low in spirits, I am up early for our return to Arnprior. I have slept little, thinking about Mary's grudging acceptance of friendship. And her galore of experience. And William's refusal to allow my reassignment.

A drunk is retching in the street. I long for the peace of the bush.

A horse's hooves strike the flagstones in the roadway, and I look up. Mister Ryrie himself is riding a strong chestnut mare, and in front of him on the saddle is a black and white ball of fluff. He reaches down, holding it out to me. A puppy with black button nose and eyes to match.

'Ghikas, an acquaintance gave me this bobtail bitch. She should be an excellent sheep herder. Extraordinary type this, with a natural bobtail. She has some kangaroo dog in her, but not enough, their breeder thinks, to cause her to hunt. Will you not take her into your care?'

As I put out my arms, the puppy leaps at me, her tongue flitting like a butterfly on my lips. Goosebumps travel from my mouth to my arms, and the hairs stand on end.

Her paws are scrambling over my chest, as if she already belongs to me. I hold her tight, pressing my nose into her fur. For once, something is mine. And for once, no one can take it from me.

So this is what he meant.

Love at first sight.

18

AT SEA

Intercepted

ON BOARD THE *HERAKLES,* South of Candia (Crete)
August 1827

I woke on the deck of the *Herakles,* my mind lingering on a dream of
Maria—she was waiting at the bottom of her father's stairs, dark eyes
searching for me. But instead of reaching for me, she frowned because my
hands were empty of gold.

It was the first of August, so today our fast for the Dormition must
begin.

The sails billowed above, like the skirts of the whirling dervishes in
Constantinople. A sultry dawn. A fresh breeze. We were running down-
wind under full canvas, the ship humming with speed.

Damos' words from yesterday remained with me. 'Put them in their
jolly boat, and let them row to Africa. Or finish them off.'

He had said it to scare them. And it had worked. But the way he said it
—the way he had thrown that boy over the cannon, the way he seemed to
enjoy it—that stayed with me.

'The English would hunt us down,' Andonis had said. 'And anyway,
Ghikas doesn't like blood.'

I pushed myself up from the deck, gripping the gunwale. My knuckles ached. Damos had made the line between man and monster seem perilously thin. I told myself I wasn't that kind of man. I hoped I was right.

And for what? Our attack on the *Alceste* had been worthless—no treasure, no ship. A cargo of pepper. Thin pickings.

Antonio would be looking for me. He might already have gone to my father. The thought turned my insides to ash. My father learning that his son had a debt with the bravos—he wouldn't know it had only happened once. I could almost see his face—cold, carved, unreadable. He'd pay the debt. But not for my sake. To protect the Voulgaris name. To protect his standing. He'd be furious. Hell would be waiting for me at home.

But here we were, still sailing across the trade routes south of Crete, chasing a decent prize. It wasn't over yet.

'Ship ahoy!'

I leapt to my feet. Maybe this was it.

My heart plummeted. The square-rigger loomed out of the darkness behind us—a giant bearing down—the brig-sloop from before, fast and manoeuvrable. She would catch us.

Now I was certain. It was the *Gannet*.

'We must close-haul,' said Andonis. 'And pray she cannot intercept.' Men scattered to their stations.

By five, she had caught us, eased herself across our bow, slowed just enough to hold position, to turn her guns on us. We were trapped, helpless.

Her officers barked orders, and her crew obeyed. She boasted eighteen ugly short-bore carronades—thirty-two-pounders, gun crews standing ready.

Two guns thundered, belching smoke that billowed and swirled across the water between us, a warning we dared not disregard. Men swarmed over her rigging like ants.

Andonis hauled the wheel to avoid collision. 'Heave to,' he shouted. 'Run up the colours!' We had no white flag.

The red and blue flag of Hydriot independence fluttered up our pole, then the blue and white ensign of Greece. I prayed the Englishmen would accept them as our surrender. Another blast could sink us.

She held position abeam, her cannons trained on us as we slowed.

Andonis spoke in a monotone. 'Men, sheath your weapons.'

They lowered their jolly boat and rowed to the *Herakles*.

Uniformed men surged aboard, muskets at the ready.

The officer spoke in English. 'Lieutenant Carpenter of His Majesty's Navy. Who among you is the captain?'

Andonis stepped forward, back straight, tone even. 'Captain Andonis tu Manolis.'

The man regarded Andonis' clothing with disdain. 'What is the name of this ship? Where is your home port? Your destination? How many are you? Where are your papers?'

Andonis shrugged. He would have understood little of that.

I stepped forward, speaking before he could. 'We are the *Herakles* out of Hydra, forty-three on board, flying the Greek flag. We are returning to our home port, and we insist to proceed.'

The lieutenant looked at me as if a dog had spoken English.

'Your name?'

'Ghikas Voulgaris, sir. Son of Nikolaos of Hydra.'

I saw a flash of recognition.

'Papers?' His moustache dragged in his wet, pink mouth.

'We have none, sir. Our government at Nafplio has disorder.'

Beside me, Nikos shifted. '*Égo*,' he said, pointing to his chest.

I stared at him. He was taking the blame.

The lieutenant was struggling to decipher my thick accent.

'No papers? That alone identifies you as pirates. Let's inspect your cargo.' He pointed at Andonis' *yataghan*. 'But first, sir, ask your men to unfasten their sashes.'

I spoke to the crew in our own language. 'He wants us to drop our *zonária*. Do not obey.'

No one moved.

Carpenter signalled to one of his sailors, who swung the butt of his rifle, landing a glancing blow above my eye. I staggered back, hand to my forehead. Sticky. Blood. My stomach rolled.

Nikos glared at the man, stepped forward with his arm out to protect me.

Andonis withdrew the watch from his *zonári,* unwound the cloth from around his waist, allowing it to fall to the deck.

The officer snatched the watch, studied the back. 'Luigi Mallia. Obtained legally?'

Andonis remained silent. The officer pocketed it.

I wiped my forearm across my forehead, gagging at the red smear on my sleeve. I withdrew my *yataghan* and placed it on the deck in front of me. An English sailor picked it up with a look of sheer admiration. He picked up my bichaq.

As we marched towards the hold, I said to the lieutenant, 'My father knows your captain, sir. Commander Brace.'

The lieutenant took no notice. He and his men inspected the ship, examined our cargo, comparing its riches with our dishevelled appearance. He asked that Andonis, Damos and I accompany him back to the *Gannet*, while his men locked the rest of our crew in the hold.

On the foredeck of the *Gannet*, a rough timber enclosure held some fifty prisoners—shouting in Turkish—sunburned and filthy, skin peeling. Although sworn enemies, we were now fellow captives of the English. So this was our end—sleeping side by side with the men we were meant to face in battle.

They called greetings and we answered.

Commander Brace stood at the taffrail of the quarterdeck, a slender man with heavy side-whiskers and one impressive gold epaulette on the shoulder of a navy jacket, a heavy signet ring on his little finger.

We must have looked as desperate to him as his prisoners in the bow.

He introduced himself in English to Andonis.

I knew Andonis wouldn't understand him.

I stepped forward and extended my hand. 'Commander Brace,' I said, 'I believe you are acquainted with my father.' I paused. 'He would expect you to allow us to continue on our way.'

He examined my swollen eye, face impassive. 'Your father?'

I continued, with confidence. 'Indeed, sir. I am Ghikas Voulgaris, Son of Nikolaos, from the island of Hydra.'

I loved the ring of the words, in any language.

'Ah yes. A fine gentleman.'

When he gripped my hand with excessive force, it brought tears to my eyes. I would not show weakness. My head still throbbed from the blow, but I could play this game. I squeezed back, watched his eyelids flicker with both pain and approval.

'What brings you to this part of the Mediterranean, boy?'

'The *Herakles* belongs to my cousin, Dimitris, sir.'

'Ah yes. Also an outstanding young man.'

Sickeningly so.

'Why did you run from the *Gannet*?'

'*Gannet* looked like Turk, sir.'

The *Gannet* looked nothing like a Turk. His forehead creased.

'Our government is offended, sir, if you will to stop our passage.'

He ignored this. 'Where are your papers? A Letter of Marque from your government? And why is your ship's name blacked from your hull?'

'The government in Nafplio has disorder, sir. We have no papers. Unfortunately.' I smiled in innocence.

'Listen, boy. This is British justice. It matters not who your father is. Your leaders are condoning piracy. It's a crime. My mission is to stop it.'

He called it justice when he was stealing the ship.

I met his gaze. 'We are not pirates, Commander Brace. We are palikaria, and we carry the prize of war, sir.' I placed my feet further apart. 'I insist we are released.'

He smiled as he sucked air through his teeth.

'You insiss you air riliss?' His officer repeated, laughing.

The captain frowned. Andonis was holding his breath next to me. Dreading my reaction.

I kept myself still. 'You mock me, sir?'

Commander Brace interrupted. 'He meant no harm.' And to his officer, 'Leave us.' He ignored me and turned back to Andonis, speaking in the *lingua franca*. 'Captain, you have no papers. No Letter of Marque. No manifest for the goods on board. Your ship's name has been painted out. I must escort you to Malta. The court will decide.' He gestured towards the bow. 'We already have fifty Turkish pirates on board—apprehended last Friday. Several of my crew are sailing their vessel back to Malta.' He ran his hand through his hair. 'I have too few men to do the same with yours, so we shall take you under tow instead. If you are on legitimate business, you may sail your ship home from Malta. If not, she will be a prize of war.'

I squeezed my eyes shut. A prize of war. Not just our skins. Dimitris' ship. They could auction the *Herakles* and distribute the proceeds between the English admiral, Commander Brace, and his men.

I swallowed and forced out another laugh. 'My father will soon arrange for us to sail home, sir.'

He kept speaking the *lingua franca* again for Andonis' benefit, but addressed me. 'You will be detained in the Lazaretto for your quarantine period, and then the gaol, until your father provides papers for your ship. I imagine he will seek Admiral Codrington's intervention on your behalf.'

Admiral Codrington. Commander of the English fleet in the Mediterranean. His son had drowned when a cutter overturned off Hydra five years ago. I knew he was determined to stamp out piracy. But it would only be piracy if we took an English ship.

My family would be frantic with worry, as would the families of our crew. My father would explode. But he would surely act to retrieve the *Herakles*.

Commander Brace spoke again. 'I have sufficient provisions only for my own men. What supplies and water do you carry?'

I answered. 'We are low on both, sir, unfortunately.'

'Your crew will be placed on half rations, sir. We shall make all speed to Malta. We should reach it within a week.'

We had begun our fast anyway. I tried to close my eyes and winced in pain.

'Take their details.' With that Commander Brace walked away.

An officer sat at a table on the deck, quill poised, scratching his armpit and yawning.

He barked at me. 'You. Are you Greek?'

'Né,' I said.

'Nay?' He frowned, crossed out Greek, and squinted up at me. 'Then where are you from?'

'Greece.'

He slammed his hand down on the book. 'So you are Greek?'

'Né.'

He stared at me, breathing hard. 'Nay, or yay?'

'Né. Yay.'

He rubbed his temples. 'God help me.' He shouted to another man. 'You ask him!'

A second officer leaned in. 'Are you Greek?'

'Né,' I said, nodding.

He threw up his hands and wrote 'Greek'.

'Bloody foreigners,' the first one muttered.

He turned to Damos. 'Name!'

Damos didn't blink. 'Frangiscos Mustachos.'

The officer looked up at our laughter, then scowled and tried to spell it. Damos twirled his moustache solemnly.

We were herded down the *Gannet*'s deck and shoved into a new timber enclosure next to the fifty Turks—packed in like sardines in a creel. The stench was appalling. Worse, we were told we'd be sharing a single head.

An officer and six men rowed to the *Herakles* to supervise the tow, and with a hawser joining the two ships, we were under way.

I overheard a couple of guards conversing. 'Two pirate ships in a week! We'll be rich!'

Panic surged through me. She was more than a ship; she was my ticket to freedom and the key to Maria's and my future. And she belonged to Dimitris.

—

The day stretched ahead, hot and uncomfortable. We would soon be as black and blistered as the Turkish prisoners. Late in the afternoon, when the *Gannet* hove to, we were given a sip of water. Meanwhile, the English tapped into a cask of spirits for their crew.

Lieutenant Carpenter approached the barricade and said to me, 'The captain invites you to join him for dinner, sir.'

Damos muttered. For a second, I considered refusing, but it presented an opportunity to learn more of our situation, negotiate better treatment in the coming days, and perhaps I could even recover Kostas' *bouzouki*—the confiscation had hit him hard. The *Theotókos* would surely understand if I delayed my fast.

Then I thought of wine, real food, and news. I stood. 'This will profit us all.'

'Or at least one of us,' said Damos drily.

Andonis, ever the peacemaker, stepped in. 'Enough, Damos. Trust Ghikas.'

I said, 'I would be delighted, sir.'

When I was seated in the captain's cabin, he poured us each a generous glass of brandy.

'I hope your father is in good health. Does your father know you are attacking friendly ships?' he asked.

'No, sir,' I answered. 'He forbids it.'

We discussed the situation on Hydra.

'My mission is to eradicate pirates,' he said. 'Like you.'

He didn't raise his voice—he didn't need to.

'We've a strong squadron of twenty-one in the Mediterranean; the Americans keep a presence of seven. Piracy will not go unpunished.'

Then, as if that topic were settled, he turned to Greek politics—naming provisional governments, leaders, testing me, measuring me.

We dined by candlelight, salted beef and vegetables, washed down with a French claret. We discussed the challenges facing Lord Cochrane as admiral of the Greek fleet. Commander Brace expressed admiration for our Admiral Miaoulis—surprised that the *Herakles* was out at sea when enemy attack could be imminent.

'I agree, sir. Yes, sir, we must make for home with all haste.'

'I am afraid not. If the Greek government can convince the governor that your actions were a legitimate act of war, they may release you. Otherwise, you will face trial in the Vice-Admiralty Court.'

'That will not happen,' I said.

He lifted his eyebrow, swallowed the wine in his glass, and set it on the table. 'Your age?'

'Almost twenty years, sir.'

He smiled again. 'Nineteen. We have something in common. We both come from families with a distinguished sailing history.'

I requested more water for the crew. He regretfully declined, citing the size of his own crew which numbered one hundred and twenty men. Neither could he increase our rations, and my request for the return of Kostas' *bouzouki* was denied. It too was a prize of war.

After two more glasses of brandy, the meal over, I rose to my feet, unsteady.

Commander Brace's flushed face turned serious. 'Boy, I must speak to you candidly. Because I respect your father.'

The room was spinning. I put my hand on the table for support.

Brace studied me, his wine glass turning slowly between his fingers. He was waiting, I realised, to see if I already knew what he was about to say.

I had no idea.

He cleared his throat. 'When you came aboard this afternoon, your primary concern was your family's ship. Not your men. You spoke over your captain. Showed no respect for his authority.'

A flush rose in my cheeks. He had misunderstood me.

Brace dabbed at his mouth, leaving a brown stain on the damask napkin. He leaned forward and twisted his wine glass between his fingers again. I struggled to focus.

'The value of the sun lies not in its height, but in its warmth.'

It took me a moment to understand. A surge of acid rose in my throat. My cheeks flamed. An Englishman, lecturing me on virtue, as if God himself had made him custodian of honour.

He thought me a boy to be schooled, not a man to be feared. I swallowed and forced a laugh.

'My father will see us freed, sir.'

I hoped it were true.

Brace smiled. 'I'm sure he will.'

I steadied myself—then turned and walked straight into the bulkhead.

19

ARNPRIOR

In Her Company

SYDNEY TO ARNPRIOR, New South Wales
August 1833

As we journey back to Arnprior with Mister Ryrie's third son Donald, Mary's initial rebuff of my friendship fades from my mind, displaced by the warm, soft weight tucked inside my shirt. I've called the pup Chara—pronounced 'hara', the Greek word for joy. She radiates heat, her puppy smell wafting up to my face—earthy, sweet, intoxicating.

My only experience with dogs until now has been the large savage kangaroo hounds chained at the back of the stables on Arnprior, eyes wild, snarling at the slightest movement.

'She's a handsome pup,' Donald says one evening, as we sit with our backs to a log, staring into the fire. 'But obedience is key to training a sheep dog. You must teach her to return to you, or you'll lose her in the bush.'

I bear total responsibility for this small life.

She perches on my boots while I take breakfast, a ball of fluff leaning back against my legs, surveying her world. I look down at her, a patchwork of black and white. She takes it all in before she moves off—every stick a potential plaything, every unfamiliar object, such as a saddle lying on the ground, a potential enemy to be outsmarted. When she hears my voice, she halts, a curious tilt to her head, her black eyes sparkling with trust, tiny tongue sticking out. Sometimes she rests her face on her paws, bottom in the air, ready to play. When she's startled, she scurries back to my lap, where I pull burrs and sticks from her coat.

'Brush her often,' Donald says, although he sees me do it each day. 'Bobtails feel the heat, so make sure she's clipped at shearing.'

Chara curls into the crook of my arm, nibbling delicately at the scraps I offer, her sharp little teeth grazing my fingers before her tongue smooths them clean. When her belly is full, she lets out a tiny sigh and drapes herself across my lap, warm against my ribs. I scratch behind her ears, and her body softens, moulding into me with perfect trust—as if she's always belonged there.

I enjoy placing the needs of another being before my own.

—

Back at Arnprior, training becomes part of our daily routine. Each morning, I attach a rope to her collar, and when I set her on the ground, we approach the sheep together. The ewes show their displeasure by stamping their feet at her. At first she's unperturbed, never dreaming she's causing this reaction. But when they advance on her, she's quick to seek reassurance, which reminds me of William's advice: 'You're spoiling that dog. When she jumps on you, do not pat her—that signals approval. If she misbehaves, you must go to her, instead of calling her to you. Her success as a sheep herder depends on you. She will be a big dog with a hearty appetite, and meat is precious.'

The threat in the words is clear.

My natural inclination is to show my affection, so this restraint feels unnatural, even cold. Yet, if this discipline is as necessary as William says, and he has the experience, I will embrace it. But I can't help wondering—is there no room to temper authority with a little more kindness?

It's a thought I keep to myself.

So when Chara looks to me, I hold back the instinct to stroke her.

Late one afternoon, as William and I finish penning the sheep, we hear the jingling of horses' harness. As a cloud of dust drifts through the gum trees and golden wattle on the ridge, he walks towards the homestead.

'This will be my father and Isabella returning from Sydney. Come. Unload the luggage.'

He constantly reminds me I am a servant. I push down a surge of resentment and follow.

Once the horses jostle to a stop in clouds of dust, the driver alights to attend to them. I place Chara back on the ground and move to untie the load. The boys tumble out, full of energy: first John, then Alexander, and last, little David. Mister Ryrie hands down his wife with his usual gentle concern, and she puts her hands to her back, stretching her chin upwards. The mail coach offers convenience but lacks comfort.

'Geeeeks,' Alexander yells. 'We have a surprise.'

I smile; the boys amuse me. They always have treasure from the road, or some absurd tale from Sydney.

William hands down young Jane, who smiles mysteriously.

And the boys are watching, hopping from foot to foot and giggling.

William extends his hand into the coach again. I glance at the door— expecting a guest.

A long skirt. A bonnet.

My breath catches.

It's Mary.

My heart leaps. I want to close the distance between us to hug her. Instead, I turn my attention to a knot in the rope, pretending to concentrate as my thoughts tumble over each other. The force of my reaction rattles me —what were these boundaries I imagined I'd drawn?

But she barely glances at me. A nod. No smile. Then she's gone, following the others inside.

I'm left with the bags—and a head full of confusion.

—

I do not see her until the following day—Sunday, our day of rest. I have rolled up my shirtsleeves to mend a gap in the bark of the hut wall. Chara is playing with a piece of bark as if it is alive, growling, throwing her head from side to side so vigorously she tips herself over. I'm laughing at her antics when I see Mary walking up the hill towards me, smiling, no bonnet, curls pulled back.

The world narrows to her, and I no longer hear the kookaburras, or Joe chopping wood.

I want to hoist her into the air.

She wears black kid slippers on her feet, totally unsuitable for the rough ground. Her stiff white apron starts at her throat and drops to her knees. No hint of the figure beneath except where she has tied the strings around her middle.

I dig my fingers into my palm. Chara runs to her and Mary picks her up, bringing the pup's face to her own, touching noses. This simple and unguarded interaction contrasts with the turmoil raging inside me.

'Oh, what a beautiful puppy!' Mary exclaims as Chara licks her chin.

I have quite forgotten the green of her eyes, the shine of her hair.

'You surprised me yesterday,' I manage to say. The neck of my shirt is too tight. I put my fingers inside the fabric and pull, stretch my neck upward and turn my head from side to side to loosen it.

She has tucked Chara under her arm and is simply looking at me, a smile on her lips.

'I thought you had a deep aversion to the country.' I roll down my sleeves.

She puts Chara down and answers with a hint of scorn. 'Not really,' she says, pushing her hands into the front pocket of her apron. 'I have a fierce aversion to being ordered about.'

'You should be a landowner's wife then, not a housemaid.'

She crosses her arms. 'And perhaps you should have been a rich man, not a convict?'

The tension breaks momentarily as I laugh. She turns her head and looks at me from the corner of her eye.

She appears to relent. 'Mrs Ryrie sounded a fine employer in her letter. Mrs Watt has deferred my employment for the time being. I may take up the position with her whenever I choose.' She puts her hands on her hips. 'So here I am. Thanks to your kindness in vouching for me.'

My head fills with questions about the emporium and Townsend's offer.

'Mrs Ryrie said you might be escorting me on a walk this afternoon. To show me around.'

'I'm busy.' Part of me wants her to feel a little of the confusion she's instilling in me.

She turns to go.

'But if Mrs Ryrie said I will do it, so I will.'

She turns back, and the dimples in her cheeks deepen.

I'm stunned. Her face is open, smiling, watching me. Her teeth are white.

I grunt. 'After the midday meal, then,' I say, regaining my composure. 'Meet me at the back of the homestead.'

She opens her mouth as if to respond, but she walks away, a bundle of contradictions wrapped in an apron.

Now I can't remember what I was doing.

—

After lunch, Mary is waiting for me with a tiny paper-wrapped parcel in her hand. 'This is for you.'

I'm intrigued. 'What is it?'

'Open it.'

Inside the paper is a small box. Inside that is a river pebble as big as a thumbnail, threaded on a leather cord. It has a hole in it, perhaps washed out by tides or currents. I place it in the palm of my hand.

'An Irish hagstone,' says Mary. 'Some call them fairy stones. Or druid's eggs. I bought this in a shop in Sydney—to replace your amulet. From this day forward, your luck will change, Ghika.'

I put my hand over my heart. 'It has, as of this moment. Thank you, Mary.'

My luck changed yesterday when you stepped out of the coach.

Superstitious as it is, I throw two fingers up against the evil eye, just in case, then slip it over my head, like impenetrable armour.

'I came because of something you said.' Mary kicks at a stone ahead of her as we walk towards the river. She wears the same ankle boots as at our first meeting, now scuffed and tattered.

'If you keep kicking your boots like that, you'll wear them clean through. You've almost done it already.'

'You said this is a wonderful, unknown country. I've come to see it for myself. And I'll leave when I've seen enough. So don't be dreaming that I've come to marry you.'

'I won't. I told you—I will return to Hydra to marry.'

'Excellent,' she says. 'We understand each other.'

I am relieved.

She smooths her skirt and tilts her chin, as if to set something straight. 'And you understand that I'll be going back to Sydney as soon as I've seen the countryside. This is a visit. Nothing more.'

'But you've only just arrived.' I am regarding her profile when she gasps.

'A snake,' she says.

I turn. In front of us, a water lizard is sunning itself. I step towards it.

'Ghika! Snake!' She grabs my arm.

I feel a surge of annoyance. 'No,' I say. 'A lizard. Surely you can see it has legs?'

It watches us with bright eyes. I take another step forward and it springs to life, scurrying away towards the river.

'Faith and begorrah, Ghika! Were you seeing that now? That lizard ran away like a person! On its hind legs!'

She claps her hands, her fear turned to laughter. Any annoyance I feel dissolves like the morning mist on the river.

I'm captivated.

—

I discover that Mary has a routine. After completing her duties each day, she sits under the colossal gum tree on the ridge near the house, legs stretched out in front of her. Chara and I begin to detour to join her. The gum's towering presence dwarfs us, casting a majestic shadow as the days lengthen and the sun sets behind the tree, its light colouring the river flat below. Finding her there each day lightens my heart like a summer song; she is part of the landscape.

But she said she would only stay a month, didn't she? It has already been three weeks.

Sometimes, I sit with her and chat. Sometimes, we walk in companionable silence. She shares details of her day, and I reciprocate with stories from mine.

Her sense of humour never fails to elicit laughter from me.

One evening she opens her hand to show me a button. Smaller than a threepence—a circle of mother-of-pearl, with a brass shank shining from years of being turned between her fingers. She keeps it wrapped in a scrap of linen, as if it might vanish. She says she was found with it sewn into her swaddling clothes. Mothers did that, she tells me, so they could know their babes again if ever they came back.

She still has it—her only link to the woman who left her—her greatest treasure.

About her past, she's guarded, offering only glimpses of the dark orphanage—a grim, airless place. She also speaks of Cork's misty streets, where people endure constant dampness, sleep beside pigs, throw nightsoil from their windows and suffer empty bellies. Where even in summer, you might never feel the sun. I encourage her to talk, but do not press her.

'The sun is so hot here,' she says. 'And the shade has holes in it.'

I tell her that on Hydra, even fewer trees grow, with less shade.

'I'm glad I never have to go there. That will be why your skin is so dark,' she offers.

She tells me again she thought she had found a family once. Her employer, Mister Jenkins in Ireland, said she was like a daughter to him. Then one day, he packed up and took his real daughter back to England for her education, gave Mary two guineas, and that was that.

'Two guineas for two years. A grand price, don't you think?' She says it as if it's a trifle, but she makes a fuss of sweeping an ant off her skirt.

I see the hurt.

I almost say it—two guineas is a handsome amount. But something in her face stops me.

What else can I say? That not everyone abandons those who love them? I can't. That would only remind her of her parents.

I simply say, 'I'm sorry.' I nearly tell her about Hydra. About the night that split Andonis and me. But what would be the point? She'd just ask

what happened, and I'd choke on the truth—not because it didn't hurt—
it did.

We have no chaperone, and we're visible from the house, so I keep my
distance.

'When will you invite me to see inside your hut?' she says.

'Never. It would be improper.'

'Why?'

'As I said. It's a matter of propriety.'

'Pooh to propriety. I'd rather think for myself.'

'Propriety matters.'

She laughs, but I don't move. Not because I don't want to—but
because I do.

We sit there, neither of us speaking, and I think of all the things I can't
offer her, even if I wanted to.

Five and a half years have passed since my trial—I've had four of them
at Arnprior—long enough for men like the Ryries to make a fortune. Like
the shipowners at home, they are the *prokriti,* the privileged few. And if I
were English, I'd be doing the same: being a friend of the governor, lining
up for my share of land grants and grazing licences. I've heard Bourke
insists the land be bought now—not given. Fair enough. But who can
afford to buy? The same men who would once have been gifted it. It's still
the same game—with new rules.

In New South Wales, you're either free—or you came in chains. Even
when your sentence is served, they call you an 'emancipist'. Forgiven by
law, but never by the men who matter. If the 'exclusives' don't like you,
they'll call you worse—an 'objectionable'. Not for what you did. For who
you were.

'It's a land of opportunity for men of action,' William often says.
'Those brave enough to take the land now will be well-situated for licences
when they're issued. In the meantime, we will shear more sheep for the
English market.'

He's right, of course, but being a man of action isn't the entire story.
Money and influence matter more. I can't help wondering, though, if there
is any end to this quest for wealth? When does a man say enough? Or is
the search for more land, more sheep, like being on a never-ending treadmill? Stop moving and you fall?

One afternoon, in the shade of the gum tree, I tell Mary of my father's expectation that a son should mirror his father—be his equal or his superior, in honour and prosperity. I confess that my failures so affronted my father that he disowned me, and now, I am driven to return to Hydra to restore my worth in his eyes.

'I'm sure your father loves you, whatever your failings.'

'Which are many?' I ask her, laughing.

I tell her about the societal restrictions on women on Hydra. How marriages are arranged, how the women of our house never venture down to the port, nor would they ever engage in any form of business. How they cover their hair with scarves, not bonnets.

'You will not choose your own wife?'

I want to defend our customs, yet I struggle to articulate a response that bridges our worlds.

'We Greeks trust the judgment of our parents. Marriage is more about business. About joining families.'

She frowns. 'Business? It's not about love?'

'Marriages based solely on love are likely to fail.'

'You are an obedient son,' she observes thoughtfully.

'My father didn't think so. But it is the wife who must be obedient.'

She laughs. 'Being a Greek wife sounds suffocating!'

She watches my face now, and our laughter fades. As if she's pulled back ever so slightly, quietly marking the line between us.

Mary and I are like two parallel lines, close but never meeting, shaped by the geometry of our differing origins.

'What do you want from life, Mary?' I ask her one day.

'A place of my own, Ghika. That no one can take away from me.'

I nod. 'Well, you've seen now what the country is like. Cleaner. Safer. Better than the filth of Sydney. Would you not make a home here?'

A kookaburra laughs in the tree above us.

She's silent.

'If you give it time, I think you'll see that Arnprior is the right choice.'

She picks up a twig and snaps it clean in two. 'Sure and didn't I tell you I am only visiting?' She watches me too long.

I watch her hands brush the snapped twig from her skirt. I don't say it, but I want her to stop calling this a visit. 'Yes, you did. But maybe in time you'll feel a sense of belonging.'

'Mister Jenkins knew what was best for me too. He made me believe I belonged at Clover Hill. Right up until the day he packed up and went back to England.'

I think about that.

'Have you decided you'll marry?' I ask, to ease the tension.

'No. Not a bit of it. Never. I'll not be trusting a man.'

'You trust me.'

'Only so far.'

To shift the conversation, I mention Laskarina Bouboulina, a Greek heroine.

'Booboo who?'

'Bouboulina. She was born in a Constantinople prison when her mother was visiting her dying father, a political prisoner.

She and her mother lived on Hydra but moved to Spetses when she was a child. When she grew up, she widowed twice by Barbary pirates, and took over her husband's fleet of ships, and prospered.'

'She prospered without a husband? I admire her already.'

'Yes, she was a man's equal—with a fleet of eight ships. When war came in 1821, she was actually the first shipowner to declare her support, while the other islands were dithering. She built a huge warship called the Agamemnon, eighteen guns, named after the leader of the Greek forces in the Battle of Troy. She was its captain and fought as bravely as any man.'

'How magnificent.'

'But then one of her sons eloped.'

'Eloped? How scandalous! I thought your marriages were arranged?'

'They are. The girl was already betrothed to a rich man, and her brothers, while pursuing the pair, shot Bouboulina dead.'

'Oh no! That's so sad!'

'Yes. You resemble her in your pig-headed determination.'

'But you said she married. I will trust no one with my heart. Ever.'

She says it plainly. Not bitter—certain.

'That's very sad too,' I say.

It's clear to both of us that our views on life, love, and duty are worlds apart.

She says nothing more. She stands, brushes off her skirts, and walks back toward the house. The next day, she's polite but distant. That afternoon, she doesn't come to the tree. Joe mentions that Biddy—the maid working for a visiting family from Scotland—has taken to Mary. He said the two of them were out in the garden, laughing over something after supper.

The following day, I pass her near the cow-milking bale. She waves, but doesn't stop.

I tell myself it's nothing.

I've been busy. So has she.

But Chara waits for her under the tree anyway.

—

One day, when I am looking out over the crops, Mary surprises me. 'Mrs Ryrie's maid mentioned a man called Earnest Bartholomew today. Did you know him?'

The name catches me off guard. 'Bartholomew?' I walk along the ridge, masking my surprise.

Mary trots alongside. 'Yes, she's glad he's gone. She said he's a villain.'

I will not speak ill of the man, but I will not praise him either. 'Hardly a villain. When William discharged him, he blamed me, and threatened to come back to even the score.'

She gasps. 'No! They've arrested him in Goulburn for brawling in the street. He's in the gaol.'

'He loves his children. I pray someone is caring for them.'

'Children?' Distress clouds her face. 'He has children?' She places her hand on her chest. 'Oh Ghika, it is always the little ones who suffer. What if their mother is sick, or with child, or cannot work? The poor little mites could be placed in an orphanage.' Doubt flickers in her eyes. 'I was one of those, once. I still remember the cold.' She looks up at me. 'No child deserves that. None. I pray someone is looking after them. But will he come back for revenge?'

'I think not. Cowards like him are all bluster and no backbone.'

Mary watches me. Then she draws three shapes in the dirt with a stick, joining them at their tips. Three love hearts.

'An Irish shamrock for good luck,' she says brightly.

I pretend interest in the crop below to hide my relief.

—

Chara and I are working the sheep when a thunderstorm rolls in, boiling black clouds marching across the sky. There's a flash of lightning, followed by a loud clap of thunder, and the sheep scatter in panic. I'm working swiftly to gather the flock, but suddenly I realise Chara is missing. The storm drowns out my calls. Through the rain, I catch sight of her, cowering under a bush. The sheep demand my attention, but I make my way over to her, rain blinding me, soaking my clothes.

'Here, Chara!' I say, but she refuses to come. At another crack of lightning, her eyes open wide with fear. I kneel, my hand instinctively stroking her fur. 'You're safe, girl,' I murmur.

She snuggles into me, shivering in fright, and we remain huddled together, the world reduced to the rhythm of falling rain. After a while, I rise, and with Chara at my heels, we return to gathering the sheep.

Sometimes compassion must overtake discipline.

—

Mary catches a chill and is confined to her bed in the maids' quarters. Concerned about her health, I visit the back of the homestead daily for updates.

Mrs Ryrie emerges one afternoon while I wait. 'Don't fret, Ghikas. She'll recover.'

Fret? A silly term. I am merely interested in the girl's well-being.

'It's her breathing,' Mrs Ryrie adds.

'Thank you, Mrs Ryrie, for being a caring sheila.'

Mrs Ryrie erupts into laughter, and I am not sure why.

That day, I pick the most pungent bush herbs I can find for a tussie-mussie, as my mother used to do. In the hope it might ease Mary's breathing, I leave it at the house.

Days later, she reappears underneath the gum tree. My heart races as she extends her hand.

'Thank you Ghika, for your thoughtfulness,' she says. 'The flowers were pretty.'

'They weren't supposed to be pretty. They were supposed to help you breathe.'

She takes my hand in hers, palm up, and lays her fingers on top of mine. They're small, finely formed, her wrist delicate, small half-moons at the base of her fingernails. Mine is black from the sun, dry and rough. On one finger, a line of blood has dried along the edge of a jagged cut. My stomach flips.

She looks up quickly. 'What is it? You've gone pale.'

'Nothing.'

'It's just a scratch.'

'Best you don't show me,' I say, forcing a smile.

'You don't like the sight of blood?'

'Not much.'

'Why?'

'Another time.'

For a moment she studies me, head tilted, as if she might press the question. Then she lets it go. Her fingers trace the line of calluses below my knuckles. I have been using the axe this week, and she touches a fresh blister. Covers it as if to heal it.

Her breath is warm on my palm.

'You have beautiful hands,' she says, still looking down. 'And you work so hard.'

I look at the top of her head, inhaling her smell. For a moment, I'm on the brink of pulling her close to me. These feelings are familiar, but intense and inappropriate, and certainly not brotherly.

She looks up at me, her eyes unguarded, expectant. Her gaze lingers on my face. 'How did you break your nose?' she says at last, smiling. 'It suits you.'

I have no intention of telling her about the York.

'It's my father's. And my grandfather's.' I almost laugh. 'My mother used to call it the noble Voulgaris nose.'

I have that same melting feeling I had on the picnic. If I lowered my head and stretched my neck forward, our lips would touch. As delicate as a butterfly's wing. I imagine the softness of her lips—imagine us breathing together.

My pulse flutters while I try to summon coherence to my thoughts. The urge to kiss her is overwhelming.

What did she say? Oh yes. How hard I work.

I pull my hand away.

'I have to go.'

—

Late one Sunday afternoon, with my chores done, I am working on a box for Mary, inspired by my yiayia's. I've used cedar offcuts from the Arnprior homestead, with William's permission. Each evening, by the glow of candlelight or scarce lamp oil, I've shaped it using Damos' dovetail techniques and the special chisel they used for the Scottish thistle design on the architrave of the homestead's front door.

The lid fits snugly, and I plan to carve into it Mary's intertwined initials, M and L for Mary Lyons. I will rub it with beeswax for protection.

It pleases me, doing something useful for her.

Since the day I first wanted to kiss her, I've thought hard about our friendship. I would never take advantage of any woman—least of all Mary. And there is one immutable truth: I will go home to marry. My affection is purely protective—I will guide her, protect her, see her safe and settled. In time she may see that marriage offers the security she deserves. I hope for an advantageous match for her—though where, in all New South Wales, she might find such a man, I do not know.

And if I feel a hollow pang when I imagine that, well, I'm fond of her.

But anyway—friendship is what she needs. Not entanglement.

Suddenly, she appears around the side of the hut. I've told her not to come here, for fear of her reputation. But she won't listen. And I don't want her to see the box until it is finished.

It's too late.

She flops onto the bench beside me.

'Don't start, Ghika. Biddy already warned me you'd twitch about wagging tongues.' She adds, 'You and your sense of propriety.' She's flushed from walking, curls loose, breath short. 'I've been stitching till my eyes blurred. I needed air.'

I rub my eyes. It's been a long day, for I have dug two new beds in the convict garden and it was hard work, for the soil was compacted.

'Ghika! You made that? It's beautiful.'

'A trifle. It's for your treasures, that button you showed me. I will carve your initials in the lid. ML for Mary Lyons.'

Her mouth opens—you'd think it was covered in jewels.

'Use it for whatever you fancy.'

For a moment she doesn't speak, her hands held together in front of her chest. She bites her lip.

She says softly, 'For me?' Her voice catches. 'No one's ever made anything for me before.'

I can feel it—what I've been holding at bay. It rises like a tide, the ache of wanting to hold her.

Her fingers hover, as if afraid to touch it. Then, slowly, she picks it up, traces the smooth edges, as if committing them to memory.

The sight of her unshed tears unravels me. I want to promise her something.

I tell myself again, friendship. Not entanglement.

She holds the box to her chest for a moment, then stands.

I want to ask her to stay a while.

'I promised I'd help Biddy tonight,' she says, not quite meeting my eye. 'She's hopeless with stitching.'

She hands it back, then she's gone.

I sit in the dim light with Chara's head on my foot.

She'll be back tomorrow.

20

MALTA

Castellania

ON BOARD HMS *Gannet* en route to Malta
August 1827

On the deck of the *Gannet*, I lay sleepless beneath a moon bright enough to read a map, the planks hard against my back. Salt in my nose, pitch in my hair, a bruise thudding above my eye.

Every breath reinforced the weight of my failure. I had not protected my men. I had not led them.

I kept reliving the arrest aboard the *Herakles*—Carpenter's orders, their boots on the deck, Nikos' hand going to his belt. The look on the men's faces when they realised we were lost.

I had to inform my father. I could already hear him grumbling about the expense of a court case. 'The only people who gain from the law,' he always said, 'are lawyers.'

The waves against the hull eventually lulled me, and I was almost asleep when I heard voices close by. 'Thinks he's quite the gentleman, that Greek, the barbarian,' said one. 'I'd like to teach him a few manners.'

Barbarian? I'd like to suggest he bathe.

A sudden commotion at the stern jolted me properly awake. Lamps swung wildly. Voices raised in alarm. Men running.

Something was wrong with the *Herakles.*

I sprang up. She'd slewed way off course astern of the *Gannet*—so far out that I could see her.

Panayiá mou. Had the tow hawser snapped? Was she adrift?

No. It was worse.

The rest of the men were on their feet now, Andonis beside me. The Turks too—all watching.

In the hard white moonlight, I could see that they'd fixed the tow hawser too low, could see the bobstay hanging loose, the iron brace wrenched away—and a raw, splintered gap in the bow where it had been.

'The bobstay is gone,' I whispered. 'The whole rig will come down.'

The *Herakles* groaned. The masts shivered—one tilting, holding for a second—then a long, low creak. Slowly, inexorably, they leaned, and then they fell. First one, then the other, each like the Colossus of Rhodes—monumental, and as tragic. A thunder of timber and canvas crashed to the deck.

My throat closed. I couldn't get a breath.

This didn't have to happen. An English crew—with all their training, all their arrogance—so sure of themselves. They'd boast of seamanship to the gods, but couldn't even tie a hawser. All their pride, and they'd splintered her.

Brace was shouting orders to cut the lines, clear the mess. Within the hour, nothing but the stripped hull remained, sails and rigging cut away, drifting backward on the moonlit sea.

The *Herakles* was a bare silhouette.

As the sailors checked the hatches, Andonis put his arm around my shoulder. I couldn't move.

Brace didn't look at me. I was glad of it. I had to stomach his men's stupidity, but I could not bear his pity.

———

The promontory of Valletta shone golden in the sun, the square outlines of its stone buildings crouched on the headland, formidable battlements rising a hundred feet from the waterline. Having sailed these waters on my father's ships, I knew the baroque palaces, the endless limestone steps, and the curious wooden balconies where the town's women hid behind shutters.

Now it glowered like a place of judgment, unyielding, unforgiving.

We anchored in the smaller western harbour, near the Manoel Island quarantine station, the Lazaretto building almost as grand as the Doge's palace in Venice.

I wrote to my father.

My dear father,

Recent events compel me to write without delay.

Our schooner Herakles intercepted the Maltese brig Alceste, laden with stores for the enemy at Alexandria, and was thereafter detained by H.M. sloop Gannet, under Commander Francis Brace, on a charge of piracy.

While under tow for Malta—and owing to a badly secured English tow-hawser—Herakles lost both masts and her rigging.

We are ordered to twenty-five days' quarantine. Your kind intervention may secure our earlier release and permit our repatriation. I entreat you to intercede with the Governor of Malta for the restoration of the ship, and to remit funds for her immediate repair.

I shall make good my debt to Dimitris and his partners from the proceeds of the cargo—and any other debt I owe.

I await your instructions.

Pray assure Mamá of my well-being.

Your obedient son,

Ghikas

I left unsaid that Brace had held the rank of commander before Malta; our capture had procured his advancement to captain.

—

Valletta
September 1827

In early September, with skin flaking off our feet and clothing in rags, the guards manacled us for transfer to Malta's Great Harbour.

As we sailed past the landmark cliffs on the eastern headland, the ferry pilot pointed a finger. 'That's Fort St Elmo, and that's Fort Ricasoli atop Gallows Point.'

On the cliff above us, an iron cage hung from chains. Skeletons swayed inside, trousers flapping as they danced a gruesome jig in the wind.

'That's what we do to pirates around here,' he shouted.

'Does he know we are pirates, Ghika?' Nikos asked, casting nervous glances back at the cage.

Our destination was the Castellania Gaol, a damp subterranean pit beneath the Law Courts in Valletta, originally a palace built by the Knights of Saint John. The head of the guard bashed on a studded wooden door on the side street and it creaked open. I dragged my elbow down the stone wall, eyes struggling to adjust to the darkness as the underground cells swallowed us whole, the heavy doors sealing our fate with a resounding clang.

The next morning, after a night in the airless cell, breathing mould and rotting straw, we met our doleful advocate, a tall, thin man with a sharp beard and red-veined cheeks. A translator accompanied him.

'Doctor Francesco Maria Torregiani, Advocate for the Poor.'

I said, 'Poor? There must be some mistake.'

Damos gave a short bark of laughter.

Nikos nodded solemnly. 'Yes, Ghika. We are poor.'

Clearly, money did the talking here. I had to convince him I was born to it.

'Excuse me, sir. My father is Nikolaos Voulgaris, shipowner of Hydra. What of the funds he has sent for our defence?'

He responded dryly, 'I have heard of no funds. I will proceed as instructed. Your case, such as it is, rests entirely on goodwill.'

He doubted my word. I straightened. 'What is the charge?'

He pursed his superior lips. 'You stand accused of piracy. Sir Edward Codrington is determined to make an example of you.'

So that was it—a public spectacle. We were to be the lesson.

'The merchants' associations and our insurance companies cannot continue to tolerate the losses caused by Greek plundering. The prices of

Maltese goods are depressed because your countrymen are flooding the market at absurdly low prices.'

And the Maltese were buying the same goods at auction.

'Not one of a hundred Greek pirates held in our gaols this year has been convicted.'

Of course not. Conviction required proof.

'Sailors like you are said to be boasting that English ships are easy prey.' He looked from one of us to the other. 'If found guilty, you will hang.'

Nikos made a choking sound—doubtless recalling the pirates hanging on the cliff face. I kept my eyes on the advocate.

He relented. 'But I am hopeful of a merciful decision.'

'We seek no mercy, sir,' I said firmly. 'Only acquittal for the forty-three of us is acceptable.' Now was not the time to yield or betray any hint of weakness. 'We are *palikaria*. Freedom fighters. If you are incapable of mounting a proper defence, we will seek another lawyer. We will not hang for your incompetence.'

When he left the cell, Damos spat out, 'Ghika, your stupidity may well have done for us. How do you plan to engage a lawyer? With your charm and a list of your ancestors?'

'We are *palikaria*, Damo. If this barrister cannot see that, we must find someone who can.'

'Ghika speaks from passion, Damo,' said Andonis. Then to me, quieter, 'But we must tread carefully.'

'Caution won't see us released,' I said.

Three days later, at ten o'clock, we stumbled into glaring daylight like newborn rats, squinting, shuffling, shackled. First, they herded us across the courtyard into the dark chapel. No tapestries, no icons, a bare rail, a chipped altar, and a lonely cross. We were granted a moment of prayer.

Afterward, we were marched into the main courtyard for identification.

'Do you think they will recognise us?' said Kostas.

I didn't answer. Instead, I crossed my eyes, sucked in my cheeks, and pulled a face so grotesque that Nikos gasped. The tension shattered. Laughter burst out—short, sharp, too loud. Damos, always the showman, threw his arms wide and bowed like a drunk bishop. Nikos pushed out his tongue and twisted his arms around his tilted head. Even the guards laughed.

Then the laughter died. The official party had entered.

A man in flowing black silk robes led them all with an air of authority that extinguished my smile in an instant. A guard whispered who he was—Sir John Stoddart, Chief Justice. At his side, Governor Ponsonby, Waterloo hero, his arm bound in a black sling like a mourning flag.

Behind him, a fourth man stepped forward—the captain of the *Alceste*.

The boys around me stiffened. Andonis went rigid.

That was it, then. The man we'd robbed stood five paces away, coat buttoned tight, mouth set like a blade.

A guard shoved Andonis into the centre of the quadrangle.

Captain Mallia pointed. 'Yes. That's the captain.'

One by one, his crew nodded.

Then it was the turn of all forty-three of us, pushed forward one by one.

They identified seven of us.

Andonis. Damos. Kostas. Nikos. The two younger sailors, Pietros Lalahos, and Pietros Bouff. The boy who'd worried his mother would be short of food.

And me.

'Bring them to my office,' said the governor.

In the upstairs room of the justice building, Lieutenant-Governor Ponsonby lifted the dead weight of his arm onto the gleaming desk. His precise English accent could have cut glass. The interpreter translated his words into Greek.

'Piracy is a serious charge. Vice-Admiral Codrington is in Greek waters now, aboard the Asia, preparing to defend your country. He fights for Greece.'

His eyes locked on mine, cold and unblinking.

Codrington fights for England, I thought, and he will invoice the Greek government later.

'His true adversary, however, is not the Turks or Egyptians. But you. Greek pirates.'

'Excuse me, sir. We are *palikaria*,' I said.

He gave me a cursory glance.

'Your advocate, Doctor Torregiani, is from an old, prestigious Maltese family. Respected within the legal fraternity of this island and throughout the wider community over many generations.' His voice dripped with condescension. 'You are fortunate indeed he will represent you *pro bono*. I understand you are from the island of Hydra?'

The others nodded.

'One of you is the son of a shipowner?' His eyes swept over the group, then dropped to the paper before him. 'Voulgaris?'

At last. My moment to be useful. 'Yes, sir. Ghikas Voulgaris, Son of Nikolaos.'

His eyes betrayed no hint of warmth. 'Ah, the same man who desires better representation. Your friends are ordinary seamen. Their deprived circumstances offer some excuse. But your participation, when you represent a ruling family, leads me to think that the leaders of Hydra have no respect for our alliance. On the contrary, they demonstrate contempt for our friendship. You, sir,' his gaze returned to me, 'and your captain, and your men, are to be made an example.'

An example. Perfect.

So much for my family name opening doors.

'You know, I imagine, that the penalty for piracy is death.'

At least it wasn't a fine. My father hated fines. The absurdity of the thought almost made me laugh—and I did, a short, involuntary snort.

The governor looked up, disapproving. As if I found the notion of a death sentence amusing.

I continued, 'Sir, we meant—'

I was about to explain that we meant no disrespect by our laughter in the courtyard, but Ponsonby silenced me with his hand.

Later, outside, Damos said, 'Why did you laugh in there, Ghika? Were it not for you, we would not be in this quagmire. You've done enough. Let someone else speak.'

Nikos opened his mouth. He would defend me.

'I saw a dead rat in the corridor,' he said.

'Enough, Damo,' Andonis said. Then, to me, quieter, 'Ghika, your father's name won't fix this. Stop acting as if it will.'

It always had before.

—

I continued to tell the others not to worry. My father would fix it.

But we'd attacked a friendly ship. Would the Hydra Council risk intervention? Would they protect us when the English had made it clear we must stop piracy on their shipping?

Then I remembered Spyridon Trikoupis. My father knew him—Greek envoy to the Court of Saint James in London. If anyone could intervene, he could.

But I could picture it too clearly: *Kyrios* Manolis, *Kyrios* Stromboulis —all the boys' fathers—standing in the cathedral quadrangle.

'Without the son of Nikolaos, none of this would have happened,' they'd say.

And my father, listening. Bearing it. Swallowing it.

Winter slid through the walls, the chill clawing at my bones as I memorised every inch of the narrow, dark cell. After two months, every crack in the limestone was an intimate companion. My cough echoed across the high arched ceiling, a deep rattle which wouldn't leave me. The suffering of my four friends was etched on their faces, and they held me responsible.

We passed the hours hunched over the *tríliza* we'd scratched into the stone—a strategic sailors' game of lines and crosses, played with pieces of rock Nikos chipped from the wall. I took a savage pleasure in beating Damos, though I let Nikos win enough to keep him happy.

'Who ate my share of the cake?' He asked continually.

There was no cake. There had never been cake.

A small, barred window sat high in the wall, opening onto the street above where the hill sloped up to the cathedral and down to the harbour. We watched boots go up and down, the world moving on without us.

It was Kostas who first heard the muffled English voices above talking about the war.

'Listen,' he said.

We crowded round, straining to hear.

Snatches drifted down: 'Navarino—Turks fired the first shot— Codrington fired back—Turkish fleet in flames—sunk.'

'They're drunk,' said Damos, but he didn't move from the wall.

More footsteps. Laughter. A second voice, clearer.

'Codrington and the Frenchman, de Rigny. The Russians too. The Turks and the Egyptians are finished.'

Then: 'Whole bloody armada gone before it could reach Hydra.'

Andonis gripped my shoulders.

'Is the war over?' Nikos said.

Kostas crossed himself.

None of us spoke. For a long time, we listened.

We'd had no news from home. Given the biggest news for years by a sailor pissing against a wall.

But if it were true—if the Turkish and Egyptian fleets were gone—then Hydra had been spared. The war on the mainland must turn too.

And all I could think was, Greece might soon be free. But would it change anything for us?

Or were we already history?

—

Valletta, December 1827

On a freezing day in December, the door of our cell creaked open. Our gaoler held a thick vellum packet.

'An envelope from Hydra,' he announced as he distributed the letters.

One for each of the others. Two for me.

I wanted to tear mine open. But Kostas was slapping his envelope on his hand, Nikos bouncing on the balls of his feet.

We sat on the floor. I read for Nikos while Andonis read for Kostas. Damos could read his own.

Nikos' father was angry over his son's decision to join the *Herakles*. His mother missed him. Nikos beamed and held the letter to his chest. Kostas' letter written by his sister in a careful hand, spoke of a sick cat. Andonis read it for him twice.

Then I opened mine.

Cousin,

News has reached Hydra of your arrest for piracy and damage to the

Herakles. I demand the return of my ship, and when you communicate its release, I will arrange credit with a Maltese ship builder for repairs.

We will discuss repayment on your return.

Should the English courts find you guilty, resulting in the loss of my ship, I will seek compensation from your father.

Dimitris Voulgaris

No more than I expected. Counting coins before people.

Andonis looked up from his letter. 'Ghika, Persephone says she misses playing knucklebones with you.'

The second letter. I checked the signature. My older half-brother, Giorgios.

Dear Ghika,

Your continued confinement grieves us all. My heart longs to visit, but the unrest at home makes it impossible.

On a brighter note, the Turkish and Egyptian navies were destroyed at Navarino before they could attack Hydra. The war at sea is over.

It sorrows me greatly that you read in a letter what I must tell you next.

Your mother has died in childbirth. The baby girl survived, and your father has named her Xanthe in your mother's memory.

The words didn't make sense.

Mitéra had died.

I read them again. And again.

Mamá was dead.

She had died.

I hadn't been there.

I hadn't said goodbye.

She would have known I took the *Herakles*.

My ribs ached with the effort of breathing.

I pressed my hand to the stone floor, trying to steady myself.

The paper crumpled in my hand. I stumbled to the door and struck it hard with my fist.

'I have to go home,' I said. No one answered.

A hand touched my shoulder. Andonis.

I shook my head. *Not now.*

I turned my back to the door and slid to the floor, gesturing for him to give me a moment alone. Everything tilted, as if the floor had shifted.

Did childbirth kill her? Or did I?

When I could see again, I smoothed out the paper.

Our father is to marry Aunt Anezo in January.

With my mother barely cold.

Maria Kountouriotis is betrothed to our cousin Dimitris.

Of course. Sold to the highest bidder. Dimitris.

The next words blurred. I had to steady the page and force myself to focus.

Our father has settled your gambling debt. He asks me to inform you that taking the Herakles without permission brought disgrace and division upon the family. Regardless of the court's decision, you are no longer his son.

I read that sentence again. He had paid the debt. The debt I still intended to repay. But erased me.

And a daughter had taken my place. Xanthe. I might never meet her.

.   .   .

However, dear brother, your siblings pray for your swift repatriation to Ýdra, and wait eagerly for your return.

I remain your devoted brother,
Giorgios

I folded the letter. Slowly. Carefully. As if by handling it gently I could keep something intact.

Some time passed before I heard Kostas ask, 'What's wrong, Andoni?'

I could hardly hear the whispered reply, 'Anastasia has married a ship's captain.'

I stood, pulled Andonis to his feet, embraced him. 'I'm sorry, Andoni. About everything.'

We stood together in silence until he murmured, 'It's not your fault, Ghika.'

I nodded, once.

I had no family name left.

—

Valletta—Friday 28 December 1827, late afternoon
The cell was bitterly cold, our breath smudged in the half-light. I was halfway through re-reading my brother's letter when a single boom reverberated through the walls and lifted the paper in my hands. On the stool beneath the high, barred window, Nikos steadied himself.

Another report followed, then a third—measured, answering. I listened to the intervals.

'Not time guns,' I said. 'They're salutes—fort to fort.'

The volleys went round the harbours until dust fell from the stones.

—

Valletta—Saturday 29 December 1827, morning
The turnkey came by with the pail.

'What caused the salutes yesterday?' I asked.

'HMS Warspite has come in,' he said. 'Bringing a Greek count on board—Kapod—Kapodistrias—he's here to see Admiral Codrington.'

The door closed on the draught.

Kapodistrias.

The man the Assembly at Troezen had elected Governor in April. For months we'd been waiting to see if he would come to Greece at all.

Now he was here—in Malta.

A Greek ship. A Greek envoy. To speak to Codrington.

No doubt he was here to thank the Admiral for Navarino. And surely they must discuss Greek piracy.

And us, surely.

Our names, our case. Maybe the count had come to insist that men who fought for Greece could not rot in an English prison.

For the first time in months, something moved in my chest that felt like hope.

To hear his name in the cell felt like a key turning in the lock.

—

Valletta—Monday 31 December 1827, afternoon

Boots sounded on the flags; a key scraped; the door swung wide.

'Collect your bundles,' the turnkey said. 'Release orders from the Admiral—the Greek count has spoken for you. You're going home.'

For a heartbeat, no one moved. Then everything—talk, movement, breath—burst loose at once. We scrambled to our feet.

Another guard shouldered in behind him. 'Not this cell,' he said, jerking his chin at us. 'These nine remain. They boarded the Alceste,' he added. 'Identified.'

The door slammed shut.

We kept our bundles on our knees, until the last footsteps faded.

Later we learned that the other thirty-four of our crew went home aboard HMS Warspite with Kapodistrias—Codrington's nod to mercy.

A fine story for his dinner table. Proof of his English fairness.

—

Hope was a dangerous thing; when it left, the cell felt emptier than before.

One hundred and seventy days since our arrest, the guards marched us to the judicial building.

Doctor Torregiani was waiting.

'In Malta,' he said, making a steeple of his fingers, 'a jury system, but only for piracy trials, was introduced in 1815. *De Medietate Linguae.*'

He said it like a gift. We stared at him.

'It means half the jurors will be foreigners—men with no ties to the merchants or the English Crown. No requirement of land. Or profession. Or wealth.'

He looked pleased with himself.

Damos said, 'What does that mean for us?'

Torregiani spread his hands.

'It means you will be judged as men, not Greek pirates.'

21

The Fracture

ARNPRIOR AND MANEROO, New South Wales
December 1833—July 1834

One afternoon, Ned comes looking for me in the sheep yards. 'You and me, lad, we are to go south with William for a couple of months. To the Coolaringdon run, to young Donald and Stewart. On Maneroo. We will take a mob of sheep and a dray load of timber for his house, and fetch back wool.'

I've been wanting to visit those famous vast treeless plains of Maneroo.

Later, at the gum tree, I hesitate before speaking. There is something in the way Mary looks at me, expectant, as if she is waiting for something more than I have come to say. But I push that thought aside.

I ask her if she will care for Chara while I'm away.

'To be sure I will. And how long will you be going away? And what if Bartholomew shows his face?'

She has settled at Arnprior almost as if she were born in the bush, but she has developed a real obsession about the man.

'A couple of months, I expect. And don't worry about Bartholomew.'

She folds her arms. 'Who said I was worried?'

The day before we leave, I find a bunch of wildflowers in a mug on the makeshift table in the hut. I've told Mary about staying away from the convict huts. She has no sense.

Joe looks at me and rolls his eyes. 'Your girl left you a love token, Ghika.'

'She's not my girl,' I say, more sharply than I intend. 'And whose mug is that?'

I stomp out, and Joe follows me, whining. 'She must have brought it. I didn't thieve it.'

When I lift my eyebrow, he goes red, and then he grins. Whoever owns it will come for it—everyone knows about Joe's pilfering. Just as well he's loveable.

—

Mary puts her index finger in the corner of one eye and says, 'Chara will be fine. You'd better hurry.' She squeezes her eyes shut. 'I have an eyelash in here. Will you take a look before you go?'

She comes close. I retreat a step, lean my head back a little and squint. 'There's nothing in it.'

Her eyes close tighter still. 'Look properly.'

My pulse betrays me—my fingers tremble. She tilts her face up, lashes fluttering, and something closes in around us. I use my thumb and forefinger to hold her eye open. Her head is still, and her other eye is staring at me. It's making me giddy, how the volume of air between us changes with each breath she takes. I want to remove all of it.

I rock on my heels.

The distance I have carefully maintained shrinks to nothing. I can no longer ignore this feeling. Perhaps it's for the best that I'm leaving.

I squeeze my eyes shut. 'I can't see anything.'

'Go,' she says, stepping backwards.

I think I will shake her hand, but she's too quick.

'Off with you. They'll be waiting.'

The breeze carries the scent of eucalyptus. Before I turn the corner of the house, I wave goodbye.

—

For the first part of the trip, the weather is dry. Willy-willies spin dust in frenzied circles ahead of us on the track, and the sun leaches colour from the land. The Creator's palette is a pale version of the original—sandy grey, subdued brown, mud black, hushed rust, shining quartz, noiseless grey-greens, desiccated silver, bleached white. There's a haunting beauty to it, but iron hides in the silken glove. The swirling dust inflames our eyes and clogs our lungs; we hawk up dirt-streaked spit.

William knows the reliable waterholes, and the sheep press forward with heads low, driven by instinct not direction.

At night, we camp near scattered settlers' huts. These are lonely souls—Ticket-of-Leave men, a few absconders—squatting on the land with their women, locked in a losing battle against the bush and the threat of bushrangers. They gather round our fire, hungry for news, or a pinch of tobacco. Most share what little they have. Often, the poorest among them are the most generous. Perhaps it's only through suffering that we learn compassion.

'Looks like rain,' says Ned.

It comes south of a place called Michelago—three days of soaking rain that turns the creeks to rivers and the soil to mud. The dray wheels sink deep and the bullocks' hooves cake with clods. We cannot move. We camp until the ground hardens, knocking dried mud from the wheels in rock-hard lumps.

One evening, when the others have retired to their blankets, William, with a thoughtful expression, breaks the silence. 'Ghikas, is there something between you and Mary?'

A wave of unease washes over me. It's true. I feel a pull towards Mary, a magnetism that's hard to ignore. A path I cannot take.

'She's a good-natured girl, William, with no family in the colony. Or in Ireland. I value her friendship.'

William's concerned gaze mirrors the conflict in my heart.

'You're still planning to marry a countrywoman?'

I nod again. 'I've been honest with Mary about my intentions. I would never dishonour her.'

Totally honest. About going home. About the wife who waits for me in

Hydra. I value honour highly. So why does the statement sit so heavily in my chest?

'I know you to be honest,' says William. 'But women are easily hurt.'

Later, under the starlit sky, I ponder his words.

When we return to Arnprior, I must have a candid talk with Mary, to ensure there are no misunderstandings about our friendship. And I must be more careful not to show any affection suggesting more than that.

Within days, a green tinge spreads across the landscape. The stock chase it, restless and unsatisfied, until the green pick thickens into grass—and then they settle. The change in feed is sudden and rich. Horses, oxen, sheep—all succumb. William calls it 'the scours'. Ned, 'the bellyache'. The sheep's hard, black pellets turn into a flowing stream of foul, greenish-yellow water.

Once the sun dries the new grass, the trouble passes. The animals buck when they run and their bodies fill out again.

Then the forest thins. And the horizon opens.

After the open woodlands of Arnprior, the sight of the Maneroo plains takes my breath away. Undulating hills roll out forever, wave after wave of grassland lit golden and mauve by the setting sun. Grey shadows lie soft in the valleys. As if the giant Antaeus has passed this way and ripped the trees from the earth with his bare hands. Low, tattered bushes dot the flats, with stunted trees on the ridges and rocky outcrops.

There's a grandeur in it that stirs something deep in me. The bare openness, the lean strength, reminds me of Hydra. And for the first time since I arrived in New South Wales, I feel at home.

We deliver the flock and our load of timber and stay for several weeks, helping Donald and Stewart with jobs requiring a team of men. We load up bales of wool to take back to Arnprior for sale in Sydney. I look forward to our return to see how Chara has grown, whether it has rained, and if the winter crop is out of the ground. But most, I look forward to seeing Mary.

We approach the Arnprior buildings late one afternoon. Nothing has changed—the house, the fences, the rolling land. And yet, I feel something shift in me. A tightening, an anticipation.

Someone has thrown a rug over the back fence of the homestead, and a figure is swinging a broom with great energy, clouds of dust rising with each stroke. Unmistakably, Mary. Putting her usual enthusiasm into her work.

My heart races. I stare, unsure what to do, how to greet her after such a long time without giving her the wrong impression.

Chara sees me first and lopes over, nearly knocking me down. I have worried about her, but she is her usual boisterous self. I scoop her up, staggering and laughing as she licks my face all over. How she has grown! No longer a ball of fluff, but heavy, with long hair, glossy and combed.

Mary's voice sings out. 'Ghika! Ned!' She runs towards us. 'You're back!' She stops ten yards short of us, smoothing her skirts. For a moment, she looks unsure. Then she squares her shoulders, chin lifting as if she has something to prove.

I smile but shake my head, meaning she should return to her duties, lest she appear negligent of her work. But beneath my casual gesture is a longing to close that distance at my fastest run, to envelop her in a close hug.

She stops ten yards short of us.

'The gum tree, later,' I say.

Her hand flies up to her mouth. 'When I am ready,' she says.

Her words knock the wind out of me. But I nod. 'Of course.'

Late that afternoon, when I have seen my flock arrive home, I take the time to complete some extra chores before I stroll to the gum tree. As I approach from behind, I see a pair of familiar ankle boots at the end of a long skirt spread out on the ground. And pretty ankles. My heart does a quick somersault.

Has she come because I asked her, or because she wanted to?

She takes fright as I round the tree. She gasps. 'Ghika!'

'Yes, it is I,' I grin. 'Did you expect a bushranger?'

She laughs and stands up, looking radiant.

'No, not a bushranger. A big Greek pirate. Chara's missed you fierce—and me too.' Her cheeks turn pink and her hand goes to her throat, but when she sees how I stare at her, she pushes her hair off her forehead, claps her hands together, slapping them back and forth, to clear them of grass stuck to her skin. Then she looks away, flushed.

'Yes,' I say. 'I missed Chara.' She turns back to me, waiting.

I hesitate. I do not want to give her a false impression, so I stand there like a moonstruck ox.

Then I choke out, 'And—and—you, of course.' I wince. Was that inadvisable?

'Oh tosh.' A deep blush spreads from the base of her throat to her face. She rubs her hands down her skirt and sits on the ground again. 'Go on then. Tell me about the plains of Maneroo,' she says, folding her legs neatly beneath her, hands on her lap, the way she did on the day of the picnic in Sydney. That thought makes something twist in my stomach. I stretch out on the ground, arm bent at the elbow, supporting my head, holding a piece of grass in my mouth. Chara flops close to my chest, and I put my arm over her. I use a stick to trace a sketch of Mary's face in the loose soil.

There are women there on the plains, I tell her, tired, worn women, burned brown by the sun. They stand by their men in the most primitive of circumstances.

'How brave and loyal,' says Mary.

I describe the rolling hills going on for miles, the pastel colours, how I felt at home. I tell her about the shepherd I met at Coolaringdon, who explained to me a novel herding style, where the shepherd leads the flock, rather than trailing behind it. He said that while it stops the faster sheep from rushing ahead, the slower ones catch up. I think it will cause losses, but I am eager to experiment, and keen to resume training Chara.

Mary, in her turn, gives me news of Arnprior.

After I left, the rain came, sheets of it. It filled everyone with joy to see the wheat finally planted on the flat below the house. James put some in at Durran Durra, too. Mrs Ryrie has been unwell, but is feeling much better, and is playing the piano again. Mary loves to listen to those faraway tunes that remind her of the green grass of Ireland. Young Jane has been riding her pony on the flat below the house, using the jumps I set up for her. And Mary has brushed Chara every day.

'Thank you for looking after her. She looks beautiful. If a little fat.'

She smiles. 'And Ghika, you'll never guess who came to the house! Not Bartholomew, don't worry. Nor Jack the Rammer. It was your friend, Father Therry. He was telling me about a convict who has applied to marry a free settler girl. At the Protestant church at Parramatta. Isn't that grand?'

I am restrained. 'Indeed.'

'Oh Ghika. They fell in love at first sight!' Her eyes glisten with emotion.

'Well, we all know that's fanciful.'

Mary stares at me. 'Yes. Fanciful. And stupid.'

But her excitement continues unabated. 'Father Therry is having quite the time in Sydney building his church, and Governor Bourke is more cooperative than Governor Darling.'

'Is that so?' I nod in approval.

Mary has discovered more from Father Therry in one afternoon than I have in several years.

'And Ghika, would you be knowing what Father Therry must do in Sydney?'

'No, I wouldn't be knowing,' I say. She is too excited to notice I'm making fun of her.

'I like the way your eyes close when you smile, Ghika. Well.' She nods her head to her chest and closes her eyes, gathering her thoughts. She looks up again. 'He prays with men who are sentenced to hang. Yes. A horrible duty. And did you know that he fights for the orphans? Foundlings like me? They shut him out of the Orphan School at Parramatta, where they were converting Catholic children to Protestants. Mind you, I'm not sure of the difference.'

'Nor do I care,' I say, 'for he is a great champion of Protestants and Catholics alike. And you know, he rides like the devil to cover the country under his care. He visits our blacks, and he tells the governor that black children need educating the same as white.'

'Oh Ghika, yes, he told me that. I like him so much. We took a cup of tea together in the kitchen. Mrs Ryrie said we may. They are not Romans, of course, the Ryries. They are Protestants. So, is Mrs Ryrie not kind? He told me a funny story about a christening he did the week before, where the child was almost a full-grown man.'

She pauses and looks at me. I don't have to wait long.

'Let me tell you more about Father Therry. He said he enjoys marrying people. His favourite job, especially for those living in sin. He rescues them from going to hell, like.'

I shift uncomfortably.

'He said, sometimes he sees a man and a woman who are made for each other. Has he ever told you that?'

I am entirely uncomfortable with the direction of this conversation. She waits again for my reaction. I shake my head.

'Well, he does, sometimes. And he tells them so. Or sometimes they tell him. And they apply, and if either of them is a convict, the Superintendent of Convicts must approve. And then he tells Father Therry, who posts the banns.' She smiles in delight. 'But he cannot tell them for sure when he is coming. So, the girl must have her dress ready!' She laughs and claps her hands together. 'Can you imagine? Rising in the morning to polish the brass and finding yourself a bride at lunchtime?'

I feel my face redden.

She is watching me now, green eyes shining, as if she is waiting for something. And suddenly, I think I know what she is thinking. And it terrifies me.

'What is wrong?' she says, putting her hand on my arm.

I pull away as if her touch burns my skin. I must be straight and honest. Leave no room for doubt.

'Mary, if you're waiting for me to marry you, you'll be waiting a long time. But you knew that. I've made that clear, right from the start.'

Her face crumples. I don't expect that. She's not angry. Not indignant. Something worse. She's hurt.

I've said nothing I haven't said a hundred times before. She's always claimed she wouldn't marry. Or have I been missing something?

'I didn't mean to upset you,' I say.

'Waiting for you? I told you—I would never marry.' Her voice is sharp now, rising.

'Then why—'

'And even if I did, what makes you think I'd marry you?' Her cheeks blaze. 'Why would I want to go to that island of yours, where girls are married off like livestock? If you think I'm waiting, you are— you are—,'

She breaks off, breath shaking.

'It's so mistaken you are! Chara's the only one who loves you. And only because you feed her!'

Her words sting more than I want to admit.

I try again. 'Mary, you deserve someone who sees the world as you do.'

She doesn't answer. A single tear drops from her chin.

I reach for her. 'I'm sorry. I didn't mean—'

She flinches back. 'To think I trusted you. Do not touch me!'

She gathers her skirts and runs in the direction of the homestead.

Four days later, the coach takes her away.

I do not see it go.

I do not go to the gum tree that day, or the next. But I feel the absence of her as keenly as an amputated limb.

—

Mrs Ryrie summons me about the garden. We briefly discuss what is ready for harvest, what we'll plant, vegetable preferences. Peas are her winter favourite, while Mister Ryrie has a fondness for cauliflower. I listen, my mind wandering, contemplating the currant tomato plants sprawling unchecked, and the ever-elusive bandicoots that defy my attempts to mend the fence. We'll soon need to repair the slats in the cellar for the potato harvest.

She remarks the artichokes are looking splendidly architectural.

'I've never cooked artichoke,' she says. 'Do you eat them in Greece?'

'Yes, ma'am, my mother used to pickle them,' I tell her.

'Really, Jigger? They look so hard and leathery on the bush. How do you prepare them?'

'You don't use the tough outside, ma'am—you peel away those leaves. And remove the choke. It's only the heart you eat.'

'Ohhh.' She smiles. 'Only the heart. I like that.'

Mary would like that, too.

'The grape cuttings have disappointed William. They are susceptible to mould.'

I hope it's not smell-fungus. I smile.

'He will buy different varieties on his next trip to Sydney.'

Sydney. Where Mary has gone. Presumably to work for Mrs Watt.

Mister Ryrie's voice breaks through the afternoon stillness, calling for Mrs Ryrie.

'Oh Ghika. Before you go, Mrs Ascham sent an old newspaper for you. It mentions Greece. I left it on the chair at the back of the house, if you care to collect it.'

'Oh, and there's a letter for you.' She pulls an envelope out of the wide pocket at the front of her apron.

I'm hardly out of the gate before I open it.

My shoulders slump. It's not from Mary. From Andonis. Ando.

Kostas has secured a responsible position with a shipping agent who has given him leave to travel to Camden Park and stay overnight. He plays the jaw harp once a week at a Sydney hotel where patrons flock to hear him. He is saving to buy a fiddle and Ando says he seems happy. I'm glad to hear it.

I collect the newspaper, but I'm thinking about my friends. I am glad they are all together now, but nevertheless, the news has knocked the stuffing out of me. That's one of Joe's favourite sayings.

I go to the gum tree. Out of habit, not hope.

I unfold the yellowed newspaper. A column headed with last year's date knots my stomach. In 1831, Hydra rose against Governor Kapodistrias —our shipowners refusing his new imposts and his plan to seize private vessels for the state. Our ships! Hydra and Spetses were blockaded; shots were traded. Miaoulis broke through the blockade and reached Poros, where, cornered and defiant, he burned the frigate Hellas and the corvette Hydra—the finest ships in the Greek fleet—rather than see them taken. Weeks later, Kapodistrias was shot dead at the church door in Nafplio.

I read it twice. Even in peace, Greece suffers.

Mary's boots have worn a hollow in the earth where she used to sit.

I sit there longer than I mean to.

The trinket box lies under my bed, abandoned.

22

MALTA

Oyer & Terminer

CASTELLANIA GAOL, *Malta*
  February 1828

The English called their piracy court *Oyer and Terminer*. Hear and determine. As if that made their cruelty clean.

In the heavy silence of the first floor room in the Castellania Palace, my eyes searched for my father's face. I'd told myself not to expect him. But part of me believed he would fight for me.

No one. He had not come. So be it.

We were lined up at the bar. The clerk mispronounced all our names.

Nikos rubbed a hand over his ribs, blinking as if focussing. 'When does it start?' he whispered, voice full of fear.

'Now, Niko.'

The usher placed a copy of the Commission on the table. As the clerk read it out, Doctor Torregiani touched the name of each commissioner with his fingertip.

Admiral Sir Edward Codrington—presiding, drenched in medals. Great friend of Greece. Out to get us.

Sir John Stoddart—Chief Justice. White wig. Black-robed and bored.
Lieutenant-Colonel Bathurst—English soldier, Treasurer to the government. Sharp nose, soft curls, a collar so high it nearly hid his mouth.
Captain Spencer—Royal Navy, *Talbot*. I knew his face. He captained her the night I left my mother in the church.
Captain Richards—Royal Navy. Blank eyes.

All British, four of the five with titles, all in uniform. The only question was how fast they'd hang us.

The twelve-man jury was *de medietate linguae*—which, we'd been told, meant half were British, half were 'aliens'.

We thought that meant Greeks.

'Where are our countrymen?' I said.

Our advocate didn't look up. Just gave a tired shrug.

'It's legal.'

'So is calling us pirates,' I said. 'That doesn't make it right.'

The jury was sworn in two languages—English and Italian—but the room was a babble of languages with translations into Maltese, Greek (for us), Spanish and French.

How could they possibly understand the evidence in this commotion?

Doctor Torregiani said the jurors would sleep each night in the palace until they reached a verdict, in what was called the Tapestry Room, guarded by sworn officers.

Proceedings began.

The judge said, in English, 'You stand accused of the crime of piratically and feloniously boarding the English merchant-brig, the *Alceste*, and taking therefrom sundry merchandise; and with having put in fear of their lives, the master and the crew. How do you plead?'

They charged us as a group; the verdict for one would be the verdict for all.

Our interpreter translated into Greek.

So, as one, we answered, '*Athóos, Kýrie Dikastá.*' Not guilty, Your Honour.

A note was handed to the judge. The crew of the *Alceste* could not identify Pietros Lalahos. He was acquitted for non-identification. Later he was sworn for the defence, but was able to add nothing.

Doctor Vella, the prosecutor, painted us as ruthless pirates of the high seas, with Andonis and Damos named as the chief aggressors. He argued that we carried no papers; we took contraband articles but also the crew's personal effects; we allowed the *Alceste* to continue instead of taking it as a prize for our government, signifying we knew it was not a legitimate prize of war; and we left the sulphur on board to continue to Alexandria.

He said that the young clerk's fear of unspeakable acts, when Damos threatened to tie him to the cannon, would have been no less because he did not carry out the threat.

Damos shouted, 'I only meant to frighten him!'

Sir John Stoddart said, 'Silence.'

Nikos stared at the floor, chewing the inside of his cheek.

Captain Mallia of the *Alceste* testified that the she had been carrying eight hundred and fifty-three gold dollars. Concealed in the ballast. He smirked with satisfaction as he said it.

In the ballast. We searched it. I knew they had gold. I knew it. His eyes met mine, and his smile burned my gut like pepper.

On Saturday, the fourth day of prosecution evidence, the mother of Pietros Bouff was waiting, white-faced, in the corridor outside the courtroom. She cried out to her son, and he ran to her. As they embraced, I looked down the corridor.

'The thoughts of Hydriots are with you all,' she said.

Only she had come. From the poorest family among us. Yet she found her way from Hydra to Malta.

The defence began—and there was precious little to be said.

Doctor Torregiani's pleas about the chaos of war and the intricacies of maritime law barely made an impression in the prosecution's argument. The Greek Government had itself proclaimed that vessels of the Greek Fleet must carry a Letter of Marque. Therefore, we were, even by the judgment of our own countrymen, deemed to be pirates.

The evidence was complete. Time for the jury to decide.

Sir John instructed them. 'To encourage a swift decision, I direct that no food shall be brought to you during your deliberations. The court will only reconvene upon a unanimous decision.'

The jurors muttered to each other, outraged.

Our lives dangled by the thinnest thread, and the court pinched their bellies to squeeze out a verdict.

As we made our way down the stairs from the courtroom, a luscious smell wafted up towards us from the door to the courtyard. My mouth watered and my stomach clenched with pain. Three cooks were standing to the side of the door, holding steaming plates stacked high. The smell filled the stairwell—meat, rice, vegetables, rich with spices. I had smelled nothing like it since home.

A guard's shout shattered any hope.

'Halt! No food for the jury!'

Like vultures, the guards swooped in, snatching the plates away and carrying them to the corner of the quadrangle, where they tipped the food into an ash barrel.

No one would eat it now.

The cooks decamped, muttering, 'Who will pay us?'

Nikos groaned. 'Just a taste,' he whispered, voice breaking. 'That's all.'

He had lost something far greater than a meal. He turned his face to the wall.

The guard spurred us into movement. 'Into your cells. Your gruel waits.'

Nikos' gruel remained untouched again that night.

The flavours from the stairwell clung to me, filled my throat—and suddenly, I was at home again: *Pascha*, last year. Easter, the most important and joyous festival in the Orthodox calendar. The Feast of feasts.

Hydra would be green from winter rains, spring wildflowers blooming.

Roasting lamb, fat sizzling on the coals, juices dripping, the courtyard smelling of roasted garlic and fresh thyme. Spiced *pilau*, the table groaning under the weight: olives glistening in oil, slabs of sharp white goat's cheese, a mountain of Easter bread, golden with egg yolk.

In the kitchen, my mother stood over the pot, stirring thick waves of yoghurt, sleeves rolled high. My grandmother worked at the pastry board, pinching perfect crescents of almond-flour sweets and dusting them in sugar.

Someone threw an orange across the courtyard; my brother caught it one-handed, laughing. I snatched a hunk of bread from the table and devoured it—still hot, crisp crust flaking under my fingers.

We spent Great Friday together in prayer. On Saturday, my brothers and I accompanied our father up the mountain to kill the lamb. The previous year, as he did every year, my father killed the lamb swiftly with a dagger and its blood spurted onto the sweet green grass. Normally, my brothers and I sliced the wool from the carcass, but he did that himself— inserted the knife at the breastbone and pushed the blade away until the glistening intestines ballooned out and uncoiled along the ground.

I raised the waterskin above my head to wash my face, letting the narrow stream of water splash me, soaking my clothes. I gasped; my brothers' mouths had dropped open.

'*Stamáta*!' my father snapped. 'You're wasting good water.'

I don't know what possessed me, for I tilted the skin again, this time more slowly and deliberately, allowing plenty of water to splash over my face. I watched it run off my legs. Then I looked at my father.

He remained silent. Triumph warmed my belly.

Afterward, we rubbed the inside with a mixture of salt, pepper, and herbs, and loaded the carcass and offal onto the donkey for the journey home. We spent the rest of the day preparing for the Sunday meal and shortly before midnight, dressed in our finest attire, we walked down to the church on the quay—the Cathedral of the Assumption of the *Theotókos*. The soft glow of hundreds of candles danced on the silver and gold icons, casting a shimmer on the silk brocade of the women's dresses and sparkling in their jewellery. The indistinct murmur of prayers filled the air, and the priest's voice flowed like warm syrup. At midnight, his tone brightened with joy as he exclaimed, '*Christos Anesti*!' Christ is risen!

The bells of all the churches on Hydra rang in unison.

After the liturgy, we gathered to break our Lenten fast with *magiritsa*— soup made from the lamb's offal—the smell of spring onions, lemon and dill rising in the steam from each bowl. And we played *tsougrisma*, the traditional *Pascha* game, a riotous affair when we each took a hard-boiled egg dyed red in onion water and hit them end to end with each other. The aim was to crack the other person's egg without cracking your own.

I gripped my crimson egg, feeling the shell smooth and fragile in my palm. This was my father's domain. He always won.

I struck his egg first. A sharp crack. He turned the broken shell over in his hands, then let out a short breath—half amusement, half disbelief.

'Well done,' he said.

He picked up his wine, took a sip, and clinked his glass lightly against mine. A brief acknowledgment, but it was enough.

I would not be there this year. Neither would my mother.

—

The next morning, Sunday, the guard brought our food late and said the jurors in the Tapestry Room were rebelling—some threatening to break down the doors to go to Mass.

A farce. Our lives hanging on men locked in a room, starving and praying.

The hours dragged. By midnight I was still awake, staring into the dark when the key turned in the lock.

I was on my feet before the door opened. The jury must have reached a verdict.

We were marched upstairs, the corridor thick with the smell of sweat and tallow. The judge called the room to order as we entered. The prosecution stood ready, hollow-eyed. Doctor Torregiani too, wig askew, jaw set.

Silence.

Then the jury filed in.

Sir John's voice was calm, deadly. 'Have you reached a decision?'

A grey-haired vagabond of a man stood, swaying on his feet, a button missing from his coat, his face raw with exhaustion. This man—this stranger—held our lives in his shaking hands. I fixed on the twitch at the corner of his mouth.

When he spoke, the blood drained from my head.

'We have been deliberating, sir, without food, since yesterday afternoon. Over twenty-four hours. One of our body has become ill and requires medicine. We cannot come to a unanimous verdict while we are ill from famine.'

Not a verdict. Hunger.

Sir John's face hardened. 'You will be attended by a physician, who will prescribe only what is necessary to prevent severe illness. You will return to your deliberations until you reach a unanimous decision. This court will reassemble at ten o'clock in the morning to hear your verdict.'

The sound of his voice echoed.

Back to the cell. The door slammed.

On Monday he asked the question again.

No verdict.

And again on Tuesday.

No verdict.

By Wednesday morning, the courtroom felt airless.

'Members of the jury,' Sir John said, 'you have been deliberating for eighty-eight hours. Have you reached a verdict?'

The room held its breath.

'We have, Your Honour.'

The foreman shuffled his papers.

'And what is your verdict?'

The foreman spoke slowly. Deliberately. 'We find the defendant, Pietros Theodoris Bouff, not guilty.'

Young Pietros fell to his knees, crossed himself. His mother wailed.

The foreman waited for silence.

'We find the defendants Andonis Manolis, Damianos Ninis, Ghikas Voulgaris, Konstantinos Stroumboulis, Nikolaos Papandreou—'

Sir Edward stood with his arms folded, hawk-like.

I stared at the foreman's lips.

'Guilty.'

The word landed like a hammer.

Sir John glanced at the clock. Codrington didn't look up. Spencer drew on his gloves.

We were remanded to custody. Sentencing still to come.

A horse whinnied in the street below. Somewhere, a bell chimed the hour.

23

Nothing Left To Hold

ARNPRIOR, New South Wales
    July—December 1834

It's Sunday. I should be patching the roof. Instead, I lie on the cot, fiddling with the hagstone on my chest. Today has been darker than most since Mary left. The walls of the hut close in, their familiar contours now a suffocating reminder of all I've lost. A man would do better to rise and find something useful to occupy his mind, but I don't.

I've thrown myself into my duties since she left, trying not to think about her. She never understood me anyway.

'Another sheep taken by dingoes last night,' says Joe.

'You can't protect them all,' I say.

Martin glances at me, his voice quiet, almost too casual. 'Sometimes, though, it's the one you lose that you should have watched.'

My fingers close tighter around the hagstone. Martin isn't talking about sheep.

Ned appears, wanting to borrow a flint. He thinks Joe stole his. I can't find ours either, and spend five minutes cursing and tossing things about. When I hand Ned's back, he studies it, then says, as abruptly as a slap, 'Do you miss Mary?'

'Is this a conspiracy?' I snap. 'People come and go. That's life.'

I think of Katerina, leaving home to marry a man she barely knew, and the words we used to whisper to each other. Stars shine brightest on the darkest night.

Not on Arnprior they don't.

Ned doesn't blink.

'You should've wed her.'

I stare at him.

'Are you daft?' he presses on. 'Mary was the one. She'd have kept you honest.'

'I—'

'You're a blethering fool, man. You act like you've lost five pounds and found a farthing. Do you know how many women you meet who make you happy? One, if you're lucky. None, if you're me.'

The words hit harder than they should. My chest tightens. I look away.

'She made you happy, didn't she?'

I don't answer. My throat's thick.

When Ned stomps out, the silence feels larger than the hut.

Joe mutters, 'He's right, you know. You were soft as butter when she was here. No use telling you—you were too stuck on your Greek wife.'

A fantasy.

The breath goes out of me. My vision tunnels. My hands clench into fists, nails biting skin. I stand. The cot creaks. The hut smells of sweat and dust and regret. I stride out into the daylight before the walls close in.

Outside, the air hits me like cold water. I walk until the noise in my head dulls. Then it comes—quietly at first, then all at once.

She made me happy.

She was the air in this place, the light in my days. And I let her go. I thought I could shape Mary's future. But she shaped mine. And now she's gone.

The thought steadies me, then breaks me open. I must find her. Tell her. She may not listen, but I must try.

Every evening under the gum tree, she was there. Every time I laughed, it was because of her. She left because of me. And now she thinks I don't care. I must tell her before it's too late.

But she's in Sydney, and the Ryries will not go there until Christmas.

Months away. Perhaps Father Therry can intervene. After all, didn't he put the idea of marriage into her head?

I buy paper from the storehouse and William allows me to use the station's pen and ink. It takes three days before I am satisfied with what I have written:

Dear Father Therry,

I regret being absent during your recent visit to Arnprior, when you made the acquaintance of Miss Mary Lyons, an Irish housemaid in the employ of Mr and Mrs Ryrie. I spoke foolish words that caused her distress, and she has since left for Sydney to enter the service of Mr and Mrs Hercules Watt.

I would write to Miss Lyons myself, but fear she might not receive—or would not open—my letter. I therefore ask, with great respect, that you speak to her on my behalf. Please tell her, dear Father, that my wish is to marry her without delay, if she will consent.

I shall await your reply with sincere gratitude and hope.
Your faithful servant,
Ghikas Voulgaris

I take a page from an old ledger and pull the pencil stub from my boot—the last inch of lead I have.

I write out a list of reasons why she should marry me.

Joe is full of advice.

'When you find her, Jigger, why don't you say to her, I'm a block-headed oaf, and I've seen the error of my ways.'

'Be quiet Joe, I'm planning what to say.'

I read it out slowly, as I write:

1. Her reputation will be safe

Joe snorts. 'Nothing says reputation like being a convict bride in the middle of nowhere.'

I ignore him and keep writing.

2. I will protect her

'From what?' says Joe. 'Kangaroos?'

3. I will try to make her happy

Joe laughs. "You done a good job so far.'

I glare at him and continue.

4. I will be a devoted husband—though not rich

'More like a pauper.'

5. When my sentence is over, we will go home

'Oh yeah, Mary will love that. Stuck on some rock where she can't open her mouth.'

I frown. 'She'll have a good life, Joe.'

Joe shakes his head. 'Jigger, you're bloody hopeless.'

I continue the list.

6. She will gain a loving family—the family she never had

7. I will apologise for implying she was trapping me into marriage

'That'll fix everything,' Joe says. 'An apology after you accused her of lying.'

He laughs like an idiot.

I look down the list. It's practical. Sensible.

It's also ridiculous.

What kind of fool writes a list of reasons to convince a woman to marry him?

I scrub my hand over my face, groaning. I drop the pencil. 'God help me, I can't do this alone.'

'Hey, Jigger?'

'What, Joe?'

He grins. 'Number eight. Tell her you love her.'

'If I had half your sense, Joe,' I say, 'I'd be married already.'

—

Joe jabbers about Jack the Rammer who escaped from the Goulburn gaol a few months ago. His gang raided young Stewart at Coolaringdon at gunpoint and took a military sword.

'É, Chara.' I pat the side of the bed.

She's at my side in a heartbeat, that ridiculous face: tilt, smile, frown, head over the bed. I try to keep my expression blank, but the corner of my mouth betrays me. As soon as she sees my mouth twitch, she's up on the bed, bringing her wriggling warmth and dog smell with her. She's jumping over me, pushing her head in my face, under my arm, licking my nose.

I hug her to keep her still. She struggles in my arms, pads moving on my chest.

She's a born herder; the sheep obey her better than they obey me.

I hold her head, and her eyes look up at me. Her fur's still matted from rolling in yesterday's puddle. I smile at her, and I swear she smiles back.

She whines, a small, soft sound that says, why lie there all the afternoon feeling sorry for yourself?

I let her go, and she jumps off the bed and wheels around and wags her tail. She wants to be running. She's such a scruff, a comic—hair flopping in her eyes.

I give in to her begging, swing my legs over the side of the cot and pat her shaggy head.

'Right, lass,' I say. I sound like William. 'A walk along the creek?'

Her tail waves a little faster and we leave the hut. Without hesitation, she turns towards our spot on the river. I laugh as she whips around, mouth open, tongue hanging out. She knows our routine by heart and trusts I'll follow it.

At the grass on the flat, I pick up a stick and throw it in a long arc. Chara bounds along, long fur flopping. She's there, almost before it lands. She loves this game as much as any pup, and she lopes back to me and drops it at my feet, tongue out, panting.

She moves her weight from foot to foot, turns in a circle.

'You're such a clown.'

She grins again.

I think about my letter to Father Therry.

I've been waiting for a letter. Nothing has come.

Perhaps she has already moved on.

Chara has stopped her antics and waits for me to throw.

I bend to pick the stick up again, but she's there before me. I fall; we wrestle. It's part of the game. I'm on my back, and she's got the end of the stick and she's shaking her head, twisting my arm, growling her ownership. In a second, she'll let me have it back. And we'll start again.

I'm up and give her a quick rub on the neck. 'Good girl. Come on. Let's go!'

I throw again, and this time the stick lands in the long grass at the river's edge. She's off in a flash, bounding after it. The stalks move as she searches.

She barks. A different bark. And again.

It's a yelp of pain.

I sprint toward her. She's out of the grass, but she grabs my trouser leg, pulling me back.

I look down. She wobbles and whimpers. I reach out to touch her head. She lowers it to nestle into my palm and that's when I see movement behind her. A snake's tail slithers away into the long grass.

I can't move. Panic narrows my mind: I should have seen it. I should have trimmed that hair. I shouldn't have thrown into the long grass. If she's bitten, I can't let her run. I must take her back to the hut.

I pick her up, and she lies limp in my arms. 'Stay with me, Chara. Please stay with me.'

Her legs swing. I whisper to her. She's still warm. Too still.

I would give everything to have the minute back—my amulet, the dream of Hydra—anything.

Her head flops over my elbow as I make for home.

'Not long, girl. Look, there's the hut.'

That won't save her.

—

I gently lift her body and kiss her head. My arms tighten around her. I lay her on her bag near the fire. She lies there, barely breathing. I stroke her, whispering, 'Please don't die Chara. Don't die.'

Joe enters the hut and walks over to where I'm kneeling. 'What's wrong with Chara?'

'A copper-coloured snake bit her.'

He stares, eyes wide. 'Christ. I've seen it. They stagger, then drop. Nothing you can do.'

'She didn't stagger.'

He crouches beside me, his hand on my shoulder. 'Jeez. I'm sorry, Jigger. You're having all the bad luck.'

The hagstone swings from my neck—a hollow promise.

She is on her side, breathing shallow and laboured, eyes closed.

I can't breathe either. I don't care if Joe hears.

'*Panagia mou*, please. You took my home, my family, my friends. You took Mary. Please don't take Chara.'

Her chest shudders. My hand moves with it. I keep praying.

'If you do nothing for me again in all my life, do this, please. I beg you, *Panagia mou*. Don't let her die.'

Her breath catches once, twice, then stills.

I press my face into her fur. She smells of river mud.

'Good girl,' I whisper. 'Brave girl.'

A sob tears out of me, a serrated blade, raw and ragged.

—

Hours pass. I can't tell if she's asleep or unconscious. Her breathing becomes deeper. I lie on the floor beside her and stroke her curls flat.

I drift in and out of sleep until Joe wakes me by shaking my shoulder.

'She's sleepin' peaceful, Jigger. You want some?' He points at the kettle.

I run my hand along Chara's fur. She sleeps on.

'Thanks Joe.'

He takes a heaped spoon of sugar and dumps it into his pannikin. 'Oh, look, they've shook me again on my rations. Look at this.' He shows me the inside of the empty sugar jar.

'Joe, you can't put three teaspoons in your tea. That's why your ration only lasts two days.'

'No, no, no. They've shook me again. Or there's a thief in the hut.' He looks around as if he might catch a culprit in the act. The man will drive me mad, but his foolishness steadies me. Good-hearted fellow, Joe, but a bit touched.

He softens. 'I'm only trying to make you smile, Jigger.'

There's a knock on the door of the hut. It's William.

'Ghikas, grab your belongings. Father Therry is here, and he wants to see you. He'll be up in a few minutes. Meanwhile, James and I are taking a team of men to Richlands to help the Macarthurs wash their sheep. You'll be joining us.'

He notices Chara and lifts his eyebrow.

'A snake bit her yesterday.'

'I'm sorry to hear that. But there's little you can do for her now. Joseph will look after her, won't you, Joe?'

Joe nods confidently. 'She'll be fine, Jigger. Ain't nothing you can do.'

I have been hoping all this week that William will ask me to go to Richlands, one of the Macarthur runs—ten thousand acres, sixty miles north of here—for I have already received a letter from Ando saying that the Macarthurs are taking them there for the same purpose. Four of us could be together. Only Kostas would be missing.

But I don't want to leave Chara.

Joe is already sitting on the floor beside her. He loves her as much as I do.

'Right,' says William. 'And we will continue from Richlands to Sydney for Christmas.' He slaps me on the shoulder. 'We leave in an hour.'

—

'Ghikas, you young spalpeen!' Father Therry booms, his grin widening as he clasps my hand in a rough grip. I make him a cup of tea, thick with the dusty dregs of my ration. He blows on it, and when the steam clears, sips as if it is the finest leaf from China.

Chara's breathing is a soft rhythm in the corner. When I tell him about her, his face changes. The lines around his eyes deepen, and for a moment, his boisterous energy dims. 'I'll pray for her, my son.'

'I'd be grateful for that, father. She's my family.'

We pray together as she sleeps on.

Back at the table, he takes a quiet sip of his tea, eyes momentarily distant. Then he shares the news of Jack the Rammer's death during an attack on Joseph Catterall's run down south. They terrified his wife, heavy with child. The Rammer is dead, and the troopers are riding after the rest of the outlaws.

Interesting news, but I clench my jaw, eyeing Joe and Martin impatiently.

'We'd best be going, Father,' Martin says, ushering Joe towards the door.

When they're gone, I say, 'Father, my letter about Mary—'

But he barrels on, speaking of road thieves on the Parramatta Road who'd swipe tea from your pannikin. He pauses, finally. 'Mary? What letter?'

'The one asking for your help with Mary Lyons.' I hate how pleading I sound. Once I would have died rather than ask another man for help.

His eyes soften. 'I received no such letter. But tell me Ghika, what did you want me?'

'I want to marry her.'

'But you broke her heart, Ghika. Mary has her own mind. She has forged her own path.'

'Her own path? What has she done?'

I lean in, eager, hopeful.

'She's engaged.'

My hand loses grip, and the pannikin crashes to the floor.

I hear myself mutter an apology, but the room has closed in. Father Therry hesitates. 'To a free man. A merchant. She has known him since her arrival.'

Townsend.

The trader. The haberdasher.

I want to laugh. Shout. Break something. Of course she'd choose him. He offered her coin, status, safety. She told me she would never marry. But maybe she just meant she'd never marry someone like me.

The race is run. And I didn't even hear the starting gun.

I slam my fist on the table, shove my chair back and stride, furious, across the floor. 'When do they marry?'

'January.'

A roaring fills my ears. 'January?' My voice is hoarse. 'That's only weeks away!'

'The seventeenth, to be exact,' says Father Therry. 'The first banns will be read at the end of December, then again on the following two Sundays.'

He says it gently as if that will soften the blow.

I grip the edge of the table. I should have gone after her the moment she left. I should have known.

I should have—

I slam my fist down again, so hard the cups rattle.

Father Therry is observing me. 'Ghikas, my son, if you love her—'

Love.

After Father Therry leaves, Joe stirs his tea with his finger. 'Don't fret, Jigger. I'll look after Chara.'

She lies quiet now.

'She'll pull through. She's a fighter, that one,' he says. Then he gasps. 'What if some bushrangers come while you're away? You won't be here.'

Joe is utterly terrified of being robbed, for reasons known only to God. He has nothing to steal except his tobacco—and even that he hides as if it's gold dust.

I nod at him, my thoughts already shifting away from his unfounded fears and toward a farewell I can hardly bear to make. My chest feels split open.

I kneel beside her, pressing my forehead against her soft fur.

'Farewell, old girl. Thanks for our journey together. May God travel with you the rest of the way.'

I stroke behind her ears. I wait. For her to lick my hand. For her tail to flick.

Nothing.

At the door, I turn back.

Her ribs rise and fall.

24

Mercy

CASTELLANIA GAOL, Malta
February—March 1828

We waited a week to be sentenced.

Each day, the clank of our chains echoed off the walls, a bell tolling the future.

Nikos barely spoke. He curled tighter each night as if the cold might crack him open.

On the seventh morning, I smoothed back his hair, tried to make him smile.

'It's not the end of the world,' I said.

'How do you know, Ghika?'

The cell door opened before I could answer.

Doctor Torregiani stood outlined in the light, his face carved from stone. Four guards stood behind him.

Damos cracked his knuckles.

I stared at the strip of skin peeling from under my fingernail. I ripped it off, the sharp pain a welcome distraction.

'Come,' said our advocate. No need to ask where.

The courtroom was colder than I remembered.

The commissioners sat like grim sentinels, expressions unreadable.

The jury chairs, empty now, looked like headstones—ours.

Sir John cleared his throat. A breeze caught the edges of his papers. He slapped them down. The sound cracked through the room like a pistol.

And I knew. Every reckless choice I'd made had led us here. I shivered.

He read, voice cold: 'Andonis Manolis, for the crime of piratically and feloniously boarding the English merchant-brig *Alceste* and taking therefrom sundry goods, wares and merchandises, and with having put in fear of their lives the master and the crew,' here he paused, his gaze piercing, and I felt my heart stop. 'I sentence you to be taken to a place of public execution and hanged by the neck until dead.'

It was as if someone had driven a fist into my stomach. I heaved.

Andonis flinched as if struck, then straightened his back, his eyes locked on Sir John with a look that bordered on defiance.

I had never admired him more.

Damos' name was read, the same sentence. Hanged by the neck until dead. The words blurred.

A rope. The drop. The crack of bone. Each image, merciless, in front of my eyes. I thought I might vomit.

My spirit floated to the courtroom ceiling, observing the scene from above, cut loose from the reality unfolding. My name must come soon.

'Ghikas Voulgaris, for the said crime,' Sir John continued, his voice reaching me through a fog, 'I sentence you to be taken to a place of public execution and hanged by the neck until dead.'

The room spun. Past and future collided in a single, sickening wave.

The room narrowed to the single word—dead. My father's voice rose from memory: A Voulgaris does not beg. I clamped my jaw, but every part of me wanted to scream.

A voice pierced the haze.

'Because you did not take a leading role or commit an act of violence, I recommend you to mercy.'

A merciful death.

Sir John addressed Kostas and Nikos, each sentence ending with the same grim decree, the same recommendation for mercy.

Their faces swam in and out of focus—boys I had led, men I had doomed. I felt nothing and everything, all at once.

It was over.

Our advocate's face was a haggard map of red veins and shiny taut skin. His spectacles came off; his weary hand pinched the bridge of his nose. When he spoke, his voice was barely audible.

'There is no reason the death sentences for Andonis and Damianos cannot be carried out tomorrow.'

Tomorrow. The word punched the air from the room.

'No!' Damos and Andonis cried together, chains clattering as they lurched against each other.

'Wait.' Our advocate lifted his hand, voice low but determined. 'We must act at once. I must write to the Lieutenant-Governor immediately— demanding a stay of execution. You must not be moved to the Grand Prison; if you are, I cannot protect you.'

He gathered his papers, turning to go. 'Say nothing to anyone.'

Then he was gone, the door slamming behind him, his footsteps fading down the corridor.

The blood roared in my ears. The place where I had torn the skin from my finger throbbed in time with my pulse.

'Ghika, will they hang us in the cage on the harbour cliffs?' asked Nikos.

We waited all the rest of that day, the silence of our cell punctuated only by the distant clanging of doors and the muffled footsteps of guards. Each hour felt stolen. Every sound from the corridor made us flinch.

When the door finally creaked open, Doctor Torregiani stood there. 'Sir Frederick has placed a temporary stay on the executions.'

Andonis sagged against the wall. Damos seized the advocate's hands, still with the letter clutched in them.

The doctor waited for the noise to die before he spoke again, his tone expressionless.

'But the governor instructs me not to raise false hope. There is not the slightest chance of reprieve.'

We fell silent.

'If there is no hope, why the delay?' Ando's voice was a blade of defiance.

'You must write to the King.'

Nikos brightened. 'The King in England? He knows about us?'

'You may have to wait months. The appeal will be a long process,' our advocate continued, his voice steady against my rising panic. 'In the meantime, you are to be set to hard labour, carting stone for the roads of Valletta.'

We would live for another day. But every step took us closer to the gallows.

—

MALTA

March 1828—Feb 1829

Months of hard labour, shackled under Valletta's relentless summer sun, followed again by another winter's biting cold, reduced us to miserable, tattered wretches. Our beards were unkempt, our hair matted, and our skin ingrained with dirt. The constant chafing of our chains left sores on our ankles.

Letters were exchanged between Malta and London—none with answers.

Every despatch asked for more particulars, more opinions, more signatures. Each one ended the same: no decision.

'They're chasing their own tails,' I muttered.

'While we wait for the rope,' Andonis said.

On a freezing evening in December, after a day when unusual snow flurries had dusted the stones we were condemned to break, Doctor Torregiani arrived.

'Gentlemen,' he began, his voice bouncing off the frigid walls of the cell, 'there's been a development.'

We gathered around, chains clinking.

'After several exchanges of letters between here and England, the Greek envoy to the Court of St James, Spyridon Trikoupis, has interceded on your behalf. His influence has reached the ears of the King.'

Trikoupis. My father's friend.

I hardly dared to breathe as he continued, 'His Majesty King George has written to Lieutenant-Governor Ponsonby.'

Doctor Torregiani paused, gauging the impact of his next words. 'You are to be pardoned—'

The golden word. A collective cheer interrupted him.

Nikos said, 'We have won?'

He held up his hand until we were silent. '—on condition of your transportation to New South Wales, or Van Diemen's Land, or other adjacent islands.'

Where? Wasn't that on the far side of the world?

We were all silent.

'Andonis and Damianos, you are sentenced to life in the colony. The rest, fourteen years.'

Pardon. I used to think the word meant forgiveness.

Now I knew better.

It meant punishment. Chains. Exile.

English mercy. They granted us life so they could profit from our labour in their colony. A rope would have been more honest.

—

The Onyx, Malta to Portsmouth
March—May 1829

They fitted us with new irons before we said goodbye to the Castellania prison, its oppressive corridors echoing as we stumbled up the stairs to the street. That sound would repeat in my dreams long after I left its walls behind.

One year to the day after sentencing, our escort, Lieutenant Decœurdeux, shepherded us from our subterranean residence into Malta's blinding light. We hobbled down the steep stone steps to the harbour, Nikos gripping the tattered remains of his book.

The troop ship HMS *Onyx* rode at anchor, bound for Portsmouth. Eight English naval officers, survivors of the British assault on Gramvousa the year before, preceded us aboard, shuffling with stiff, painful gaits. One leaned heavily on a crutch, his face grey with pain. Another wore shining braid, though his uniform sagged on his slumped frame. A third had the vacant stare of a man who had left half of himself behind in battle, his right sleeve sewn to his shoulder.

Neither this sorry sight, nor the prospect of lice-ridden bedding, could dampen our high spirits—we were back on the sea. A flicker of my old self was returning. Yet I sensed that deep down, my friends believed it had been my family connections that had sealed our harsh treatment by the English. It was an ever-present undercurrent of tension.

Damos, as if reading my thoughts, said, 'I'll wager they'll give you a soft bed in Port Jackson, eh, Ghika?'

'Absolutely,' I said. 'And a welcoming committee.'

The *Onyx* had a joyful run through the Mediterranean on a favourable easterly Levante. After enduring the cold and cramped cell of our prison for so long, the exhilarating pace was invigorating. Even the grey chop and driving rain couldn't touch us—the fresh air filled our lungs like new blood.

Nikos climbed the rigging with an easy grace, stretching his arms wide, letting the wind buffet him like a man tasting freedom for the first time. 'This is it, Ghika!' he called down.

Lieutenant Decœurdeux shared news of our fame on Malta. 'I heard you pirates had your death sentences commuted. Transportation, eh? Lucky you have friends in high places.'

Damos, ever blunt, grunted. 'Friends in high places didn't prevent life sentences in the colonies, Lieutenant. But not you, eh, Ghika? What was your sentence again? Fourteen years?'

I ignored Damos and answered the Englishman. 'Our advocate did a fine job of defending us, sir, but it was Spyridon Trikoupis who interceded on our behalf in London. He's a friend of my father's, and the Greek envoy to the Court of Saint James. However, the appeal took a year.'

'While we wasted away in prison,' added Damos.

While my mother had died, knowing she couldn't come to me, knowing her husband wouldn't. He had left me in that cell for a year and a half.

The lieutenant, an attentive listener, questioned how a person born into a wealthy family could end up facing a piracy court. This conversation bored my friends, but I welcomed his interest. We were *palikaria*, I told him. If he were in London, could he pass the word to any friends of Greece who might intercede on our behalf.

'Yes, Lieutenant,' drawled Damos. 'Do let us know about the Greek Committee, sir.'

Let Damos rant; he'd accepted having his death sentence commuted—thanks, no doubt, to my connections. I was finished interceding for him. Let him say what he wanted.

Sensing the tension, Andonis spoke. 'We're in this together, Damos. Ghikas' connections have been our lifeline. Don't bite the hand that feeds you.'

Questions for the lieutenant shot out of me like a barrage of cannon fire from a warship. Did he know anything about New South Wales and Van Diemen's Land? Would they imprison us or put us to work in a chain gang? Was there any sentence reduction for good behaviour?

'I know nothing of the Antipodes,' he said. 'I'm sorry.'

After six weeks at sea, our ship anchored on the Motherbank outside Portsmouth Harbour, in the straits between England and the Isle of Wight. Lieutenant Decœurdeux summoned us to the deck. 'You will be housed on a hulk, not the finest of accommodation. These decommissioned ships have had their masts removed and are anchored in the marshes west of the harbour. Mudflats lie beyond.'

Every man was listening.

'They classify convicts according to behaviour. Misbehave and you'll find yourself with the worst class of men, packed twenty to a bay in the bowels of the ship. Hulk fever runs rampant down there, and the air is so foul, a candle will not remain alight. The *York* is the worst, for she accommodates five hundred.'

Five hundred. The world was shrinking again. My breathing turned shallow. Jerky. I had thought exile was the worst of it. But there was always another level of hell. I shuddered at the thought of so many men crammed into the confines of a prison ship with no fresh air. My skin crawled with imaginary bugs.

Lieutenant Decœurdeux's expression softened. 'I will do what I can.'

Nikos sat with his back against the gunwale. His hands were busy—tying knots, rolling a coin over his fingers. He no longer spoke first. He was listening.

The next day we sailed into Portsmouth Harbour. The township lined the eastern shore, the thriving home base to the English navy for seven centuries—with barracks to house a thousand troops. Near the Naval dock-yard was a veritable forest of the masts of English men-o'-war. To the west lay Gosport, where the line of hulks leaned in the water, stretching away like the corpses of dying animals, no longer recognisable as the fine ships they once had been.

We dropped anchor near the dockyard, where Nelson's mighty *Victory* lay at berth, her 104 guns silent but her presence commanding.

The lieutenant returned several hours later, face sombre.

'Ghika, you are fortunate. You will be shipped to Port Jackson aboard the *Norfolk*, departing at the end of May. You are fortunate you will spend only two months in Portsmouth.' He hesitated. 'Because your accommodation is on the hulk I told you about. The *York*. May God have mercy on your souls.'

Fortunate. The word must mean something different in English.

I stared at the hulks rotting in the marsh.

I smelled the stench before I breathed it. Felt the press of five hundred bodies. The crawl of lice. The suck of breath in a space with no air.

Fortunate meant nothing—not with the *York* waiting.

25

An Invitation

RICHLANDS AND SYDNEY, New South Wales
December 1834

As we journey to Richlands, although my soul weeps for Chara, the anticipation of reuniting with my friends buoys my spirits. When we arrive, we make camp on the flat below the homestead, but a wave of disappointment grips me when I realise my companions have not arrived.

Burra Burra Lake, though vast, shallow and teeming with thousands of water birds, is not suitable for our purpose.

For ten days, we attend to the sheep—a tedious job—washing them in Burra Burra Creek and then manhandling the unwieldy weight of the wet sheep on land. They're herded onto grassy pasture to dry, ready for shearing.

Mister and Mrs Ryrie, the boys, and Jane, arrive to join William for the trip to Sydney. Late on the eve of their departure, William comes to me, saying, 'You may come with us, Jigger, to help Ned. I know you're worried about your dog—and you may return to Arnprior if you wish. But I'd pursue Mary. Let me know in the morning.'

Mary? Father Therry must have told him. Perhaps the good reverend is more involved than I realised. William is kind when he chooses—but he wants to keep me at Arnprior.

Just then, the crack of a whip echoes around the hills. I turn toward the sound, shielding my eyes against the glare. A dust cloud stirs on the ridge —movement. They come into sight like three brothers, nut-brown, curls unkempt, convict slops caked in dust. We are missing only Kostas. As if on cue, they raise their arms and shout, '*Eleftheria i thanatos*!'

I wish for a pair of pistols to fire into the air. Instead, I run. We fall on each other, laughing, shouting.

'*Yamas*!'

Joy bubbles up.

William approaches with a flask of rum. 'Good to see you boys have finally arrived. Jigger has worn a long face all the week.' He hands me the bottle. 'Enjoy your evening.'

'I like your boss!' says Damos as William walks away.

'For someone convinced of his own superiority, he does well enough,' I say. 'You've dodged the work, you lot.'

Damos laughs loudly. 'Thinks he's better than everyone else? Does that sound like someone we know?'

Nikos looks serious. 'Not Ghikas. He's my best friend.'

I push him in the shoulder. We hug.

Andonis says, 'It's good to see you, my friend. They gave us extra rations for making this journey. We will stay a few weeks. I hope you do too.'

'Bad luck for me. I leave for home tomorrow.'

Later, around the fire, Ando gives me his news.

'Once I have my Ticket of Leave, William Macarthur says he will allow me to share farm, Ghika, which means I take a share of the profits. As if the land is mine!'

He says 'mine' as if his residency is permanent. As if he belongs here. I grin and thump his back, but something twists in my gut. He's not coming home. Even if he's pardoned, he's not coming with me.

'Isn't the land yours, Andoni?' says Nikos.

'No, Niko,' says Andonis. 'It belongs to Mister Macarthur.'

'The Sydney newspapers are full of it,' says Damos. 'The fight over land. Who can own it. Who can't.'

'Bravo, Ando.'

'And what about you, Ghika?'

'There is no chance of sharecropping the poorer soils of Arnprior.'

Our conversation continues long into the night, way after the liquor is gone. We relive the good old days of sailing the seas. We sing the old tunes and wish Kostas were here with his jaw harp. *Kapetánios* Damos has us laughing once more with his comic tale of being captured on the Wellington.

Nikos shares more news. 'Ando is going to build his own hut, and marry his Elizabeth. Aren't you, Ando? She's Irish.'

This is indeed news. Nikos could not be prouder if this Elizabeth were to be his own wife.

'The Reverend Samuel Marsden will read the banns,' he adds.

'When?' I ask—excited.

Ando scuffs the dirt in front of his boot. 'No hurry. She's a friend. Nothing more.'

His tone shuts discussion—he will share when he is ready. I put my hand on his shoulder and squeeze.

'And you, Ghikaki?' he says.

I smile to hear this term of endearment after so long, but then I sober. 'A snake bit my dog, Chara, this week. My friend Joe is looking after her. It will break my heart if she dies.'

They make the sign of the cross, murmur their sympathy, slap my back.

'But what about a girl?' says Damos. 'Any on Arnprior?'

'Yes, I found one. But it came to nothing.'

Damos sits up. 'Nothing? What do you mean nothing?'

I shake my head, look away.

'Doesn't matter.'

But Nikos won't let it go. 'Was she Greek, Ghika? From home?'

I sigh. 'No. She was Irish, Niko. Like Ando's Elizabeth.'

'Irish?' Damos laughs. 'An Irish princess? A convict heiress?'

I smile, but my heart isn't in it. 'Neither. A housemaid.'

'*Ouáou!*' says Ando. 'No dowry? Is this the new Ghikas? Did she know how lucky she was?'

'No. She went back to Sydney. And she's marrying a *malakas* in January. Good riddance, I say.'

They snort with laughter. We are fifteen again.

Nikos smacks his forehead. 'You don't care?'

'What's wrong with you, Ghika?' says Damos. 'You said Ryrie wants you in Sydney!'

'Yes, Ghikaki, you must fight for her,' says Ando.

'Yes!' says Damos. 'Fight!'

'Fight!' says Nikos.

I want to return to Arnprior in case Chara is still alive.

It is not until near dawn, when the wood has burned to a few glowing coals, and the mosquitoes are biting, that we stretch out on the ground to sleep. Lying on my back, staring at the black velvet sky dotted with twinkling stars, I hear Ando whisper, 'Are you awake?'

I raise myself on my elbow. 'It's been too long, Ando. My heart is full.'

'For me as well.' He pauses, then drops his voice. 'Look, Ghika, I know how much your dog means to you. But you'd fight the sea if it challenged you, but now you won't fight for the woman you love?'

As I drift off to sleep, Ando's soft snoring is a comforting background.

Of course I must go to Sydney.

—

We arrive on Monday the 22nd of December, without having been robbed or bogged on the Parramatta Road, to find the town awash from a deluge two days before. Potholes brim with water; mud stains the hems of the ladies' skirts; wheelwrights busy themselves with repairs to broken wheels. Instead of camping as usual with Ned at the carters' barracks on common ground south of the town, I am to sleep in the garden hut.

When we alight at the house, the staff are lined up at the back door and the Ryrie boys run to Cook, who winks at me. Miss Jane disappears immediately, presumably to join society.

Mrs Ascham, the housekeeper, wears a black dress with a long white apron, her hair pulled into a tight bun on the top of her head.

'Madam,' she says to Mrs Ryrie, 'with Christmas Day on Thursday, market day this week has moved to tomorrow—so it's my last chance to buy provisions. If you are not too fatigued, might we discuss menus tonight?'

'Mrs Ascham, that is an excellent idea. I'm eager to see the new market sheds. I'd be delighted to join you. Ghikas will carry our purchases.'

Mrs Ascham looks doubtful. 'Are you sure you wish to come, madam? It's a rough sort of place.'

'I will enjoy the diversion.'

The next morning, the streets closest to the harbour still reek of last night's ale—from publicans tossing buckets of water across their door-ways. As we climb past the military hospital on the ridge, the air sharpens, cleaner. Ahead, the great blades of the windmill catch the breeze and turn steadily. Past the parade ground, the market comes alive—farmers unloading drays piled high with vegetables, voices rising in barter. Bullock teams groan and heave, hauling wagons up from the Cockle Bay wharf below.

Mrs Ryrie marvels at the handsome design of the four new buildings: the floors are stone, and inside each, stallholders face each other across a central corridor, with the roof allowing cooling breezes. The first building contains meat, poultry, eggs, butter and cheese, and the next has fruit and vegetables.

My thoughts are elsewhere. The stable hand knows where the Watts live, and I will call there, but I'm afraid Mary may be reluctant to give me an audience.

Our first stop is Smith's Butcher Shop across the way. The floor is a carpet of sawdust, and a group of Aboriginal people are leaving the premises—Mrs Ascham whispers about a few locals who throw stones—but Mister Smith, an ex-convict, conducts fair trade with them. They sell their freshly caught fish and give him news from the waterfront.

In the market, there is no lucerne hay, but good supplies of straw, oaten hay, and maize.

When we enter the fruit and vegetable hall, Mrs Ascham says, 'You may wish to put your hands over your ears, madam. The shouting of the vendors is quite hideous.'

Trays are piled high with pyramids of fruit and vegetables in all colours: the greens of cabbages, cucumbers, beans, peas, pears, gooseber-ries and apples; oranges and lemons, peaches, carrots and apricots, and purple plums. Currants, prunes, sultanas, raisins and rich spices for

Christmas puddings are stacked in baskets, fresh from a ship. Potatoes are scarce, but Mrs Ascham has a good store of them in the cellar, brought from Arnprior. Mrs Ascham is formidable in her pursuit of the best price, and Mrs Ryrie's hand flies to her throat in shock each time a figure is mentioned. 'Lemons at *two shillings* for the dozen! I don't believe it!'

Mister Ryrie always jokes about her Scottish blood. As if he weren't just as careful with money.

In the meat hall, the air is rich with the aroma of cured hams and bacon. An array of poultry—ducks, geese, and turkeys—hangs from wires, and vendors have stacked fine cuts alongside Bathurst cheese, known for its excellence. Mrs Ryrie's eyes widen at the sight of the plump geese, ideal for Christmas lunch, but she gasps at the price. Mrs Ascham hastens to convince her of its value.

I've left my cart under the watchful eye of the constable on the corner, and I take out a bag of coal, and one of apples. The shops are opening, and in a window display nearby is a little earthenware jar like a Brown Betty—with a coin slot in the snug-fitting lid—perfect for Joe. I'll buy tobacco for Martin.

Back in the market, I have the extraordinary feeling I am watched.

I turn to look.

Everything blurs but one person—Mary.

She stands still at a stall, basket on her arm, eyes locked on me. A passerby jostles her, but she doesn't move.

She shines as if the day itself is conspiring to reveal her at her most radiant.

Every longing of these past months finds expression in my broadest smile, while my pulse thunders.

She clasps her hands to her mouth.

'Mary,' I say. 'Mary. You—'

She lowers them. 'Ghika.' A breath. 'You're looking well.'

She's holding something back—regret, surprise.

Not anger. Relief floods my body, my shoulders relax.

'Thank you. And you have been in a—'

I stop myself from saying 'good paddock' and flash a smile. 'Sydney agrees with you.'

Her deepening dimples show she remembers the day at the Bloodsworths'.

'And Chara? Would she be herding the sheep by now, while you take your ease on the verandah?' That impish grin.

The strength goes out of my legs. 'Nearly—although a snake bit her.'

Her hand flies to her heart, and she gasps, 'No!'

'She was ill when I left. But Joe is caring for her.'

'Oh, Ghika. I'm so sorry. Will she survive?'

I shrug.

'You'd miss her terribly.'

'Almost as much as I miss you.'

Her face pales. She grips her smock, frozen for a heartbeat—throat working, lips parting—then smooths the fabric with slow, deliberate care, as if she could press the moment away.

'I am now in service with Mrs Hercules Watt, wife of the currier, on the other side of the Tank Stream, near the Governor's house. And—'

She hesitates.

'And?'

'I am engaged to be married.'

Her words slice straight through me as her fingers close around a silver ring.

'You said you would never marry.'

'Yes, Ghika. I was daft to think I could make my own way in this world. It's not the same for men. They sail off and build empires. We women are followed in the market if we speak too boldly. You said as much the day I met you.'

I read the resignation in her eyes. I did this to her.

'Do you love him?'

'Marriage is not about love, Ghika. It's a contract. You taught me that. You never stopped talking about how you're going home to marry, to join your houses.'

My fingers curl into fists. I steady my breath, but my pulse is hammering.

'I am not.'

She lifts an eyebrow.

'I have found a wife here.'

Her surprise is evident.

'She's not obedient, however.'

Her expression tightens. I can see into her soul. She's hurting.

'Compromised, then?' She is stoic. 'Where did you find her?'

'At Arnprior.' I watch her closely.

A sceptical lift of her eyebrow. 'Really.'

'She is Irish.'

Mary stills, one hand tightening on the basket strap. She has a slight furrow in her forehead.

'A foundling. A very annoying one.'

She blinks, face still impassive.

I open my mouth, then close it again. Not here. Not like this. But if not now, when?

'It is you, Mary. I want to marry you.'

I have spoken too loudly, and a nearby servant girl nudges the red-nosed waif beside her. They both giggle.

Mary lets out a huge breath of distress.

'You wait until you lose something, Ghika, before you value it.' She breaks off, blinking, jaw tightening. ''Tis too late.'

She loves me. No matter what she says. I see it in her hands. Her eyes. The way she steadies her voice.

I step closer. She steps back, palm raised. I'm tempted to remind her that this is an insult in Greece, but I think the better of it. Let her raise her hand all she wishes.

'I'm committed to Mister Townsend. He is a good man, and he guides me. He helps me fix my flaws. That is that.'

Her voice cracks, matching the feeling in my chest.

'Flaws? You have none! He guides you? Don't you deserve love, Mary?'

'It's safety I have now. And certainty. And I'm grateful for it. 'Tis worth more than any excitement.'

'Safety? Is that what you truly want? Please don't marry him.'

'The banns are set to be read. It's done.'

I'm boiling now. She loves me, but she will marry him?

'He's rich.' I whisper it.

The servant girls gasp. Mary's eyes flash.

'Are you suggesting—?' Her voice could frost glass. 'Unlike you, Ghika, I'm not one to judge a man by his money.' She shifts the basket handle in a brisk movement. 'Excuse me. I have more interesting business to attend to. With a dead duck.'

The servant girl and her friend both laugh loudly.

I stand there, gutted.

Mary is looking past me.

I turn. A slow clap breaks the spell. Clap. Clap. Clap.

Townsend stands near the market entrance, peels off his gloves, slaps them together.

'Quite the performance, my dear.'

Mary stiffens. I turn. Black cutaway wool coat, velvet lapels in the Sydney heat; white linen shirt, silk cravat, new, tighter style of fly-fronted trousers, as William Ryrie wears. Watch chain.

The type of man who assumes the prize is his.

He guides her beside him, eyes me up and down with a flicker of disdain. 'And who might this be?'

'Mister Townsend, I'd like you to meet Mister Voulgaris,' Mary says.

Our handshake is a battle, my grip unyielding until his eyes twitch.

'Ah yes. The shepherd. Mister Bull—?' His tone is condescending.

'Indeed, sir. And your profession is in *trade*, if I'm not mistaken?'

Mary catches her breath. Townsend goes red in the face. 'Trade, sir, is the backbone of Sydney.'

'On the contrary, sir: it is the men who work with their hands who create a nation's wealth.'

He fixes his gaze on the hagstone around my neck. 'It's amusing how the lower classes place their faith in superstition, rather than hard work.'

I step forward. Slightly. Just enough.

Townsend holds his ground.

'Perhaps if you wore a hagstone, Mister Townsend, you might have made a profit on that last silk consignment?' Mary cuts in, smiling.

His jaw tightens. 'Nonsense.' He peers into her basket. 'Mary, where is the duck? The oysters?' He glances at the empty space in her basket. 'I trust you haven't been—distracted.'

I suck in my breath. She won't like that—treating her like a servant, reprimanding her in public.

Then I see it—the smallest flinch when Townsend's fingers graze her wrist.

Mary swings the basket out of his reach. 'Please don't concern yourself, Richard. My errands are well in hand,' she says lightly.

Something has changed in her demeanour. Her shoulders square. Her tone sharpens. She's not performing now.

She turns to me. 'Hercules and Mary are hosting a supper this evening. Will you join us?'

Townsend goes a bright shade of tomato. He blusters, 'Convicts roaming the streets at night? Out of the question, my dear.'

I lock eyes with him. 'I'll be there.'

'Six o'clock, then,' she says. 'The second-last house on Phillip Street.'

The wind has changed. And this time, it's at my back.

26

The York

MALTA TO PORTSMOUTH
April 1829

With each stroke of our oars, the *York* loomed closer—a carcass of rotting timbers and rusted iron, less a ship than a floating tomb. Beyond it lay only desolate marshes. There would be no escape here. A wooden staircase zigzagged up the outside of the dark, discoloured hull, winding past ancient gun ports barred with iron lattice like missing teeth. As I gripped the iron rail, I thought briefly of the polished marble steps at home.

The sound of washing flapping on ropes slung between the mast stumps banished the thought. Sandflies swarmed on nearby mudflats. On the top deck, the bosun, a bloated, dishevelled fellow—and a convict like us—sat with a pen poised over a stained vellum-bound book, the top of the page marked '4th April 1829'.

Our guard handed over our names and the letter from Lieutenant Decœurdeux.

I nudged Andonis. 'Who is your fat friend?'

Nikos laughed loudly.

The bosun's head snapped up. 'Who said that?'

'I did,' said Andonis.

'No, I did.' Damos, Kostas and I spoke at the same time.

'It was me,' Nikos bellowed—which made us all laugh.

The bosun went red in the face. With a sharp snap of his fingers, he signalled for silence. He would decide who wore shackles and who wouldn't.

With thick fingers pinching the quill, he scratched an inky star beside Andonis' name. I had made the joke; Andonis would bear the mark.

I leaned closer to the desk. 'Sir, it was I who spoke.'

He pointed to a set of heavy shackles on the floor. 'Shut up and stand back, or he'll have it worse.'

I stepped back. He read the letter.

'So, we have an important guest. Now—what's his name?' He scratched his beard as he looked down again to read. 'Burglary. Which one's him?'

Someone snorted with laughter, but someone groaned—once again my friends felt singled out because of me.

'That's Ghikas,' said Nikos, pointing. 'He's important.'

I stepped forward. 'Sir.'

'Ah, pity. The hero. Don't like your name, don't like your face.'

We were off to a good start.

His laugh revealed a gold tooth, a veneer, we discovered later, hammered from jewellery he had filched from prisoners. He looked me up and down.

'Any coins, Burglary?'

Damos snorted, unable to help himself.

The bosun turned to him, his tone laden with malice. 'What's amusing you, bilge rat?'

That wiped the smile off Damos' face.

The bosun looked back at me. 'Any valuables, rich boy? Give them up now.'

I considered offering him my talent for sarcasm, but thought better of it.

With his quill, he transferred our details to the book until he had blotched the page. 'Thank your friend,'—he tapped the lieutenant's letter —'for your berths. But one foot wrong, and you'll be in the orlop.'

He closed his book. 'Now, delousing.'

—

An hour later, our heads were almost bare of hair, hacked tufts remaining, our bodies red, raw flesh, in places bleeding. The smell of lye soap mixed with blood nauseated me.

'Looking pretty, you are,' said the bosun.

He saw my expression and smirked. 'Did you expect a tailor with epaulettes?'

Slops came in one size. The trousers were tied with a belt or rope at the waist, and they dwarfed slight men like Andonis. One pair of trousers, one misshapen grey jacket marked with an arrow to denote government property, a coarse linen shirt with the texture of a rasp, a pair of thick stockings, a hat and a handkerchief.

I turned to Nikos. 'Be honest, Niko. Does this suit my eyes?'

He was about to answer, but then he laughed fit to burst.

Our cleaner, softer clothes would doubtless go to the wardrobes of our captors.

A blacksmith appeared, holding a clutch of clanging leg irons. 'One each. Right leg. No chain.' He let them fall to the deck with a loud crash.

They dragged on our legs twice as heavily as the ones on Malta, which still featured in my nightmares.

'That's the end of our running races,' I said.

'Ain't about running,' the blacksmith said. 'Try swimming.'

He dropped a heavier set at my feet.

'Fancy those?' He clicked his tongue.

Nikos crouched and felt their weight. 'You'd sink, Ghika.'

The guards pushed us to the stern. As we passed each companionway, a powerful stench rose like a solid wall. I gagged, hand over my mouth and nose. There must surely be dead bodies below. The captain emerged from inside his cabin, an affable man with an unhealthy wheeze.

'So you're the Greek pirates,' he puffed. 'Welcome aboard the *York*. Remember, no convict may own property of any sort. Betray that trust, and you will find a home on the orlop deck.' He rubbed his hands together as if expecting an entertainment.

At ten o'clock that night, a commotion broke out on the deck above our heads, then the unfamiliar sound of a feminine laugh.

'Was that a woman?' Damos jerked upright.

'Probably,' drawled one of our cellmates. 'The captain goes ashore at night and the crew bring slatterns aboard from Portsmouth Point.' His voice caressed the words.

'We hear them taking their pleasure,' sighed another. 'I love the sound of the Irish girls the best. Their laughter's like sweet music.'

Damos sighed like a man at his last rites.

We had already learned to identify accents: the cut-crystal English accent of the well-born and educated, the jerky speech pattern of the Londoner, the musical lilt of the Irish, and the almost unintelligible gibberish of the Scots. So were Irish girls different? I would have given anything to hear the softness of a woman's voice. I pushed aside the thought of what was going on above our heads.

The following morning, we rolled up our hammocks and stored them in a corner of our cabin. At the first of two breakfast sittings, in the huge chapel-refectory at the other end of the ship, with the now-familiar stench in our noses, the footfalls of two hundred and fifty men thundered on the boards. A kitchen hand slopped bitter cocoa into my jar as I took a twelve-ounce lump of bread, rich with pink and black mildew.

Not the worst breakfast I'd ever had. But close.

We found space on an unoccupied bench, its surface a mosaic of old stains.

The bosun thumped the table with his fist, a chaplain gave a blessing, and we ate our runny grey oatmeal in silence. My mind drifted back to layers of succulent eggplant *moussaka*, spiced meat.

A giant of a man was approaching, bending now and then to speak in a low voice to another convict. He and his two followers appeared to be exempt from the quiet rule.

He stopped in front of us. 'Ah'm Donald. Ah'd best git straight tae the point, new boys,' he drawled in a rolling Scottish burr. Fair-skinned and red-faced, he had a gap between his two front teeth and a slight whistle in his speech. A narrow halo of ginger hair bordered a shining bald pate above his ears. Gaping holes in his earlobes must once have held earrings.

He smiled with genuine warmth. 'You need tae ken two words on the *York*. Respect an' grief. You gie me respect, and a tithe of the wages you earn at the dockyard, an' I'll nae gie you grief. Ma friends will call to collect.'

When he saw a guard approaching, he shuffled off.

Who ran the *York*? The guards? The bosun? Or Donald?

As I finished the stinking slop in the cup, feet scraped the floorboards outside the refectory. Two convicts passed the door carrying a lifeless body by the arms and legs.

The wretch across the table from me had his arm crooked around his plate to protect it. He stared at me, as if sightless, out of swollen red eyes, hollow cheeks bulging as he chewed. He leaned forward to utter a confidence. 'The poor sod will have died on the orlop deck. Fever. Or—' He rolled his eyes right back until I could see only the whites. 'The strong prey on the weak. 'Tis how it is. Don't tell them I told you.'

On the way out, guards suddenly surrounded the giant red-haired Scot. One hit him on the side of the head with the butt of his musket and he fell to the floor, writhing. 'That's for talking during breakfast, Donald.'

When another guard went to kick him in the ribs, I put out my leg, taking the blow. I took a musket blow to the head for my trouble.

Donald took my offered hand to pull himself up as the guards walked away. 'I'll make them pay. Ye're a braw laddie. Any trouble, you let me know.'

The guards laughed as they walked away, the sound echoing through the deck.

Nikos nodded solemnly. 'They laugh a lot here.'

I said, 'And they only hit convicts at breakfast. That's restraint.'

All hands were put to scrubbing the decks with sand and seawater. A guard tossed me a bucket. I thought of the day Andonis and I, as ships' boys, had filled a drinking water bucket with seawater. My father was first to take a sip and blew it out like a blowhole.

At morning roll call, an officer addressed us. 'Your wage at the dockyard will be a biscuit, one pint of small, and a half-penny worth of tobacco.'

'Small' was a weak, tasteless beer, safer to drink than water.

We rowed across the harbour to Portsmouth dockyard, a sight such as I had never imagined. Two thousand convicts worked on backbreaking tasks inside the high brick walls. A three-basin dry dock area occupied a vast tract of land reclaimed from the sea. A menacing forty-six-gun frigate was taking shape—and two ten-gun brigs. And smaller craft. Horse-powered chain pumps relentlessly drained murky water. Convicts worked on tread-wheel cranes unloading goods. An enormous steam engine belched forth smoke and steam.

Our guard, knowing we were sailors, pointed at a building. 'Ten men make one hundred thousand pulley blocks a year in there, on special machines.'

At home, we made them by hand.

He pointed at another. 'That's a thousand feet long, that rope building. They spin the yarn on the highest of those three floors, and wind it into rope below.'

We watched in awe as eighty men emerged from it, handling a single rope.

A team of us grunted and strained, hauling a tram loaded with one of three masts to the dock, ready to be fitted to a man-o'-war.

I saw one of Donald's boys slip him a copper. Donald grinned. I watched them from then on—I worked out he had a system—his boys helped smaller convicts for a price. They paid him in coin when the guards weren't looking.

Returning to the *York* for our midday meal was a journey into despair —our food came by rowboat from what the guards called the Gosport Weevil Yard. Rations passed through so many hands that the lowest class of convict received only a quarter of his allowance.

As we rowed back to the dockyard again for the afternoon detail, the guards were deep in debate: should Irish Catholics be allowed to sit in the British Parliament? They hadn't done so for a hundred years.

'Nothing but rabble, them Irish,' said one.

Unlike Greeks, of course. Scholars. Philosophers. Gentlemen.

I'd thought that our war—Christian against Turk—was the only one still being fought. But here, Protestants crushed Catholics. The Irish wanted the English gone. One guard said the French king was jailing anyone who spoke against him. Everywhere, someone had their boot on someone else's neck.

Weeks dragged on. Any hope of contacting London—or Spyridon Trikoupis—withered.

As our time on the *York* drew to an end, we trod carefully. Smuggling contraband from the dockyard was a dangerous sport—if suspected, you earned the lash or a new set of irons. A man coughed too loudly at muster and the bosun made an example of him: one lash for every guard on deck. Thirteen, that day.

Luckily the hay fever was bad that week.

Donald, bless him, gave us a few coins for the colony. I sewed mine into my slops—they might be the last coins I'd see. Later, stretched out in my hammock, the ship creaking around me, I felt the coins pressing against my thigh. Nikos slept beside me, talking in his dreams.

I thought of home—an ache like a rope burn.

A shot cracked through the night. Then another. Silence. Somewhere, a man had gambled on freedom—and lost. Another drowned in the black water. A third was dragged back aboard, ribs showing through shredded skin. One hundred lashes. Then death.

They went into the orlop on their feet and came out as corpses, bunks refilled before the bodies cooled.

We had, so far, avoided the fever that nested in the bowels of the *York*. With luck, we'd stay that way.

At muster one morning, the captain announced: the *Norfolk* would sail for New South Wales in two weeks.

We had two weeks to keep our heads down and mouths shut.

Two weeks to survive.

Then we'd be on the open ocean.

We'd say goodbye to hell—although we wouldn't exactly be heading for paradise.

27

A Single Soul

SYDNEY, New South Wales
   December 1834

Mrs Ascham claps her hands with delight when she hears of the invitation. 'Supper, you say? Well. You must give me a full account of the evening. Every detail.'

'Of course you must attend, Ghika,' says Mrs Ryrie. 'A man like Mister Watt, rising by his own effort—that is the kind of example this colony needs. We must give credit where it is due.'

Mrs Ascham insists on lending me clothing belonging to her husband —including a jacket that might tear under the arms if I so much as inhale. I nick my chin shaving, of course, and blot it with a cloth to prevent staining the collar. My curls spring up behind the comb, as they always do. Cook gives me a black velvet ribbon to tie them back and picks the fluff from my sleeve. When she licks her finger and reaches for my chin, I pull away, laughing.

Between them, they do their best. I will never pass for a gentleman, but at least I will not embarrass Mary.

Miss Jane comes into the kitchen. 'You're looking quite the gentleman, Ghikas. Mary will surely be impressed.' And then she winks.

She knows about Mary? This family seems to know more about me—and my intentions—than I do myself.

The Watt's house, a stone's throw from the Bloodsworth's, boasts an Indian verandah style common to prosperous parts of the town. I arrive as the watchman calls the sixth hour.

On the front wall, a sign:

HERCULES WATT

Currier

Leathers: sole, kip, calf, kangaroo, harness and basils

Orders executed with punctuality and despatch

My knock is louder than I intended. My worn rawhide work shoes are almost black from the linseed oil I applied this afternoon. At least they look clean.

The door of the house opens and the sound of laughter drifts down the hallway.

A child of about ten years stands before me in his night clothes, red hair slicked down, freckles sprinkling his nose. 'Good evening, sir,' he says, in an Irish accent.

Peeking out from behind him is another boy of about five. The older boy points and says, 'He's Hercules. Same as our da. I'm John. Please follow me.'

'How do you do?' I shake both their hands. 'Please call me Ghika.' They drop their chins behind their hands to hide their giggles.

I follow them along the hallway until John points into a room on my right. Hercules points too, like a shadow.

'Your servant, John.' I bow from my waist. I turn and bow again. 'Your servant, Hercules.'

John bows back. The smaller fellow puts one bare foot upon the other.

I step into a smoke-filled room, alive with Irish voices. Emerald green and wine-red velvets gleam against polished wood, and a Persian rug muffles the noise. I don't see Mary. Then a rotund man with freckled skin

292

and wispy ginger hair steps forward, hand outstretched. I take him for the boys' father.

'Ah, the Greek pirate!' he roars. 'Everyone, meet Mary's friend.'

His wife's hand lies limp in mine as she tries my surname. 'It's so wonderful to meet you, Mister—'

The stiff collar rasps my skin and the necktie feels like a noose. If I'm to die tonight, I'd almost rather it be at Townsend's hands than strangled by borrowed finery.

'Friends,' says my host in a loud voice again, 'I introduce Gerkas Boolgary. Mister Townsend, whom I think you know.'

I step forward to shake the hand of the man who presumes to marry Mary. A diamond-studded pin shines in the folds of silk at his throat. His hand closes on mine in a vicious grip, and this time I crush much harder in return.

As I scan the room, a twinge of disappointment hits me: Mary isn't here. I turn my attention to mingling with the other guests, introducing myself to Mrs Watt's family—the jovial Kennedys and their wives. By the look of their flushed faces, they've already indulged in the rum bottles on the side table. Despite Mary's absence, I find myself gradually drawn into several overlapping conversations, trying to understand the thick Irish accents above the chatter, answering questions thrown my way.

The chief topic of conversation is the death of Jack the Rammer, and their sympathies lie with the bushranger, even though he was not an Irishman. I learn he was transported for stealing a bucket. I learn too of the Kennedys' convict lineage, proudly traced back to a conviction for forgery which brought their father, along with Hercules Watt, to New South Wales. Kennedy's daughter Mary eventually followed, becoming Hercules' wife. Her brothers followed too, one for sheep stealing.

One jokes that, were it not for the dullness of the Irish constabulary, they'd all be convicts.

Mrs Watt's brother Hugh asks about my work as a shepherd, and the quality of the wool at Arnprior. 'I hear Botany Bay fleeces are so fine,' he says, 'that any clod of an English broker can identify them by touch alone.'

I sense her presence before I see her. She is beside me, giddying in her nearness.

She stops short when she sees me, as if she hadn't expected me to come.

'I am glad you came, Ghikas.'

Her voice is breathy from hurrying. 'Baby Louisa would not sleep until I read her *Mother Goose* and sang her a song.'

The thought of Mary singing to a child catches me off guard. I can almost hear her voice—soft, lilting, filling a quiet room. A voice she shared with me only that once. The day we met. Maybe that's why I'm so affected.

She looks at her employer. 'I tucked the boys in, too. We read a page of *The Swiss Family Robinson*.'

'Thank you, Mary,' says Mrs Watt.

Townsend appears. 'Mary, my latest shipment of imported silks—come and tell Meg which you prefer.'

Mary raises an eyebrow at me, and I roll my eyes at her. It's an old game we play.

Townsend notices and his smile tightens. 'You two seem—familiar.' He takes a slow sip of wine. 'I suppose that's the bush for you. It has a way of making people forget their place.'

Townsend raises his hand toward a curl at Mary's temple. I freeze—but he stops short and adjusts his cuff instead. The pounding in my temples is so loud they must hear it.

He steers Mary away while Mrs Watt keeps me busy with introductions.

When dinner is ready, we move into another room across the hallway. I stand aside, hoping to take Mary's arm, but there is no standing on ceremony here. Men and women jostle in together.

Lamplight and candles reflect in the gleaming wood, the sparkling glass and fine china. Hercules slides his hand along a fine oak table which almost fills the room. 'I bought this at an auction down near the wharf. From a manor house in Scotland. It comes apart in pieces, otherwise it would not have fitted up the corridor!' He laughs and picks up a fork. 'And the silver. Bought that too.' He hooks his thumbs in his waistcoat.

'Handsome,' I say.

'You should attend the auction in Pitt Street next week, Hercules,' says Townsend. 'I dare say you will find much to interest you there.'

The currier sits at the head of the table, with Mary next to him. Mrs Watt bids me to sit beside her at the other end, yet when I pull out the chair for her, she seems surprised. Then she smiles. I sit to one side of her, Townsend on the other.

'I confess I prefer to eat in the kitchen, as we always have.' She places the flat of her hand on her napkin. 'But Mister Watt is more cultured than me. His business is prospering.' She looks at him with fondness.

Hercules thumps the table and, without waiting for silence, gives thanks to the Lord for our meal. The Kennedy boys argue good-naturedly about some cattle they have purchased. Or *duffed*. I am not sure. The soup is thick in consistency, flavoured with butter, carrot and onion. Some guests run their fingers around their bowls, licking their fingers. Although their manners are rough, the banter and enjoyment are sincere, with Hercules' voice loud enough to reach from one end of the table to the other, when he quiets his guests.

Townsend and I exchange polite words with our hostess and the people on either side, but not with each other. The tension lingers, casting a shadow over the otherwise pleasant conversation.

'I worry about robbers,' Mrs Watt confides. 'Four young rogues smashed the windows of a house halfway along the street last week, and at four o'clock in the morning. The owner is offering a five pounds reward.'

A princely sum. Half of what the Ryries offered Mary for an entire year's work.

'Mister Bul—Bul—sir, please take care when you return to your accommodation later this evening. These vagabonds hide in wait for the unwary. There is talk of lighting our streets, for which we will pay upkeep of a penny a night, but as yet, it is only a proposal.'

In Sydney, high boundary walls are a necessity of life. I saw one earlier today with its top studded with pieces of broken glass.

Mrs Watt leans forward. 'Tomorrow, Mary and I are going to see Mrs Hordern in King Street.' Her voice has a consumptive wheeze. 'She has a new shipment. I worked as a dressmaker before I became Mister Watt's wife, and Mary helped me choose the fabric for my gown. She witnessed our marriage.'

She and Mary smile at each other. I am pleased that Mary's employers are her friends also, and interested in her welfare.

'And now I take the same joy in helping her. We share a love of these things. We particularly want to look at the shoes from Denmark and Morocco.'

I know how Mary loves ribbons. I should, for it was Townsend who offered to stake her the funds for an 'emporium'. The soup turns to paste in my mouth.

The second course is roast pork with crackling, fragrant, crisp and oozing with fat.

'A rare treat,' says Mrs Watt, 'from the market today.'

Townsend wasn't granted his wish for duck.

Hercules' voice booms along the table.

'Townsend, did you see that Richard Lang's house in George Street is to be auctioned in a week? Ten rooms, verandahs, wonderful position with extensive views, one of the healthiest positions in the town. Recommended for those with weak constitutions.' Everyone laughs. 'You'll be needing a home for your new wife?'

I think of the size of my father's house, and the hut on Arnprior. I think of Townsend and Mary living together as man and wife. I'd like to kick my chair back and pound him to a pulp with my bare fists.

His face reddens. 'It's true that Mary and I will need space, Hercules, for the sons we plan to rear.'

Mary turns scarlet and her hands drop into her lap. 'Richard,' she chides. Not a plea. A warning.

He ignores it. But his grin falters. He looks back at me. For half a second, there's a flicker of uncertainty, maybe even regret. But it passes.

His smile resets, broader than before. 'Yes indeed, we will need a spacious family home. Lang's house is fine at that. What do you say, Bulgary?'

He bangs his glass on the table.

He has drunk more rum than I realised.

'What size do you think Mary and I will need for our brood of children? Larger than your home back in Greece, I'll wager?'

I feel every eye shift toward me. The thought of this oaf making children with Mary fills me with rage. I squeeze my glass so tightly I fear it will shatter in my grip. Mary stares at me, face wretched.

I control myself. 'My family's home was smaller than most in our class. But on our island, one does not brag about the size of one's dwelling, sir.'

Townsend has a slight tic at the side of his eye. 'Perhaps because one has nothing to brag about?'

An intake of breath along the table.

He is emboldened. 'What is the name of this island?'

'Hydra, sir. It's a small island off the Argolic peninsula.' He looks blank. 'Off the Morea.'

Townsend puts his hands against the table and pushes his chair back as if bored. 'Never heard of it. I suppose on Hydra, a man's status is measured by the size of his house?'

I dig my fingers into my thigh.

Mrs Watt places her hand on Townsend's arm. 'Mister Townsend, might I be offering you—'

He shakes it off, eager for my answer. Our host is frowning in disapproval; one of the Kennedy boys shakes his head; Mary twists her napkin. I do not wish to spoil the evening or upset her. I must handle this delicately.

'Respect and status, sir, aren't bought at auction,' I say.

His tic twitches again. 'In my experience, that sort of thing is usually said by a man who has neither.'

'I say, Townsend.' Hercules raises his hand. 'There's no call for rudeness.'

Townsend waves Hercules' comment away, the chair creaking as he leans back in triumph. 'And what was your trade, sir, before you became a convict?'

'I worked on an Ýdriot family's fleet of ships. Schooners, brigs, three-masted polaccas.'

'A fleet?'

'Nine of them. And smaller craft.'

'My dear sir,' he drawled. 'Nine ships? Belonging to one family? Preposterous.' He looked around the table, enjoying his moment. 'And what family would this be, with such vast wealth?'

I murmured in Greek, '*I oikogéneia tou patéra mou.*'

'Speak English, man.'

'The family Voulgaris. My father and his brothers.'

His mouth already hangs open, ready to laugh. Instead, he grabs his wine glass and drinks the contents in one gulp.

Hercules roars with laughter. 'Got you then, Townsend! Mary, we need some port!'

But it's his wife who rises to fetch it. The guests rock on their chairs, slap the table, snort with hilarity.

Townsend's face has gone purple. His arrogance deserved a knock, but I didn't mean for it to turn into a spectacle. I unclench my hands.

In the hubbub, one of the Kennedy boys raises his glass to me, '*Sláinte*!'

But he tips his glass sideways and the contents spill over his wife's skirts. She stands abruptly with a good-natured cry, her chair clattering against the wall.

'John, you oaf, my new gown!'

'Arrah, what a waste of grog!' He laughs and wipes a clumsy hand over the stain.

Mary smiles at me again. She dips her napkin in a water glass and moves to sponge the fabric. The chatter continues. The dessert is a rich plum pudding laced with more rum.

I trust we will soon leave the table to allow me the chance to speak to Mary. But the Kennedy boys are in high spirits—the law imposes unnecessary restraints on the questionable enterprises of these loveable rogues.

One of their uproarious tales involves riding a stallion into a bar, where the publican's wife says, 'May I fetch you a rum, sir? And for your horse?'

They howl with infectious laughter and almost fall off their chairs.

The youngest brother's wife shares a tale of her husband's run-ins with the law for selling sly grog in Wollongong. When she warned him of potential arrest, he said, 'Send the troopers one by one. I'll handle them!'

That sends another wave of laughter around the table.

Near the end of the meal, Hercules calls for a toast. A scrape of chairs, a clink of crystal glasses. 'To Townsend and Mary. To a long and happy marriage.' Townsend smirks.

Mary lifts her glass—then pauses. Slowly, deliberately, she sets it back down, untouched. Her eyes scan the table. Then flick to mine.

I allow myself a glimmer of hope.

'And loyalty,' Townsend adds, and his eyes don't leave Mary.

At last, we move back into the parlour. I thank Mrs Watt and Hercules, say goodbye to the Kennedys, shake hands with the men, who are louder now, and quite drunk.

I leave Mary till last. She approaches me at the door of the parlour.

'Thank you for being here tonight, Ghika. I loved it when you spoke Greek. It's such a beautiful language.'

Cheekbones pronounced. Those green eyes. A sprinkling of freckles all over her face, so faint they could be imaginary. That smooth throat.

'Will you see me out?' I ask.

We walk together, neither of us speaking.

I stop beside her at the door.

'In the words of Aristotle,' I murmur, '*Miá psychí dyo sómasin oikoúsa.*'

Her eyes shine with delight and she claps her hands in front of her chest, holding her palms together. 'Yes, it sounds so beautiful! Those soft s's. I love them! What do they mean?'

She smiles in that way that makes me want to crush her to my chest— yet cradle her like porcelain for fear she will break.

'Do you really want to know?'

'To be sure, I do!'

I lower my voice, feel it vibrating in my chest. 'It means that you and I are one soul, living inside two bodies. A single soul.'

She breathes in sharply, as if she's been struck.

Her lips part, but she says nothing. Her hands press to her heart. For a moment, I think she will cry.

Then she blinks, straightens, and laughs—quick and light.

'Oh, Ghika,' she says. 'That's beautiful. To be sure.'

I'm about to propose marriage again, when her smile fades. 'Beautiful words Ghika. Words a girl might have wanted to hear. Once.'

I take her hand, certain I can turn her mood.

She is looking at me. Really looking at me. My chest tightens. I want to pull her close, to promise—I will make no more mistakes.

She says quietly, 'When we spoke this afternoon—about marriage being a contract—I meant it. A soul has no place in a business bargain.'

I flinch. I'm such an oaf. 'Mary, I—'

She lifts her fingers to my lips. 'I can't speak of it now. Tomorrow.'

She hasn't said yes. But she hasn't said no.

Her hand in mine—her eyes—it's done.

Or near enough. I just have to get her to say it.

But she slips her hand free and closes the door in my face for a second time.

A flutter of doubt stirs in my chest.

28

PORTSMOUTH

A Piece of Cheese

THE HULK *YORK,* Portsmouth, England
    April-May 1829

I was already clammy when I climbed aboard the *York*—the fever had begun, and my stomach cramped from insufficient rations and bad water. When I saw the bosun's cheese lying on his table, I didn't think. I grabbed it and stuffed it into my mouth.

Andonis caught up with me as I strode away along the deck, trying to swallow. 'What's that in your gob? You didn't take the bosun's cheese, did you? It's only a week until we leave for New South Wales! We must stay out of trouble.' He blinked, as if he wasn't sure whether I was joking or had lost my mind.

I tried to respond, but the cheese lodged in my throat. I coughed and laughed all at once. 'Yes. Want some?'

He cast a wary look behind us. 'Ghika, have you gone mad? He'll notice it's missing!'

My punishment came the next morning. By then I was drenched in sweat and shaking, and I barely made it to the refectory, where I fell onto a bench at the table.

The bosun's voice reverberated through the room, stern and commanding.

'Someone took my cheese yesterday. If the thief does not confess, all aboard will go without rations for three days.'

I tried to stand to own up to my deed, but a swarm of black spots crowded my vision, and the world went dark as my forehead met the wood with a thud.

—

I woke choking on my own tongue. Men groaned in hammocks around me, bilge sloshing beneath and the stink of death in the air. The orlop.

No light. No fresh air.

Shapes emerged in the gloom. On instinct, my hand reached for the amulet. Of course it was gone. My hammock was hemmed tight on both sides.

Head pounding, eyes half-matted shut, so thirsty I could not swallow, I croaked, 'Water.'

'We all need water,' said a voice, 'except for him next to me. He's dead. Wait, like the rest of us.'

I fell back, exhausted. The face of my mother hovered above me, hand cool on my forehead. My eyes closed to breathe in her perfume.

The same voice cut across it. 'Ain't you the scabby mongrel who let 'is mate cop it?'

I turned to face two disembodied eyes in the darkness. I closed my eyes.

'It's all over the ship. You're a coward. You stole the bosun's cheese.'

My eyes flew open. Understanding washed over me, ice-cold yet scalding.

'Gave him fifty lashes, left him in short chains—he stood for days. He's finished.'

'Who?' But I knew. Andonis.

With a groan, I shoved against the hammock next to me, opening up enough space to tumble into bilge water inches deep below. No ports, no ventilation. My hand hit something foul. I gagged.

On trembling legs, I grabbed one hammock rope after the other and shuffled towards a sliver of light at the end of the cabin. There, I pounded weakly on the door.

A gruff voice challenged from the other side. 'Who wants a floggin'?'

My voice was a hoarse whisper. 'Ghikas Voulgaris.'

The lock clicked and the door opened slightly. A candle lit the guard's face.

'Need air, do we?' He sneered. 'Fancy a turn around the deck?'

He pulled me though, kicked the door shut and snapped the bolt.

'They dumped you in here when the hospital overflowed—the fever deck, the ship's belly,' he said.

As I steadied myself, I heard the slosh of water in a bucket.

I grabbed, tipped, choked—and spilled most of it.

'You have friends with coin to spare, you have. Paid to get you out of here.'

I stared at him.

'Your rich mates. Greek mates.'

Nothing made sense.

He lost patience. 'Move along. Before I change my mind.'

Gasping for air, muscles screaming, I climbed the ladder, driven by a single thought. I had to find Andonis.

Finally topside, I stumbled to the gunwale and leaned over the side, gulping breaths. When the world stopped spinning, I looked up. The sun was sinking below the horizon. I turned around, wiping my mouth with the back of my arm, head bowed, dizzy. When I opened my eyes, a ring of legs and bare feet stood in front of me.

I looked up.

Damos, Kostas, and Nikos.

'Thank you for getting me out of the orlop. Where's Andonis?'

'He's in the infirmary. He took the lash for you.' Damos spat on the boards. 'Short chains. No food. They left him standing for days. God knows what else.'

I staggered, reaching for his shoulder. He stiffened.

'I must go to him.'

His shove sent me back against the bulwark.

'You lost his father's boat. You took his girl. And now you'll be the hero to rescue him? You make me sick.'

I pushed past him.

'He would die before he let this happen to you. And the worst part? He still thinks you're worth it.'

I nearly fell down the ladder to the gun deck. The infirmary door stood ajar, unguarded. Andonis lay on his side, face black, swollen nearly beyond recognition, bony feet curled in silent agony.

'Andoni,' I whispered. I touched his arm, afraid of causing more pain. If only I could take his place. Shield him from harm.

But I'd sent him into it.

He turned his head towards me, one eye closed. An open gash on his chin.

He was cowed. They had broken him.

'In the name of God, Andoni. You took the lash for me? And bashed as well? I'm sorry.'

His lips spread in a slow smile. 'You should see the other wretch.' He coughed.

A surge of tenderness threatened to reduce me to a fool. I touched his arm, afraid to squeeze it.

He whispered, 'The captain told us what happened to the *Herakles*.'

I stared in surprise.

'It was in the *London Gazette*. She brought two thousand pounds. Proceeds to the crew of the *Gannet*.'

He coughed again; the rattle echoed in the cabin.

I had no care for the *Herakles*. 'Andoni. I am sorry about the cheese…'

His eyes softened. A vortex of guilt and gratitude drained me, leaving me light-headed and unsteady.

His eyes widened in fear as someone shoved me from behind and a shadow moved past.

Andonis whimpered, 'No…'

The bosun tipped him out of the hammock.

Then he swung toward me, musket over his shoulder. 'Out of the orlop, are you, Greek bastard? You filthy mongrels never know when enough is enough. Get out of here. I've business with your friend.'

Andonis curled into a ball, one arm shielding his head.

I stepped forward and struck the bosun square in the face. My knuckles met bone, and he reeled back with a snarl. The musket butt rose in the same breath and smashed against my temple. Light burst behind my eyes. I went down.

'Get up,' he barked. A boot nudged my ribs. 'Up!'

I dragged myself upright. He spat, wiped his mouth, and drove the musket into my face again. Pain split through my nose and I fell against the ladder. The last thing I saw was his boot and the closing door. The key turned in the lock.

Silence. The deck pitched. My hands came away wet when I touched my face. Blood. I retched.

When Andonis needed me, I was again absent.

Up on deck, I fell heavily.

Nikos and Kostas pulled me up. I struggled free.

'His brains are rattled,' Kostas said.

'They broke his nose,' said Nikos.

Damos stood with his arms crossed. I couldn't read his face, but his fists were clenched.

'You always think one grand act will clean your slate. Friendship isn't a single moment, Ghika. You have to live it every day.'

He was right—I hated him for it. I wanted that moment anyway—a single blow that would undo everything I'd done.

I swallowed, tasted iron. 'I tried—'

Damos cut in, his voice rising. 'It's too late. You betrayed him again.'

Fury filled me. 'I have never betrayed him. I'd kill for him. He's my brother.'

Damos spat on the boards. 'You have no right to say that. *Den eisai dikós mas.*' You are no longer one of us.

Nikos looked at me, then at Damos.

'*Den eisai dikós mas,*' he repeated.

I couldn't speak. Nikos looked away.

That night, we were allowed to take Andonis back to the cabin. His shirt was black and stiff with dried blood; fresh red spots had begun to spread on the cloth. As we helped him, the others watched me cautiously, sensing a storm brewing. My face throbbed where the musket had struck; the pain fed my rage and remorse until I could barely see.

Andonis caught my eye, his grip weak on my hand. 'Your face looks pretty.'

I forced a smile. 'Not as pretty as yours, my friend.'

'At least I still have my handsome nose.'

Our words were light, but my mind raced with thoughts of revenge.

—

The following morning, we helped him to the washhouse. Nikos and Damos held him while I soaked the back of his shirt, peeling it carefully off his shoulders, mindful of his pained grunts and the clinging scabs.

As he reached to put his arm through the sleeve, Kostas stiffened, his stare fixed behind me.

I turned.

The bosun was at the door. Eyes locked on Andonis. A dog circling the weakest sheep.

'What's this? Can't even put on your own shirt?'

He barged through our cordon and seized Andonis by the hair.

My vision swam with red, boiling anger. I sprang, knocked him to the deck and pinned him down.

My hands went to his throat. I squeezed.

I tightened my grip. His eyes widened in panic, hands flailing and clawing at my fingers and arms. I clenched my jaw, focused on the red veins in his eyes, and squeezed harder. I could feel life ebbing under my hands, the rasping of his breath. My knuckles whitened. The world narrowed to the sound of my own blood.

I let go.

I don't know if my arms failed from the fever, or if shame pried my fingers open.

He twisted, gasping, and wrenched free.

'Git oot o' mah way, Greek boy,' came a voice behind me. 'Ah'll finish what ye started.'

Donald shoved me aside.

He didn't hesitate.

One punch. Two.

The bosun slumped.

Donald crouched over him.

'He'll wake sore. But not yet,' he said.

None of us moved.

'You saw nothing,' he said.

Damos muttered, 'We didn't see a thing.'

'And we don't ask,' Kostas added.

'We don't ask,' Nikos repeated.

None of us looked back.

At the other end of the deck, Captain Lamb appeared with a sheaf of papers.

'Prepare for immediate transfer to the *Norfolk*.'

He read a list. Our names were on it. Donald's was not.

As we lined up, Andonis tried to smile, and failed.

Donald caught my eye and gave a faint smile. 'Ye'll no' be blamed,' he said in a low voice. 'Hae a guid trip, laddie.'

He finished what I'd started.

There was no victory in this.

Laughing Moustaches

SYDNEY AND ARNPRIOR, New South Wales
December 1834—June 1835

It's the morning following the Watt's supper, and I sing a Greek song as I waltz Cook around the kitchen.

'A grand evening, laddie, was it?' she asks, tidying her hair as she tips a fried egg onto my plate.

'Indeed, Cook. I believe she'll say yes.'

She lets out a shriek, wiping her hands on her apron. 'Yes? To marriage? To be sure and isn't this the best news I've heard this year! I remember how bony and sick-looking you was, when you first came here. Who's the lucky girl? The one you took on the picnic?'

'The very one! She shares your Irish blood.'

She clasps her hands to her bosom. 'Oh, Jigger, this warms me heart. We must take a wee drop to celebrate, you and me. When is the day?'

'Six months, at least. Once I have my Ticket of Leave and enough savings to support a wife.'

'Ample time to ask Madam if I may cook a cake! I'll steep it in a little whiskey,' she says with a wink. 'That's the secret!'

This offer touches my heart. At home, even the humblest family provides an extravagant feast. But here, even a simple celebration is an unattainable luxury.

'Cook, I'd marry just for your cake.'

Another chop lands on my plate.

—

I hurry my chores and walk to Phillip Street, with Mrs Ascham's permission. Mary appears, closing the door behind her, dressed in a mob cap and apron over her blue maid's uniform. My throat tightens at the look of her.

'Hello, Ghika.'

I saw her only hours ago, yet still she takes my breath away. Sydney is part of heaven.

'Mary. What a grand morning. Cook is delighted.'

She tilts her head. 'Delighted with what?'

'My singing!' I grin, waiting for her laugh.

She raises her eyebrows. 'Really?'

'No,' I admit. 'That we're to be married, of course! If you'll have me.'

Her fingers tighten on the doorframe.

My smile vanishes. 'Mary?'

She doesn't answer.

'You agreed we were one soul, Mary.'

'I said it was a beautiful thought. We need to talk, Ghika.'

I was ready to tell her all our plans, but I decide against it. We fall in beside each other and walk silently along Phillip Street.

At the corner, I stop. 'I thought last night meant— I want to marry you, Mary.'

Her voice is low and careful. 'I understand. But I've not given my word—not yet. Ask me properly.'

I look around. Heat climbs in my throat. 'Mary,' I say, voice even and determined, 'will you do me the honour of becoming my wife?'

She studies me for a long moment, eyes searching mine. 'If you truly mean it, you must take me as I am. No shaping me to suit. Can you do that?'

I meet her gaze steadily. 'I can try.'

'Not try, do. And please don't decide for me—about Hydra, about anything—without asking.'

'But my dream is to take you home.'

She raises a brow.

My jaw tightens. 'I'll ask. And I'll listen.'

I will try to be patient, yes—but I am not given to total surrender.

'Mister Townsend came this morning,' she says. 'I told him I was breaking our engagement.'

My heart stops.

'He said I embarrassed him. That he'd never marry a woman who couldn't hold her tongue.'

She lifts her chin. 'So be it. I wouldn't marry any man who'd try to silence me.'

Then she looks at me, softening. Her voice drops. 'Ask me again.'

The street noise fades; even the gulls seem to hush. I steady myself. 'Mary Lyons—' the words stick in my throat, 'please marry me.'

A long pause. Then—'Yes.'

I stand there like a fool, robbed of breath and words alike.

She lets the moment settle, then turns. 'Come. Let's walk. Did you sleep last night?'

I shake my head. 'No. At dawn, I dived into the waters of Cockle Bay.'

She is already kicking stones. 'I wish ladies could bathe without censure.'

I gently touch her fingers. 'That would be most improper. Besides, I had to be quick, for there's a heavy fine after 6 a.m. To protect the ladies' delicate sensibilities.'

She laughs. 'Ghika, you could never offend. I did not sleep either. Thinking about us,' she squeezes my hand quickly and lets it go. 'But I was also contemplating the public embarrassment that Mister Townsend will suffer now that our understanding is broken.'

'I can find no regret for Mister Townsend.'

What I regret is that I cannot offer Mary the same as he could.

'Well, that's as well, for he shares your sentiment. He paid me a visit this morning and said I must be away with the fairies to refuse a life of luxury—fine house, servants, a haberdashery shop, travel to the East.'

She pauses, hand flying to her open mouth as she gasps, 'Oh my goodness. What have I done?'

Her laughter fills me with joy. Like the warmth of a fire after cold water.

'I bring you none of those things.'

'I choose the man,' she says at last. 'A single soul.'

'Mary, love alone will not feed us.' I smile and point at her feet. 'Or buy your shoes. I must secure my Ticket of Leave. I must regain some freedom.'

'Tis not honour nor freedom that holds me, acushla. 'Tis yourself. And I'll put my hands to work too, if it helps.'

'*Acushla*?'

'*Acushla* means "darling". *Acushla machree* means "pulse of my heart". Do you mind?'

Mind? When I thought I couldn't love her more. I am giddy with happiness as we arrive at the gates of the prisoners barracks.

'You once said you would never marry,' I say, but I'm smiling.

'Only because I believed such a man did not exist.' She's smiling, too.

'And what of that shop you dreamed of?'

'I have had a better offer. From a pirate.' Her eyes crinkle up. 'Besides, I find ribbons giddy and frivolous. Except when sewn on a wedding dress.'

She always reassures me. I feel like a giant.

'What of your dream of marrying an obedient Greek girl?' she asks, smiling again.

'*Agápi mou—*'

Now it's her turn to look puzzled.

'That's 'my love' in Greek.'

Tears spring into her eyes.

I continue, 'I prefer a touch of chaos.'

She mimics my gesture against the evil eye, as she has seen me do. I laugh.

'Before the chaos. Tell me. Who said that about a single soul? I couldn't understand the name last night.'

I answer, pronouncing each syllable. 'Arrrr-ree-stow-tell-ee.'

She pulls a face. 'Are-ree-stow-who?'

'Our famous Greek philosopher!'

'Spell it.'

'A-R-I-S-T-O-T-L-E.'

Delight spreads across her face. 'Ahhhhh. Aristotle!' she says.

At that moment, the barracks gates swing open, out strides Mister Hely.

He smiles warmly as he extends his hand. 'The Greek!'

'Merry Christmas, Mister Hely. May I present Miss Lyons.' I am bursting with pride. 'My fiancée.'

'Good day, Miss Lyons. Bulgary, is it? Delightful news. Glad to see you building a life in New South Wales.'

'It's only temporary, sir. We shall return to Greece when my sentence is over.'

'And when will that be?'

'Eight years, sir—1842, if all goes well.'

Mary draws in a small breath. She'll come to agree.

Hely continues, 'I've heard favourable reports about you Greeks. Except for that Ninis fellow, but the treadmill sorted him out. We need men like you, Bulgary. I hope you'll stay in New South Wales. Send your marriage application to my office. Good day, Miss Lyons. Bulgary.'

'Happy Christmas, Mister Hely.'

He touches his forehead.

We walk past Saint James' Church and Mrs Hordern's shop.

'Ghika, a small gift for you. For Christmas.'

'How did you know I would come to Sydney?'

'I bought it this morning.' She pulls a flat, tissue-wrapped parcel from her reticule.

'I have one for you too,' I say, presenting my gift, 'but I made mine months ago.'

I've wrapped it in a piece of cloth and tied with string. We stand on the corner of Market and George streets, feeling the festive air of Christmas. She unwraps the wooden trinket.

'A shamrock!' She beams. 'Or three love hearts?'

'The ones you drew in the dirt.' This makes her smile. 'Happy Christmas, Mary.' At last, I have a fiancée with whom I may share the season's greetings.

'You knew they were love hearts, didn't you?'

I remember we are in a public street, so I gently withdraw my hand from hers.

'I almost burst out laughing last night at your story about your father owning ships.'

I smile. 'He does.'

She stares in disbelief. 'What is this?'

I nod.

'That's a shock, to be sure.' She grins. 'A shipowner?' She shakes her head. 'Doesn't matter. I love you regardless. Open your gift.'

It's a fine white linen handkerchief—an extravagant, utterly pointless luxury.

I have an overwhelming desire to kiss her, but I press the handkerchief to my lips instead.

Her dimples deepen.

—

We attend Mass to share news of our betrothal with Father Therry. I arrive early, my heart sinking with a cold flutter of doubt when I cannot see her. Then I feel that familiar lurch in my stomach when I spot her in the shadows. I slide along the heavy pew towards her, but her hand moves along the wood, marking a respectable gap between us. Her face glows, eyes twinkling, as she whispers, 'Like the day we met, remember?'

I whisper back, 'Yes. It was you who set the distance that day. But one day, we won't be in public. Then I will ravish you.'

She blushes, brings her hand to her mouth, mock horror in her eyes. 'You wouldn't.'

'I might.' My lips twitch in a half-smile.

We don't move. A meeting of eyes.

After the service, we join Father Therry in his cottage, over steaming tea in simple white cups.

'Father, Mary intends to return to service at Arnprior. And we'll marry once I secure my Ticket of Leave and build a hut. Would you conduct the ceremony please?'

Mary blushes as Father Therry nods.

'If I'm still at St Mary's, certainly. But first, I must baptise you both. Will you stay in New South Wales?'

'No, Father. Once I'm free, I hope to take Mary back to Hydra, to my family.'

I follow Father Therry's gaze to Mary. Her fingers are white around her cup.

'We shall speak of Hydra when the time comes,' she says, to her tea.

On the walk back to Phillip Street, we discuss our future. Her optimism, ignoring potential hardship, is both heartening and unrealistic.

'You were quiet back there, Mary. You didn't drink your tea.'

'It was too hot. And 'tis not seemly to cross my husband before company.'

'Mary, here, I have nothing. On Hydra, I can give you comfort.'

She squeezes my hand. 'Ghika, you worry too much. We'll manage.'

I smile. 'I must provide for you. I have a list of items we will need.'

She gives a small laugh. 'You and your lists. But it's a long way off yet. And I've put a little by myself.'

Mary thinks love will fill an empty cupboard, and she mocks my lists. The future will not take care of itself. She's maddening.

'Mary, your savings are yours. It's my duty to provide the necessities —bedclothes, saucepans, flatware, furniture.'

A deeper concern troubles me. Once I secure my Ticket of Leave, the convict rations end. And government clothing. We'll slaughter and salt our own meat. But I must negotiate for a wage, and buy staples at the prices set in the Arnprior storehouse. We must live on my earnings.

I hate the thought of Mary working long hours for the Ryries, serving others. Our children growing up in a bark hut with a dirt floor.

What would my father think of his daughter-in-law living like this? Of his grandchildren raised in poverty?

Mary interrupts my thoughts. 'What's the use of wealth, Ghika, if it doesn't hold love in it?'

—

Christmas passes too quickly. Soon I must leave Mary behind and return to Arnprior. The thought of leaving her in Sydney sits like stone in my gut—we've only just found each other, and already I'm walking away.

Even the thought of Arnprior without Chara, who's been in my mind every day I've been away, weighs on me.

I will carve a wooden cross for her grave.

When I step inside the hut, grief hits in a wave.

Her sack still lies where she used to rest, the fabric wrinkled with the shape of her body. My heart sinks. Why did Joe leave it there? It's a cruel kindness—a reminder and a comfort both.

Her absence is a gaping wound that nothing will heal.

I imagine her face, her black nose, those soulful black eyes.

I take the sack up and clutch it to my chest, trying to capture a hint of her smell.

This is harder than I imagined.

I hear movement outside and hastily compose myself.

Joe appears at the door, his face alight. 'Hey Jigger! How's Mary?'

'Joe, where did you bury Chara?'

A black-and-white streak barrels through the door.

'Chara!' I drop to my knees as she throws herself into my arms, licking my face and whimpering with joy.

Joe waits for me to look up again. 'Ned says she might walk funny for a while, but she's made it this far, so she should recover.'

Chara doesn't know what to do to show her affection. She wriggles, whimpers, presses her face into the crook of my arm, races around the hut. I hold her face and bring it close to mine, kiss her nose, and hug her tightly.

'Thanks, Joe,' I say. 'Look in my bag. There's something in there for you.'

'Jigger!' he yells. 'You bought me a scratch jar!'

He shakes it, the penny inside rattling.

'Now I'll be rich like you!'

—

February arrives, and with it, the heat. Mrs Ryrie has invited Mary back to her old position at Arnprior, and we've arranged for her to follow me once Mary Watt's persistent lung complaint improves.

One afternoon, after I've counted the sheep into the fold, I go as I always do, to sit beneath our tree.

She is there.

My heart stumbles at the sight of her.

Chara dashes to her side.

'Mary,' I stammer. 'Mary.'

How I've missed you.

She stands to hold out a black and white puppy, its fur soft and shining in the afternoon light.

'It's a boy. From the same breeder near Parramatta. I walked all the way to the farm to collect him—past Duck Creek Bridge.'

For a moment, all I want is to hold her. The scent of her, the warmth of her presence.

There is so much I want to say, but I hear her words again, and a cold knot of fear tightens in my stomach.

'You went to Duck Creek? Alone?'

My heart leaps into my throat. The Parramatta Road is notorious—last month an auctioneer was robbed, and a clerk was held up at Duck Creek Bridge.

'I cannot believe you would venture along that road alone, Mary. You could have been robbed. Or killed.' My worry spikes to anger. 'I beg you not—no, I forbid you—to do that again.'

It's my father's imperious voice—but she's so reckless.

Her smile fades and she stiffens. Slowly, she lifts the pup between us like a shield.

'I knew I could never replace Chara, but clearly there's no need.'

I take it.

'Did you say 'forbid,' Ghika? There's the old you again. I know the road and its risks, but I won't be shut away like a chest with a key. And I cannot promise Hydra—' She puts her hands on her hips. 'I don't take orders, remember? I'll mind your counsel—but not your commands. Remember what you promised. Ask, don't decide.'

We have so far to bend to reach each other. I shrug. 'You're impossible.'

She turns her back, still bristling, and sits beneath the tree.

I say nothing.

'I'll vow to love, honour, and keep you, Ghika. God willing. But obey in all things? I will not promise what I cannot keep.'

Her independence is admirable, and yet it frustrates me beyond words. But anger will not solve this.

I grin. 'Better an honest rebel than a silent servant.'

After a moment, I say, 'Yes, I'd cage you if I could. But I won't. Can we at least agree on precautions?'

Her expression softens, and she steps closer, her hand finding mine. 'Very well, let's talk about precautions.'

She's still stubborn, still impossible. But she's listening. I squeeze her hand, and the moment passes.

Kneeling, she kisses Chara's head; the pup sniffs at her and wriggles.

'Ghika, how perfect. Do you realise? A husband for me and a companion for Chara.'

Chara's bobtail wags like a runaway rudder. Mary offers the puppy. I take him, but my gaze is fixed on her.

Mary. I still can't believe my eyes.

'When did you arrive? You look like Aphrodite.'

'Just now. There's a coach through Goulburn now. Mary Watt is better. I'm so happy to be here.'

'Not as happy as I am.' Cradling the puppy, I caress Mary's face.

Those green eyes.

Chara is jumping up. The pup is sober and alert, one blue eye, one brown, resembling Chara, but with a squarer head.

'This is the most beautiful gift.' I don't just mean the pup.

'What about your hagstone? And your handkerchief?'

I slap my forehead. 'My favourite possessions!'

We both laugh.

I hold the puppy close and touch my lips to Mary's forehead. The puppy squirms. Mary leans into my neck but I step back, reluctant. Her reputation still matters.

I stroke Chara's head to reassure her she is not being replaced. Mary kisses the pup between the ears. I feel the weight of responsibility—not just for this new life, but for all the ties that bind us now.

'Did you notice his odd eyes? The others cost more than I could pay.'

I rub my thumb between his ears. 'Odd eyes signify strength and loyalty—Andonis, for example. And so did Alexander the Great's horse, Bucephalus.'

She laughs. 'You know such curious things, Ghika.'

'Does the pup have a name?'

'I've been calling him Mister Jenkins. After Mister Jenkins in Ireland. He had an odd eye too.'

'Then Jenkins it is. Chara and Jenkins. Our family. Now, tell me the news since I saw you last.'

I can't push her away. Not this time.

—

The same cheerful determination marks Mary's return. Mrs Ryrie is so pleased you'd think she'd arranged our engagement.

On a sweltering afternoon, in the convict garden, Mary is sitting on her haunches, bouncing on her heels, her skirt spread around her. Jenkins, full of puppy exuberance, jumps into her lap. A flurry of emotions sweeps through me. My breath quickens and my heart races.

'Mary, William says not to pamper him,' I caution her.

Mary's face is impish. 'Perhaps he's wrong. Jenkins is like us. He needs affection.'

'Mary, you will spoil him. William knows what he is talking about.'

Ignoring me, she continues cuddling Jenkins and pulls a weed, then leans her head back. She brushes wisps of hair from her cheek and trails her fingers down her throat. They rest lightly in the hollow.

My mouth is dry. I can't even think straight.

'Ghika, why have you stopped hugging me? No one ever hugged me as a child. Except my foster mother. But I barely remember her. They took me away when I was tiny and returned me to the foundling hospital, lest I become attached. After her, only my friend Lizbet, who died. I miss that warmth.'

Her face is open, trusting. I think of my own childhood, full of affection. Mary has been denied so much. I want to make up for what she's missed.

We stand and I open my arms. When she steps into my embrace, my hands go to her back, her waist; her soft curves press into me, bringing with her a sensuality so intense I lose my footing, and we topple into the carrots.

She sits up, laughing, but her smile fades when she sees my face. Concerned, she touches my leg. 'What's wrong?'

Desire, love, hunger, reverence sweep over me like a *meltemi*. It's too much, too fast. The weight of her in my arms, the warmth of her skin through her dress, the scent of sun and sweat and laughter. I want her.

And that is why I have to speak. She trusts me. And I won't break that trust.

When I can speak, I say stiffly, 'Mary, I long for you. But we must wait until we are man and wife. I say this out of love and respect.'

'Oh is that all?' she says, trying for lightness. 'I'm glad, Ghika. That fornication business is so dull. Rolling about in sweat and silence.'

She wrinkles her nose.

I can't help my face registering my shock.

Uncertainty creeps into her voice. 'You understand, don't you?'

My desire evaporates like a drop of water on a hot skillet, replaced by a wave of protectiveness. What she must have endured. I hold her close, determined to keep her safe. Her past matters not—only her happiness.

'I only want to make you happy,' she says.

'I am already delirious. On Hydra, we say, 'my moustaches are laughing'.'

—

The Ryrie family has no fondness for shepherds with their reputation for unreliability, yet they already pay me a modest wage, provide extra rations and a cash bonus during the busiest periods like shearing, lamb marking and sheep washing, and branding calves.

But other convicts say employers often block Ticket of Leave applications—for it ends their payments from the governor. William won't want to lose any allowance. He knows I'm his best man and my lambing rates speak for themselves. But he cares naught about my happiness—only his profits.

My frustration reaches boiling point. One day, without knocking, I march straight into the station storehouse.

'Sir, I request a Ticket of Leave.'

I'm puffing as if I've run from one end of Arnprior to the other.

He calmly hands me a signed application and a pass to travel, directing me to the magistrate in Bungonia. Surprise flickers through me—I'd expected resistance.

'Take Diablo. Be back in two days.'

I've gone red in the face. Not every man is my father.

'Forgive me for barging in. That's good of you. Thank you.'

He raises an eyebrow. 'Did you expect anything less?'

The ticket arrives on the ninth of June. I can live anywhere within the district, leave Arnprior if I wish, visit the Sydney markets, travel beyond the region twice a year, provided I present myself to the authorities each quarter, with proof of my income.

Freedom.

I secure from William a promise of thirty-five pounds a year, rations, plus a one shilling bonus for every lamb above three hundred.

Humming, I head back to the hut and spot Mary watching from the shadow of the homestead. She breaks into a bright grin.

'Ghika,' she says softly. 'Your moustaches are laughing again.'

I smile. We understand each other.

30

AT SEA

The Transport

ABOARD THE *NORFOLK*, Portsmouth to Port Jackson
May 1829

I wasted no time pushing my few possessions into my canvas bag, heart thudding. My legs were still unsteady. The fever had broken, but left its mark—a tremor in my hands, a tightness in my chest, the sense that I wasn't entirely back inside my body.

My ears strained for a shout that didn't come. We were being transferred from the *York* to the *Norfolk*, hired by the English government to transport two hundred convicts to New South Wales. We rowed in silence —a heavy pull through grey water under a grey sky. No one spoke.

The only sounds were the oars, the slap of water, and the dull throb behind my eyes.

I kept expecting a musket shot. A summons. A name shouted into the wind.

Nothing came.

Donald had dealt with the bosun. I hadn't.

The guilt sat in my gut, sharp and heavy.

And the others? Would they even speak to me now? Would they continue to blame me for Andonis' flogging? Or would they move on?

I shifted on the bench, breath shallow.

We came alongside the transport at anchor on the Motherbank—off the Isle of Wight, sheltered and still. I was last in line on the *Norfolk* as the clerk wrote laboriously in the ship's muster while I watched on with a kind of detachment. I steadied myself against the table.

When he asked for my name, I said 'Ghikas Voulgaris.'

He frowned. 'Can you read and write?'

I nodded. 'Of course.'

'Write your name here.'

I wrote Βούλγαρης.

I heard laughter behind me. Then I realised.

'In English,' he growled.

I crossed it out and wrote 'Bulgaris' instead.

A guard peered over the clerk's shoulder. 'Pale and sickly, broken nose and two black eyes, speaks Greek. We'll know him anywhere.'

I kept silent.

He scrawled 'RW' beside it. Reads and writes.

I kept Andonis upright as we moved deeper into the crowd. I'd heard of a convict ship where one quarter of the convicts had died before they reached Sydney. He could not afford another setback.

Anything would be better than the *York*.

Light drizzle beaded on our shoulders, the heat of our bodies stirring the odour of damp wool. Our leg irons dragged across the boards, drowning out the murmur of excited chatter around us. The planks gleamed with new pitch. My head throbbed and my nose was so clogged and swollen that my breath dragged in as a shallow rasp. I could taste blood.

Beside me, Andonis swayed. I reached for him. 'It's over, my friend.'

He sighed—a small, shuddering breath of relief.

'Andoni, I want to show you something,' said Nikos, guiding him carefully away, grip steady, steps slow. I watched them go.

Then came Damos' voice, sharp. 'It might be over for you. It's not over for Andonis.'

A gut-wrenching truth. Nausea washed over me.

I couldn't fix this.

I stared down at the deck. Then up. 'I know, Damos. I will make it up to him. Somehow.'

'You can't. That ship has sailed, rich boy. No inheritance can bring it back.'

A knife pushed cleanly into my gut.

'Listen, Damos,' I began, but was interrupted by a convict jostling me. A gentleman and two ladies, one carrying a toddler, were approaching. Passengers. A brush of fabric. A breath of perfume. A life I'd nearly forgotten.

Kostas' voice was loud in my ear. 'I wonder, are there any female convicts on board?'

A man behind said, 'Ain't no doxies on this ship, ducks. Will I do?'

Kostas grimaced.

Nikos returned with Andonis, and I took his arm again. The captain, a stout man with mutton-chop whiskers, appeared behind the rail on the poop deck. Not Royal Navy but merchant marine, dressed in a dark blue jacket with gold braid, black cravat tied carelessly under his collar, polished boots, one planted on a coil of rope. He waited for silence.

'Welcome aboard,' he announced, as if to invited guests. 'I am Captain Alexander Greig, commander of the *Norfolk*. We are bound for New South Wales.' He waved towards two grim-looking officers in brilliant red jackets, 'With a guard of the Sixty-third Regiment.'

'I do not call you felons. Men live up to the names we give them.' His gaze travelled over the crowd.

He was right. I had lived up to my father's dismal forecast I would be a nobody and a nothing.

'This is my second voyage to New South Wales, and I intend to deliver all two hundred of you safely. The other passengers—Mister Hallan, and families of officers of the guard, will take air on the poop deck, out of bounds to you.' He swept his hand behind him for the benefit of those unfamiliar with ships, most of our fellow convicts.

'Surgeon-Superintendent Dickson, who has made three voyages to Port Jackson, will care for your health.' He pointed to a pale, thin man in a red beret with a yellow band, who acknowledged the introduction with a nod.

'The crew will provide vinegar to keep your accommodations clean.

Failure to use it will result in heavier leg irons. Mister Dickson will conduct regular bodily inspections and issue lime juice to prevent scurvy.'

'Good behaviour will see your present leg irons removed in a week. Finally, this voyage will take three months, with no landfall. Not at Tenerife, nor at Rio de Janeiro, nor at Cape Town.' He waited for the muttering to subside. 'No landfall.'

An ambitious plan, but no doubt they had done it before. And the Roaring Forties south of the African continent—strong westerly winds that made for fast sailing—were reliable. If the ship survived them.

After settling Andonis in the cabin, I searched for Damos and found him chatting to a seaman on deck about his last voyage.

'A word, Damo?' I said.

When we were alone, he stared out to sea, the wind whipping his hair.

'What did you mean earlier?' I asked, keeping my voice steady.

He turned to glare at me, eyes cold. 'Andonis is broken, Ghika.'

'I have apologised, Damo. It was only a piece of cheese. And I would have confessed, if I hadn't fainted.'

He shook his head, disbelief in his eyes. 'Did it ever cross your mind you would drag all of us down if they caught you?'

'Why are you making this bigger than it is? Where were you, anyway, while the bosun was beating Andonis?'

There. That hurt.

He struck back. 'Bigger than it is? Andonis was beaten nearly to death. You think one heroic act made up for that? I have news for you. To earn friendship, you must be a friend.'

My head still ached, but his words hurt worse than any blow. Pain flared when I spoke, but my anger burned hotter.

'Damo, you ungrateful worm. Who bought you your carpentry tools? Who rescued you from the trouble with that girl's father?'

He looked out to sea again.

'Me!'

'You speak of everything in terms of money,' he spat through clenched teeth. 'Andonis took that beating for you—sacrificed himself—because you were too selfish to think beyond your own nose. Andonis was punished for losing his father's fishing boat. And he was punished by losing Anastasia. But you've forgotten all that.'

'Of course I haven't,' I muttered.

His eyes burned into me.

He thought he was so righteous. 'You're wrong about Anastasia.'

His face flushed with fury. 'You call him your best friend. But only when you need him.'

He leaned in, stabbing his finger into my chest, voice rising, breath hot and sour.

'How did you think it affected his family when we lost the *caïque*? Did you think your father's money fixed that? And what about Anastasia? Why didn't you buy your way out of that, too?'

The realisation was slow at first, like a fog lifting. I was shaking, but not from rage. The world shifted beneath my feet. I'd spent my life thinking money could fix everything. Now I saw the truth. Andonis had sacrificed his health for my reckless mistake, and now, I had nothing to give in return.

'Who cleans up your mess, Ghika? Me and the boys!' He was shouting now. 'You dream up the schemes; we pay the price. Where was your rich father when we got the death sentence?'

I felt my teeth grind. His words rang in my ears as he turned on his heel and strode away. I stood there, shaking.

The silence was deafening.

But then he was back. Voice calm. That was worse.

'You think you hold us together. It's Andonis. It's always been Andonis.'

He shouldered me out of the way.

I wanted to answer him: I was a protector, a leader. But the truth was— I was neither. And I'd dragged Andonis down with me.

Nikos appeared beside me. He said nothing at first—but put his hand on my arm. 'I'm here, Ghika.'

I pressed hard on a callus in my hand and nodded, but the words still rang in my ears. *You're not one of us.*

I climbed down to our cabin, with its sharp stench of vinegar, where Andonis lay in his sling. He looked up at me, eyes tired. 'What's wrong?' he rasped.

I wanted to tell him everything, beg his forgiveness, but the words stuck in my throat. He didn't need my guilt—he deserved better.

His voice was soft, steady, patient. 'Ghika?'

His eyes held no anger, only concern. That crushed me more than blame ever could.

'I'm seasick,' I lied.

I had used money as a shield my whole life. But even if I had it now, it would be useless. It always was.

I turned my face away, unable to look at him.

I had hurt everyone I cared about.

I fell into the darkness of my own making. The stink of the ship, the groaning timbers, the cold, the damp—nothing compared to the weight of my failure.

I would carry this with me.

And so would Andonis.

The hull groaned. Somewhere below, a man retched. The voyage had begun.

31

Terms of Agreement

ARNPRIOR, New South Wales
June—August 1835

In seven years, when my sentence is over, I'll be thirty-six—still young enough to make my mark at home. If my father won't give me a ship, one of my uncles will. And if they don't, I'll build one myself. Andonis said he'll stay here, even if he's given a pardon, but once he sees the others join me, he'll come to his senses.

By then, I will be established, with coin in my pocket and a fleet on the way—ready to hire them as crew. I'll pay them a fair wage plus a share of the profits—better than they've ever known.

In the meantime, I must improve my position on *Arnprior*, put money aside, keep Mary safe. Simple.

She talks of planting trees, sewing curtains, keeping chickens. It settles her. Good. She deserves that much. But when the time comes, she'll go where I go. She's marrying me—not Arnprior.

Martin and Joe are helping me build a hut. The frame was already up when carpenter Seamus Johnson arrived to work on the Arnprior homestead, but he's lifted our standard of workmanship. He shows us how to make neat cuts, tight joints, and a fancy finish. He's a square-built man, with skin like walnut, and hands made for this work. And he always has a story about 'Paddy'.

'Hey, Jigger,' he calls out. 'Did I tell you about the time Paddy was walkin' along behind a gentleman?'

Every joke involves Paddy and often with thievery.

'No, Seamus, you did not,' I say.

'Well now, the gentleman drops a receipt book, and Paddy picks it up and sneaks out a ten-pound note. Then he calls out, "Beggin' your pardon, sir, here's your book that you dropped on the footpath. But some thief has stolen ten pounds out of it!".'

His howls of laughter draw a smile even from Ned.

I laugh, and say, 'It's a wonder Paddy hasn't done more time than all of us.'

I nod at Seamus. 'You're sure you're not related?'

Mary admires our new hut. She's less impressed by the sawdust and plaster dust Seamus trails through the Arnprior homestead—but she is curious about his lath and plaster walls.

'Ghika, might we have two rooms in our hut? With a wall, and wall-paper like the Ryries? And a lock on the door in case Bartholomew comes?'

I almost say, 'One day', out of habit. I'm actually remembering a rumour I've heard that Bartholomew's wife has died, and he's taken up with a convict woman—they say she's a healer.

But then I see the set of Mary's shoulders. I'll make concessions for now, but our passage to Hydra is as good as booked.

'I'll add a lock to our next goods order. Right below the china.'

She beams.

'You're full of surprises, Ghika. I would have sworn you'd say no.'

'So would I,' I admit. 'Soon you'll be calling me Gentle Jigger.'

She laughs. 'Not likely.'

I fold my arms. 'Careful, woman. I've agreed to a lock, not a palace.'

'Good,' she fires back. 'I'd hate a palace. Too much cleaning.'

For a heartbeat we look at each other, half-smiling, half-challenging—neither of us conceding the last word.

'Wait until you see my family home,' I say. 'The houses on Hydra are decorated in the Ottoman style—gilded panelling, frescoes of flowers, carved ceilings.' I picture the gilded panels.

'It must be beautiful,' she says, but she as pauses and her fingers stroke the rough wall.

And suddenly I wonder—does she expect me to see this hut as our home?

Outside our hours of labour, we work side by side. Mary kneels on the dirt floor as I fetch soil from an ants' nest. She mixes it with crushed cow manure and water into a thick slurry. Despite her peeling hands, she refuses my help, letting each layer dry to a hard, gleaming shine.

'Let me do it,' I say.

'Oh no, Ghika,' she says. 'I love doing this. I've worked for other people all my life. This is my home. Our home.' She smooths the floor with her palm. 'Here, I decide.'

She says it lightly, but it's not a joke. I hear the warning bell, and I mark the reef.

We make a list of household goods, and I take it to William in the storehouse.

'Do you have time to help me with an order?' I ask.

'I'll make time,' he says.

It arrives on the mail coach in August. William is there again, sleeves rolled up, untying canvas and rope.

'Thanks, William,' I say.

He shrugs. 'Think nothing of it.'

'You don't have to help,' I say.

'I know,' he says, as he prises open a crate. 'But I like making you say thank you.'

We check the contents—everything as described, and unbroken.

Mary's eyes light up at the sight of the silk ribbon I ordered for her from Mrs Hordern—a luxury. Yet it's the extravagance of a water kettle that really delights her. I'm pleased that it will be safer for her than our billy. Together, we re-wrap the household goods and stack them in the new hut like precious jewels.

One Sunday afternoon, Seamus takes a sweep with the adze to a joist. The blade bites, glances, and opens his leg to the bone.

For a second, even the wind stops. Then the blood comes—hot, bright, too much. It gushes down his leg, splatters the plank, turns the sawdust into a red paste.

'Hold it—press!' he hisses.

I'm already tearing my neckcloth, shoving the wad hard to the wound. My hands are slick. The blood surges around my fingers as if I'm bailing with a sieve. The iron stink hits the back of my throat—heavy, metallic—childhood and shame. My stomach lurches.

'Press it, Jigger,' Seamus grunts through his teeth.

I press harder. The cloth slips. The wound yawns again and spills. Heat rises behind my eyes. The edges of the world blur.

Mary's voice cuts clean through me. 'Move.'

I don't. I can't. The red is everywhere. I blink, fighting the wave.

'Ghika.' Not timid. A command. 'Now.'

I snatch my hands away. She is already there—apron ripped in two, clean strip folded, heel of her palm planted on the artery like she's stopping a leak in a hull. 'Joe—boil the kettle. Martin—give me a shirt, the cleanest you own. And vinegar. And keep him talking.'

Seamus tries to chuckle and hisses instead. 'Paddy once said—'

'Save Paddy for later,' Mary says, not unkindly. She keeps pressing. The bleeding slows. My useless hands hover.

'Put a pillow under his leg,' she says, and Seamus raises it. She wraps the second strip tight, knots it flat, then braces her weight with both hands. The adze lies where it fell, blade sticky.

I step in, wanting to help, and the smell surges up again. The room tilts. I take a breath, and another, and hate myself for my weakness.

Mary doesn't look at me. She murmurs steady words of comfort— 'Good man, nearly there'—until the ooze gives up and the cloth stays white at the edges.

Only then does she glance at me. Not scorn—worse—pity softened by love.

Seamus exhales, colour crawling back into his face. 'Mary,' he says, making a joke even now, 'remind me to hire you as my foreman.'

'Hire my mop to clean the floor,' Mary says, smiling, and ties off the last knot.

When it's finished, Seamus thanks me first—because I'm the man— and Mary next—because she saved his leg. Mary smiles.

I nod, jaw tight. I can captain a deck in a gale, but one cut undoes me. She did what I could not.

—

A letter from Father Therry arrives, giving notice he will visit Arnprior in late September or October, and if it suits us, he will conduct our marriage ceremony. He has indeed been banished—too 'Irish' in his dealings, too ecumenical for the Catholic Church's liking, so they have replaced him with an Englishman, a bishop no less.

He writes from his new parish at Camden. So now he's Ando's priest.

Mary reads the letter and folds it carefully. 'Poor man. He did everything for his flock, and they stripped him of his parish.' She looks up at me. 'Makes you think, doesn't it? You do your best, and someone else decides your fate.'

She slaps her hands together. 'I've had enough of other people deciding mine.'

Good. Better to row the boat than wait on the wind.

Martin has new life in him, sparked by Sarah, a woman whose jagged hair marks her time spent in the Female Factory at Parramatta. They settle in a lean-to made of bark until we can build them a hut, and Martin, perhaps for the first time in memory, is caring for his appearance. I have not seen Sarah up close, but from a distance she has a wild and hunted look. Mary worries that Sarah's away with the fairies.

Last time Mary visited her, Sarah said, 'They kept me a year past my sentence at Parramatta. They don't let you go when your time's up. It's not like you're real people.'

Martin is buoyant, hauling timber with the strength of an entire team of oxen, and he sings loudly.

'Do you think Sarah is happy?' he asks me.

I keep my doubts to myself, but if anyone can coax a smile from her, it will be Martin.

Mary's presence on Arnprior makes me more aware that bad news can be a constant companion in the bush. Despite the good rains of last September and October, the first half of 1835 has been relentlessly dry. Dust storms besiege us and the grass turns to powder under our feet.

Waterholes shrink and the grey aprons of mud around them widen and crack like honeycomb, each piece curling up at the edges.

Herding the flock has become a daily struggle for survival—we roam the landscape, seeking the best of the remaining grass. The only safe watering place for the sheep is the sandy ford at the river, and I must prevent them from straying into muddy waterholes where they might bog. The shock alone can kill a weak ewe.

In the suffocating stillness of midday, they seek shelter in the shade, panting.

Entire branches on the trees turn brown and die.

At night, wallabies, smaller cousins of the kangaroo, invade our vegetable gardens. The local Aborigines at Kurraducbidgee have vanished, some say to the coast. Others say they've gone south. In June, tantalising showers of rain tease us, stirring the fragrance of damp earth and bringing a short green pick.

The ewes chase it until they're exhausted.

Seamus' explosive bursts of laughter are a relief from the drought, but there's more bad news to come.

Late one afternoon, as Martin and I are walking home along the river, he confides his worries. For all his might, he is a gentle soul, and on this day, he speaks of his Sarah as one might of a wounded bird. He's troubled by her solitary habits and her nightmares, and he fears she is not thriving.

'Wait,' he says. 'I'll fill my water flask.'

As he removes his boots and rolls up the bottom of his trousers, I notice an empty rum bottle lying on the bank.

An agonised cry brings me rushing through the reeds to the river's edge. His Sarah is floating face down in the shallows, dress drifting. Martin lifts her and brings her from the water, her head hanging over his arm.

He stumbles forward, eyes locked on his hut, never once looking down at her face. He is Orpheus, undone by grief. Her legs swing. Her skin is blue. Her hair drips down his arm. Barefoot, groaning like a wounded animal, he carries her. I pick up his boots and follow.

The commotion draws the others from their huts. We fall in behind him, a silent procession. Martin lowers himself onto their bed, cradling Sarah like a child, rocking her limp body as water pools at his feet.

In the crowded doorway, I glimpse Mary's stricken face.

We help him dig a grave on the hill behind the huts, below her favourite tree. He fashions a beautiful wooden cross to place on the cairn of stones.

A child dies of lockjaw; a neighbour near Coolaringdon perishes from poisoned blood; another child is lost in bushland and not found for three agonising days; a convict on Durran Durra meets his end from snakebite. Mary, observing Mrs Ryrie, suspects she has consumption.

Yet she remains unbroken, even when I go away with the Ryrie brothers to help neighbours, even with the threat of attack by bushrangers.

'Don't fret about me,' she says. 'I'll keep busy sewing. And I'll plant flowers instead of your eternal vegetables.' Her bravery extends to the wild —she is not afraid of the dingoes, nor of the natives, and she uses a broom or a stick on goannas and snakes. But she does admit to a fear of Bartholomew.

I am heartened when she befriends Seamus' wife, although Annabella is also a source of concern.

'She's the kindest soul, Ghika, but so frail, and thin as a pratie dibble, even though she's heavy with child. Her hair is already grey, her shoulder bones stick out, and her dress hangs off her body. And the way she stands, with her hands propped at the back of her waist. So tired, and looking off into the distance. I think she longs for Ireland.'

One August evening, Mary rushes towards me, breathless.

'The Ryries and Jane are away at Coolaringdon. Quickly Ghika, Annabella's baby is coming too soon. Ned's gone to Braidwood to fetch the midwife, but who knows how long she will be.'

We search for the native women at Kurraducbidgee, but we find none.

'I must go to her,' Mary says. When I offer to accompany her, she stops me.

'No Ghika, there might be blood. You'll be no help if you faint on the floor.'

That night, Seamus comes to wait with Joe and me. I am shocked by the depth of Annabella's agony as she screams through the night, unnerving and exhausting everyone.

The midwife arrives in the early hours. Too late.

As the sun rises, Mary comes, pale and sick, to the hut. 'Seamus. Annabella is fine, but I am so sorry—the baby—'

Tears spill down her cheeks.

He puts his head in his hands, then rises to go to his wife.

Before he goes, he says, 'Thank you. To both of you.'

My first reaction is disbelief. An innocent baby. The depth of Seamus and Annabella's loss is unimaginable, and the thought of Mary witnessing such a tragedy fills me with something close to grief. I feel helpless. All I can offer is my presence.

'What you endured last night, Mary—you are far stronger than I.'

'I never thought I could face a night like that, Ghika. It's amazing what you can do when you must.'

Her voice drops. 'The baby's hands, Ghika— Why does it always happen this way? To the people who deserve joy, who never did anything to deserve punishment? Why them, Ghika?'

I have no answer for her. There is none.

Seamus refuses my offer of help and carries the tiny form to the convict graveyard, a lone figure against the hill, to lay his child to rest.

Sometimes I long for my siblings. I wonder if Katerina is happy. Giorgios is twenty-three years old, Makris nineteen. Are they married?

Mary says, 'Ghika, why does blood unsettle you so?'

I've always tried to hide my aversion to blood.

But this is Mary.

I don't even want to think about it, but I take a deep breath. 'I was about five,' I begin. 'I went to visit Mamá in her bedroom early one morning—I didn't know it, but she had given birth to my little brother Giorgios. My father was angry I had entered without knocking, so he pushed a basin at me, pressed it against my chest. It sloshed over me, spilling its contents—blood, dark and hot—and something heavy slid against my wrist, soft as liver. Later I learned it was the afterbirth.'

I swallow.

'It covered my feet; lumps stuck to my nightshirt. That metallic smell —it was everywhere. Like the plague that killed my grandfather.'

I breathe in through my nose.

"Pick it up. Take it outside," my father said. So I did. I left it in the vegetable garden where it stayed until Lambros removed it. I still smell it.'

'Oh Ghika,' Mary says. 'I'm so sorry. A child shouldn't see such things. No wonder you carry ghosts.'

'Didn't do me any harm,' I say. Lies sit easier if you say them fast.

'Ghika, can't you be happy here?'

I brush that off. 'You'll love Hydra.'

I will never belong here. Am I asking too much of her?

I tell her about Malta. About the letter from my brother, my mother's death, my father paying the debt. The death sentence.

She understands—and that is almost worse.

That night, I wake with the taste of iron in my mouth. My arms are punching the air above me.

The rattle of chains clangs in my skull, tighter, tighter.

I can't get air—

'Jigger.'

Joe's voice. Close. Real. 'Jigger.'

My eyes fly open and the ceiling of the hut swims into focus. I reach down to feel my ankle. Nothing but scars.

'You were fighting someone,' Joe says.

My throat burns. I try to laugh, but it comes out jagged.

'Some nights I'm back on the *York*—I can feel irons.'

—

Another message from Father Therry lifts our spirits. God willing, he will marry us in the middle of September. Mrs Ryrie even offers the front verandah, and she says her climbing roses may be flowering for the ceremony.

I pen letters to Andonis, and Kostas, sharing the news.

Later, as I help William Ryrie build a fence, he pauses to light his pipe. 'Jigger, you're about to take a wife, yet you seem downcast.'

'I have no capital, no future.'

He blows out a cloud of smoke and shakes his head. 'Maybe it seems so to you. But you've earned respect here, from my family, from the other men.'

'William, this life is hard for a woman. Mary could have been comfortable in Sydney.'

'Mary didn't choose Sydney.' He knocks the tobacco out of the bowl of his pipe. 'The fortunate few live in comfort, Jigger, but most struggle.'

Yes, but Mary doesn't deserve to struggle.

He continues. 'What is your father's business back on your Greek island?'

Only now he asks. After all this time. 'Merchant ships. Before the war, he prospered.'

'Ahhh, that explains your bearing.' He leans on the fence post. 'So, you are not as financially secure as you wish? You have a mind for business. You will do well.'

He can't know how the thought of illness knots my gut—the fear, if I were taken, of leaving Mary with nothing.

'It's easy for you to speak, William. You've never had to start with nothing.'

He steps back, his tone turning serious. 'Ghika, listen,' he begins, sounding much like Yiannis when he's about to give me a lecture. 'I knew a man once—rich as Midas. Couldn't stand to eat dinner with his own family. Never saw his children.'

He looks at me. 'Not all riches are in coin.'

For a moment, I think of his quiet evenings at Durran Durra alone. Does he envy what he thinks I have?

'Love doesn't feed a family,' I say.

'No,' he agrees. 'But I've seen men who would trade every acre they own for what you have.'

For what I have? Is he blind? What do I offer Mary? A hut with a dirt floor, clothes no better than a convict woman's slops, and perhaps a trip to Goulburn once a year—if we prosper.

She deserves better.

And I'll be damned if I give her less.

—

The evening air is cooling when I find Mary sitting beneath the gum tree, back against the bark, knees up, skirt spread around her. Jenkins runs to her, Chara follows. Her hands are busy—she's very kindly mending one of my shirts, needle and thimble catching the last of the light. I don't ask her to do these —she seems to take pleasure from them.

I sit beside her, stretching my legs out in front of me, arms resting on my knees. We do this often—sitting, saying nothing. I watch the slow shift of the sky, the way the light catches her hair. She looks content. Settled.

She glances up from her stitching. 'You were talking to William for a long time.'

'He was giving me a lecture.' I smile. 'He thinks I should be grateful for my lot.'

'He's right.' Her dimples show in the fading light.

'Don't tell me you've joined the William Ryrie's band of admirers.'

She nudges my arm. 'Oh no, you're still my favourite stubborn man.'

I grin, but something about her words stays with me. I scratch the back of my neck, glancing toward the hut.

She keeps her eyes on her sewing.

A moment passes before she says lightly, 'I was thinking we should plant more trees near the hut next spring. It becomes too hot in the afternoon.'

She thinks she'll still be here when they are big enough to cast shade. She's planning a life here. I'm plotting our escape.

I study her profile, the curve of her cheek, the way the last of the sunlight catches the pale freckles on her skin.

'You think we'll be here long enough to see them grow?' I ask, keeping my tone light.

She ties off a stitch.

I wait. Something rises in my throat—not dread, exactly.

'Mary.' I shift to face her.

At that, she looks up at me, her expression unreadable. 'Don't say it.'

Something prickles at the back of my eyes. 'Mary, you won't have to work in someone else's house. You'll have family. Comfort. You'll be given respect.' I smile. 'But I can't guarantee no mending.'

She exhales sharply, shaking her head, her hands pressing into her lap. 'How do you know?'

'Know what?'

'How do you know I won't hate being a wife in your father's house? Expected to pour coffee and remain silent?'

I open my mouth, but no words come.

Her throat moves as she swallows. 'Ghikas, you presume you know what's best for everyone. You don't even ask. You just decide. I won't be dragged there.'

The words sit heavily between us. I watch her face, but she doesn't look away this time.

I do know what's right for us. But the truth is, I don't want to argue.

She shakes her head again, softer this time, reaching for my hand, lacing our fingers together. 'We shouldn't argue about this tonight.'

The edge has gone from her voice, but not from the words. They are lodged in my chest—'you presume you know what's best for everyone'.

Something twists inside. Not anger. Just the ache of being judged without a hearing. When I'm trying to do what's right for everyone. Like on the night of the wedding.

I stare at our joined hands. 'There's something I've never told you.'

She waits.

'On Hydra—at Kostas' sister's wedding,' I say. 'We were all there. Ando and the boys. A girl lied about me—she said I took liberties with her. Andonis believed her. He never asked me what really happened. None of them did.'

Mary's needle pauses above the cloth. 'Have you spoken to him about this?'

'There is no point.'

She looks at me—steady, not unkind. 'You still bleed.'

I start to speak; she cuts in softly. 'You have to tell him.'

'And if he doesn't apologise?'

'You won't know unless you try.'

I squeeze her hand, press my lips to her knuckles, and let it go. I will think about it.

This is our home. For now.

A mooring. Not the home port.

32

AT SEA

Calmer Seas

ABOARD THE *NORFOLK,* en route Portsmouth to Port Jackson
   May-Aug 1829

We'd barely weighed anchor from the Motherbank and sailed down the
Solent, past the castle on the headland and out into open sea, when
contrary winds drove us back. Two days later, the captain tried again.

When we finally set sail for New South Wales, I fell into a black mood.
The events on the *York* hadn't left me—they were lodged in my chest. It
wasn't just the guilt of Andonis' beating. The fever left me with pounding
headaches and waves of nausea. I could only sleep curled on my right side
—lying flat on my back made the world pitch.

Where the English Channel met the Atlantic, a nor'easter hit, and the
ship reared and plunged like a donkey with a burr under its saddle. Most of
the convicts had never been on a ship before. The stench of their vomit
rose from below like steam and clung to the boards.

Confined to a space little bigger than a cupboard, with a ceiling too low
to stand upright, I lay in my hammock, staring at the beams above, feeling
every shift of the ship in my bones. Light and air reached us only when the
hatch was open.

Even the thought of sailing on an open ocean would normally fill me with joy. Now, it didn't.

I'd barely left my hammock or spoken a word in two days.

At night, Kostas' hammock thudded against the bulkhead in time with the swell.

'Would you care to take my sling, Kostas?' I asked.

'Why? It's in the best location.'

I shrugged. 'The airs offend my nose. Or what's left of it.'

He grunted, rolling out of his, 'Then I'll change places, before it offends it further.'

He swung out of his hammock without another word.

From the shadows, Nikos said, 'Ghikas always gives away his best things.'

I looked away. Not always.

Andonis' forehead burned under my palm. I pressed the cloth to his temple cool him, but it was still warm from the last time.

'Drink,' I urged, holding the tin cup to his lips. He coughed, turning his face away.

'Try,' I said again.

He did. A few drops, then a weak smile.

'Nikos will think I'm drinking all the rations,' he said.

I forced a laugh.

I kept to myself—scrubbing the cabin, dousing it in vinegar, squashing bedbugs. Nikos helped me in silence.

On the sixth day out from Portsmouth, a cry of 'Land ahoy!' went up. The island of Madeira was Portuguese, and famous for its wine. We sailed past without stopping. Then came the Spanish-owned Canaries, with Tenerife's towering volcano. After that, the Cape Verde Islands—once the centre of Portugal's slave trade.

On the seventh day, our irons were struck off. The hammer rang along the deck, sparks flying in the sunlight. When mine fell away, I rubbed the raw circle around my ankle—the skin red and ridged. Around me, men did the same—half laughing, half wincing, testing the lightness of their step, as if learning to walk again. We were no longer animals.

A warning shout came from the rigging. I looked up to see a young seaman lose his footing aloft. I felt the jolt underfoot as he landed—one leg grotesquely broken, an arm twisted behind his head, a strange, frozen smile on his face. Sailors ran from all quarters, forming a hushed, sombre circle.

Grief settled over me—for a stranger. We were celebrating our freedom; he'd fallen to his death..

The burial at sea was swift and brutal.

'We commit his body to the deep, to be turned into corruption—'

His corpse slid into the ocean with barely a splash. Days later, the chief mate auctioned his belongings at a Dead Man's Sale.

It reminded me of what I had once considered a morbid saying—a favourite of my mother's.

'In death, we are nothing but the sum of our service to each other.'

Certainly, no purse could ransom a man from the sea.

And I disagreed, a little. Surely personal achievements meant something?

—

As we left the northern latitudes behind, the air turned mild—temperate breezes and soft skies.

One morning during the exercise period on deck, a gust caught the topsail and left a crewman swearing and tangled in ropes. Kostas was already climbing—bare feet sure on the ratlines, hands moving from years of practice. The rest of us followed.

From that day on, the captain allowed us to work on deck, even carry out repairs. The crew nicknamed us 'the pirates', or 'the Greeks'.

Freed from chains, I worked with a frenzied intensity, deliberately avoiding Damos.

The crew painted vivid pictures of Port Jackson. 'The water is so blue it hurts your eyes, and so clear you can see the bottom. And the water is warm! Not murky with shit like the Thames. And in the harbour, bay after bay with sandstone rock faces, and stretches of pure white sand—so fine it blows like dust.'

One day I found Kostas lying in his hammock, feet swollen, soles split and bleeding. In the palm of his hand was a dab of salve from the surgeon.

I gritted my teeth. 'May I help with that?'

He pulled his legs away in refusal—but after a brief pause, he reconsidered, extending his legs towards me.

'Thank you, Ghika,' he murmured.

I applied the salve, knowing the others were watching open-mouthed, knowing my shaking hands betrayed me.

It turned my stomach—but afterwards, I felt something close to pride.

Nikos wore a mischievous grin. 'Look at this, Ghika.'

He yanked up Kostas' other trouser leg.

The skin was raw, weeping, peeling at the edges like old paint, reopened by the removal of the leg irons.

I recoiled. 'For the love of God—'

Even Andonis smiled. 'You're green, Ghika.'

My skin crawled. I grabbed the vinegar and cleaned the wound.

After I'd wrapped it in a clean cloth, I collapsed to the deck, exhausted. Kostas continued what he had been doing before he went to the surgeon—making a musical instrument from a scrap of wood, stringing it with fishing line.

'Where'd you find that line?' I asked.

'Traded my biscuit.'

Nikos settled beside me, holding up his book. 'Let *me* read *you* a story, Ghikaki. You've had a big day.'

He tapped the drawing. His tone was confident—the way I always read to him. 'Look, Ghika, the doctor's saying: "Hold on tight, boy. I'll cut off your legs so you can fit in the bed."'

The others laughed.

I smiled. 'Your reading skills are truly impressive, Niko.'

He nodded. 'I know.'

He was looking after me as I had always done for him.

—

As we neared the equator, the weather became as unpredictable and as hostile as Damos. Dark clouds brought squalls, a twisting waterspout, and sheets of rain that washed the decks clean. Then, as quickly as they came, the skies cleared, with steam rising from the wood in the suffocating heat.

Watching the women and children on the poop deck at dusk brought me comfort. The toddler waddled like a drunken sailor and when she spotted her father—a uniformed officer—she stood on tiptoe, arms outstretched.

The sight of it twisted something in my chest.

Word spread that one of the lady passengers had been taken ill with catarrh. When a guard told us the doctor had blistered her chest with a caustic paste, we pitied her more. Surgeon Dickson swore by the practice.

That afternoon, while Andonis was sleeping, Kostas said, 'How's your stomach problem, Damo?'

Any sickness could threaten Andonis, so I said, 'What stomach problem?'

Damos was quick to answer. 'Why the sudden interest, Ghika? Scared you will catch it?'

'No. If it's infectious, Andonis could catch it. I'm thinking about Andonis, you arse.'

Damos snorted. 'Well, that's a change. Ghikas Voulgaris thinking about someone else.'

I didn't rise to it.

He added, more quietly now, 'It's not infectious. My stomach's always been bad. Worse since the *York*. Runs in the family.'

Then, with a shrug, 'If I'd gone to America like I always said, I'd be well-fed by now.'

I hadn't known about this dream either. I realised then how little I knew about my companions—how much else had I missed?

Kostas spoke. 'Why are you so low in spirits, Ghika?'

He caught me off-guard. 'Kosta, I got you in this mess.'

He sat up and hit his head on the bulkhead. 'We would have been hanged if not for you.'

'You can't be sure of that, Kosta,' I said.

Now Nikos spoke. 'You taught me to read, Ghika.'

Oh Niko. You can't read now, you loaf.

He went on, solemn. 'And you're kind, Ghikaki. You share your food with Andonis. You're a saint.'

Damos, I felt sure, remained unconvinced.

'I wouldn't go that far.' Kostas grinned. 'But I like your foot rubs.'

—

We were coiling rope on the main deck—real work, not punishment detail. The five of us, just like the old days.

Kostas checked the lay of the line and corrected Nikos, who'd doubled the slack too soon. No one snapped.

Damos took the lead, directing Andonis to the forward end. I followed his hand signals without a word. He glanced over his shoulder.

'You're not barking orders,' he said.

I paused. 'Should I be?'

He shrugged. 'You usually do.'

I kept working.

He grunted. 'Didn't think you had it in you. To follow, not lead.'

The sweat stung my eyes.

He just said, 'About time.'

—

Later that week, Damos and I chanced to collect our rations together.

He spoke. 'I have something to say.'

I stiffened, waiting for another low blow.

'You've lost some of that hot air.'

'You haven't called me "rich boy" in three days.'

He hesitated. Then he smiled and held out his hand.

I looked at it, looked up at his face. Then I took it.

'Thanks. It's been hard,' I said.

'You think it's been easy for us?'

'I want to be a better friend. I'm sorry for everything.'

'A better friend? Start by apologising to Andonis.'

'He's too sick to talk about it.'

'Try anyway.'

—

The next morning, I was the last to climb topside.

As I reached for my boots, a half-written letter fluttered from Andonis' hammock.

I picked it up.

One glance at the Greek letters, and my breath caught.

Ghikas reminded me this week of your bravery. Do you remember that day we asked you to hold the bitter orange while we chopped it in half with our father's yataghan?

It was to his sister Persephone. In an instant, I was twelve again. We had skewered an orange with a stick and asked Persephone to hold it for target practice. A shiver travelled through my bowels as I remembered her eyes squeezing shut, waiting for the blade to fall. What courage. She would be a woman now, perhaps a wife.

'It was good fortune, not skill, that we did not chop your arm off.

I do not know what I would do without Ghikas on this voyage. Or ever. He fusses over me like a yiayia, washing my clothes and making sure I've had enough to eat.'

I folded the letter and slid it back into place.

It gave me hope.

—

Andonis' health improved, but slowly.

Day and night were of equal length. Humid heat sapped our vigour—moving became an effort. The crew worked without shirts, sweat glistening on their skin, running off their flaming red backs in rivulets. The paying passengers stayed in their cabins, conserving energy. On calm evenings, they paraded on the poop deck, the women in bonnets and light-coloured dresses that blew against their bodies, arms resting lightly on their husbands' sleeves, their carefree voices carrying on the heavy air.

'Oh, look at the phosphorescence!' A woman's tinkling laughter.

Andonis was no longer the carefree youth who had laughed at danger. Not the boy who jumped off cliffs, or raced me to the top of the mast, or stood toe to toe with bullies. His hands shook; he jumped at loud noises; he was quiet and withdrawn, unwilling to take the lead or offer an opinion. During the day, I guarded him from being jostled and assisted him topside. At night, when he woke from a nightmare, as he often did, I was there.

But there was little to do for his spirit.

Bathed in sweat that refused to dry, our tempers frayed. Near the equator, ships are often becalmed for days or even weeks—but the gods were kind and the winds favoured our passage.

The day we crossed the equator—a sailor's rite of passage—Captain Greig allowed one of the crew to dress up as Neptune, Roman god of the sea. He burst onto the deck with a mop for a beard and a wooden trident, flinging seawater from a bucket at anyone who didn't duck fast enough. We laughed, darted, slipped, and shouted as he gave chase. For a moment, we weren't prisoners—just sailors again. The ladies stayed on the poop deck, out of his reach.

On the rare days when our sweat dried, white salt lined our convict slops.

In the middle of the South Atlantic Ocean, Captain Greig changed course. Now we headed south-east away from the American coast and the nights were cooler. One night, we were permitted to stay on deck and the crew pointed out the Southern Cross—the most brilliant constellation in the southern sky. Four stars, like the stay ropes on a mast, tilted slightly, always pointing south. The Milky Way was far brighter here in the southern hemisphere than at home—and it ran clear from one horizon to the other.

As the *Norfolk* surged along, porpoises swam alongside, smaller than the dolphins at home, threading in and out of the swell, appearing and disappearing, clicking and blowing like carefree children.

Andonis' strides grew longer each day. As if, bit by bit, he was reclaiming himself. And in that incremental recovery, I found joy and hope.

During the exercise period one day, as he and I walked along the deck alone, he said, 'Ghikaki, I want to talk.'

Good. He still looked grey and ill but I was ready to tell him how sorry I was.

He added, 'About the night of the wedding.'

I had no intention of accusing him when he was still so ill, so I said, 'I'd rather not.'

He looked at me then, eyes dark. 'Maybe I need to.'

I said nothing.

The silence stretched. Eventually, he sighed and looked away.

He had stuck by me since we were small boys, always defended me, even when I was wrong. Without him, I would be an outsider, alone. Without my family's position and wealth, stripped of my identity, who was I, really? A nobody. My friends were all I had.

I could have apologised again for the *York*. But with his wounds still so fresh, I didn't want to put him through it.

Instead, I said, 'There's something else, Andoni. Damos said something to me the other day. He made me see the real motive for all that 'generosity' in our childhood. It wasn't for you. It was for me.'

He went to speak, but I cut him off.

'Let me finish. I wanted to be liked. So I bought it. Yiannis was right. Money can't buy respect.'

He nodded. 'You've always been more than your wealth, Ghikaki. Don't doubt yourself now. You never talk about the times you saved my life by being brave. Remember that time in Constantinople? When we were ship's boys for your father? And that janissary took me for a thief in the bazaar?'

An image flashed through my mind—Andonis kneeling, the janissary's long silk coat open down the front over ballooning pants, a huge feather arching backwards from his tall cap, raising his *kilij* sabre to strike the back of Andonis' neck. I'd reached them just in time, driving my shoulder into the man's legs. Then we were running—ducking, weaving through the crowd, losing the janissaries in the tangle of men—until we reached my father's ship.

On a freezing day in early July, a westerly arrived and the captain changed course. We would sail to a point one hundred and fifty miles south of Cape Town, then head due east—our final leg to New Holland.

We were now in the path of the Roaring Forties—the ferocious, freezing winds that circle the globe between forty and fifty degrees south. The crew said they would batter us and hurl us five thousand miles across the bottom of the world, through the southern Indian Ocean.

They also crowed about the treacherous currents and reefs in the strait to the south of New Holland. 'Wait until you see the boiling seas in Bass Strait—it's littered with shipwrecks!' they said. 'Captain Greig will take it anyway. It's quicker than sailing south of Van Diemen's Land.'

The following day, in a mountainous grey and white ocean, another mishap occurred. The ship rolled, and the boilers below deck broke from their fastenings, pouring boiling water over the seaman beside them. In the middle of the night, he was still screaming from his burns.

A Scottish voice called from the next cabin, 'Will you nae put the man out o' his misery?'

Mercifully, he succumbed in the early hours. We stood by in silence for the second time as a body slid off a plank into the depths.

Andonis looked at me with sad eyes. 'Ghika, let your soul be at peace.'

But peace was not easily won.

During the long winter nights, when the ship rolled violently, the boys begged for stories of home.

I told them we'd sail the seas again, build ships, catch fish, grow olives and grapes, lemon trees and oranges, make gardens and wine. Our wives would bake amygdalota for us and raise hordes of healthy Greek children who'd swim at Avlaki and Kamini, as we once had. And when we were old, we'd sit together on the quay and relive the memories of our youth, as old men do.

Each night, they wanted more.

Days blurred. Captain Greig announced the ship was making two hundred nautical miles a day. Flying.

The ocean turned into mountains—waves so huge we held our breath, sure they'd send us to the bottom. The Virgin Mary alone knew the depth of these black waters.

Each day we woke to the sound of howling winds and driving rain. The temperatures stayed above freezing, but we were chilled to the bone—skin chafed raw by salt wind and damp wool, faces red, lips peeling, bleeding chilblains swelling our feet.

When the navigator allowed us a look at his charts, we shared his jubilation at passing abeam the tiny Île Saint-Paul—halfway between the continents. A miracle of navigation in a featureless world of grey.

The five of us came down with colds. Andonis ran a high fever and developed a hacking cough that exhausted him and kept the rest of us awake. I sat with him at night, wiping his forehead.

He was admitted to the infirmary, where men groaned on narrow bunks, skin raw with rashes, sweating with pleuritis or pneumonia; others lay silent with catarrh, dyspepsia. One man wept as the surgeon lanced an abscess on his leg.

When I went to collect Andonis, I found him propped against the wall, pale and trembling. Dickson had given him an emetic to induce vomiting and diarrhoea.

'Did it help?' I asked.

He gave a weak smile. 'No. But it took my mind off the cough.'

On the twenty-first of August, we sighted New Holland—Cape Otway to larboard. There were cheers on deck as we entered Bass Strait in mild weather. But the mood changed quickly. The crew's eyes stayed fixed on the water beneath the hull, and farther out. They spoke in clipped voices. 'Watch for shoals. Reefs everywhere. One mistake and we're gone.'

No one slept.

Captain Greig knew these waters. Still, no one relaxed until three days later, when we sighted Cape Howe—and the cheer that rose came from the gut. We were still afloat.

We sailed up the east coast under brilliant skies, the Pacific failing to live up to its name as the most boisterous of oceans.

Late on the twenty-sixth of August, with magnificent sandstone cliffs abeam, the ship buzzed with excitement. We were south of the entrance to Port Jackson, below an elegant lighthouse more suited to a European headland.

We soon changed course by ninety degrees to pass between the harbour's twin headlands, and anchored in a small bay near the lighthouse-keeper's cottage.

We were allowed to remain on deck to watch the escarpments turn pink at sunset. Waves crashed against the rocks below them, sending spray into the air.

As night fell, the lighthouse pulsed from the ridge—a beacon promising people, buildings, order, and civilisation.

Andonis was regaining his strength; his laughter was more frequent; the colour was returning to his cheeks. The others were showing further signs of trust again, even camaraderie. They chattered excitedly, pointing out every detail—the scent of land on the wind, the way the water no longer heaved beneath us, the glow of the lighthouse against the dark.

I felt almost part of them again. I needed more time.

A tight knot of dread had formed in my stomach.

I couldn't bear the thought that our days on board were nearly over.

That I might lose them again.

As the pink sky faded into night, a guard behind us spoke to another. 'You couldn't cut them Greeks apart with a sword.'

I wanted to believe that. We had come through eighteen months locked up together. Survived a death sentence together. Even the disaster on the hulk, although it came close, hadn't split us apart.

I had to make sure New South Wales didn't do it either.

33

Untangling Lines

CAMDEN PARK, New South Wales
Late July 1835

I accompany William Ryrie to Sydney once more as Ned's offsider. Mary hands me a shopping list as long as a squid's tentacle and as hard to grasp, accompanied by verbal instructions.

This will be my last opportunity to see my friends before I become a husband—to give them notice of the date—so they can request a leave of absence.

We arrive at Camden Park on a Saturday evening, and on the following morning, under an overcast sky, all four of us take up makeshift fishing rods and head to the river. Then, while the others cast their lines farther along the bank, Andonis kicks off his boots and wades calf-deep into the water. He flicks his wrist, and his line sails through the air, hitting the surface in the shadows of the river gums.

I sit on the bank, rod propped against a log, the line disappearing into the water. We fish quietly with no need for speech until I pull in a small fish. I carefully remove the hook from its mouth and release it.

'There you go, little friend,' I say, watching it swim away, its silvery form disappearing in the muddy water.

Andonis lifts his line off a submerged branch and wades back to shore. The hems of his trouser legs are wet. Water droplets roll down his ankles and run off his feet, making dark spots on the earth.

He lowers himself next to me and pushes his rod into the dirt, the line still trailing in the water.

'So, when's the day?' he asks without looking at me.

I glance at him. 'In the middle of September.'

'So soon?' Nikos calls from farther up the bank. 'We'll barely have time to write you a toast.'

'You don't have to write anything,' I call back. 'Just be there.'

There's a silence. Andonis sighs.

'Ghika,' he says gently. 'That's lamb marking at Camden. Every man's needed.'

'No leave, even for a wedding?' I ask, forcing a smile.

He shakes his head. 'Not even for a hanging.'

My stomach sinks, but I nod. 'I understand.'

'I wish it were different,' he says.

Nikos walks back, crouches beside us. 'We'll send something. A bottle of rum. Or a bucket.'

'Or advice,' Damos adds dryly from behind us. 'He'll need it.'

'We'll be with you in spirit,' Andonis says.

'And maybe next winter,' Kostas offers, 'we'll come.'

I nod, throat tight. I had pictured them there—teasing me, brushing my coat, raising their mugs.

Andonis shifts on the bank, rod steady in his hand. 'Tell Mary we're sorry.'

'I will,' I say. 'She'll understand.'

The others move back upriver to where they've cast their lines.

'You and William Ryrie seem to be familiar, these days,' Andonis says.

I shrug. 'He's not the pompous ass I thought he was. Knows his land. Fair. Doesn't waste words.'

Andonis raises an eyebrow, a smirk tugging at the corners of his lips. 'You almost sound fond of him.'

I glance at him. 'I'm not writing him a testimonial.'

He doesn't bite. Just says, 'There was a time you thought yourself better than him.'

I poke at the dirt with a stick.

'There was a time I thought a lot of things.'

'You've changed. For the better.'

I shrug modestly, trying to mask the warmth spreading in my chest. 'Or I've run out of excuses.'

Andonis nods thoughtfully, then hesitates before speaking again. 'And you'll soon be a husband. Didn't think I'd live to see that.'

'Neither did I. Mary's the brave one.'

I thought courage was loud. I was wrong—it's in the quiet.

He chuckles, but the smile doesn't linger. He picks at the hem of his trousers, eyes downcast. 'It's strange, isn't it?'

'What is?'

He exhales, tilting his head towards the river. 'Sitting here like this. Almost feels like old times.'

I glance at him, catching the edge in his tone. Andonis, who took a beating for me on the hulk. The same man who believed Anastasia that night.

'Almost,' he repeats, quieter now. 'But it's not, is it?' He hesitates, then looks at me. 'It's never been the same since the night of the wedding. Back on Hydra.'

'That was ten years ago,' I say quietly. 'The autumn of 1825. And no. It's never been the same.'

He says nothing for a second, and then, hesitantly, 'And we've said nothing about it since—'

I turn to face him. 'What was there to say?'

He exhales, staring at the water. 'I saw her follow you outside, Ghika. She came back crying, saying you'd—you know what she said.'

The air is still. He speaks again. 'Was she telling the truth?'

My fingers tighten around the rod, knuckles white. The current makes small sucking sounds against the bank.

'No.'

He looks at me.

'She followed me. I told her what I thought of her. She went back inside and lied.'

He stares at me, blinking as if I've hit him.

'I believed her, Ghika. I couldn't believe you. If I did, I'd have had to hate her.' He shakes his head. 'I always thought I was the wronged one.' He exhales heavily, dragging a hand through his hair. 'I should have listened to you. I should have known better. I was too busy feeling wronged.'

I glance at him. 'You weren't the only one.'

He lets out his breath. 'I told myself you wanted her, Ghika. That made it easier. But you never did, did you?'

'There's only ever been one woman I've wanted like that. Mary.'

'You are lucky Ghika. I was miserable after that night—couldn't eat, couldn't sleep. My cousin finally hauled me off to a woman of the streets.'

That draws a laugh from me, despite myself. 'And what did you learn?'

'She yawned halfway through.'

We both laugh.

'It was a trade, nothing more. No warmth, no tenderness.'

He tilts his head, studying me. 'Isn't that what it's about? Warmth?'

I meet his gaze. 'I wouldn't know.'

I've had chances enough. Other men went to women after a voyage. I always stayed behind, pretending I'd had my fill elsewhere. Truth was, after that night, the risk of another humiliation wasn't worth the price.

He frowns.

I rub my thumb along the line of calluses. 'That night—it's never left me.'

I look down the river. If I say the words, it will make it real.

'I've never been with a woman, Andoni.'

He laughs loudly. Then, when he sees the expression on my face, he frowns. His eyebrows lift. 'Never?'

I watch the river swirl.

His voice cracks slightly. 'My God, Ghika. I don't know how to make that right.'

I let the silence settle before answering. 'You can't.'

He starts, 'I wish I—' But then he stops.

The river keeps flowing. The ache in my heart eases a little. It's not gone, but lighter.

I say, 'Give me a better rod, and we'll call it even.'

Andonis' eyes crease. Then, finally, he laughs.

'Fine,' he says. 'But don't expect bait too.'

We sit in silence, fishing rods in hand, the years slipping away like the current.

34

A Bush Gathering

ARNPRIOR, New South Wales
  September 1835

It's Thursday the seventeenth of September—our wedding day.

Sick with nerves, I stand on the verandah of the Arnprior homestead. The late afternoon sun warms the boards, and new roses climb posts behind me. At one end, a small table waits, draped in white. The idea to be wed here was Mrs Ryrie's—no small thing—just a quiet nod to her husband and a word to Mary. It was a kindness we didn't expect, and we'll not forget it.

It will be a fine ceremony. I have told myself it doesn't matter that the boys cannot be here. Their absence is no great thing. But the truth is—I've pictured them here, teasing me for being anxious, Ando brushing my coat, Nikos trying not to cry.

Father Therry rode in after dusk two nights since, and Mister Ryrie and William agreed weeks back to stand as our witnesses.

Mary Watt insisted on sending a length of silk from Sydney months ago for Mary's gown—an extreme luxury no maid, or convict like me, could ever afford. Mary said she would not wear it—people would think she was dressing above her station.

Mrs Ryrie overheard. 'Of course you must use it, Mary. I'll not hear a word otherwise.'

Mary is grateful Annabella helped her to cut the cloth out by lamplight, and together they stitched it. They had enough for matching slippers.

I almost ordered a suit of clothing by post from Mr Townsend's tailor in Sydney, but when Mary confessed she'd rather see me in my work clothes than in a frock coat, I tore up the letter. I was relieved, all the same, when Mrs Ryrie—as kind as ever—pressed one of Mr Ryrie's cast-off jackets into my hands.

But none of his collars fit me, and I own none myself.

Back on Hydra I would have dressed in black *vraka* tucked high at the waist, a flowing white shirt with immaculate cuffs, and a *geléki* of midnight velvet shot through with silver thread. A scarlet *zonári* sash, silver-buckled *tsarouchi*a shoes, and a new *fési*—my soft red tasselled cap.

But without any of this finery, not even a collar, I still feel remarkably grand.

The wedding party will consist of Father Therry, Mister Ryrie and William, Mary, and me.

I check my pocket for the rusty nail—protection against the *mati*, the evil eye, and around my neck is my hagstone, sacred to me because it's blessed, as much by love as superstition.

I wait. Time drags. I want the thing done.

I'll just go up to the fold and check the sick ewe. It will only take five minutes.

No, I'd better not.

There's a noise at the verandah's edge.

It's Mary.

She rounds the corner of the house, Annabella beside her adjusting her hair. When it's done, Mary kisses her on the cheek; Annabella waves and steps back out of sight.

Mary's smile could launch five thousand ships. Her cheeks are flushed, curls pulled back from her face, roses in her hair, and a small bunch of flowers in her hands. The fabric of her dress is the colour of bleached whalebone kissed by the sun—soft and filmy, swathed across her form and caught high above her waist. Tiny puffs of sleeves start on her shoulders, and the dress drops straight to her ankles, grazing the slippers.

Her eyes are on me. Only me.

I take her other hand. It's cool. My stomach fills with fluttering butter-flies. Mary has fretted over her dress, and whether she should wear a bonnet—and now I tuck her hand in mine to reassure her—she could wear sackcloth and still outshine them all.

Father Therry emerges through the front door, prayer book in hand. 'My boy, my boy. Mary,' he booms, as if delighted. 'Good to see you both. Are we ready?'

Mister Ryrie follows, waistcoat buttoned, hair neatly combed, solemn dignity in every step. William comes behind him and makes a soft whistling shape with his mouth when he sees Mary.

The four of us shift a little closer to the table. Dust glints in the sunlight. A laughing jackass cackles high in the gum tree, and a faint clang carries from a far paddock.

'Don't be nervous,' Father Therry says kindly, beckoning us forward. He lifts the book and begins. 'In the name of the Father, and of the Son, and of the Holy Spirit. Be attentive to our prayers, O Lord, and in your kindness, pour out your grace on these your servants, Ghikas and Mary, that, coming together before you—.'

His voice folds into the rhythm of Latin and English. Mary's fingers find mine again, and I don't care who sees—I grip her hand tightly. She's trembling. So am I.

There's a reading from Saint Paul—love, patience—and another where Jesus commands us to love one another. I hear the words, but they wash over me like the creek in flood.

Then the moment comes.

'Dear children of God,' says Father Therry, 'you have come today to be joined in matrimony, to pledge your love before God and before the Church, here present today in the person of your priest and your friends.'

I take Mary for richer or poorer. My voice catches, but I manage to speak.

When it's her turn, she lifts her chin and says clear as a bell, 'I do.'

Everyone laughs, including Father Therry.

He opens his notebook. Our names are written already. I take the pen. There's a flicker of hesitation—a second—under the name he's put down for us:

Mister and Mrs Ghiera Burgara.

I swear, since I left Hydra, I've never seen my name spelled the same way twice. It doesn't matter.

It's as well I'll never be famous—for no chronicler will ever find me. I sign.

Mary takes the pen with no hesitation.

Then Mister Ryrie, with firm strokes, and finally William, in his fast scrawl.

When Mister Ryrie passes back the pen, he grips my shoulder, the wrinkles around his eyes deep with kindness. His voice is low. 'You've done well, Ghika. We wish you and Mary every happiness.'

I can only manage, 'Thank you, sir.'

Father Therry raises his arm in the sign of the cross. 'Go in peace and glorify the Lord by your life.'

And so, it is over. And there stands my wife—the very essence of beauty, and the centre of my world.

The front door opens. Mrs Ryrie steps out with Jane behind her, bearing a tray of china and a steaming teapot. The scent of black tea and dried citrus peel drifts on the afternoon air.

Mrs Ryrie clasps her hands. 'Mary,' she says, her admiration unmistakable, 'you look exquisite. That silk was made for you, my dear.' Then she turns to me with a smile. 'And you, very handsome, Jigger.'

Jane sets the tray of china on the table, eyes shining. 'Oh, Mary,' she breathes.

Mary lays down her flowers and moves to take the handle of the teapot —but Mrs Ryrie lays a gentle hand on her arm, smiling.

'Today, Jane will pour.'

Mrs Ryrie offers us slices of fruitcake—finely cut, laid on small plates with a napkin beneath. The aroma is rich with spice, a reminder of Sydney Cook's promise at Christmas. She has kept her word, sending it from Sydney on the mail coach, wrapped in oilcloth, with a note praising the Arnprior pumpkin she used in it. The rest—flour, sugar, dried fruit—would have been given by the Ryries. Otherwise we'd never have it.

William Ryrie clears his throat, and the group stills. 'Today,' he says in his usual abrupt voice, 'we have witnessed the marriage of two of our most valuable staff. Jigger and Mary, may your journey together be as fruitful'—here he coughs—'and as prosperous as your contribution at Arnprior.'

Mary blushes.

'Thank you again, sir,' I say. 'And thank you for everything, Father.
'

I nod with respect at our employers.

'And you, sir, ma'am.'

Mary inclines her head, fingers brushing her gown. 'I'll never forget this day, thank you kindly, sir, ma'am,' she whispers.

Jane places a wrapped slab of cake into Mary's hand. 'For your celebration,' she murmurs.

'We shall take our leave,' I say, bowing. 'Thank you again, ma'am.'

Mrs Ryrie offers a final, warm smile. 'Enjoy your evening with your friends,' she says. 'It's a fine thing to be well loved.'

Mary and I step down from the verandah, the boards giving way to soft earth.

I hear William's voice behind us. 'Jigger, one moment.'

When we turn, he holds out a creased envelope. 'I almost forgot. This came in the last mail. Addressed to you.'

I nod, throat tight. 'Thank you, sir.'

Now he holds out a cloth-wrapped bundle. 'A gift for you both. Something useful.'

He turns to Mary. 'Forgive me, Mary. Jigger will use this more. But I hope it serves you both well.'

I take and shake his hand. 'Thank you, sir.'

William gives a half-smile. 'You've come a long way, Jigger. You and Mary both. We're proud to have you.'

A nod, then he's gone.

I slip both into my jacket pocket. I'll open them later. Our friends are waiting.

Mary doesn't speak, but her hand slips into mine, and I can feel the smile in her fingertips. We follow the path toward the convict huts, the air cooling now. Shadows stretch across the paddocks and the sky glows orange over the ridge.

'Congratulations, *agápi mou*,' Mary says. I kiss her hand. The murmur of familiar voices drifts down the hill. We're going home.

A fire burns low outside our hut. Smoke lifts in ribbons above the roof, curling toward the darkening sky.

I see figures gathered—silhouettes moving in and out of the light. Their voices reach us in snatches—laughter, a joke, the scrape of something being shifted.

'Here they are!' Joe shouts.

And then I see them.

Two chairs.

Not stools. Not crates—chairs. Real chairs. Sturdy, bush-timbered things with arms and slatted backs—wood smoothed and pegged at the joints. Made by hand. Made by them.

Sitting like thrones beside the fire.

Mary lets out a breath. Her hand is still in mine.

Seamus is the first to move. He straightens up from where he's been tending the coals. He's grinning like a schoolboy, wiping his hands on his trousers.

Joe bounces beside him, unable to stay still. 'You're late!'

Mary crosses to the chairs and glides a hand along the back of one, firelight outlining her smiling face. She hesitates, eyeing the seat with the caution of a woman wearing silk.

'Smoothed with a stone,' Seamus says quickly. 'Rubbed it right down. You won't be catchin' your stockin', Mary, if that worries you.'

'These two chairs,' Martin says, 'are from all of us. We made them. Together.'

Joe lifts his mug. 'To Jigger and Mary!'

'To Jigger and Mary,' they all chorus. The sound fills the clearing.

I raise my mug in return. 'To friends—both present and absent.'

They cheer—quietly, but with feeling. Someone claps. Someone laughs. The fire crackles.

I catch Mary's eye, and we both smile.

My father had a handsome chair carved with lion's heads and velvet arms. This chair is mine.

Martin gestures. 'Take a seat, Mary.'

'It's beautiful,' she says and lowers herself gently.

I sit beside her, my hands resting on the arms.

'Thank you,' I say. 'This is the finest gift I have ever received.'

Mary looks around. 'Thank you all.'

Ned comes forward, both hands holding something that looks like a tray. It's a board, with two neat holes carved into each end for lifting. Not quite a tray, but close enough. A bullocky's version of one. The surface gleams faintly for he's rubbed it with oil, maybe, or wax.

He sets it down on a stump beside the fire. 'It's not silver,' he mutters, not meeting our eyes. 'For you to put your cakes on, Mary.' Then he reddens and clamps his pipe between his teeth, as if lost for words.

Mary touches his sleeve, then the board, with gentle fingers. 'Thank you, kindly, Ned,' she says. 'That is, without a doubt, the loveliest tray I've ever seen.'

Ned's mouth grimaces in a grin, pipe still clenched in his teeth. He tips his head.

Above the coals of the fire, a pot swings gently from the iron hook, lid clinking as steam lifts it. Joe stands and pulls it off with a flourish.

'You didn't think we'd let you starve tonight, did you?'

Inside is a thick stew—mutton and barley, seasoned with onion. Annabella has a ladle in hand, already dipping into the pot and serving it into tin bowls while Ned tears the damper apart and passes them around, crust charred, centre warm.

Mary perches on the edge of her new chair, bowl balanced on a cloth in her lap, laughing at something Seamus says. I watch her in the firelight— she looks even younger tonight, lighter. My wife. She feels me watching, and smiles. For me.

Seamus uncorks a bottle with a flourish. 'Where would we be without a tot? To Jigger and Mary, may your cow never run dry.'

The toasts grow rowdier, the mugs keep refilling, and laughter rings louder. Ned, face flushed, raises his mug toward us, then forgets what he meant to say.

Mary slices the cake and every hand reaches for a slice.

Seamus sniffs his. 'Fruit! And rum!'

Joe takes a bite and closes his eyes. 'Oh, Lord above.'

Joe and Seamus sit cross-legged on the ground, elbows braced on knees. Seamus is in full flight—voice rising, waving his hands like a harbourmaster bringing a ship into port.

'No, no, listen, I swear on me grand-mother's grave. The pig were dead when they put it in the cart! But when they got to the market—'

Joe snorts, already laughing. 'Dead?' he gasps. 'And they still sold it?'

'Well, they told 'em it were a bit sleepy, didn't they?'

Joe slaps his knee, howling. The sound makes something relax in my chest.

Martin's talking earnestly about ploughing ground—something about the angle of the furrow—but Ned is nodding with the distant look of a man who understands none of it and doesn't care. I laugh. Properly, freely, head tipped back, breath stolen by the sheer, absurd joy of it all.

Joe taps his mug against mine. 'You said you wanted a fancy party for Mary, Jigger—and by God, it is.'

We sit in our chairs, faces flushed from the fire and feet warm, stew in our bellies, our friends around us.

I could not wish for more.

One by one, they rise.

Joe lurches to his feet and offers a crooked bow. 'Goodnight Mister and Mrs Bulgary.'

Annabella kisses Mary's cheek. 'You are beautiful,' she whispers.

Seamus shakes my hand.

They go arm in arm, Joe and Seamus drifting into the night, voices fading into the dark.

Martin and Ned stay a moment longer, then slip away, holding each other up.

Mary brushes her hands together and looks around. The fire's a bed of red coals. Empty bowls sit near the log. The last crumbs of the damper lie on the tin plate. The oilcloth wrapper rests beside the stump—the cake is gone.

Mary looks at me, smiling. 'Shall we tidy up, Ghika?'

As if we do this every day. My pulse thunders.

She gathers the bowls, setting one into another. I move to help, folding the cloth, raking the coals into a pile with a stick. Neither of us speaks.

A breeze lifts the last of the warmth and scatters it into the night.

When the last bowl is stacked and the fire left safe, we step inside.

She is radiant. But one day, when the roses wilt and the dust settles, when she sees me as a man without a name, without position, will she still be smiling at me?

It is then that we hear a noise outside the still-open door.

'What's that?' Mary is frightened.

Then—another crash. A muttered curse. Both dogs lift their heads.

I know what she's thinking—Bartholomew. She has nightmares about him. I step in front of her, looking for something heavy to use.

A shadow shifts in the doorway.

I push her further behind me, take a step forward, fists clenched.

It's Ned.

He stumbles in, still clutching his mug.

'Left my flint on the log,' he says, a silly grin on his face. He claps me on the back. 'That was one cracker of a day!'

We're both laughing now. He winks at Mary and stands there, swaying slightly.

'Ah. Right. Well then. It's time I went.'

I walk him to the door, close it behind him.

I reach into my pocket. The letter is still there.

On the back, in careful writing: 'For the bride and groom'.

I open it. The paper is thick. The writing neat.

Andonis' hand.

'Read it out,' Mary whispers.

Ghika,

    We trust this finds you in good health.

    We send our congratulations to you and your wife Mary.

    We wish you both great happiness.

    God willing, we will come next winter.

    Until then, keep safe.

    Your Greek brothers

    PS If Mary ever grows tired of your Greek temper, tell her she can come and live with us.

I hand the letter to Mary. She reads it, then presses it to her chest.

I take out the small paper-wrapped bundle William gave me.

It's a folding knife. Plain wood handle. Sturdy. English. On the blade —*Sheffield*. It opens smoothly, closes with a clean snap. The sort of knife a man will have for life.

I turn it over once in my hand, then set it gently on the table.

We don't speak for a long time.

We don't need to.

It's us—my wife and me.

Our house. Our room. Alone.

For the first time ever.

We smile at each other.

My heart's hammering. I've faced storms with steadier hands.

The whole night stretches before me. And I don't have a compass.

35

Nightfall

ARNPRIOR, New South Wales
September 1835

In the soft lamplight, Mary glows—her features luminous, almost ethereal. It's in the line of her throat, the elegant angle of her jaw, her bare shoulders. She moves with the grace of a schooner slicing through calm seas.

I marvel. This is my wife.

I've been longing for nightfall, yet now I'm seized by nerves. Everyone else in her life has failed Mary. Not me. Not tonight. I remove the jacket and set it over the back of the kitchen chair.

My pulse pounds in my ears and the rehearsed words fly out of my head. I pick up the trinket box from the table and hold it out.

'Oh, Ghika.'

She slides her fingers over our initials, not M and L for her name as I first planned, but our initials instead: M and G.

She clutches the box to her chest. 'I will treasure it beyond anything I have ever owned. I'll keep the button in here. It's the only part of my mother I have.'

Her hands fall to her sides. 'Acushla,' her voice falters, 'Father Therry said that you'll want to consummate our marriage tonight. I am ready. If it kills me.'

'If it kills you?' I blurt, confused.

A look of doubt flickers across her face.

'We don't have to rush if you feel uneasy,' I say, but a weight crushes my chest.

'I'll be fine.' She hesitates. 'But things can happen.'

'Like what?' I brush a stray hair from her forehead. Surely it's a straightforward procedure.

She shrugs. 'Complications.'

I try to make her laugh. 'Like tangled bedclothes?'

'You know—like dogs,' she says with a nervous laugh, clasping her hands like a hinge.

I'm stunned. 'Mary, we aren't dogs.' My solemnity lasts two seconds. I choke on a laugh. 'That would be worse than tangled sheets.'

She blushes deep red. 'I know. Sorry. I'm— Annabella said it can be painful.'

My stomach churns. 'Wouldn't you be telling Annabella?'

Now it's her turn to look confused.

'With your galore of experience?'

She twists her hands. 'I have no experience, Ghika. None. Only what my friends have told me.'

My mouth drops open.

'But Annabella says it's also like heaven,' she adds quickly.

I'm still back on 'no experience'.

'You told me at the picnic in Sydney that you had a galore of experience.'

She groans, covering her face. 'I wanted to shock you.'

'You lied?'

She huffs. 'You assumed I had experience, so I invented it. I learned how to move out of a room. How to make myself plain. How to make them laugh. I was lucky. It worked.'

I open my mouth, close it again.

'I've never fancied anyone until you.'

I let out a slow breath.

'Mary—I've never done this either.'

Her mouth drops open. 'You haven't?'

I shake my head.

She stares. 'Oh, thank the Lord.'

We both burst out laughing—relief, absurdity, all of it bubbling up and washing the fear away.

'Lizbet said it's like wrestling a slippery eel.'

That hits like cold water. I pull a face.

'Sorry, sorry, Ghika. It's just that I'm frightened.'

'My love, don't be,' I say. 'People have been doing this for centuries.'

'Are you wanting to do it—now?' She punches her fist into her open palm with a loud smack that makes me flinch. But her question gives me strength, though my heart knocks against my ribs.

'Yes. Very much.'

Her green eyes meet mine. She reaches for her reticule and withdraws a small button hook, placing it in my hand. Then she turns, lifting her hair to reveal dozens of tiny buttons running down her back. 'Help me out of this dress, Ghika.'

I wonder if my legs will hold me. I glance at the hook. I've used one often on my jackets at home, but my fingers feel thick and useless.

'Unbutton me,' Mary says. 'Annabella fastened them.'

There must be forty silk buttons down her spine.

I close my arms around her. She shivers. I lower my head, brushing my lips against the curling hairs at her nape. The perfume of flowers rises from her skin.

Her body tenses.

My fingers tingle. I rub my hands down my thighs to calm myself. I begin, but I can't even undo the first loop.

'Mary, it is impossible. They're too tight. How did Annabella do them up?'

'Take your time, acushla.' Her voice is liquid, soothing.

I try again. My fingers fumble at each loop as she brushes her fingertips against my legs. Halfway down, I shake out my cramping hands. One by one, the buttons come loose, the dress gaping further. At last, it's open from top to bottom. The smooth valley of her spine. The satin of her skin.

I feel faint. I press my hands to her waist and close my eyes.

'Don't stop.'

I slide my palms up, parting the dress, gliding over her shoulders, easing the silk down her arms.

She turns. The dress falls to her feet.

Now I cannot breathe. Giddy, I pull her close, steadying myself with her warmth. I slide an arm beneath her knees and lift her onto the bed.

She exhales in a long sigh. So small. So vulnerable.

'Ghika, please place my dress over the back of the chair. And I haven't put on my nightdress.'

I obey, and turn down the wick. The hut goes dark. 'I can't see—even if you had.'

She reaches out to touch my shirt. I pull it over my head and throw it aside. The night air raises goosebumps on my skin, but Mary's hands are warm as they skim my ribs.

We lie face to face, lips touching, breath mingling.

Her breath catches again. I press my forehead to hers.

'I love you, Mary,' I whisper, words I've never dared say before.

'I love you too, Ghika,' she says, her breath warm on my cheek.

'Together, *agápi mou*,' I say.

We kiss—slowly. It's awkward, uncertain. But something sparks between us, something deep and fierce.

I pause, steadying myself, wishing only to be gentle.

I hold her. In that quiet, I feel it: not power, not possession—belonging. A single soul. Together.

In the middle of the night, I slide my fingers across dark marks under her arm—she says they're numbers.

'Two hundred and ninety-three. I've had those for as long as I can remember. All the children in the Foundling Hospital had marks like that.'

'You poor wee thing.'

'Hush, Ghika. We were but scraps, and they had to tell the babies apart. We didn't feel it.'

I sing her favourite song—the old Greek lullaby my mother used to sing to me. Quietly, so the sound will not carry, as though my voice might soothe the pain of being abandoned, marked, counted.

She lies across me, the side of her face cushioned on the hair of my chest. 'Your voice makes my lips shiver,' she says.

She lifts her head. 'Promise you will never leave me behind?' The words are soft. Almost a whisper. 'I've been left before, Ghika. I have the fear in me it will happen again. Even when everything's perfect.'

How could she even entertain the thought?

I lift her hand to my lips. 'Mary, I promise,' I say. 'Not even if the ship goes down. We will drown together, with me there beside you.'

'Not tonight, I hope!' she says.

We talk about our vows, and Father Therry, and his spelling of our name in his book, and how kind were the whole Ryrie family. And we laugh about Joe looking for more fruit cake, and Ned giving us such a fright at the end. We hide our heads beneath the bedclothes to muffle our laughter in case we disturb those in the other huts.

She sings to me, in a sweet breathy voice, a song about a faraway Irish battle. When she's finished, she cups my face in her hands. 'Ghika, are you happy?'

'I've never been happier, *agápi mou*.'

She snuggles up and a sense of peace settles over me as if all the worries of the world have melted away, leaving only this perfect moment of connection.

I pull her closer and the world feels still, as if this moment could last forever.

I breathe her in, feeling something change inside me—something I've never felt before.

For the first time in my life, I'm not alone.

'Mary,' I whisper, 'I'm not afraid any longer.'

'Neither am I,' she says.

From this moment on, there will be no looking back.

I cannot wait to show her to my family.

36

At Our Door

ARNPRIOR, New South Wales
September 1835—July 1836

Each morning, when I leave the hut, I half expect to find the world changed to match the shift inside me. Married life is steady—chatter, laughter, comfortable silences. Being together is joy enough.

After months of drought, the weather finally yields to weeks of steady, thrumming rain. Rain drifts across the plain in silver threads, stitching sky to earth. Frogs dormant for years begin a deep, joyous croaking, an army of them answering one another in a reverberating chorus. Sheep collapse under the weight of sodden wool; some do not rise. I grieve their loss. But when the grass grows long enough to grab mouthfuls, the others leap and buck for the sheer joy of living.

I feel the same. Time no longer drags—it has a rhythm.

Work pulls the convicts together. In drought we haul water, in flood we dig drains. I've learned to listen—to the men who know this country better than I ever will. I used to think I carried others; now I know I'm the one being carried.

Late one day, when I come in from the convict garden, Mary stands by the table with a billy of water. A single waratah leans sideways in it, its crimson head catching the light.

'There are plenty on the ridge,' she says. 'They seem to like growing near each other, and only in the roughest ground.'

I touch a petal—as thick as leather. 'It's a wonder they survive up there. The soil's so dry.'

She smiles. 'Maybe they survive because of each other.'

I look at her hands, scratched and rough from work. 'Like us.'

On another winter afternoon, as I'm about to go down to the homestead to collect Mary at the end of her work, the door swings open, letting in an icy blast. She steps inside, rubbing her hands, cheeks flushed, breath rising in small white clouds.

The stew I've prepared is bubbling—fresh mutton, potatoes, carrots, onion, and a bare bacon bone for flavour.

'Oh, Ghika, that smells grand.' She has a rough blanket under her arm. 'This was by the door. I think Ned must have left it for you. I told him you say I always pull the blankets off you.'

'He's a good friend.' With Ned, friendship often sounds like silence.

I grin and pull a letter from my pocket. 'And now, there's other news. He's coming!'

She blinks. 'Who? Faith, don't say Bartholomew!'

We've heard that Bartholomew has visited Arnprior with his new woman to ask for his old position. Without his children. William, of course, denied him.

But this is good news. 'No. Ando. And Nikos, Damos, Kostas.' I wave the letter. 'They have applied for leave. They'll be here in July. If all goes well.'

She fumbles at the buttons of her coat, and I help her slip it off and hang it on the nail by the door. She folds her arms on the blanket on the table and drops her head on them. When she lifts it again, her smile is bright—but her eyes scan the hut. 'We'll be needing more chairs. Plates. Maybe a rug—'

'They won't care about rugs,' I say. But her unease mirrors my own.

Her voice drops. 'You're not ashamed, are you, Ghika?'

'No.' But the word catches in my chest.

She touches my hand softly. 'Then no more am I.'

But I can't help thinking of ships, houses, servants.

None of it real.

I will enquire if William has a catalogue from Sydney—one with rugs. I want Mary to smile.

She glances toward the shelf near the fire—where her prayer book still holds the letter from Hercules Watt. The one telling her that Mary Watt, her closest friend in this country, died in April. Forty years old. She wept only once—silently, shoulders trembling. Then she pressed her lips together, folded the letter, and tucked it beneath the candlestick.

She pales.

'*Agápi mou*,' I say. 'Is there something amiss? Don't you want my friends to come?'

She touches my arm. 'No, let them come. I want to know all of it. I want to love them all, so I do.' She grips the back of the chair.

'So?'

She takes a deep breath. 'It's tired I am. A bit queer in the stomach, that's all. I have been for a while.'

Queer? My heart stops. No, this cannot happen to us. I drop to my knees beside her, my hand around her shoulder.

'I haven't had my courses for two months.'

A dozen tales of women dying crowd my head. Please, dear God—not Mary.

'I don't know if I have it in me to be a mother, Ghika.' She swallows. 'What if I die?'

A mother? She is with child? I heave a sigh of relief. Then wonder. The first of our sons. Or perhaps a girl.

'You won't die, *agápi mou*. We'll manage,' I say, and stop myself there. 'Tell me what you need.'

'I was left at the gate of the Foundling Hospital. I've never had a mother. Or a father. I don't know how to do it.'

I open my mouth to reassure her—to say that her parents must have been in desperate conditions to leave her. But that won't answer her worry. What do I say?

'I know you've had no one to show you, Mary. But you've loved others well. You loved your friend who died. You love Jenkins. You love me. And now—' I take her hand. 'You'll love this child.'

She bites her lip, but she smiles.

Memories flash through my mind: the bloody basin; my mother's death; my father's first wife; Ando's aunt; Annabella's baby.

The danger.

'I forbid you to work in the homestead,' I hear myself say.

'Nonsense,' she says. 'Maids work until their babies arrive, if their mistress allows it. Ghika, having a baby is not an illness. And let us be clear—'

She stands up and looks me straight in the eye.

'You forbid me nothing, husband.'

I let my hands fall. 'Right. Then tell me what help you want—and I'll do it.'

'Don't be worrying, Ghika. You're right. I'll manage fine.'

She reaches for her precious kettle, but I gently take it from her hands.

She cups my face, fingers warm against my cheek. 'I prefer to be here. With you.'

One day, I will give her everything she has done without.

I thicken the stew with flour and water.

—

Mary's belly shows only a hint of her pregnancy and she continues working in the homestead. Her nausea passes. Her skin glows.

To prepare for the visit, we save our salted beef and conserve our sugar ration. I pay special attention to the vegetable garden and borrow additional plates and pannikins from the other huts. Three blankets, too, from the Arnprior storehouse. The cook promises eggs.

Mary plans to make hotcakes, like Yiannis used to cook for Ando and me. She folds blankets, fills jars, teaches Jenkins tricks with quiet joy. We're preparing together.

I take over the cleaning.

It niggles at me. They're coming—in the dead of winter. They must sleep in the same room where Mary and I cook, eat, wash, and sleep.

They won't care, but still, it's no *archontikó*.

—

July 1836

I walk up the hill, the scent of wood fires telling me I'm nearly home. Sleet needles my face, wet and biting. I pull my coat tighter and lower my head. Sydney had an inch of snow in June; Coolaringdon had two feet.

The cold affects the sheep, especially those with lambs.

This morning, Chara sniffed out a newborn tucked away in the grass. A young ewe can reject her lamb, but when Chara stepped closer, this mother stamped her feet in agitation. The lamb, still unsteady, tottered to its feet, bleating. It knelt to suckle, tail wagging like a rudder.

For a shepherd, there's no sight more heartening.

Lost in this joyful thought, I almost miss it—the tantalising smell drifting down the hill towards us. Roast beef. Mary's own way with it. I know what that means. I quicken my pace.

Inside the hut, four bare-chested figures sit by the fire, steam rising around them like a Turkish bath. Mary fusses over them.

All four. Even Kostas.

They stretch their arms toward the flames, except for Nikos, who huddles under Mary's blanket. Their wet shirts hang on the wall to dry.

I stand in the doorway. 'Kostas!'

Ando reaches me first and hugs me hard. 'Ghika!'

Kostas grips my arm with his quiet strength, Nikos lifts me clear off the ground. Damos slaps my back with his usual swagger.

Their joy is real.

But as we sit and talk, something shifts inside me.

Andonis speaks proudly of his share farming. He's done exactly what I would have chosen for him. Kostas describes the tavern where he plays his music. Nikos beams—he's learning to read. Even Damos, restless as ever, is happy in his own defiant way.

They've made lives. Without me.

That realisation sits uneasily.

I've always thought their happiness needed my hand to guide them. But here they are.

I take off my coat, hang it alongside theirs, and drop onto a chair. They produce a flagon of rum. We warm our bellies with it. Mary drinks tea. Jenkins puts his head on Nikos' lap, and that giant hand scratches between his ears.

When Mary clicks her fingers, he spins in circles.

'Show-off,' I mutter.

She laughs. 'My favourite boy.'

I raise an eyebrow.

She laughs. 'After you, of course.'

Chara remains by my side.

My wife, our dogs, my friends.

Ando says, 'I'm sorry we have no gift, Ghikaki.'

Mary puts her hand on his arm. 'Your presence is the only gift we want.' Then she touches his sleeve. 'Ando, what did you call Ghikas?'

'Ghikaki, Mary. It's a term of endearment. He hates it.' Ando grins.

'It makes me sound like a little boy,' I say.

'Well, I love it.' She tilts her head, eyes twinkling. 'Ghikaki, you make a handsome husband.'

The boys laugh and I roll my eyes.

Damos nudges Nikos, who blushes, fumbles in his coat, and pulls out a smooth skipping stone.

'For you, Mary. To remind you of me.'

She takes it gently. 'I'll keep it forever.'

I offer water to Nikos. He's surer of himself, growing up. He doesn't wait for me to speak first.

The firelight catches deep lines at the corners of their eyes, white creases from years of squinting into the sun. Their hair is long, beards thick. Each different, yet the same—ruddy faces glowing, arms muscled from work, skin pale above the elbow, dark below. Their hands, like mine, are rough and callused, the knuckles cracked.

Seeing them again is like stepping back into a familiar painting. I know these men. I know their families, the streets they grew up on, the tricks they played as boys, the dreams they spoke of in the dark. I don't have to ask their stories. I carry them with me.

We once talked of ships and sailing. Now, it's crops and livestock. Instead of cargo and wind, it's soil and rain. Our roots lie in whitewashed houses built on solid rock, but now our bark huts cling to dry soil plains.

But not everything changes—they work with good cheer, dress neatly, and carry music in their souls.

We've come so far. We've built lives with our hands.

'One day,' I say, 'I believe people here will say we Greeks made a difference. We helped build this country, even as this country shaped us. And more Greeks will follow in our footsteps.'

'Hear, hear,' says Ando. He is at ease in a way I have never seen before. His shoulders, usually so tense, have relaxed. He speaks of Camden like a man who has made the place his own—not just a place to wait out a sentence.

'So how goes it, Jigger?' Damos asks. I smile at the name. 'Ploutos, thárros, gámos?'

Wealth, bravery, marriage. The things I once thought made a man.

He takes Mary's hand. 'You have the important one.'

She takes mine with her other. 'My husband has saved every penny since he came here. We're making a tidy little life together.'

Ando lifts his cup. 'Your wealth is in your wife, my friend.'

Mary blushes.

I ask the same of them, and they shake their heads, laughing.

'No wealth, no bravery, no marriage,' Kostas says. 'But I have something better. My music.'

Damos kisses Mary's hand. 'Now we've met you, Mary, we want to take you back to Camden Park with us.'

Mary withdraws her hands, smiling. 'Oh, I think not.'

We laugh, the fire flickering, the dogs sprawled out snoring. I lean back, listening to the banter, feeling the warmth of the fire settle into my bones. This ease, this laughter, the knowing each other so well that words are almost unnecessary—this is what I've missed.

And now Mary is here, part of it too.

Ando speaks as if he has known her all his life. 'Mary, how is it you accepted this oaf?'

'I set a kangaroo dog on him to bring him down.'

They all laugh.

'Lucky man,' says Kostas as Mary returns to her meal preparations.

'Jigger,' Nikos laughs when he says this name. 'William Macarthur lets me count the wool bales onto the dray,' he says, chest out. 'I'm slow, but he says I never make an error.'

I offer my hand. Nikos beams and grips it. I place my other hand over both. I glance at Mary—she knows how I've worried about him.

'I have news of Greece,' says Ando. 'From the newspapers. Would you like to hear?'

'You know I would!' I lift my voice.

'You know the new Greek king is a Bavarian—a Roman Catholic? His taxes are higher than the Sultan's and the foreign debts remain. It's a disaster—no constitution, no democracy. They sentenced our Hydriot war heroes to death and only pardoned them under pressure.'

Damos says, 'Didn't you read that Ghikas' friend, Spyridon Trikoupis, is petitioning the English king to pardon men who fought in the revolution?'

Bitterness heats my face. 'He had a chance to do something when we were in Malta. He's forgotten we exist.'

Ando continues. 'Well, they shifted the government to Athens, still in rubble. And they speak French instead of Greek. They wear western dress.'

I struggle to picture this.

'Hydra is in a worse position than before the war.'

I place my mug on the table. 'So, Ando, are *you* still Greek?'

'Even if I were to be given a pardon, Ghika, I will stay in New South Wales. I sell my first crop of wheat this year. One day I will buy my own land.'

Ando has built something of his own. He's rooted here now. I feel proud—but something twists inside me. I thought our futures were tied together, tangled like two ropes on the deck. The knots are loosening. I didn't expect it to sting. It does.

Mary, ever the diplomat, nods in agreement, 'It's a wise path you've chosen, Ando.'

Then, folding her arms with a hint of mischief, she says, 'But dinner will wait until those shirts are back on. Or you'll give me the heartburn.'

We heave the table over to the bed to make room for everyone. Mary has prepared salted beef with her special technique: soaked to remove the saltiness, part-cooked in the pot, and then brown-roasted to crispness with potatoes, pumpkin, cabbage and carrot—saved especially for this day. And she's made a rich gravy from the pan drippings.

Mary passes me a plate. 'They came all this way for you, Ghikaki,' she whispers, reading my thoughts. 'For yourself alone.'

Her words pierce deep. Have I fallen short of their expectations, or my own? Am I too proud to congratulate myself on a modest success?

A dessert of warmed preserved plums and a sweet white sauce, rich, sticky, and utterly unnecessary, fills us to bursting.

'And for breakfast, boys,' says Mary, 'we're having *tiganites*.' She mimics a thick Greek accent—to make them laugh. 'Ghikas tells me you love them.'

Their applause fills the room. Nikos slaps his belly.

Kostas takes a small iron instrument from his bag, holds it to his mouth and flicks the end—long, pure, vibrating notes. 'A jaw harp,' he says. When he plays one of our old favourites, we hum softly, rocking in time, voices rising and falling in harmony.

Mary claps her hands.

Nikos stands and we follow, slinging our arms over each other's shoulders. Our steps are slow, deliberate—feet tapping forward and back, side to side. The fire casts flickering shadows on the hut's walls. Damos beckons Mary; she laughs and claps in time. Kostas picks up the tempo, and we follow, easy as breathing.

With a final slap on the wood, Kostas ends the song. We collapse into laughter.

Andonis nudges me with his elbow. 'You still have the footwork, Ghikaki.'

As the laughter fades, Kostas drifts over to me, a cup in his hand.

'You always tried to fix us, you know,' he says, voice low, and then he pauses.

'But you never let us fix you.'

I glance at him, surprised. There's no accusation in his voice—only understanding.

'It's good you have Mary to carry you now,' he says. 'You're not alone any longer.'

'It's good to see you, Ghika,' says Damos.

'A good night,' says Ando, and the others nod. Mary yawns.

I let the talk wash over me. Old arguments can wait.

We continue talking in front of the warm fire, the rain gently pattering on the bark roof above us. The hours slip away, and Mary lies down in her clothes and falls asleep within minutes. The boys, content and weary from their journey, eventually lie on the floor, arranged head to toe, and I cover them with blankets. They drift into peaceful slumber.

Ando and I remain awake.

'I'm delighted you are prospering at Camden, Ando. Are you still seeing your Elizabeth?' I ask.

'Yes,' he says. 'One day we might marry, Ghikaki. One day, perhaps.'

'Mary and I are expecting a child, Ando.'

He grips my hand and a silent understanding passes between us.

'Thank you, friend,' I say.

But then he shifts the conversation.

'Ghika—Mary might not want to go to Hydra,' he says softly.

Mary coughs. She's listening.

He falls silent.

There is nothing to discuss tonight. But the ember of it glows.

I stare into the fire.

We sit silently for a long while. He speaks again, gently. 'You know, Ghikaki, when we were children, I always wanted to sleep at your family home. And here I am, finally doing it. On the other side of the world, on a dirt floor.'

His words bring a familiar sting—not quite shame, but a quiet awareness of how simply we live. Mary shifts in her sleep, murmuring softly, and I feel something deeper stir. Pride. Gratitude.

'You know, Ando,' I finally say. 'We're doing our best.'

He nods slowly, smiling. 'I know it. We all are.'

Mary's voice, half-asleep, says, 'It's enough, Ghikaki.'

I nod in the dark.

For now.

37

The Freedom to Choose

ARNPRIOR, New South Wales
October 1836

Spring is finally here.

We've had newborn lambs taken lately, so Joe and I are camping out with the flock, keeping a watch for dingoes. Mary is close to her time, but I'm not worried. Annabella is sleeping in our hut in the light wooden cot Seamus and I carried over. The two women enjoy laughing together, and I'm close enough to fetch if needed.

The day is done, and the flock has camped, a sea of rounded white shapes in the moonlight. They're quiet except for an occasional bleat. We sit in the soft loose soil in front of our campfire, backs propped up against a log, the warmth radiating outwards in the cool night air, casting an orange glow on Joe's freckled face. Heat ripples upward from the flames, warping the air and blurring the flock beyond. Chara and Jenkins have eaten and are lying beside me. Chara's asleep, and I suspect she's in pup. Jenkins, the father, gazes at her as he rests his head on his legs.

I picked peaches this morning from the tree in the convict garden, but the skins are thick and furry—best for stewing. My hand seeks my knife on the log beside me. The one William gave me—it's not there.

Joe's busying himself by the fire, whistling like a saint. Too innocent by half. I catch the glint of steel as he slides something into his bag.

'Have you seen my knife, Joe?'

His eyes widen. 'No, but we better find it. You'll need it if a bushranger attacks us! Hey, Jigger! We can catch one and earn the reward!'

'We won't catch one with a little knife, Joe.'

'You're right Ghika. Ain't none in the district, anyway.'

'No, not unless you count one with a gap in his front teeth.'

He grins into the flames. Fine. Let him think he's fooled me. I feel around. As if I think it's fallen off in the dirt. 'It can't have gone far,' I say. 'I'll look in the morning when it's light.'

I put the peaches aside.

When the fire dies down to glowing embers, we cook our mutton chops over the dancing heat, mouths watering as the meat sizzles over the coals. I take a small piece of folded newspaper from my bag and carefully unfold the precious salt. Joe takes a huge pinch and rubs it between his fingers, sprinkles the meat, then slaps his hands together, sending salt everywhere. I refold the remaining salt into the paper for breakfast.

We eat the smoky chops with our fingers, sucking out the marrow before tearing meat off with our teeth, gnawing until the bones are white. We wash down our meal with cups of sweet black tea made in the billy. The fire pops softly, a background to the crickets and a distant owl.

Jenkins crunches on a bone. Joe's presence warms the night.

Now and then, sparks shoot upwards toward the stars. The Southern Cross holds steady in the south, and the Milky Way—no longer Hera's milk or a sea route home—stretches out like a flock of trailing sheep. The gums tower above us, their ghostly silver trunks and twisted branches casting long shadows.

'What are you thinking, Jigger?'

'Nothing much.'

He looks disappointed.

'My savings, Joe.'

'How much you got in that pouch of yours?'

'I don't know.'

'Yes, you do Jigger. I see you counting it. How much?'

I hesitate. 'A few pounds, maybe. To take home.'

Joe's mouth drops open. 'A few pounds! That's a king's ransom! What are you going to buy at home? A palace?'

I laugh. 'Not enough for a palace, Joe.'

Joe pokes the fire with a stick and more sparks fly into the air. 'Will your da be happy then? If you take home some money? Hasn't he got enough?'

'No.'

Joe grins. 'Ever thought of stealin', Jigger? It's quicker than savin'.'

He knows how to rile me.

'You know what I think you should buy with it, Jigger? A ship! Your father would love a ship.' He looks doubtful. 'I suppose he's got all the ships he wants.'

We sit in companionable silence. The idea of taking my savings home —proof of my success—is deeply ingrained. No matter how far I've come, some part of me still aches for his approval. Or perhaps I want to show him I never needed it.

'Hey, Jigger, you know what would be funny?'

'What, Joe?'

'If we put a frog in Willie Ryrie's bed.'

I laugh out loud. 'Joe, that's not funny. That's silly.'

'Can you imagine his face when he found it?'

I don't reply.

Joe pouts. 'You're no fun.'

I shake my head. 'You're incorrigible, Joe.'

'Thanks, Jigger.'

'It's not a good thing, Joe.'

Joe grins. 'Jigger, you know how you always think money is so important?'

When Joe lights on a subject, he worries it like a bone. 'Yes, Joe.'

'Well, what would I do with a heap of it? Apart from buying tobacco and the like?'

'Well, Joe, when you earn your Ticket of Leave, you'll need it.'

Joe jabs a thumb towards the homestead. 'Why do I need a Ticket of Leave? I'm staying here. I'll pinch everything I need from the Ryries.'

I let out a bellow of laughter.

'Sometimes I think them Ryries can't see me,' Joe says.

'What do you mean, Joe?' I'm licking my fingers.

'Well, sometimes they walk right past me like I'm not even there. Yesterday, William comes up to me and asks where the sheep brands are, and I tell him, clear as day. Then he walks straight past me and asks you.' Joe's voice rises. 'But Jigger, I already told him.'

'I don't think he means any harm, Joe. He's thinking about other things.'

We lapse into a comfortable silence for a moment.

'You may wish to marry, one day, Joe. You'll need money for that.'

'Nah, Jigger. I told you I had a sweetheart once, and she din't stick around. She weren't keen on me pinching.'

Joe tips the last of his tea onto the coals. They hiss and spit, sending up a curl of steam.

He continues, 'Nah, that little betty you gave me is all the wife I can handle. She's hard to keep a lid on. Of course, she's empty again. But there's a rascally Greek around here who sneaks coins when I'm not looking.'

He puts his hand over his mouth to conceal his laughter. I roll my eyes and smile.

'But you're dead keen on going back home, right, aren't you, Jigger? To your island?'

'Yes, that's the plan.'

Joe pauses for a moment, staring into the fire. 'Mary speaks Greek, does she? '

'Not yet. But she will.' I must start teaching her. But what if she doesn't want to learn?

'I'm glad it's not me. I can't even speak English. And I'm daft. I'm a nobody.'

That word again. I think of my father. I think of Yiannis. 'Having money doesn't make you a man, Joe. You're kind, Joe. That makes you more than a nobody.'

Didn't I just tell him the opposite? That money makes the man?

Joe grins. 'Aye, mate. That's what me mother used to say. The swells have fancy titles and silver spoons, but they're no better'n us. And they're never happy.'

I nod. 'Your mother was right, Joe. But money does give you the freedom to choose—to say 'no', so other people don't make your decisions for you.'

'I like you to make my decisions, Jigger. You're clever,' Joe says, scratching his chin.

If I were, I'd still be at home.

But then there'd be no Mary.

Each time she places my hand on her belly, it occurs to me that perhaps this—the family we're building—is a success far deeper than the wealth and recognition I once sought.

And perhaps, in the end, it's these men—Joe, Ned, Martin, Seamus— that have taught me what strength truly is. I once believed they needed me. The truth is, I'd never have managed without them.

I pick up the peach again. 'I wish I could find that knife.'

Joe grins and pulls it from his bag like a magician at a fair. 'Look what turned up!'

I take it, shake my head at Joe, with his sheepish grin.

'Anything else of mine in there?'

He lifts the bag, shakes it. It clinks.

I shake my head and start to peel. 'Good thing we're mates.'

38

The Storm

ARNPRIOR, *New South Wales*
  December 1836

It's been raining for hours.

Mary has thrown her arm across me, and where our skin touches, we stick to each other in the stifling heat of the hut. She complained of cramping and backache earlier in the night, a tightness low in her belly, but waved me off when I suggested it might be the baby. Cook told her last week that her belly hasn't dropped yet—whatever that might mean—and that the birth is likely some weeks hence. I was glad to hear it.

Eventually, Mary's restlessness gave way to sleep, her nightdress hitched up to cool her legs. Before she drifted off, she placed my palm on her belly, as she often does. Suddenly, it jabbed against my hand—as if the child means to punch its way into the world. Surely a boy.

The Ryrie family and the domestic staff have gone to Sydney for the Christmas season, and the Aboriginal people to Maneroo for a 'Bogong' festival, where it is said they gorge themselves on a type of moth. Young James remains at Durban Durra to oversee the place, though there's little enough to do.

I need to go outside.

Easing Mary's arm off my stomach, I slide from the bed and pad to the doorway. The night is black as the inside of a cow's stomach. The rain has eased, fat drops still dripping from the eaves. Lightning flares in the south, bleaching the hut white for an instant, followed by the long, rolling crack of thunder. I stand there listening.

Chara, soon to be a mother herself, sits at my feet, while Jenkins, the father-to-be, sleeps on.

A footstep crunches in the darkness. Chara barks.

'Who's there?'

Moonlight breaks through the clouds, casting a ghostly light on the trees. Chara barks again and gives a low, menacing growl. Jenkins is here too now, alert, watching. The shape of a man melts out of the shadows—clothing in rags, feet bare, a gaunt face topped with a mop of ginger hair.

For a moment I can't believe it. Bartholomew. How did he cross the river? How long has he been here?

I move from the shadow of the hut. 'What do you want?'

Without warning, he lunges at me. As we grapple, Chara leaps on him, seizes his arm, shaking her head as her teeth dig in. Jenkins is here too, latching onto the man's trousers with his teeth. Bartholomew curses as he slips in the mud, trying to shake them off. He's on the ground, yelling. 'Get these stinking dogs off me!'

I wait a second before I catch both by the neck and pull them back.

He rises to his feet, breathless. 'My wife died, Bulgary. Alone in a humpy. Did you know that?' He is almost sobbing. 'After Ryrie got rid of me, they took my children away to the orphan school in Sydney. Did you know that? Do you know what that is like? To lose your children?' His voice breaks. 'But what would you care, eh?'

His grief is raw, his fury wild enough to wake the dead. The poor wretch. Widowed and childless. I think of Mary then—he's lost a wife and children, she lost her parents and siblings.

'I am sorry. I truly am.' I take a step towards him.

'Stay where you are!' He pulls a cloth bag from inside his shirt. 'See this? From Ryrie's safe. I know where the old man keeps the key.'

'Bartholomew, don't make it worse for yourself, man. You will hang. Put it back.'

'They'll not catch me. I will find my children. With this, I can support them. We will be a family again.'

But his wife is dead.

He guesses what I am thinking.

'With a new mother. This here's Milly.' He beckons behind him and the dogs bark as a figure limps out of the darkness around the corner of the hut to stand beside him. She's pale and haunted, with black hair hanging lank to her waist.

He hands her the bag and turns to me, his voice carrying over the sound of the rain. 'It's your turn now.' A knife appears in his hand—probably from the Arnprior kitchen. 'Don't make me use this.'

The old anger surges through me. The way he's moving suggests he's drunk, and the knife looks harmless, but the sight of it stirs every instinct in me to strike first.

'Bartholomew,' I warn, 'put it down.'

He steps closer, the blade wavering. Before I can think, my fist flashes out. The crack of it sickens me. The knife drops. He stumbles, then collapses in the mud.

I stand over him, breathing heavily, fists still clenched. For a moment I'm frozen. Rain and thunder fill the silence. I've done this before. Too many times.

'Get away from my Ernie!' the woman cries, striking at my chest.

Bartholomew groans. She drops to her knees beside him.

He's not a wicked man. Just broken and foolish. He's up on one knee, and she's helping him struggle to his feet. He's so groggy I could push him over.

'Bartholomew, put the money back. Do it for the sake of your children.'

He shoves the woman aside and staggers toward me, one finger stabbing the air. 'It was you that cost me my children. I can't get them back without a job. I need money—'

His woman interrupts. 'He doesn't care what you need, Ernie—but he'll tell them it was us, and they'll hang us. It's over, Ernie. We must put it back.' There's despair in her voice.

Bartholomew's shoulders slump. 'You're right, Milly.' Hand in hand, they begin to slink away.

I think of his children—faces pressed to orphanage glass, waiting for a father who won't come.

Joe had it right. What's money worth? My father's pride was built on collecting it. I've despised men like Bartholomew—all bluster and self-pity, always the victim. But as he stands there soaked and desperate, I see the ghost of myself the day we took the Herakles. So sure the world owed me respect when I hadn't earned it.

If I walk away from Bartholomew now, I stay that man forever.

Recklessness has ruled my life. Let it serve something better than pride. Let it cleanse rather than destroy.

I take a deep breath. If I stop to think, I won't do it.

'Wait,' I say.

Bartholomew stops, turns back. The woman too.

'Wait there.'

I turn. Mary is standing in the door's shadow, holding a dark shape heavy in her hands. She steps forward into the moonlight. The leather pouch with our savings. She has read my mind.

'Are you sure?' I whisper to her.

'It's Bartholomew isn't it? I overheard. You can't bear it, Ghikaki—his children. And nor can I. No child should be left without a father. He must get them back.'

I have already decided. This confirms it.

I take the bag from her and squeeze her hand. Bartholomew is still waiting.

I hold out the pouch. 'Bartholomew, have this. Our savings. But first, you must put Mister Ryrie's money back.'

'Is this a trick? You yell "thief" before you murder me?'

I wait. He and the woman murmur to each other.

'We'll take it,' she says.

Mary says, 'Come inside, Milly, out of the rain. I'll make you a cup of tea.'

Bartholomew turns and walks alone towards the homestead while his woman takes the pouch from me and follows Mary into the hut.

Rain beats on the roof. My hands tremble. This will delay our return to Greece. I feel hollow, yet oddly at peace. Bartholomew will regain his children. As any father should.

The dogs lie near the door, still alert.

Mary gives a low groan that lifts the hairs on my neck. She folds over her belly and grips a chair until her knuckles go white.

'Mary!' I'm at her side. The dogs are whining.

Her eyes lock on mine—clear, shocked. Another wave takes her; she clamps down on my arm. 'Now?' I say. A whisper. 'Now?'

She can't speak. She nods—once—and drags in air through her teeth.

Bartholomew steps back as if Mary has the pox.

The river is up. There is no one to help us. Mary has been adamant right from the beginning that Annabella, ill in bed herself, must not be involved in the birth.

'I must go for the midwife,' I say, as the rain beats on the roof like a thousand drums.

Mary cries out. 'No, Ghikaki. Stay. Please.'

I look at Milly. She looks back, blank as a wall. 'No man can cross that river tonight,' she says. 'Would you make your wife a widow?'

'You,' I say. My voice cracks. 'You're a healer. Aren't you?'

For a heartbeat she doesn't answer. Then she barks a laugh with no joy in it.

'I put people to sleep. I draw the devil out of them. I don't deliver babies. Isn't there anyone here who can tend to her?'

'No.' I stand there like an idiot, trying to think what to do.

Her eyes flick to the bed—Mary is a sheen of sweat, pale lips, body curled up.

Something shifts. 'Well, there's no stopping her now, is there?' She shrugs. 'I've seen a few babies born.'

She throws the blanket off her shoulders, shoves the sleeves of her mud-streaked dress up to the elbow. Her bare feet slap the floor, hands black with grime, nails overgrown. The sight of her makes me shudder.

I light the lamp.

'Clear the table,' she says. 'Boil more water. And pray your wife is strong.'

My mind flies back to Hydra. My mother welcomed guests to our home by pouring water over their hands, a sign of ablution. I pick up the bucket, aware that this water will be precious, for once we use it, any refill from the river will be brown.

'Wash your hands, Milly,' I say, tipping a little into the basin.

She snaps, 'I'm not your maid, am I?'

But she obeys.

I give her a cloth.

She laughs and flips her hair back over her shoulder. 'It's a finger-smith, you want, is it?' She lifts both hands and waggles her fingers.

The nausea surges again.

'Find some rags.'

I swallow the lump in my throat. Mary has already organised a birthing box, filled with baby clothes she has stitched, and clean torn cloths.

'Now, where's my tea? Any damper?'

Mary moans behind me, and Milly asks about food.

Mary refuses tea, squeezes her eyes shut, and grips the side of the bed. As a wave of pain takes hold, she arches her back with a low moan. I'd give anything to take her place. I put her tea on the table.

Milly pats Mary's hand as she drinks. Then she rummages through the box, throwing the delicate baby clothes aside, keeping only the rags. She tears two long, thin strips with her teeth and catches me staring at her. 'For the cord,' she says. 'Leave the hut. This is for women.'

Leave Mary to this harridan? I shake my head, take her hand again.

Mary opens her eyes, shining with tears. 'Go on out, Ghikaki. If I call, you'll come. But I've work to do now.'

Milly grunts approval. Mary has dismissed me. I must entrust my world to a stranger. The urge to push that woman out through the door is overwhelming.

Mary touches her fingers to her lips and turns them to me. I feel the force of her, her formidable strength, like a wave.

My heartbeat slows, as if calmed by a potion. 'Call me. I will be waiting.' I kiss her forehead, willing every ounce of my strength to flow into her, an invincible shield. Her fingers trail through my hand as I pick up my clay pipe, tobacco, and the leather pouch from the table. Bartholomew and Chara follow me outside while Jenkins stays beneath the bed with Mary.

I sit on the slab bench beneath the lean-to roof. I drop my head into my hands, the heat of my palms against my forehead. Lightning slices the sky, followed by the rumble of thunder. The river will not go down tomorrow. Mother of God, please protect her.

Bartholomew falls onto the bench beside me without a word, clothes reeking of alcohol and sour sweat. If the gods chose me to be a saint handing out money, they might have given me someone sober to save. I already regret it. Or so I tell myself. But in truth, I'm proud I did it. I have years to earn our passage home. And our needs are few.

Who would have thought—Ghikas the Redeemer. Patron saint of thieves.

I let out half a laugh, half a cough, and pull tobacco from my stick— offer him a twist. We rub our palms in silence.

'How did you get across the river?' I ask.

He grunts. 'We waded across before it came up. We waited in the timber at Kurraducbidgee for nightfall. I wasn't leaving the district without what is owed me.'

I nod, too tired to argue. 'I'm sorry you haven't been able to find work.'

He gives a short laugh. 'I'm too much like my father.'

I glance at him. 'Your father?'

'He liked a belt. With the buckle. Every day, whether we'd earned it or not. I ran when I was nine.'

He holds out his arms. I've seen the scars before. Now I know.

'And your mother?'

He shrugs. 'She was drunk by breakfast.'

I say nothing.

'I was proud of being an overseer. But I had to keep control with the whip. That's what I thought, anyway.'

We remain in silence until a scream lays open the night. Mary! I fly to my feet.

Bartholomew leans back. 'It might take all night. It did with my Charlotte.'

I pace outside the hut, helpless.

As the hours pass, Mary's cries are more regular, then louder, longer, more urgent. When I think it is over, they are weaker. Then stronger. There is no end to it. With every scream, I think my chest will burst. I smoke my pipe. I pace.

Towards morning, Milly appears in the hut's doorway, arms slick with blood. I feel the colour drain from my face. I look at the ground, at her curling toenails. Bartholomew is asleep on the bench beside me.

'I need your help. Both of you.' She shakes Bartholomew.

Mary, Mother of God, please give me strength.

'You must hold her down.'

She doesn't need to tell me that my wife and child might die. I know from her tone.

'I've buried two of my own,' she says. 'We'll not see another die tonight.'

I want to run away, but I'm anchored here.

Mary needs me.

I feel a surge of power.

Of course I can do this. I will not fail her.

We follow Milly into the hut filled with the iron reek of blood. My precious girl is lying on the table. She looks at me, hands gripping the edges. Her knees are raised, legs apart. Milly stands between them, blood covering the front of her dress. She has strewn blood-soaked rags across the table—even the white handkerchief Mary gave me. Milly lifts a limp wrist to push the hair off her face.

Mary seems beyond caring that Bartholomew is here in the room, seeing her like this.

So much blood. I choke down a wave of nausea and attempt to disguise my horror. Mary needs me steady. Not struck dumb as I was with Seamus.

The iron tang fills my throat, but Mary's cry is sharper; I force myself to look at her.

'Don't just stand there, Ghikaki!' She grinds out the words.

I go to stand at the side of the table with my hands on her shoulder. Bartholomew stands on the other side near the wall.

I push the wet hair off her forehead and speak with a confidence I do not feel. 'Don't fret, *agápi mou*. Milly knows what to do. We will help.'

She lifts her hand to me, exhausted. I kiss it, fold it, put it back. I turn to check the lamp for oil.

Milly leans over Mary, one hand pressing her belly, brow furrowed, pushing this way and that.

'I think the baby is lying sideways. It can't come out.'

She straightens, wipes her face. 'I saw it once. The midwife put her hands up inside to turn it straight.'

She shakes her head. 'I can't do that. I'm not trained—I might kill her.'

I feel the ground tilt beneath me. My heart's hammering. Mary lets out another cry, weaker this time. 'Do it,' I say.

She stares at me, eyes wide.

'Milly. Please.'

For a moment, she doesn't move. Then she nods, once, face grim.

'Hold her,' she says. 'Don't let her twist.'

I nod, sick with fear. Bartholomew nods.

'Right.'

Mary groans. A terrible shuddering takes over her body, her face becomes distorted, her chin digs into her chest, and she lets out a long, grunting groan from the depths of her soul that goes on and on. Milly bends between her legs, one hand reaching inside my wife. I close my eyes and force myself to breathe; I will the nausea down, find a point in her face to fix on so the rest of the room falls away. I feel Mary's body being pulled, pulled, pulled.

Mary lets out a scream, a long, hoarse scream. Her mouth closes, her teeth grinding on each other. Worse than any nightmare I could ever imagine.

She relaxes again, gasping, panting, her body collapsing on itself. Milly stands up, panting too, heaving the air from her body. Now she's pressing on the baby again while Mary grunts. I stroke her forehead, no longer caring about the blood on her face. Please, *Panagia mou*, let this be over. Let her live.

Milly leans forward. 'Good girl. Next time.' Her hands reach again between Mary's legs.

Oh my God. Next time. It is going to happen again. I squeeze my eyes together, swallow, ready to hold my breath.

Mary shakes her head, her fingers clawing at my wrist. She grunts out between her clenched teeth, 'No next time—.' She lets it all out in a grinding scream, 'Now—.'

She grits her teeth and goes rigid with another paroxysm of pain, summoning a guttural scream beyond anything she has uttered before, on and on and on, pushing air out between her teeth. Her voice changes note each time Milly leans into her. Her head bumps up the table. I press hard on her shoulder to keep her still. Bartholomew does the same. Milly works between her legs.

'Yes! YES!' Milly cries.

The force of it is terrifying. A slick, bloody mass expels from Mary with such violence I fear it will shoot off the table. But Milly catches it, fumbles, holds it up.

I cannot move. It is a baby. Covered in blood. Ears flat to its head. Black hair. Wrinkled and blue, red and purple. Is it dead?

Milly crooks a finger and cleans out its mouth. It scrunches its eyes, opens its mouth—silent for a moment too long.

Then, a breath. A furious wail splits the air, fierce and alive.

Milly's mouth opens in triumph. She takes a cloth and wipes the worst of the mess off the tiny glistening body, lays it back down.

'You have a girl.'

Mary gives a sob, holds out her arms, but Milly is still busy. She takes a strip of rag and ties a knot, repeats the action, then saws back and forth with a knife. Now she is coming towards us, holding the slimy newborn. It lets out another angry squall.

The blood doesn't make me gag. Not anymore.

I thought it was the sight.

It was never the sight. It was the fear.

She croons softly to the baby, 'There now, little one, the hard part's over.'

I step aside and she places the infant on Mary's chest. 'No need for thanks.'

'My wee one,' Mary says. 'Thank you Milly.'

Mary is safe. Our daughter is alive.

At last, it is over.

I gaze at my precious Mary.

Not a son. A girl. She has arrived, furious at the world already.

I grip Mary's hand. Something shifts inside me, deep and permanent.

I look at Milly, and I am flooded with gratitude.

Where I saw grime and insolence, now I see grace.

Sunlight streams through the open door.

39

The Measure Of A Man

ARNPRIOR, New South Wales
December 1836

A laughing jackass penetrates the silence of dawn. Light filters through the window above our bed, where Mary is still sleeping, casting shadows on the polished floor, rippling like liquid. That pane of scratched and bubbled glass—once meant for grander purposes in the Arnprior house—gives us a modest view of the world outside our hut.

When I installed it, the whiting and linseed oil William gave me to mix as a sealant filled the hut with a fresh, nutty fragrance, and Mary and I stood together, marvelling at it, luxuriating in the sun's warmth without the wind.

Wisps of fragrant smoke drift around the hut, twisting away from the hearth, where I've set the kettle to boil.

I'm filled with a deep sense of peace. I touch the hagstone at my neck. No gleam of silver now, no Saint George on his dragon. Just a tumbled stone. Mary's choice. And mine.

The gentle light moulds her features, still pale from her recent ordeal, and I'm reminded of her strength. Baby Xanthe, named after Mamá and also the little sister I've never met, lies swaddled in a box on the table, a new chapter of our lives. As I bend to inhale her intoxicating baby smell, the tiny lips purse into a sucking shape, and her eyelids flutter. She is so miniature I cannot believe she has a beating heart.

This life on Arnprior—rough, makeshift, miraculous—has made me more than I ever was. I give thanks to God.

Chara peers at me from her crate, one eye open, while Jenkins dozes at the door. Their puppies, round-bellied and usually attached like limpets to Chara, are now softly snoring. We have takers for all of them, here on Arnprior.

My little family. In the hut we built. The thought of leaving it in seven years tugs at my heart. But the promise of Hydra—of taking Mary and Xanthe home one day—makes it sing.

As if sensing my thoughts, Mary turns over with a sigh.

I smooth the dust off the letter in my hands. Expensive cream parchment paper, my name misspelled as always.

Ghika Bulgary
    c/o Stewart Ryrie Esquire
    'Arnprior'
    District of St Vincent
    New South Wales

I turn it over. The official governor's seal is perfect in outline, fixed off to one side, holding the flap secure. William has delivered it on his way back to Durran Durra after staying last night in his father's house to collect his mail.

'Maybe the governor is offering you the position of Colonial Secretary,' he joked, handing it over with a smile.

Absurd. Although Governor Bourke is known for his favourable attitude towards ex-convicts, unlike Macleay and the Macarthurs, who see emancipists as perpetual underlings. It matters not—my heart is set on Greece, not colonial politics.

My curiosity outweighs my patience. I take Mary's vegetable knife, careful not to wake her, and slide it under the seal. The wax gives, and I gently unfold the page. A second sheet flutters to the floor.

The signatures at the bottom are unmistakable: Governor Richard Bourke and Alexander Macleay. But it's the top of the page that holds me —the English king's coat of arms, a lion and a unicorn standing guard.

Below it, two words hit me like a wave:

ABSOLUTE PARDON.

I clutch the page to my chest. My heartbeat pounds in my head—at this rate I must surely suffer an apoplexy. Blood rushes to my face. I check my name again. I pick up the other sheet, my thoughts a muddle. I have only just earned my Ticket of Leave. I won't qualify for a pardon of any sort, neither conditional nor absolute, for another seven years.

Then I read the second page. And I understand. Emotions flood through me—confusion, disbelief, freedom.

Gently, I nudge Mary awake. She smiles when she sees my face.

'Mary,' I say, holding the sheet. 'It's a pardon.'

'A problem?' She looks at Xanthe and puts her fingers to her lips. 'Shhhh. What is it, Ghikaki?'

'A pardon! I am free.'

'What?' Startled awake, she casts off the bedclothes and rises, movements swift. I hand her the papers and she turns away to the light, scanning them. I wrap my arms around her and read the words again over her shoulder. I assume Ando and the others have received a pardon too. Free passage home. London, then Greece. It's real. No cost. We could leave Arnprior tomorrow.

'We can go home.' I point to the page, heart galloping. 'The English will fund our travel to London, and the Greek government will see us the rest of the way. This must be the work of Spyridon Trikoupis—he's one of the King's ministers now, and our envoy to London.'

'It might be the work of your father.'

'Not him,' I say. But even after all these years, I still haven't extinguished a flicker of hope.

She scans the words, fingers playing along the edge of the page.

She looks up—no joy, only pale shock.

I am already picturing it—Mary standing at the rail on the ship beside me, Xanthe in her arms.

'So then—when is it you'll be leaving?' Her voice is flat.

'Would you like to sit down?'

I take her arm, but she remains standing.

'Soon, as quickly as I can arrange it. There are often ships to London. We can be in Hydra by the northern summer.'

She says nothing. Of course. The passage is for one.

'You and Xanthe will take my berth. I'll sign on as crew,' I assure her, my thoughts running ahead.

I close my eyes and heave out a sigh. At last. I will secure work as a sailor as soon as we land. I can hear the strains of the bouzouki already, the cries of seagulls wheeling above the port. 'We'll take the dogs with us.' I'm picturing Chara and Jenkins running on the quay.

Her face portrays a stillness I fail to interpret.

Until she says, 'Have you considered my wishes?'

She lays her hand on my arm to gain my attention. 'I want to raise Xanthe here.'

Raise Xanthe here?

'I assumed—I thought—now we have a child—it's different—it's Xanthe's birthright.'

'It changes nothing.'

'Mary,' I begin, clutching the pardon, 'You always knew Hydra was my dream. You've always known I want to take you home.'

Her face is blank.

I'm pleading. 'Xanthe is half Greek.'

She collects her thoughts. 'She is also half Irish. But that doesn't mean we'll go back to Ireland. I understand your feelings. Yes, our children should know about their Greek and Irish roots.' She pauses. 'But you need to realise the worth of what we have here.'

She sweeps her arms around the hut.

'Mary,' my voice breaks. 'Our children can grow up with aunts and uncles, cousins to play with, a love of the sea. It's the way of life, the freedom, the history, it's being Greek. It's me.'

'You, Ghikaki. Not me. I don't even speak the language. And the life for women there, as you've described it—well, I will lose myself.'

She lowers her head and presses her fingers into her closed eyes.

She looks up again. Tears spill down her cheeks and her mouth twists.

'I knew you'd leave me one day.' She drags in a breath and opens her mouth to speak, then closes it again.

She squeezes her eyes closed and turns away, gripping the back of the chair with both hands. The knuckles of her right hand are white. In her nightdress, she is so small and fragile.

Her words have taken all the air from the hut. I nod slowly. I keep nodding. She has cast me off. I turn and walk out of the hut.

Outside, I double over—hands on knees, gasping, fighting for air.

She means it. She will let me go.

I clutch the pardon. Everything I ever wanted. But it will tear apart everything I've built—everything I've made, from nothing.

I straighten slowly.

My mouth is dry. My thoughts are hard and bitter.

Mary does not behave as a wife should. She would dictate where we live. Decide our course. Take the wheel. Strip me of my manhood.

That's a mutiny.

I am the man. I decide where we go.

It's clear. I have no choice. I must go alone.

A stab of pain shoots through my chest.

It's not a threat. It's the only course left.

Ships are always looking for crew for the return voyage to London. I'll take Chara. Jenkins will stay.

I close my eyes. Is that too cruel? To split the dogs up?

They will pine for each other.

So will we.

I stare at these foreign trees, my mind painting Hydra—the sharp tang of sea air, the cobbled quay alive with voices, the slap of ropes against masts, white-washed houses rising steeply behind. I see our children diving off the rocks, our ships moored tight along the harbour wall.

I try to hold on to it. My home. Where I will build ships, command them, and walk with pride again.

But as I stare at my surroundings, the gum tree's silver bark gleams in the morning light, its shadow stretching across the ground, flies buzzing in the heat.

This is what I know now.

This landscape has soaked into my being—the pungent eucalyptus, the magpies warbling, the relentless sun over the sprawling, open terrain. It's become a part of me.

Both places are part of who I am.

I see myself stepping off the ship, the quay below me.

No Mary. No Xanthe. Just me.

My breathing stops.

Hydra means nothing without her.

The vision fades.

I stand there, empty-handed.

And I see it.

I've been building this dream for years. And it's always been about me. My name. My ships. My honour. I've circled back to the man I was before I met her.

The family inside the hut—Mary, Xanthe—that's a home.

Ando said he's staying here, whatever happens. He knows it. This is his home.

Hydra is a dream.

This is real.

But she said she expected me to go. Without her.

I step back through the doorway. Mary hasn't moved. Her cheeks are wet. She says nothing.

I pull her to me. Her body stays stiff in my arms.

'I know you told me,' I say. 'I knew Hydra wasn't your dream. But I thought—' I shake my head. 'When I read those words, I thought it would change things. That if our passage was free—if it was now—you'd say yes.'

I ignored her wishes. Her opinions.

I was certain I was right. I still think I am. But she doesn't.

She still says nothing.

I draw back and look at her properly.

'You said you'd let me go,' I say, voice breaking. 'You'd let me go alone.'

She lets her head into my shoulder. I want to bridge the gap. Crush her rebellion against me. Kiss her doubts away. She's still, but I feel it—she's bracing. Not for my anger. For my leaving. She is in my arms but she might as well be on the other side of the world.

'That's what undoes me, Mary. Not that you didn't want to go. That you'd give me up.'

She pulls away again and stares into my eyes. She takes a deep breath. When she speaks, her voice is low, ragged—but sure.

'You're right. I don't want to go. I hate the idea. Hydra will consume me—you know it will.'

Would it? Would it really?

She continues speaking. 'But I will not lose you. Not to your father. Not to your past. If you return—then we all go. All of us.'

My knees could give way.

Her gaze is steady. 'We will go when I am mended. And we will speak about it. I will not be put away in a women's room. I am not choosing Hydra, Ghikaki. I'm choosing you and me.'

'Even though that's not what you want?'

She smiles. 'Perhaps I'm learning obedience.'

I raise an eyebrow. 'And hogs might fly through the air.'

I place my thumb dark against her pale cheek, wipe her tears and kiss her.

I gaze at the pardon—the free passage home. Images flicker in the flames: my father, my brothers, the quay at Hydra.

I have wanted this more than anything. But I want her happiness more.

I hold the sheet above the fire. The flames crackle—burning steadily now. One move, and I sever everything I thought defined me as a man.

I used to blame them. My father. Townsend. Hely.

But it was never their fault.

It was my own doing.

My thumb wavers against the edge. I don't have to win.

I let go.

The paper floats, lands, blackens, curls. It pales inward as the fire swallows it.

But even as it burns, I wonder: are we truly mending a rift—or covering deeper cracks? Have I chosen love, but lost the last piece of myself?

It drops as ash. Then—nothing.

My hands curl around each other, my thumb finding the old ridge of calluses. I press them, one by one.

I turn back to her with a grin. 'Close your mouth, *agápi mou*. You're catching flies.'

'You fool,' she says.

I give a half-smile. 'Yes.'

I feel the thrill of a sudden change in course, when the ship surges forward, sails stretched by new winds.

She doesn't speak; her body softens against mine, as if something in her has finally let go.

I'd be nothing without her.

Ando was right. This colony is being built not just by men like us, but by women like Mary.

She draws back, enough to meet my eyes.

'And what of your grand dream, Ghikaki—to be the richest man on the island?'

I stretch out my arms. 'Look at me, Mary.'

I whisper into her hair. 'I already am.'

THE END

Author Afterword

My husband discovered his Greek heritage in the most unexpected way. During a visit to the Monaro district, our son was told about an ancestor we didn't know existed—my husband's great-great-grandfather was transported to New South Wales in 1829 as one of seven sailors from Hydra convicted of piracy.

But was he really a criminal—or a freedom fighter? Did bad blood run in my children's veins, or the blood of a revolutionary?

The Research Journey

Ghikas' trail led me across continents—not only to study the historical records, but to see the locations he lived in or passed through. I travelled to Hydra to understand how an island so small, steep, and barren built one of the most formidable merchant fleets in the Mediterranean. I began to sense the toughness that hardship had bred—the ingenuity that made it thrive. Ghikas became real: a young man shaped by his environment.

In Valletta and Rabat in Malta, I propped vast tomes on cushions in the National Library. In its National Archives, I turned the brittle pages of the trial records and colonial correspondence. I visited the Maritime Museum. In the Castellania Palace—once the Knights' court and prison, now the Department of Health—I climbed to the upstairs courtroom and descended to the musty underground cells. I located the site of the lazaretto where the men were first held.

In England, I sat in seat 44B at Kew Archives for weeks examining Admiralty and Colonial Office papers, including correspondence with the rulers of Hydra, and I photographed the *Norfolk* and *Gannet* ships' logs. I used the daily latitude and longitude recordings to plot the voyages. I also discovered there were forty-three pirates on the Herakles, not nine as the existing literature claimed.

In Ireland, I saw what remained possible birth record in a small rural church in County Cork.

In Australia, a kind local helped me locate the Arnprior homestead near Braidwood, and I was shown the possible foundations of one of Ghikas' houses on the Monaro; I searched archives and libraries across New South Wales and the ACT, including Hugh Gilchrist's papers in the National Library.

I read court records, captains' and surgeons' and ships' logs, ships' musters, newspapers, manifests, convict indents, birth and death certificates, books by travellers of the period, Greek novels of the era, and both contemporary and modern histories. I accumulated a library on convicts, pioneers, bushrangers, agriculture in NSW, hulks, the early dogs of Australia, convict slang, and the history of the Voulgaris and Ryrie families.

The Historical Puzzle

In real life, Ghikas' name is absent from the Voulgaris family records. As historian Gilchrist concluded, and I agree, the most likely explanation is that he was disowned. One alternative—that he gave a false name when arrested—seems far less probable, since there is no record of a named son disappearing.

If Ghikas had been a freedom fighter, surely his father would have honoured him. No Hydriot shipowner would erase a son who fought for Greece. There had to be another reason for his disowning—one rooted not in heroism but in pride, defiance, or disgrace.

I chose to write this story as fiction rather than nonfiction because fiction allows me to explore the reasons for his actions—to imagine what the documented history leaves unsaid. Ghikas and Mary's personalities are my invention.

Patriot or Pirate?

For those who may wish to see Ghikas and his companions as patriots rather than pirates, I understand that impulse—I felt it myself.

During the Greek War of Independence, the British Admiralty used the word pirate as a legal catch-all for any ship operating outside official naval commission—regardless of loyalties.

Many Hydriot captains fought under local authority or on self-funded expeditions. To the Greeks they were part of the struggle for freedom, but to the British, they were outlaws. In that charged climate, the distinction between patriot and pirate was often one of paperwork. Ghikas and his companions were caught squarely in that grey zone—sailors whose cause was Greek but whose papers were not.

Even so, the surviving evidence, fragmentary as it is, tells a story: they carried no legal papers, as Greek law required; they left behind a cargo of sulphur—a war requisite—bound for Alexandria, where it could be used by the Egyptians in war; they took personal belongings from the crew of the Alceste; there is no record of Ghikas' father interceding on his behalf at Malta, which surely he would have done if his son were a freedom fighter; Ghikas' name is missing entirely from his family's history; and he did not return home when he had the chance.

History, particularly in wartime, is rarely clear-cut. I've tried neither to defend these men as freedom fighters nor to condemn them as pirates, but to imagine what the historical silence conceals. The truth, I suspect, lies somewhere in the murky space between heroism and opportunism, between principle and survival.

Creative Choices

As for Mary, I found records of servant girls who stood up to magistrates in court, so she's a plausible counterpoint to the cliché of the downtrodden, subservient maid.

I made two deliberate changes to the facts for narrative flow:

— I reduced the number of Greek pirates from seven to five. I already knew them well, so it was akin to amputating my own limbs.

— I had Mary arrive in the colony alongside Ghikas, though in reality she came three years later.

Other dates, locations, events, and outcomes come from the historical record.

I had enormous fun weaving in real historical details. Many appear exactly as recorded—from Father Therry's diary entry recording their marriage to the assassination of a Hydra shipowner at his son's wedding; from the printing press on Hydra to Damos' attempt to escape as described in the newspaper.

A Note on Representation

Son of Hydra does not speak for Indigenous Australians. While Ghikas would have encountered Aboriginal people—especially during his time at Arnprior—such interactions are not central to the story as I've chosen to tell it. I focussed on sources that intersected with his limited world: period newspapers mention Aboriginal people selling fish to the butcher near the Sydney markets, which Ghikas visits; the wonderful Father Therry wrote about Indigenous education; records from Arnprior include names from the Kurraducbidgee community. I also read Grace Karskens' *People of the River*, among other books, to understand the broader context.

Ghikas reflects briefly on dispossession and on his own dislocation, but I've avoided giving him implausibly modern attitudes. This novel reflects one historical perspective; many others—particularly those of Indigenous communities—lie beyond its scope.

Final thoughts

Even within the known historical facts, the possibilities are endless—this is just one possible imagining.

I thought I was in charge of the plot—until one day Ghikas leaned over my shoulder. 'Step aside,' he said. 'This is my story, and I'll tell it.' The love story that followed was entirely his doing. I'm grateful he allowed me to watch.

I always tried to reflect only what I could verify and checked for anachronisms. But any mistakes are mine.

If you have questions about my research or the choices I made in telling it, feel free to email me at shelleydarkwriter@gmail.com—I'd love to hear from you.

I hope reading *Son of Hydra* brings you even a fraction of the joy it gave me to write.

—Shelley Dark
2025

About the Author
AND A REQUEST

If you enjoyed *Son of Hydra*, I'd be very grateful if you'd leave an online review—they make a huge difference to a book's success.

You can do it on Amazon, Goodreads, or wherever you bought the book—search for *Son of Hydra* by Shelley Dark, then find the *write a review* button.

So not only do I wait you, my friend—I wait your review.

Writing this story has been a journey every bit as life-changing as the travels it describes. After a lifetime raising cattle on Queensland's Granite Belt, my husband and I left life in the bush behind, and I turned to full-time writing and travel—including a solo trip to the Greek island of Hydra in the tourist off-season.

I'm a member of the ALLWRiTE Club, a dynamic and supportive writers' group of memorable characters worthy of a novel on their own. And I'm part of Writers on the Coast who meet at the local Noosa Library.

When I'm not writing, you'll usually find me planning another journey —preferably involving photography, an island, an archive, or all three.

My books include *Hydra in Winter* (2024), which tells the story of my journey to Hydra to search for Ghikas. Soon to come is *Daughter of Cork* —the story as told by Mary. I have more travel memoirs to write, and my short fiction appears in anthologies.

And I'm always hot on the trail of a perfect cream bun.

List of Characters

Names in italics are fictional, while an asterisk (*) denotes real people not included in the novel.

Protagonists:
Ghikas Voulgaris: sailor, Son of Nikolaos
Mary Lyons: free settler Irish housemaid

Ghikas' Siblings: (it's thought he had at least eight, including Katerina, Dimas, Andreas, Yiannis, Petros, and three Giorgios)
Katerina Voulgaris
Giorgios Voulgaris
Makris Voulgaris

Hydriot friends:
Andonis Manolis (Ando): purser, Ghikas' best friend
Damianos Ninis (Damos): ship's carpenter
Konstantinos (Kostas) Stromboulis: sailor
Nikolaos Papandreos (Nikos): sailor
*Giorgios Vassilachis: sailor
*Giorgios Laritsos: sailor

Arnprior friends:
Joseph Little: pickpocket
Martin Armstrong: labourer

Others:
Nikolaos Voulgaris: Ghikas' father, shipowner and gentleman of Hydra, Greece
Xanthe Voulgaris: Ghikas' mother, and Nikolaos' second wife
Eleni Ghika: Ghikas' paternal grandmother
Giorgios Voulgaris: Ghikas' deceased paternal uncle, previously Governor of Hydra
Frangiskos Voulgaris: Ghikas' paternal uncle
Dimitris Voulgaris: Ghikas' paternal cousin (later Prime Minister of Greece)
Maria Kountouriotis: daughter of Lazaros
Lambros: manservant to the Voulgaris family
Despina: maid to the Voulgaris family
Stewart Ryrie: Deputy Commissary General of New South Wales
Isabella Ryrie: Stewart Ryrie's second wife
William Ryrie: his elder son (first wife)
James Ryrie: Stewart Ryrie's son (first marriage)
Stewart Ryrie: Stewart Ryrie's son (first marriage)
Donald Ryrie: Stewart Ryrie's son (first marriage)
Jane Ryrie: Stewart Ryrie's daughter (first marriage)
John Ryrie: Stewart Ryrie's son (second marriage)
Alexander Ryrie: Stewart Ryrie's son (second marriage)
David Ryrie: Stewart Ryrie's son (second marriage)
James and Maria Bloodsworth: Mary's first employer
Hercules and Mary (Kennedy) Watt: Mary's second employer
Richard Townsend: Mary Lyons' fiancé

Glossary of Greek terms

Aderfáki: affectionate term for little brother

Amygdalotá: almond biscuits, often scented with orange blossom or rosewater

Archontikó/Archontiká: grand traditional mansions, especially on Hydra

Bába: daddy or papa; a child's term of affection for father

Bichaq: double-edged dagger of Ottoman origin

Blaktzákis: blackjack, a gambling card game

Bouríni: a violent storm

Bouzouki: long-necked stringed instrument

Burlótta / Burlótto: fire ship

Caïque: traditional wooden fishing or sailing boat

Chará: joy

Efcharistó: thank you

Ego: I, me

Elefthería í Thánatos: freedom or death; motto of the Greek War of Independence

Fíle mou, sto kaló: my friend, go well; a farewell

Filoxenía: obligatory kindness to strangers

Foustanélla: traditional white pleated skirt worn by Greek men

Gámos: wedding or marriage

Gávros: a small, silver fish—anchovy-like—often served whole

Geléki: Greek vest

Hydraïkí / Ydraïkí: of or from Hydra

Ímoun ántras í kotópoulo?: was I a man or a chicken?

Kai se eséna: and to you too

Kaliméra: good morning

Khanjár: curved blade or dagger of Middle Eastern design

Kilij: a curved sabre used by Janissaries and Ottoman cavalry

Koufiokéfalos: empty-headed; a fool

Kýra: madam or Mrs; a respectful term for a woman

Kýrios: sir or Mister; a respectful term for a man

Lingua franca: mixed sailor's trade language (here, of the Mediterranean)

Malákas: vulgar insult

Mantíli: kerchief, handkerchief, or scarf

Mati: the 'evil eye', a belief in a curse or negative energy transmitted through a malevolent glare

Meltémi: strong summer wind from the north

Mítera: mother

O Theós na evlogí: may God bless you

Ómorfo korítsi: beautiful girl

Pála: broad fighting knife or sword

Palikári / palikária: brave young man / men; gallant, honourable, freedom fighter(s)

Panagia: the Virgin Mary (often with 'mou' added meaning 'my')

Papoú: grandfather

Patéra: father (vocative)

Philotimo: pride in self, family, and community, expressed through dignity, decency, and doing the right thing, even when no one is watching

Piástre: coin of Ottoman currency

Ploutos: wealth, riches

Prodótes koloi: treacherous bums

Qamá: curved dagger used in the Caucasus and Balkans

Ráki: strong spirit made from grape skins or figs

Scio: now known as (the island of) Chios

Siderénios: iron-strong

Souvlák(i): skewered grilled meat
Stamáta: stop it!
Stifádo: slow-cooked stew with onions and tomato
Tiganítes: pancakes or fritters, often sweet
Thánatos: death
Thárros: courage
Theotókos: the Virgin Mary
Ti: what
Vráka: traditional baggy trousers worn by island men, usually black
Xíphos: short, double-edged Greek sword
Yatagán(i): curved sword with double-edged blade
Zonári / zonária: waist sash / sashes

Acknowledgments

I extend my sincere thanks to the people who live in this novel:

My husband John—thank you for believing in me, for your love and patience, and for being my staunchest ally and promoter. Please take pity on the members of your croquet club who I suspect take the brunt of your pride in me. And thank you for allowing me to steal your ancestor.

My family, my friends, and the social media followers who've encouraged me to fly before I could even walk.

The members of the ALLWRiTE Club—an Australia-wide writers' group of the most loving, insightful, loyal and funny people I know—for your generosity, your wisdom, and your brilliance. Each of you owns part of this novel, as does each editor and beta reader who's ever given me feedback. And to Writers on the Coast, my local tribe, thank you too for your encouragement.

The many people who have generously supported this project with their time, expertise, encouragement, and hospitality.

And finally, you, my readers—especially those who've waited seven years for this novel—thank you. I wrote *Son of Hydra* for you.

GREECE
Maria Voulgaris—for her knowledge of Hydra's history, and for sharing family knowledge and welcoming me as 'aunt'
Dimitris A. Mavrideros—distinguished member of the Heraldry and

Genealogical Society of Greece, for confirming Ghikas' ancestry through his knowledge and expertise and through his gracious correspondence
Eleni Mavroudhkou—Hydra Archives
Panagiotis Amarianos—Hydra Archives
Father Giorgos Vlachopoulos of the Saint (Aghia) Varvara
Mrs Dina Adamopolou—Hydra Archives
Stamatis Kalafatis—Hydra Archives
Sotiris Fragidis—for his tour of Athens, and his gift of *The Companion Guide to the Greek Islands*
Apostolos Delis—for his knowledge of Greek maritime history
Heraklis Kalogerakis, Vice Admiral (ret) Hellenic Navy and Naval History researcher—for his cultural and historical insight

MALTA
Pauline and Monica—Malta Archives, for help and kindness
Louis Cini—Malta National Library
Judge Giovanni Bonello—historian and advocate for Maltese heritage
Michael Cassar—historian
Martin Morana—for the introduction to Michael Cassar
Emanuel Barbara—for the guided tour of Castellania prison
Frank Theuma—historian

AUSTRALIA
Adam Franklin—for encouraging me from the beginning
Dr Liz Rushen—historian and author of Fair Game
Dr Perry McIntyre AM—historian and author of Fair Game
John Higgins—research support
Lois Gorman—research support
Shirley Tunnicliff—for sharing Bloodsworth family history
Robyn McGill—for sharing Bloodsworth family history
Beverley Earnshaw—author of *Australia's Greek Pirates*
Helena Folidis—her research support
Gail Davis—NSW State Archives, Kingswood
Staff of the State Library of New South Wales—for assistance and access
Rachel Kerr-Mackey—Parramatta Tourist Information Centre
Trisha Dixon—for hospitality, knowledge of local history and guidance

Elaine Lawson—for hospitality, knowledge of local history
Howard Charles OAM—Cooma, for the tour of one of Ghikas' properties
Barbara Dawson—historian
Chris Batten—Cooma Historical Society
Trish Cooper—for being my Braidwood PA, an angel, for hospitality, research assistance, generosity and moral support
Ian Vardenega—for the tour of Arnprior homestead
Julie Coleman—Braidwood Historical Society
Brian Mongan—oral history
Geoff Mongan—oral history
Tim de Mestre—Merigan, Mt Fairy, for his hospitality
Bernadette Foley—tutor at Australian Writers Centre
Chris Grace—manuscript assessor
Nadine Davidoff—manuscript assessor
Kyra Geddes—for her advice and encouragement
Kathy Alexopoulos OAM—for her support and introductions to the Greek Australian community
Dean Kalimniou—for his encouragement

ENGLAND
Staff of the UK National Archives at Kew—archival access and assistance
Duncan Hazell—for information on maritime life and his knowledge of the Mediterranean, and introductions on Malta
Jackie Parry—for generous guidance and historical and local knowledge in Portsmouth
Rear-Admiral Chris Parry RN—for sharing his naval expertise and historical insight
Clare Harvey—manuscript assessor

USA
Rob Cerecedes—for his marketing expertise
Maria Karamitsos—for publicity in the Greek Community and her cultural insight
Lisa Poisso—plot development editor

CANADA

Geoff Affleck—for his marketing expertise

CORK, IRELAND
Steve Skeldon—Cork City Archives
Bart Bambury—for locating the rare book *In the Shadows*
Father Tom Hayes, Parish Priest of St Mary's Church of the Immaculate
Conception, Enniskeane—who opened the parish safe and brought out the
original two-hundred-year-old baptism register so I could read Mary's
possible baptism record.
Theresa O'Driscoll—for being an angel, my Irish PA and for extraordinary
help and introductions
John Joe Lyons—for local history and Lyons family connection
Ursula Lyons—for local history and Lyons family connection

*And my thanks to all the others who have helped in so many ways
and whose names I never knew or have forgotten.*

Any errors or omissions that remain are mine alone.

I wait you.
shelleydarkwriter@gmail.com